Celtic Fire

Witch of Appalachia Series

Book 6

Francesca Quarto

Printed in the United States of America

Dedication

For all who have discovered the enjoyment of reading a good book is not found in the story alone, but in bringing a new world to life as you step into the pages, rather than turn them. I invite them to jump in with both feet and eyes wide open!

Chapter 1

Total mayhem descended on the gathering of the Council of Green Wizards. The marble walls encircling their chambers resonated with vile shouts and accusations and finally, calls for the immediate appointment and empowerment of an External Censor Officer. The ECO wizard would be tasked to investigate any unlawful use of magic within the ranks of the Council members themselves, making this a dangerous move for all, especially the guilty if they stood among them.

This sensitive inquiry only occurred once before, in the thousand plus years of the existence of this body of wizards. That ended with the ECO Officer executing three prominent Council members, discovered emmeshed in the Dark Arts for their own empowerment and wealth. The stink of that investigation never left the airy rooms of the great Citadel and hung in the smoky air of today's Council Chambers.

The present uproar was over the brutal murder of Master Bretton Clawson. The Claw as he was known, had been a living legend among the Greens and almost a god to the troops of Outlander Wizard Scouts he led. This elite unit of specially trained, soldier-wizards, was guided by Clawson for over half-a-century, under the glint of his steely discipline and unwavering loyalty to the Green Mother.

The Scouts acted as eyes and ears for the Council of Green Wizards. Using their well-honed military skills and traditional Celtic magic, these men and women roamed the Emerald Isle like ghosts.

Assigned to designated sectors by Master Clawson, they ranged over these territories, guarding against demonic intrusions from the fourth realm, into the first realm of Natural Order.

Bretton Clawson was the best of the best. His reputation among magic users on both sides of the divide was cemented in his ruthless, unforgiving approach to evil.

His murder was unimaginable and had all the council members looking over their shoulders. Prior to the assassination of Master Clawson, a threat had been reported by Sir Alex Portchamp, the Arch Wizard, of a coming bloodbath within the ranks of the Council. It had to be taken seriously, coming from their most successful spy.

Only the Arch Wizard received the spy's information, but their intelligence reporting was highly accurate, in spite of occasional speculation on the part of some members.

Like the other Greens, Sir Alex wasn't sure who among the sitting Council or their auxiliary staff was acting as their undercover agent. All reports were transmitted to him in hologram form, by a figure shrouded in mist. A filtered voice concealing even that form of identification. This spy was self-appointed and had proven reliable over a long span of time.

The Arch Wizard had his suspicions, but never spoke a name.

In response to the latest dire warnings he'd conveyed to the Sitting Council, each of the members had taken radical precautions to protect themselves with wards and spells. Their torch-lit chamber glittered with talismans hanging from golden chains and the heavy aroma of magic-infused powders and waters sprinkled liberally on robes.

A palpable dread permeated the room, like a shapeless creature moving among the robed figures. The Arch Wizard, as always, was accompanied to Council Chambers by the eccentric wizard, Corky Cochran. Sir Alex retained his services as a safeguard within the chambers, to help put the others at ease and keep order during their meetings. He unilaterally appointed him to the newly created post of Sergeant at Arms.

Corky was well known to the others. He had a reputation as a cunning sorcerer, with a penchant for stealth and trickery when it came to defeating enemies. This extended to devilish Woodland Hags, or an opponent sitting across from him at a Cribbage board. He was quite proud of the bounty placed upon his head by the denizens of the Fourth Realm. His only complaint about the reward was that it wasn't high enough.

A loud thumping sounded on the flagstone floor of the chamber.

Corky, as Sergeant at Arms, brought the heavy Yew limb down three times, to restore order and silence. They sat around the gleaming U-shaped table, the hush that followed heavy with unspoken fears.

After a drawn-out pause, the Arch Wizard said, "My fellow Wizards of the Green, may the blessings of the Green Mother ripen the fruits of our labors and act as a shield, against Her enemies and our enemies." Finishing this brief entreaty to officially open the meeting, Sir Alex looked from one Wizard to the next, searching their eyes to be sure of their undivided attention. "We have been visited by an evil so great, it reached out and struck down one of our finest, Master Bretton Clawson."

Immediately, there was another outburst of disbelief and outrage in equal measure, at such an unimaginable deed. Holding up a jeweled hand, the Arch Wizard stopped the deluge of comments and continued.

"Known to friend and foe alike as The Claw, Master Clawson served the Council of Green Wizards for an impressive span of years, even by our standards of longevity. Now, his shield of protection as the leader of the elite Outlander Wizard Scouts, has come to an untimely and unexpected end. A bloody end! A murderous end!"

He took a long breath and the others knew he was wrapping up his remarks. These last words were spoken in a near a whisper, all eyes riveted on his face. "We Greens must take action to find and punish, the evil doers. We must root them out and send them howling, back to the Dark Pit of the Sleepless Dead!"

The Arch Wizard's face looked strained and deeply worried to one of the Council members in particular. Mercy McNaughton was the Council Scribe, recording every word spoken at these meetings by using her incredible gift of instant recall. As she observed Sir Alex during this lull in his comments, she saw him looking intently at Will Farley, recently installed to the Council of Greens.

Mercy didn't know much about the new man, except for a vague rumor he was a kind of mercenary soldier-wizard, before joining the Council. However, when he was recruited by Sir Alex, he was given the portfolio of Council Historian. This was odd, to her, considering his less-than-scholarly demeanor. Will Farley had the look of a rugged explorer, with handsome, craggy features, a deeply tanned face and a well-muscled build that made Mercy think he'd never stepped into a university library.

His dark brown eyes were the only thing that seemed to move as she surreptitiously studied him. He was as still as a statue, while those eyes constantly shifted around the table.

Despite her innate caution around strangers, Mercy couldn't help but feel drawn to the good-looking newcomer, Will Farley. His shifting eyes suddenly settled on her before she could look away and she blushed deeply.

Sir Alex stood up from his ornately carved chair. His voice was strong and filled with resolve. "We need to call upon the services of one who has established a reputation for thorough sleuthing and fearless victories over the Dark Forces. Our Council lies under the viable threat of extinction, as reported by our reliable spy. We cannot disregard this warning. We have already suffered the loss of our chief protector against demon incursion into our realm. Have no doubts! Each of us has been marked for a similar fate!"

There was low murmuring among the others seated around the table. One of the older Council members stood to speak. "We need to fill the position of Master for the Outlander Wizard Scouts immediately. Do you intend to raise one from among their ranks? And what about the ECO investigator?"

The Arch Wizard blinked slowly as if to take time to formulate his answer.

Mercy recognized his tell-tale manner, and guessed Sir Alex already had his man. He just needed the words to overcome any objections. "We cannot waste precious time trying to get a new Master up to speed and taking one from among the current thirteen would mean weakening the sector they are assigned to protect. No, no. We shall use the services of one wizard, to act as both Interim Master and as the ECO officer heading our investigation into Clawson's murder. By the Mother's grace, we already have a wizard serving the Green Mother, schooled from birth in Wizardry and whose parents both served this Council. The mother, as an Outlander Wizard Scout herself, and the father, a legendary wizard in our Masters of Wizardry Annuls." His voice was strong, his tone had a final ring to it when he said, "The Witch of Appalachia, Cathleen O'Brien, shall become our temporary Master of Outlander Wizard Scouts and ECO Investigator. She is our designated Protector of the Green!"

Chapter 2

Cathleen wasn't sure what awakened her. She sat for a moment on the edge of the bed, listening and searching the room in the watery light of pre-dawn.

Not wanting to wake her husband, Jason, she quietly slid off the cooling sheets and onto the wooden floor. The carpet that was supposed to be there was lying under her Irish Wolf Hound, Cromwell. He'd taken possession of the heavy braided rug immediately upon her installing it on her side of the bed. But who was going to argue with a one hundred fifteen pound dog claiming squatters rights?

A chill ran through her as she carefully edged around the sleeping hound and she wasn't certain it was totally due to the cold boards.

Snatching her robe off the headboard, she stepped into the dark hallway. She closed the door silently behind herself, not wanting Cromwell to dash after her and distract her from some possible threat.

Their bedroom was on the second floor, at the head of a long staircase. Standing perfectly still, her senses shifted into high alert. Aside from the usual creaks and groans of a century-old house, it was so quiet, she could hear the clock ticking on the kitchen wall just below their bedroom.

I know I heard something. Better check it out while I still have the element of surprise, she reasoned.

Certain the intruder was below, she pushed up a sleeve of the heavy terry cloth robe. She would use her skin's surface like a sensory devise, something her dad taught her to do. Her training under him in the Druid tradition had given her use of many arcane tricks as a wizard.

She placed a bare foot on the first step. The bedroom door behind her opened and closed. A shift in the air current confirmed Jason's presence.

He leaned his six-foot-four frame down to whisper in her ear, "You know I can feel when you're not in bed. Did you hear something?"

Cathleen noticed his right arm was held close to his side, which meant he came armed to this party. As Sheriff of their county, that was to be expected.

Speaking into his ear, hidden under a tuft of curly dark hair, she told him she was sure there was a presence in the house. "Probably in the living room," she added.

Whenever Cathleen used the word presence, Jason went into demon alert mode. His gun would make holes in the walls, but other than that, would likely be useless.

He slipped it into the waist of his sweatpants at his back, joining his wife on the landing. A quick finger nudge and the black eye patch snugged into place over his left eye. He was ready to face whatever waited down there. He nodded once to Cathleen.

They crept down the staircase like two cats on the prowl, then stepped gingerly onto the cold tiles in the foyer. The sharp, cool scent of burning pine wafted in the air as the two moved toward the living room on their right. A mellow light poured out from the partially open pocket-door, painting a long shadow on the wall directly across the way.

Standing in front of the flagstone fireplace covering the far wall, a fire crackling merrily at his back, was a House Buddy. His eyes were closed as he rocked back and forth on his shoeless, flat, webbed feet. He realized he was being observed and his dreamy look of total contentment vanished.

He made the dramatic gesture of clearing his throat and attempting to smooth a mop of tight red curls, springing from the very top of an otherwise shiny, bald head.

To Cathleen's eyes, he was rather tall as House Buddies went. His legs, long and knobby-kneed, peeped out from under rough-spun pants, tied with a thin leather strip over a blousy top the same dull brown color.

He had the look of a gangly doll, huggable and comforting, but Cathleen knew House Buddies could be a fearsome lot when their Masters were threatened.

"Greetings, Cathleen O'Brien and mate!" he said in the high, sweet voice of a choir boy, though he might have already outlived the deep forests around them.

"The following is a message of grave import, sent to you by the Arch Wizard himself and entrusted to me, Parsons, to be delivered in all of its properties and verbiage."

He paused to take a breath. Cathleen and Jason stared, waiting.

"Ahem."

Using all the correct emphasis to impart the serious nature of his message, he began. "You are desperately needed and must accompany my House Buddy, Parsons, back to the land of your ancestors post haste!" Parsons stopped talking so abruptly that both Cathleen and Jason were still leaning forward to hear the rest of his well-memorized order from the Arch Wizard, Sir Alex.

Cathleen studied the slightly built House Buddy, wondering why Sir Alex had entrusted such an important message to a conjured being. Though House Buddies often served their masters for years, even staying with a family for multiple generations, they were known for their capricious natures and fun-loving dispositions. Not the best emissary to deliver such a summons.

She noted the glittering eyes of the elfish being, seeing intelligence there, as well as the characteristic prankster they were known to be.

Jason nudged Cathleen's arm to rouse her to give an expected answer.

"Parsons, I greet you as the loyal servant of Sir Alex. You have fulfilled your task well, but I have questions and hope you can answer them." Cathleen smiled reassuringly at the spindly-legged being.

"I have been told by my Master that you would likely have questions of me, but that all will be explained upon your return to the Emerald Isle and at your appearance before the Council of Green Wizards."

Cathleen glanced over at Jason to see how he was reacting to Parson's new information. In spite of the early hour and being roused from a sound sleep, Jason looked wide awake and deep in thought. Cathleen knew her husband understood there was no turning down a request from the Council of Greens.

He spoke softly, answering her questioning look. "Cathleen, I think you need more information from this little guy before going back to Ireland."

Jason turned back to Parsons, who'd been shifting from foot to foot like a sprinter ready for the gun. "Parsons," Jason spoke in the calming tone he used to interview witnesses. "You're probably one of the most trusted servants of Sir Alex. What rumors have you picked up around the Council chambers that might help Cathleen before she leaves with you?"

In his careful method of interrogation, Jason unlocked a flood of information. The House Buddy lit-up like the logs in the fireplace, his webbed feet shuffling about in a little dance of excitement.

"Oh, my. Well, you understand, we House Buddies never like to gossip, but after all, you are the famous mate, of the famous Witch of Appalachia that I'm speaking with. I have lots of sweet tidbits for you! The murder of Master Bretton Clawson started the whole terrible situation!"

"Wait," Cathleen interrupted. "The "Claw" has been killed? When did this happen? Have they captured his killer?"

Parsons told them how the Master of the Outlander Wizard Scouts had been found murdered along with his orderly, by another Scout investigating a report of demon intrusion in the area. He sent the bodies back to the Council, for a closer study of their deaths and to begin the investigation.

"Well, enough talk! We must be off on the Time Thread Sir Alex provided me," Parsons rushed to say.

"I need a few things, Parsons. You will wait for one hour of time in this realm. Stay here until I come back for you."

Cathleen and Jason returned to their bedroom where they both dressed warmly for the blistering cold, they'd surely encounter traveling on the Time Thread.

She made a quick call to their Vet, asking in her message that he pick Cromwell up for an indefinite boarding period. The Vet was a good friend and would use his own key to collect his furry ward. He'd done this on many out-of-the-blue occasions. Cathleen knelt beside Cromwell to prepare him for their departure. "You will be fine at the Doc's for a few days, Cromwell. He'll be here in a little while to get you. Ok, my boy?" She kissed him on his gray head, stroking his wiry fur. Cromwell blinked his eyes twice, putting his head back on his paws. He looked resigned to his fate, but that stoic appearance seemed to be the perpetual look of all Irish Wolf Hounds. With a final pat, she jumping up to stuff a few items into her leather backpack.

Jason didn't need to tell Cathleen he'd be along on this investigation. He moved efficiently around their bedroom, stuffing his own backpack. He and Cathleen had formed a very successful detective team, long ago. Where she went, he went. No argument. No discussion needed. His Deputy loved the over-time and never questioned Jason's quick trips out of Iron Mountain. A terse text message to his Deputy's cell phone and Jason was cleared to take off.

They were shoving enough clothes for a few days into their packs, when Cathleen finally spoke. "Whoever is responsible for murdering such a powerful wizard as The Claw, has sent the Council of Greens a strong message, sweetie. He or she, has powerful dark magic and they are gunning for the rest of the Council."

Chapter 3

Twenty minutes later, they found Parsons sitting comfortably on the hearth rug, staring into the yellow and orange flames. He wore a faraway look on his round face, his pointy ears pinkening from the fire's warmth.

"Parsons, Jason and I are ready to make the journey back to the Council's Citadel. Do you need my help to find the Thread?"

"No, Mistress. I have it right here," he said cheerfully.

Setting his webbed feet firmly, the House Buddy raised his arms straight out in front, his hands together as if praying. The lilting words of the Old Tongue reverberated in the stillness of the house. "Sli sruth bhua." He pulled his hands apart, drawing an arc-shape as he lowered his arms, which left a shimmering trail hanging in the air in front of him.

Cathleen and Jason slipped their arms through their pack straps, each grabbing hold of the rainbow-like Thread with both hands. This form of spatial travel was well known to both of them, but as Jason took a deep breath, Cathleen was reminded that this would always be a hair-raising experience for her husband.

When Parsons took his place next to Cathleen, the Thread shuddered and the room vanished into a silvery fog.

Jason felt the pressure of being squeezed between two realities, he closed his eye trying to ignore the stress the shift to another place in time, was putting on his body.

Cathleen watched him closely. They all felt the familiar bump, when the realities melded at some point along the Thread and she grabbed his arm. "Honey, how are you doing?" she said close to his ear.

"Well, I know I'd make a poor astronaut. Don't think I'll ever get used to Time Threads."

They began looking around. Parsons mumbled some arcane words and the colors of the Thread coalesced until it became a single dot and disappeared. "We are here, Mistress," Parsons said, smiling broadly at the pair.

"And where exactly would that be, Parsons?" she said bringing the House Buddy's attention to their surroundings.

They found themselves staring across at a green wall of woodland, so thick, it looked nearly impenetrable. Directly behind them was a steep canyon, the precipitous drop throwing back echoes of winds howling below.

"Oh, dear. It would appear the Thread deposited us too soon. Tsk. Tsk. How disappointing."

"Parsons," Cathleen said, beginning to feel a little nervous at being deposited in an area she didn't recognize. Though she'd traveled extensively over the Emerald Isle, she intuitively knew this was no where on that beautiful land. "Do you know where we landed? This place doesn't look at all familiar to me. In fact, it doesn't even feel like our..." Just as she was about to say "reality," a chilling howl filled the air, sending a ripple of alarm through the trio.

Jason slipped his hand to his side in a natural response, finding no holstered weapon to draw and defend. He felt the same vulnerability every time they went on these paranormal investigations. And every time, he knew his gun would be no defense against the dark arts that Cathleen went up against.

"Parsons, do you have any idea where we are and what made that howl?" Cathleen asked the House Buddy, exasperation tinging her words.

He was turning in a slow circle, looking about himself like a tourist in a new city. "Oh, indeed! I am quite certain of our location," he answered, his eyes roaming over the barrier of trees ahead of them.

Jason stepped closer to him, towering over the elfish creature saying, "Then tell us now, before we have to face that thing in there!"

Clearly rattled by the turn of events and Jason's near proximity, Parsons admitted, they had somehow deviated from the course set for the Council Chambers. "In fact, he continued, "we are standing between the Precipice of Doom and the entrance to Chameleon Woods."

Jason was watching Cathleen for her response to this news. Her face showed little reaction, but he knew her well enough to recognize that she was struggling for composure before she spoke.

"I'm familiar with the legends about this place. According to those, a magic user finding themselves here can only escape the cliffs by trekking through the forest."

"Mistress, you are correct, but the creatures that live in the woodlands are most fierce. They can be quite devious, changing their appearance to blend with their environment, or putting on a new body entirely, to look as harmless as a kitten, while they hide a saber tooth tiger beneath. No. No. There must be a better way."

Jason stepped closer to Cathleen. "Can't we just fly from here to safety, or catch another Thread?"

"No sweetie. When a magic user finds themselves dropped into the dark side of a Thread stream, as we have, their power is reduced. It's like a battery, slowly draining, or losing power, because it's exposed to extremes in cold for a long period."

"Cathleen, are you saying your own powers are diminished here?"

"I don't know to what degree, but yes. As surely as that Blood Bird is perched on that boulder over there, watching us."

Jason spun around to see the fantastical creature cocking its head, watching them.

About the size of a turkey vulture, the plump body and long tail were covered in deep, crimson plumage. Its head topped a long, flexible neck, allowing it to turn at impossible angles and directions while it studied the new arrivals.

Cold, reptilian eyes, studied the trio like possible buffet items. The whole time he looked them over, a long, black tongue darted in and out of the sharp beak, giving the impression he was tasting them on the air currents.

"What's our plan, here?" Jason said without taking his eyes off the predator.

"We'll have to make our way through that wall of trees, Jason. As soon as we do, I'll try to conjure another Thread directly into the Council Chambers."

Turning to the silent House Buddy, she added. "Parsons, I'll need you to act as guide through the forest. I know you can pop in and out of existence at will and if anything threatens you, you can disappear until I deal with it."

Parsons puffed out his thin chest at the honor of leading the important pair through Chameleon Woods. He had already forgotten that it was his mistake that placed them all in jeopardy to begin with, returning quickly to his genial self.

Cathleen and Jason readjusted their backpacks and she told Parsons they were ready to start.

As they moved off, Parsons tried to sound self-assured.

"It will only take an hour of time in the natural realm, to cross through this wood," he said over the narrow slope of his shoulder, to his companions.

Jason grunted, following close behind Cathleen. He was searching the forest floor for a heavy limb to carry as a weapon if needed.

Cathleen glanced over at him, guessing at his desire to have something besides his wits to fight with. She didn't have the heart to tell him that while they were stranded in this dark realm, her magic might prove as weak as the limb he secured for himself.

The giant Blood Bird seemed indifferent to their departure, leaping from his perch and making slow, lazy circles over the Precipice of Doom.

Jason caught sight of it just before they entered the fastness of the woods, thinking the bird was likely searching out poor souls like them, that ended up between a rock and a hard place.

They had no choice but to walk single file due to the way the trees grew in thick orderly rows. Weaving their way through was slow going and Cathleen wasn't sure they'd even made it to the mid-point when they heard another howl.

They stopped and Parsons quickly shifted position, to stand slightly behind Cathleen.

Jason peered into the shadowed trees ahead, before speaking quietly to his wife. "Whatever creature that was, that howl was different from the first one we heard. It was a call, or signal to a pack."

Cathleen knew Jason's lifelong connection to the rugged forests of Appalachia made him an expert on hunting and tracking. He was especially well-versed in the nature of the greatest pack-predator of those mountains, the wolf.

The only challenge to his expertise in these woodlands was that these wolves, if that's what they were, could change form, going from predator to partridge, in a blink. This ploy would catch any intended prey off guard. And Cathleen knew, they were the prey. It was time for her to try some simple magic, testing to see how diminished her power might have become in the cursed forest.

Cathleen told Parsons to get behind a giant, moss covered trunk, lying slightly off their path. She wanted no distractions from the chatty House Buddy when she attempted to test her power.

Jason stood behind and to her left, waiting to see how blunted her magic had become under the influence of the Chameleon Forest.

Cathleen began a slow, lilting chant. Two, then three more howls filled the wood-scented air around them. Trying not to be distracted by a gnawing feeling of exposure to an unseen danger, she continued speaking in the Old Tongue. She asked the Green Mother for a champion to fight off the approaching pack of creatures. Gratefully, she saw a form begin to take shape directly in front of her. The shape became more substantial and Cathleen could make out a tall male. His head hung down, a thick head of salt and pepper hair obscuring his face. She watched while the shimmering body solidified into a muscular, broad chested man. He stood like a soldier, his feet planted wide apart, his arms folded in front.

He lifted his head to meet her gaze.

"Greetings, Cathleen O'Brien, daughter of Liam and Brighid, Master Wizards of the Greens. I am Will Farley, Council Historian, at your service."

Chapter 4

Cathleen shot Jason a look with a question attached. Who needs an Historian?

The Historian's eyes were riveted on her as he awaited her response.

Cathleen finally found her voice. "Greetings to you, Master Historian. Please forgive my obvious confusion, but I was trying to summon a warrior to stand beside us when we faced the coming pack of wolf creatures."

"Ah, those would be the false mongrels, known to me as Shredders. The name infers much. Like all in the Chameleon Woods, they are part of this "foidin mearai," this little place of confusion, where much is dangerous, disguised as innocent, the converse being true also."

While he was describing the pack of hunters, still calling from different parts of the woods in sharp barks and howls, Jason stepped up beside Cathleen. His presence was met with a thick, raised eyebrow by the broad-shouldered Historian. Jason was on his guard, knowing not everything here was as it appeared.

Cathleen gave him a quick nod, quickly introducing him to the Historian.

"We were unaware your mate would be joining you on this assignment. As a sworn Protector of the Green, you may pass into other realms where his mortality will be in great peril."

Jason spoke, keeping his voice casual. "While I appreciate your concern for my safety, Historian, Cathleen and I have been working as partners on many cases requiring the same amount of diligence and care. I'm still here to testify to our success."

Will Farley seemed taken aback for a moment with such bold comments, but quickly covered his annoyance with a brisk nod of his head.

"My research on you, Jason Tate, tells me you are an enforcer of the laws of the first realm. This will be a welcome talent on this case."

Cathleen stood by quietly, while the men sorted out status and position in the game of macho chairs. It was a tiresome display, but one she tried to be patient with, for the sake of male pride.

She finally broke into their conversation.

"We need to move, right now, Historian, but I am still in need of my answer. Why were you sent in response to my summons?"

Her directness brought a quick smile to the rugged features of the man, making him even more handsome. "In another time, I served the Greens as a Detached Outlander Wizard Scout. Some called me a Mercenary. I am still used in that position on special assignment, unbeknownst to all, but the Arch Wizard, Sir Alex. I share this, only to quiet your concerns regarding my abilities."

Cathleen was happy he cleared up her doubts and relieved with having more than a scholar at her side.

"And now, let's get through these hateful woods and quickly. I smell the Shredders as they close in," he said looking into the deeply shadowed hallows in the trees.

He started to move off when Jason called out, "Wait up! Where's the little guy?"

Cathleen watched as Jason moved to the tree trunk. He looked back at her and shook his head.

"Historian," Cathleen called to his retreating back. He'd already set a quick pace. "The Arch Wizard's House Buddy, our guide, has disappeared. We can't leave here until we find him," she called after him.

Not waiting for his response, Cathleen and Jason hurried toward the large tree trunk where Parsons should have been. Not finding him there they headed back toward the Precipice of Doom, thinking he might return there for safety.

"Protector!" the Historian shouted.

Cathleen turned her head in the direction of his voice, catching movement from the corner of her eye. The rotting trunk that she sent Parsons to hide behind earlier suddenly sprang up from the ground, shaking like a wet dog, flinging thick lumps of spongy moss in every direction. When it ceased these gyrations, a squat green creature stood before them.

It was no taller than Cathleen, but its thick, greenish body and limbs rippled with brute force. Something resembling a fleshy, wild mushroom cap, sat where a head would be found. Several antennae protruded from this, waving like sea kelp under water.

Cathleen stepped slightly in front of Jason wanting to assess this potential threat.

It looked innocent enough at first glance, no teeth showing, no hands ending in sharp claws. Just a tree stump that suddenly became animated, though for no apparent reason. And it definitely had something to do with the House Buddy's vanishing act.

The next minute, she knew it wasn't as innocent as she assumed.

It moved so quickly Cathleen barely registered it was charging her like a battering ram. At the last second, she jumped to the side, falling against Jason. He was standing with his legs set firmly, ready to fight and was able to catch her, before she fell to the ground.

The fast-moving being made a sharp turn, charging them both just as she regained her footing. The creature had a little surprise in store for them when the soft head opened into a rubbery mouth, displaying several rows of ragged teeth. The air carried the rank odor of rot coming off it as it closed on the waiting pair.

Cathleen shouted a charm bringing the sacred Celtic Fire to her hand, hurtling a spinning mass of green flames into the gapping mouth of the monster.

Suddenly, the woods were filled with its shriek of agony. The flames consumed it from the inside, until it imploded into a gray ash heap.

It was over as quickly as it began. Cathleen stood next to Jason as the Historian approached from where he'd been watching.

Looking down at the oily gray smoke rising in a column from the ground, he turned a cool eye on Cathleen as if appraising her. "You did well, Protector, but were foolish to turn back without me. I could have told you this was a Forest Watchman. It is a carnivorous being that preys on the unwary entering Chameleon Woods. Was Parsons anywhere near it before he disappeared?"

Cathleen smarted from his comment about her being foolish, but knew the remark was meant to instruct her and not as a rebuke.

Jason spoke up before she could answer.

"Historian, we would have appreciated that warning when you came to us earlier, so we might have been more alert about running into a Watchman. And yes, the little guy was hunkered down behind that stump thing."

The Historian turned his steely gray eyes on Jason.

To Cathleen's surprise he spoke in a mild tone.

"You are correct. I should have told you but be warned now. Everything in here should be viewed with suspicion, no matter how innocent it might appear. This is, after all, called Chameleon Woods for good reason."

A loud popping sound interrupted any response on Jason's part.

Parsons suddenly returned from wherever he'd taken refuge, a broad smile on his face.

"Mistress, I am back! I needed to hide in the In-Between, when I felt the lifeform inside the tree trunk. Please forgive me for abandoning you and your mate, but it seemed wiser to go to that safe place, than stay here and face whatever was pretending to be a hollow stump."

The elfish House Buddy caught sight of the Historian, standing quietly next to Jason. After a great intake of breath, he made a low bow to the powerfully built man.

"Master Historian, this humble Parsons greets you. Can I assume you are here at my Master's behest?"

Cathleen said, "I summoned another Wizard and the Historian answered. If you will lead on Historian, I think we're ready to get moving now."

Turning his back to the small group, the Historian set a fast pace, never looking to see if they followed. Cathleen and Jason put Parsons between them and hurried after him.

"This is highly irregular, Mistress," Parsons said to Cathleen.

"The Historian is only good for quoting the great Wizards of the Greens and sharing facts about the Council of the Greens and the Green Mother. What good can he possibly offer our tiny band?" he asked solemnly.

Cathleen looked back at him, answering, "We'll get to see in a few minutes, Parsons. There's something besides the butterflies in these woods."

Chapter 5

The Historian led their little caravan as they trekked through the silence of Chameleon Woods.

Parsons was now walking in the footsteps of the Historian, anxious for his protection and not sure of Cathleen's abilities, she figured.

Jason, ever alert, spoke softly to Cathleen, walking slightly ahead of him. "Cathleen, have you noticed there are no bird calls and we haven't flushed any critters out of the bush, moving through these woods?"

Cathleen slowed, letting Jason catch up to her before answering.

"I agree, it's very odd. I haven't heard anything except our breathing and the sounds of whatever we crunch under foot. It could be these woods have no natural life, like we'd have back home. But stay on the lookout for anything that might have blended into this woodland, like the Forest Watchman did."

They'd been moving for the better part of an hour when the Historian held up his fist, signaling to halt.

Cathleen and Jason both moved carefully over the debris on the forest floor until they stood beside the other wizard and the anxious looking Parsons.

The Historian peered intently at a large boulder, set in the first clearing they would cross. The sunny area was crowded with lush, flowering bushes, covered with the fluttering wings of hundreds of huge, multicolored butterflies. In any other woodland, this would have been a delightful discovery, but here in Chameleon Woods, the scene put everyone on alert.

Parsons crept closer to Will Farley, but the Historian barely took note as he mutely studied the scene.

He pulled on the rucksack he wore fastened across his broad chest and back, never taking his eyes from the tranquil display before them.

Reaching into the leather pouch, he took out a handful of withered berries. Popping them into his mouth, he chewed a minute.

Jason and Cathleen watched intently. Jason raised his eyebrows wondering what the other man was doing. Cathleen gave a shrug, showing she was as much in the dark as he was, with the Historian's odd actions.

Still without speaking, the Historian bent down and picked up a rock, big enough to fill his large hand. He briefly looked over at the bemused faces around him and then hurled the stone at the boulder. It hit hard, making a thwacking sound that reverberated around the silent forest like thunder rolling through the trees.

Cathleen focused like a laser on the gray, mossy boulder. A tremor rippled through it, from top to bottom.

The butterflies that were darting peacefully among the flowers nearby all froze, their slender bodies hanging in the still air. In a coordinated movement, the colorful multitude turned as one, to face the direction of the missile's launch. With some unheard command, they began lining up in front of the boulder. They formed a solid, multicolored line, resembling mounted troops waiting to charge.

Cathleen slipped into her Inner Eye to better study this odd apparition. She was shocked to see small, gnome faces staring back at her.

Parsons shouted, "Grim Faeries! That's what's been following behind!"

Too late, the Historian slapped a hand over the House Buddy's mouth.

As if his yell had been the signal they waited for, the colorful line arrayed in front of the huge rock, charged.

High squeals blew like bugles from tiny mouths, filled with pointy teeth. Blackish, forked tongues darted in and out while they flew pell-mell directly at the startled group.

Jason tugged on Cathleen's arm to point to the boulder, now standing on two hairy legs and holding a spiked cudgel at its side. Any skin that wasn't covered in a thick mat of soot colored hair, was a dull gray. The head had the appearance of a pitted boulder, set atop a stump of a neck.

Cathleen shouted, "Historian, do something with the Grim Faeries, I'll handle the other."

"It's some kind of Rock Hobgoblin!" she shouted over to her husband.

"Jason, help me distract it before it joins the little monsters attacking the Historian!"

Jason never hesitated, moving quickly into the small glade. He grabbed a dead limb lying nearby. Standing with legs apart like a batter in Wriggly Field waiting for the next pitch, the first of the pixie demons came into range. His swing connected with the Grim Faerie, sending it hurtling through the trees.

The Rock Hobgoblin jerked its over-sized head in the direction of the newest attacker and the squeal of the pixie demon. It was moving faster than Jason thought its stumpy legs could carry it. It lifted the spiked cudgel, ready to take off Jason's head.

Cathleen came out of the woods behind the attacking creature and threw a powerful binding spell over it. This stopped it mid-stride. Its own momentum and overly stout torso finished the job and carried it to the ground. As soon as its body hit the earth, all but his head was bound to the earth. It opened its cavernous mouth; a yowl of rage shook the trees and feathery ferns where it landed.

The Historian didn't bother to check on the wizard and her mate, knowing full well she could handle herself. His attention was riveted on the swarm of Grim Faeries that he was carefully luring into his trap.

Parsons stood behind the Historian, peeping out from behind his broad back and unknowingly becoming the bait in that snare.

Knowing the massing Grims would be attracted to the fresh blood of the conjured being, the Historian jumped aside, exposing the House Buddy to the greedy mouths of the horde.

For all their innocent looks, the Historian knew how they earned the nick name "Vampire Imps." They lived off the life blood of magical beings and those created by magic like the House Buddy. He'd destroyed many of their kind when he roamed the various realms as the Detached Outlander.

Parsons went rigid watching the approaching mob of Grim Faeries. His eyes were wide with terror as the horde buzzed around him, their razor-sharp teeth flashing like tiny daggers. He was almost too stupefied to pop into the In-Between until the very last second, when his arm was grazed by a long incisor.

He knew that empty place was safer than facing a swarm of blood-thirsty Grims and vanished from sight just as the greedy creatures closed in.

That was the Historian's cue to act. He infused the blood berries he'd ingested earlier, with a specific power through his incantation.

"Neallta fola!" the call for death and annihilation rang in the air.

Immediately, a thick red cloud shot from his open mouth. The mist enveloped the swarm of Grims, surrounding them in a dense blanket, they couldn't break through.

With his Inner Eye, the Historian watched as the confused Imps flew into one another, becoming disoriented and enraged. They began to blindly lash out, tearing into the wings and slender bodies of other Grims colliding with them.

After a few minutes, the Historian raised his hand and the mist lifted. The grassy glade was littered with the tattered remains of the Grim Faeries. He studied the carnage they wrought upon themselves, reminded once more, how lethal the little demons really were.

There was a popping sound as the House Buddy reappeared next to the Historian. He looked around at the destroyed Vampire Faeries, giving a small shudder.

"I am tiring of all these narrow escapes, I can tell you!" he said indignantly.

The Historian looked over in the far corner of the glade where the Rock Goblin lay, pinned to the ground under Cathleen's spell. The beast had gone very still, as if waiting for sentence to be passed over it.

The Historian moved to the creature's head, looking over at Cathleen. Without comment he began another chant to destroy the captive.

Jason was watching Cathleen for her reaction to the Historian's actions. He knew she wasn't a wizard who appreciated being side-lined by another magic user.

"Wait, Historian!" she said firmly.

The Historian passively waited as Cathleen and Jason came over to him.

"We won't destroy this creature. He's already subdued and can't break my Binding spell. He may actually be useful to us, if we're ever to get out of these woods. The killer of Master Clawson will certainly be using the time we lose in here, to cover their trail."

"And exactly how would you use this creature, Protector?" he asked with more than a hint of skepticism in his tone.

"Actually, I will ask him to take us through the rest of the forest."

Without waiting for the expected reaction from the other wizard, Cathleen crouched down beside the hobgoblin's knobby, gray head.

"Hear me, beast, I am the wizard who binds you to this ground. If you want to be freed and not destroyed, you will do as I say. Guide us safely out of the Chameleon Woods. You must swear this to me under the eye of the Green Mother."

The hobgoblin blinked eyes resembling small mud balls and answered in a surprisingly smooth voice.

"Release me Wizard. I will serve. I swear this, under the eye of the Green Mother."

Cathleen got to her feet, looking down into the dark face, she reversed her spell and stepped back.

The Historian immediately raised his arms, ready to call down another spell if this mythic being, turned on them.

For her part, Cathleen sensed something in this Goblin that was more curiosity than killer. She didn't break eye-contact as it got to its lumpy feet.

"I was called Dunny, by the Druid wizard who placed me here. That was in the Dark Times of the first realm. I am a rock fort, like my given Druid name."

No one of the small group was prepared for such a human-like sharing by the hobgoblin.

Jason was the first to speak. "We welcome your service, Dunny, and are glad for your help in our travels here."

The creature made a snorting sound that might be taken for a pleased response. "Dunny will lead now." He turned, leaving the glade, and heading back into the thick tree line.

Cathleen walked beside Jason with the Historian close behind. The returned Parsons trailed the huge figure of the hobgoblin as he led the group.

"What did you do to make him so compliant, sweetie?" Cathleen whispered.

"I treated Dunny like an undercover informant. What he's doing puts him in jeopardy too and we needed to recognize that sacrifice."

The Historian interjected from behind, "But he got his freedom, what else could he want?"

Jason's answered simply, "Respect as any living creature I suppose."

Chapter 6

Dunny stopped suddenly, causing Parsons to bump into him. The rock creature was oblivious of the contact, but Parsons rubbed his head. They were standing in a very dense part of the forest, with only a diffused light filtering through a canopy of foliage and thick limbs. The natural dome acted as an effective baffle, keeping all sounds from penetrating and any from escaping.

"Harpies Haven. Dunny doesn't like this place," the huge hobgoblin grumbled quietly.

They all followed Dunny's gaze toward a rough slope, leading down into a rock-strewn ravine. The Historian pointed out a cave, a heavy curtain of trees, almost completely camouflaging its presence.

From where they stood, the opening to the cave appeared small, maybe big enough for a man to pass through on hands and knees.

"Are these Harpies something your familiar with, Cathleen?" Jason asked while the group studied the lay of the land.

"They were considered mythical creatures at one time, with women's heads and the bodies of birds of prey," she answered quietly, but the Historian's sharp hearing picked up every word as she continued.

"The Green Wizards found proof of their existence during the Dark Times, when Dunny was put here, I suppose.

They discovered covens of them, scattered over the known world. Reports from the earliest Outlander Wizard Scouts, talked of gnawed human remains, found in caves throughout the hill country, of what would come to be called, Ireland."

The Historian came over to where they huddled.

"You are well informed, Protector, but there has been an evolution of sorts among the Harpies since the Dark Times. They have developed keener senses, especially their sense of smell and hearing. It is said they can hear a rose bud open and smell the scent of fear in a rabbit. There is no doubt they know we're in their forest."

Dunny was watching the cave for any movement, when a large shadow passed directly above. It darkened much of the ground and cast into shadow, the mossy ledge jutting over the cave's opening.

A high, eerie call and the sound of heavy wings, flapping in a slow, strong rhythm, preceded the appearance of the Harpy, just above the hidden cave.

The watchers dropped to their stomachs, creeping forward in single line, stretching out along the ridge.

For all his size, Dunny was remarkably quiet in his movements, and his dark matted hair, proved a perfect concealment among the shadows.

The Historian was watching Cathleen from the corner of his eye, leaning closer to whisper.

"If need be, Dunny can revert to his boulder form. Let us hope he will stay as he is. We may need his brute strength."

Cathleen shot a quick look at the Rock Hobgoblin, noticing how Parsons had crept closer to the imposing creature. The little House Buddy was wriggling around on his round middle, trying to get comfortable on the rocky ground.

She wondered how much Parsons knew about these Harpies. He was supposed to guide them through these woods safely and that bit of knowledge seemed pretty darned relevant, though he never bothered to share it.

The Harpy circled the area just below them and finally landed on the outcropping of overgrown rock and scrub grass, before hopping down in front of the cave.

With its humped, feathered back turned toward the silent watchers, it appeared   the body was as large as a good-sized vulture. Folding in its wings, the feathers shone an iridescent gold and purple, with wing-tips a deep blue.

This beautiful array of color was diminished when a human-like head swiveled around on a long, scaly neck, cautiously looking behind itself.

The head was like no mortal woman Cathleen had ever seen. She noticed how the Historian winced, when he caught sight of its face. Jason's similar reaction included a deeper scowl of apprehension.

Clumps of hair dangled from a boney head, dark and lank against a dull-green scalp. The skin on its face hung loosely from sharp cheek bones and a high forehead. Its folds created a greenish hue resembling algae clinging to the side of a pool.

For Cathleen, it was the small, darting eyes that betrayed the raptor this creature truly was. They were black holes in the sallow face, empty of any natural life.

Cathleen had a disturbing thought.

That cavern is likely filled with these creatures!

They all waited for the demon-beast to enter the cave. It began to lower itself to scoot through the small opening, when it hesitated and began sniffing the air around itself. Its head bobbed up and down as it tasted smells through sharp nostrils.

Suddenly, it stopped.

The hideous face swung in their direction, though still looking directly in front and not above, where they all waited in utter silence. The Harpy seemed satisfied there were no enemies lurking about, tucked its huge head into the feathered chest and began to enter the low cave opening.

Parsons, like the others, watched the Harpy closely. When it stretched its long neck, its head partially inside the opening, the House Buddy shifted positions. This movement resulted in dislodging several small rocks from under his belly, sending them cascading down the incline toward the cave site.

In the hush of the thick woods, the stones sounded like the hooves of running horses.

The Harpy pulled its head out of the entranceway. Spinning around on its three toed feet, sharp talons dug ominously into the hard dirt, making deep gashes in the earth. Its forked tongue darted out, tasting the air in every direction.

The little group on the ridge froze in place, trying not to make a sound. Parsons, still lying on his stomach, crossed his spindly arms over his head and squeezed his eyes shut.

The Harpy stopped twisting its head and shut its mouth. Slowly, it raised its hideous face and stared up at the ridge.

The Historian shot a look over at Cathleen and Jason. They were as still as cadavers.

His eyes traveled over to Dunny, discovering the Rock Goblin was partially morphed back to his boulder shape, his head and shoulders looking part of the scattered rock formations.

Parsons was quivering where he lay, his arms wrapped protectively over his head, his eyes closed tight. The Historian was certain the vibrations of the House Buddy's trembling body, would be felt by the Harpy.

Cathleen had followed the Historian's eyes and reasoning, knowing these mythical creatures had supernatural senses. Wondering what it would do next, she didn't have long to wait.

The Harpy began to open its wings, spreading them to their five-foot span. Using strong leg muscles, it launched itself into the air.

"She wants to see what's up here," Cathleen whispered into Jason's ear.

He still held the heavy limb he'd retrieved from the forest floor earlier. Cathleen saw him tighten his grip, when he gave her a knowing look.

Cathleen was going through several of her mom's favorite recipes, as she referred to her effective, most often deadly spells.

That's when she realized they had an alley that could easily take on the Harpy, but she needed to get Dunny to do it before it attacked. The element of surprise would be with them if he could disable the flying menace before it called for back-up.

Cathleen raised her head slightly calling out to the Goblin. Though half of him was transformed, she hoped he could still hear her.

"Dunny! We need you to take this Harpy down, now!"

The horrible face of the bird-woman rushed at them through the sparse branch cover of the ridge. They lay sprawled out, looking like easy pickings to the raptor's hungry eyes.

Its mouth was wide open, showing yellowed incisors as it flew directly at Parson's quaking body. Tucking the huge wings close to its body, the Harpy dove at the beacon-red, mop of curls at the top of Parson's head.

Cathleen and the Historian were on their feet instantly, shouting in the ancient language.

Whatever spell he used was ineffective and Cathleen's call for a Dome of Protection for Parsons, failed to produce more than a shimmer around his cringing form.

"What's happening? Why aren't our spells working?" Cathleen called over to the Historian a few feet away.

The Harpy, startled by the two wizards shouting, pulled up from its dive long enough to judge the threat. It immediately flew back to the quaking House Buddy, hooking its talons through Parsons leather belt and began to carry him off, screaming and pleading.

Cathleen grabbed for Parson's dangling legs as they passed over head. While she hung on, the Harpy flapped its wide wings, struggling against the drag of Cathleen's added weight.

Jason leapt up and gripping the stout limb, swung at the Harpy's green head.

It connected with a wet thump, causing it to drop the House Buddy where Jason stood ready to deliver another blow.

The Harpy came down in a pile of feathers, one wing bent at an odd angle, obviously broken. There was a deep gash covering the forehead, oozing a thick yellow blood.

The three humans stood over the fallen creature, while Parsons and Dunny watched from a distance. Cathleen was wondering why Dunny didn't help them when she called over to him. Then it dawned on her.

He's frightened out of his wits!

She'd need to inspire some confidence in the hulking creature if he was to be of any use in the cursed woods.

The Harpy was regaining consciousness and began babbling a few words in a language unfamiliar to Cathleen. The Historian gave a sharp chuckle.

"It's saying Thor struck her down with his golden hammer," he said smiling at Jason.

Cathleen asked, "What language is it speaking?"

"It's a barbaric mix of tongues, both human and avian, becoming those chirping, sharp sounds you hear throughout. My time as an Outlander Wizard Scout introduced many such oddities into my lexicon.

Dunny and Parsons didn't move while the three studied the dazed Harpy, wondering what to do with it.

Cathleen suggested they bind her there, buying them time to make it out of the woods.

"The others will find her soon enough," she concluded.

A few words and the creature lay bound to the earth and muzzled against alerting any of the flock to their presence.

"Let's move," Cathleen said after the last word of her spell.

She was certain it was working properly this time, unlike the others she tried to cast.

Dunny took lead once more, though he hadn't spoken since they confronted the Harpy. Cathleen wondered if her assessment of the big creature was correct; that he was afraid.

Something didn't add up in her mind. When Jason came up beside her, he confirmed her misgivings, though in a totally different way.

"Listen love. Don't think I'm being overly suspicious, but there's something not right with the big guy. I get the feeling he knows something he isn't telling us."

He said the last, looking at the Rock Goblin's broad back. The muscles there were bunched in clusters, like rock formations, giving him an air of invincibility.

"I agree, sweetie. I need to test your theory and something that's been bothering me too."

They were walking single file through a field of tall, yellow grasses. The woodlands seemed to have dropped away for good and they found themselves in peaceful glens and sweet-smelling fields, such as the one they passed through at the moment.

Parsons told them they would be back to their Time Thread as soon as they crossed this sun-lit patch of ground.

Dunny was still in the lead, trampling out a clear path with his wide feet and helping them move at a faster pace.

Jason was behind Cathleen in line, taking rear-guard position. Cathleen slowed down, signaling to Jason she was ready to make her move.

"Parsons, walk with me awhile," she called.

The Historian glanced back at her, a quizzical look on his face, but he kept walking without comment.

The House Buddy went to the back of the line, matching Cathleen's speed and obviously waiting for her to speak.

Abruptly, she grabbed a thin arm in a tight grip and began an invocation for discernment of things hidden in clear view.

"Fais-tine!"

The House Buddy squirmed under the pressure of her hand and Cathleen felt the skinny arm become rough under her fingers. A pungent, fish odor, began to come off Parson's body as he protested the mistreatment by the wizard in a whinny voice.

Cathleen repeated her charm three times. Finally, with her Inner Eye, saw she was holding a tentacle and not an arm, with three others where an arm and scrawny legs should have been.

The creature in her grip had bulbous eyes, protruding from stems at the top of a head the size of a deflated volleyball. Its mouth was a deep slit, in an otherwise, blank face.

She let go of the slimy appendage, dropping a Net of Nettles over the odd creature at the same time, warning it not to move, or pay the consequences in extreme pain.

The Historian heard her spell making and knew what she was doing, but until he looked with his own Inner Eye, he couldn't fathom why.

Jason came up to Cathleen as soon as she grabbed Parson's arm. He couldn't see what she discovered, still looking down on the terrified Parsons.

"Drop your guise immediately creature, or suffer the costs," Cathleen said sternly.

An odd, octopus-like being, stood in front of them, on two tentacles gone ridged as boards, its mouth turned down and looking defiant. Its camouflage dropped away for all to see.

"And now we need to find Parsons," Cathleen said under her breath.

Chapter 7

"You have captured a creature transported here from the deep waters of our Lochs," the Historian was telling Cathleen.

"Do you think that's where he's stashed Parsons?"

The Historian stopped to consider her question.

"No. I believe the House Buddy is in fact, a convenient face for this being to wear. Am I correct...Guardian?"

"You have discovered my true identity, so likely guessed at my mission, Historian," the one he named, Guardian responded.

Turning to Cathleen, it bowed slightly. Cathleen removed The Net of Nettles before it could pierce his gray skin.

"It is as the Master Historian has said. I am, what you humans might call, a morphing secret agent. I am known as the Guardian by the Council of Green Wizards. They only call upon my presence, when there is substantial threat to the Mother's order. In this instance, the murder by unknowns, of Master Bretton Clawson, better known as The Claw.

None on the current sitting Council has ever seen my true form as I constantly change my appearance. It's more palatable to you humans I suspect to see me as one of you."

Jason stepped closer and asked, "But why the disguise as Sir Alex's House Buddy? Didn't the Arch Wizard trust Cathleen's magic? Does Dunny know who you really are?"

"Ah, your mate is a suspicious one, Protector," he said swiveling one eye on its stem in her direction, the other studying Jason.

"Indeed! Sir Alex has full confidence in your magic, Cathleen O'Brien. And combined with the Historian's powers, you are formidable indeed. No, I took the image of the House Buddy, Parsons, to pass among you untethered to the protocol of rank. I always operate alone and this arrangement of guiding you was the simplest way I could act without drawing much attention.

Dunny may appear as dumb as a...well...rock, but he sensed long ago, at my subterfuge, but played along nicely, with a bit of encouragement from me. You'd be surprised how frightened these big oafs are, of finding themselves in a gravel quarry."

This comment fell flat and the scowl on the Historian's face was enough to bring the Guardian back to the point.

"When Parsons went into The In-Between, he was merely detained there, so I could assume his identity. It was a harmless exchange and he's back at the Council Citadel, sleeping in his own cot until I finish here.

But more importantly than the House Buddy's whereabouts, I discovered from my contacts in the Lochs, dark forces have been assembling for a major assault. They are massing, even as we stand here, on the precipice of escaping this dreadful woodland.

Their plan is to wipe out every Outlander Wizard Scout they find. They could take over the frontier, when the force protecting the first realm is destroyed. This would allow them to open the way for the dark minions of the fourth realm.

As the Council's secret agent, I do not want my cover as Parsons, to become useless. In this mission, we need every advantage we can muster. So, if you don't mind, Protector..."

With a slight jerk of his deflated round head, the tentacled creature was transformed yet again, into the meek House Buddy, Parsons. He slipped right back into his part as if there'd been no interruption.

"Are we ready to move out of this awful place, Mistress? I don't wish to spend a second longer than need be and I can feel the tug of the Time Thread, nearby."

Cathleen, cleared her throat, wanting to carry out her part as normally as possible.

"It looks like we are nearly clear of Chameleon Woods, so let's get moving," she responded smoothly.

Jason was quick to follow Cathleen and the restored House Buddy. He shot a quick look over his shoulder at the Historian, who called out a thanks to Dunny for showing them the way.

For his part, the Rock Hobgoblin was looking as relieved as a hairy Goblin might look. He turned toward the tall grasses and the forest beyond, without a second glance at their retreating forms of the interlopers.

Cathleen dropped back to make sure the Historian was bringing up the rear. He nodded as he passed by her and Jason and took up his lead position with Parsons once more, walking behind him.

This assignment gets more interesting by the minute, she was thinking.

As he so often did, Jason seemed to read her mind.

"It's OK, love. Just think of all the boring work waiting for us back home."

They stopped when the Historian held up his hand and conferred quietly with Parsons.

He signaled for Cathleen and Jason to join him where they created a small circle.

They held hands, with Cathleen between Jason and the Historian. Parsons stood next to the Historian and reached out his arm. A violent spasm ran through the group, before total blackness enveloped them.

Jason felt the familiar pressure against his body, as if being squeezed like a tube of toothpaste. His eyes were tightly closed against the sharp, but brief pain.

Within a few heartbeats the shift was completed, with the usual loud pop. They were delivered to the edge of the Emerald Isle, a place where the Outlander Wizard Scouts hunted for demon incursions.

They were all acclimating to normal breathing when they slowly became aware, they stood in front of a fantastic scene.

A barrier, created by a wall of surrounding sea water.

They saw every manner of sea creature suspended in its blue-black depths. Following the curve of the monster wave with their eyes, it appeared endless, hanging there, several stories above their heads, threatening to be released from its motionless state, any moment.

"It's worse than I feared, Mistress," the Guardian said, totally in his Parsons persona.

"The Dark Ones have begun to corrupt the Mother's elements in this remote part of our Emerald Isle. It won't be visible to any human eyes, without the power of discernment, such as the Inner Eye. It will appear normal and natural looking out to sea. Therefore, no warning will be given to the innocents about to be drowned and swept away like so much debris."

"Is this what they plan to do, Parsons? Ring the land with these invisible tsunami waves?" Cathleen asked, not able to keep anxiety out of her voice as she craned her neck to find the white cap of the curling waters.

He answered, "You surely have perceived at least part of their plot, Protector, but I fear the Dark Ones have only begun. We must hurry to find their power base, to stop them perverting the other elements."

 Cathleen speculated they were operating from somewhere close by, since this was the only aberration they discovered thus far.

Jason heard that and interjected his own thoughts.

"Couldn't this just be another diversion, keeping us from investigating the murder?

"If it is, it's a very effective one!" Cathleen responded.

The Historian cleared his throat to take their attention off the fearsome sight of the waters.

"Jason's idea has merit," he said joining the conversation at last.

"I think I should go ahead and investigate the source holding this water in suspension, while you three carry out the murder investigation.

Surely both our roads will lead to the same culprits and we'll reunite at that point."

Jason was secretly pleased the Historian was leaving the small band. He couldn't explain, even to himself, his instinctive dislike for the man, except he didn't tolerate arrogance well.

The Historian was definitely haughty, mostly treating Jason like an appendage of Cathleen's, rather than her partner in this investigation. He didn't like being thin-skinned, and usually wasn't.

This place is sure having an effect on me, he thought as he watched the Historian approach the tidal wave, passing through the opaque, frozen waters, to be quickly lost from sight.

Chapter 8

The band shrank to three when the Historian vanished into the frozen waters of the fantastic tsunami waves. His goal was to locate the source threatening the Emerald Isle in a deluge of massive proportions.

The Guardian reverted back to his own, authoritative voice, though he maintained the persona of the House Buddy. The tentacled secret agent, insisted they call him by that name, to help maintain his cover.

It took both Cathleen and Jason a while, before they grew used to his new, rather bossy voice.

"We need to proceed with this investigation as quickly as possible, else all the viable clues will vanish like the morning mist over the seas," Parson's was saying, as they moved toward a line of hills.

Cathleen was unusually tense trekking through territory unknown to all but the Outlander Wizard Scouts. An unnatural twilight had settled around them, coloring the slopes ahead in shifting tones of red, blending around their base, into a deep rust. This might have seemed quite lovely anywhere else, but struck Cathleen as reminiscent of pooled, dried blood. She wondered why she was having such morbid thoughts and tried to shrug them off. Yet, strange, unsettling feelings of slaughter and mayhem kept invading her mind, as she studied the landscape of her beloved Ireland.

Jason noticed Cathleen give her head several shakes, wondering about the odd behavior, but remained silent. The trees thinned out. Hardy, low-growing vegetation taking their place in the moist environment. They were moving along a rough, narrow path, leading upward to higher hill country. Jason finally spoke into the silence, speculating they might be following some kind of animal trail. Getting no feed-back, he kept any other observations to himself.

They followed this natural track, while the dusk deepened around them, now splashing plum-purples and shades of rich blues, across the meager grasses and scrub trees as they climbed higher.

"This sunset isn't normal, Cathleen," Jason said in a low voice as he walked behind her. "It's been twilight too long, as if something is holding back the night."

Cathleen looked around. She'd been experiencing a strange, distracted feeling. It kept intruding on her thoughts, making her mind wander. They stood at the bottom of a steep incline, leading up to a broad plateau, mid-way to the top. She had a minute of panic. This hike is more of a serious trek and we're getting nowhere fast.

She took Jason's arm, that creeping panic in her eyes. "Honey, we need to make it as far as that level ground above us and reconnoiter around these hills from a better vantage point. I don't know what's come over me, but I feel disoriented. Hopefully, being off this open ground will help clear my head."

"Now that you mention it, love, I've found myself feeling anxious and feeling aggressive, for no apparent reason. Is it possible this place is having an emotional effect on us?"

Before she could answer, Parsons called back to them in his new, authoritative voice. "We must hurry. Our light will soon fade and we must cross these hills to reach the section of borderland The Claw was patrolling, when he met his death. The longer we dawdle, the less evidence will be available to you for your investigation."

The two hurried after the House Buddy, as he curled his bare, webbed feet, around the sharp grasses, climbing the hill like a sure-footed mountain goat. When they all reached the rocky plateau, Cathleen told Parsons about the emotional changes she and Jason had been experiencing. "Does it have something to do with this place?"

"It would appear you are both sensitive to the workings of the Leaspain, the Phantom Faeries that roam these outer boundaries. They are beings composed purely of light in every color of the spectrum. They can be deceptively lovely but are quite mischievous and enjoy causing confusion and harm to intruders in their lands."

Jason asked, "Is that why we have this false twilight?"

"Oh, yes! They do enjoy playing with the Mother's palette of colors. But you mustn't be drawn into the chaos they produce in other creatures, especially the thinking ones, like wizards and human visitors."

Cathleen remarked, "They are called by the Druid name for "dancing lights," but can they be made to show themselves as physical beings?" she went on to ask.

Parsons assured her, "They are loath to appear without their glorious colors, but it can be done. Shall I?"

A curt nod from Cathleen and Parsons began speaking in clicks and grunts. Cathleen had no understanding of this language, making her feel unprepared for what followed.

Suddenly, the air surrounding their position was swarming with dots of color, some whirring around them, leaving colorful tracks in the still air. One by one, the colors came together and a line of creatures formed in a loose semi-circle in front of the three. They were the size of the beautiful Colossus Faeries, almost as tall as Jason, but there the similarity ended. From the multi-colored rainbow they'd seen churning around them, came a mix of flat browns and dull grays. Looking more like willowy monks than the handsome Colossus sprites, they stood with heads drooping as if ashamed.

Cathleen counted seven and approached the shortest among them. She spoke several words in the ancient tongue of the first Green Wizards, choosing them carefully, not wanting to be misunderstood.

The Phantom's head snapped up. It studied Cathleen's face, several inches below its own. Its voice was soft, but Jason and Parsons could both hear the words spoken in perfect English.

"My humble apologies, Protector. We regret taunting you and your companions. We thought you were intruders. My clan and I give you fair welcome."

Cathleen said, "Your help will be enough compensation for trying to confuse our thoughts and perceptions. As Protector, you understand my right to seek your aid?"

The Phantom smiled, "Whatever you ask and it shall be given."

Cathleen said, "We need you to tell us about the murder of the Outlander Wizard Scout, Bretton Clawson. He is known to you, as The Claw."

The leader of the group shifted his eyes from Cathleen to study her companions. Without speaking, he approached Jason, reaching up to lay a thin, grayish hand on his head. "This companion of yours is the one who'll guide you to the place of dying you seek. I have given him the knowledge." Without another word, the Phantom Leaspain Faeries all vanished, leaving a shimmer of glorious color behind like an echo.

Jason gave his head a small shake to rouse himself and began to tell Cathleen and Parsons the information planted by the Phantom. "We need to get to a place called Mandragora's Den. That's where the body of The Claw and his orderly were found by one of his men. I don't know what this place is, but I have an uneasy feeling just saying the name out loud."

Cathleen explained to Jason why this was important information. "Mandragora is Latin for the Mandrake plant. Some wizards believe it has magical properties if harvested during a lunar eclipse, when they'll store hundreds of the plants for their use in ceremonies."

Parsons chimed in, "Many of the Dark Magic users find the Mandrake useful when calling forth demons from the fourth realm as well. Perhaps The Claw uncovered a horde of this plant and was killed to keep the location a secret."

Chapter 9

With the new information, the trio resumed their climb through the hill country, eventually making it to a crest overlooking a deep valley.

"I don't know this place," Parsons was saying as they all studied the tranquil scene below.

"There's smoke coming from somewhere beyond that stream, Cathleen," Jason pointed out.

"Yeah, and that would mean someone was home. Let's get down there and see if they know anything that could help us."

Cathleen started down the steep incline of the hill, Jason and Parsons falling in line behind. Fifteen minutes later they were following a fast running stream, headed in the direction of the smoke column, Jason spotted earlier.

Cathleen spoke quietly to the others as they approached a small cabin. "I don't think we should all go knocking on the door of the cottage. I'd like to stay undetected for now, while you two talk to whoever lives here. I'll be close by, if your welcome gets too warm!"

Parsons led the way through scraggly trees and a smattering of flowering bushes, to the front door of the small, roughly built house. There was one, pane-less window in the front of the cottage, its shutters hanging at odd angels and obviously of no use.

Jason noticed the front door wasn't closed all the way, leaving a small gap which he tried to look through. As he bent low to peer in, he noticed a single candle, shedding a weak light in a sparsely furnished room.

He crept a little closer for a better look, when abruptly the door flew open.

A beautiful woman looked back at him, a broad smile on her lovely face.

Jason was quick to explain he meant no harm but was trying to determine if there was someone at home. His explanation was a bit halting, as he tried to recapture some dignity after being caught snooping.

"You needn't upset yourself so. My door is always open to visitors. I am Neidin, please enter my humble little nest." She stepped aside so Jason and Parsons could enter, closing the door securely after them.

Parsons cleared his throat saying, "Your name is from the old tongue and tells us this place is meant to be a place of rest, peace and safety."

Neidin turned large brown eyes on the House Buddy, staring at him openly. "But of course, you would know this my elfish friend. My name is indeed of the ancient Druid language. You are now safe from any Dark Ones, that might roam this frontier. And you, you are no Outlander Wizard Scout my friend."

She turned toward Jason, studying his face closely.

Before he could respond the front door blew open.

"Ah, another visitor. Welcome wizard. You have found a place of peace within my walls."

Parsons searched the dimly lit room for the visitor, but Jason understood immediately that Cathleen was under a Shadow Wrap. She wouldn't reveal herself until she was sure of a safe reception.

"Wizard, you can drop your concealment. I am the Mother's own daughter and provide a safe venue for any of Her natural beings."

Cathleen immediately dropped her shadows, closing the door with a flick of her wrist.

"Forgive my caution, but I felt the use of magic and had to be certain my companions were safe. I am Cathleen O'Brien, daughter of Liam and…"

"Brighid! How wonderful to have you here. I knew your mother from her days as a Scout and young wizard. She often came here for conversation and rest when she traveled in the borderlands. She was a remarkable wizard indeed."

Cathleen enjoyed hearing about her mother, but quickly turned the conversation to their search. "We're hunting the place where Master Bretton Clawson's body was found by one of his Scouts. I've been tasked with bringing his murderer to the Council of Greens and any information you can share might help in my search."

Neidin suggested they sit around a small table, while she poured a cup of tea for them. "Then we can speak comfortably," she added reassuringly.

Cathleen and Parsons sat. Jason stood behind his wife's chair; his hands folded behind his back like a soldier at parade rest. His vigilance wasn't lost on their hostess as she made a point of smiling sweetly at him.

A large kettle flew out of the hearth, where it'd been hanging over hot coals. Their hostess snatched it by its handle, placing it on the table. She looked briefly at Jason, her expression friendly, but stiff.

She closed her eyes for a blink and four cups and saucers appeared in front of each, with Jason's next to Cathleen's.

"Madame," Parsons said. "We cannot tarry here sipping tea, but need to be on our quest with haste. My Master, the Arch Wizard, will be anxious for results."

The beautiful brown eyes slid over to the House Buddy's frowning face. She gently laid a hand on his thin arm and immediately he relaxed into his chair.

"I shall not detain you for long, my little friend. But let us drink our cup and enjoy a moment of peace together, first."

Jason picked up one of the steaming cups Neidin placed in front of Cathleen. But rather than drinking, he held it to his mouth as if sipping while it cooled. He looked down into Cathleen's cup a minute later and found it nearly empty. For some reason, that put him more on edge.

Neidin placed her cup back on its saucer and was toying with a silver spoon placed near the sugar bowl.

From where he stood, Jason could see her lovely red mouth was shaping whispered words while she gently waved the spoon from side to side.

A heavy silence came over the room, the breathing of the three visitors became the background to Neidin's whispered chant.

Jason didn't move a muscle, but his mind was racing with anxious thoughts of deceit.

He glanced over at Parsons, sitting to Neidin's right. His eyelids were drooping and then closed. A serene smile had replaced the concerned look he wore before the tea. When he looked down at Cathleen, she appeared to have gone rigid in her seat. He was jarred out of his thoughts at the sound of their hostess speaking.

"Well, my handsome friend, it seems only you have not succumbed to my brew," Neidin said, getting to her feet to confront Jason. Casually smoothing the front of her long gown, she added, "This could only mean you didn't drink my tea and that means, you don't trust me."   He actually felt uneasy from the moment they stepped through the cottage door, sensing something there wasn't as it seemed. Now he knew his instincts were right. He backed away from the table, to better move in the close quarters of the small room.

"Don't be foolish, human. I also entertained The Claw on his sojourn through this borderland. Like you, he was on his guard, leaving before my plans could be carried out against him. I've had greater success with others of the Outlander Wizard Scouts, however."

She gave a low, purr-like chuckle as she watched Jason's reactions to her duplicity.

Without warning, the woman lifted her arms and Jason saw a black streak of jagged light shooting from her long fingers. She was whispering more words of magic when Jason rushed her.

His body was thrown backwards when his hand wrapped around Neidin's slender arm. The sound of her shrill laughter filled the small space of the cabin. She raised her arms again, this time gathering the black energy into a spear shaped bolt, ready to hurl into Jason's exposed mid-section.

With her attention drawn from the two at the table, Neidin didn't see Cathleen come off the chair behind her. She didn't turn toward her until the words of another spell casting floated above her own in the small cottage. Green Fire shot from Cathleen's hands, hitting Neidin with the force of a blow torch. Green flames enveloped the slender woman in a burning sheath. Her own dark fire was snuffed out by the winds from the intense blaze enveloping her body.

The beautiful Neidin collapsed to the floor, followed down by an earsplitting scream.

Cathleen watched through the flames as Neidin's face began to melt away like tallow. A chill ran through her when the last thing she saw was Neidin's mouth pull back from her teeth, in a grotesque parody of laughter.

The door exploded from its hinges, landing outside the cottage with a loud crash.

While Cathleen watched, a black light rose up from Neidin's smoldering ruins. Before she could act, it flew out of the cottage where it was lost among the clustered shadows.

Chapter 10

Jason held his wife for a minute, while he collected himself. The shock wave that tore through him from his contact with Neidin's arm left him rattled mentally and shaken physically.

Sometimes he wondered how he was still alive after one of these altercations with a Dark Magic User. This was one of those times!

Cathleen was never surprised at her husband's resilience. She'd been told by her mother, Brighid, this man had hidden depths of power, but even she was unable to fathom them. "Jason, we have to get the little guy and get out of here. The real Neidin likely became a victim of the Deceiver and whatever demons he's called." She walked over to Parsons and whispered a few words to rouse him out of the spell induced by the tea.

"Protector, I thought I was back in the In-Between." He looked around and asked where their hostess was.

"I'm not sure that was the real Neidin, Parsons. If it was an impersonator, I'm afraid Neidin is lost to this realm."

Cathleen wanted to monitor Parsons a few minutes, to be sure the effect of the spelled tea had worn off.

Jason began to look around the rough cottage for any clue that might point them in the right direction for finding The Claw's murderer. He moved to the alcove at the back of the cottage. A narrow bed and small table, were the only furnishings. There was a variety of dried herbs and odd smelling spices on the table. When he picked up a jar with brightly colored berries, he uncovered a square of cloth with strange symbols painted on it.

He brought this to Cathleen, who immediately showed it to Parsons. "Can you read these symbols Parsons?"

"Naturally, in my true form I am conversant with every tongue used and written in the sphere of magic."

Jason realized he'd forgotten that this wasn't the true Parsons, but a tentacled creature in the guise of the House Buddy.

Sometimes I hate magic, he thought frowning.

Parsons voice brought him out of his musing.

"This speaks of a place within a long walk from here, Protector. It's named, Spirit Crusher and from this one symbol, it appears to lie across a bridge. Yes, a bridge. The bridge spans a deep ravine between the final boundary on this side and a pathway into the other realms, including the fourth realm and the Dark Pit of the Sleepless Dead."

Jason listened to every word and felt an unwelcome chill run down his back. He felt alarmed at how close they were to that demon-infested place of horrors.

"That won't be where The Claw was murdered, Parsons. We'll have no need to cross the bridge," Jason heard Cathleen state firmly to his great relief.

He knew it wasn't cowardice, but experience that gave him a bad case of trepidation. He'd seen his share of demons that slithered their way into the realm of the natural, but he'd never been this close to a crossing they might travel.

"Cathleen, it's getting close to full sunset," he said looking out the small window. "I think we'll want to locate the murder site, while we still have some natural light. Your Green Fire might tip off any demons hanging around this place"

"Yeah, good point, sweetie. Parson's put that parchment someplace safe so we can refer to it later if needed." Cathleen held her hand over the door as they exited the cabin, returning it to the doorway and shutting it tightly. She knew the once safe haven would never serve that purpose again, unless the Council appointed another wizard to act as caretaker. Sadly, this was no longer a peaceful respite for the Mother's own.

Cathleen wasn't convinced the creature they found in the cottage had anything to do with Bretton Clawson's killing. The black spirit that fled the ashes, could have been a corrupted Neidin, for all she knew. It was worth future consideration and she tucked that notion away.

They managed to walk at a good pace until the sun topped the mountains in the distance, turning their summits into golden miters. Cathleen would have noted such a beautiful display but was too consumed with the notion of finding the killing ground of the Master Outlander Wizard Scout.

Parsons sat perched on top of a flat rock, waiting for Cathleen's next order while Jason stood quietly, looking at the distant horizon. The clouds above them were tinged with the pinks and bruised purples of the early evening.

Parsons watched as Cathleen brought a small flame of Green Fire to her hand. He surmised she was ready to move out and they'd be investigating underground, whereupon he sighed deeply at the thought of being forced to enter a totally alien environment. Even living in the persona of the House Buddy, the Guardian felt uncomfortable about going into dark caves or under rocky overhangs.

Sure enough, Cathleen called out, "Let's investigate that string of shallow caves, Parsons. We're still miles away from the bridge according to your description of the geography of this area."

Without another word, she led Jason toward the first in a line of four, deep impressions in one of the nearby hills. Parsons followed with another sigh of resignation..

Cathleen figured the Green Fire was more than enough to scour the small area for any sign of a murder and wouldn't be noticed as they moved about inside the caves. After going through three, they approached the last wind-blown hole, with less hope and little enthusiasm for the task of searching for clues. The twilight passed into an inky darkness as they made their way to the fourth cave.

Jason still felt uneasy with the lack of sounds of animal life in the open fields, forests, and hills they crossed. He gave acute attention to the stillness around them. Listening for a single note of a night bird, his keen ears finally picked up something beside his own breathing.

Cathleen's head jerked to the side as she picked up the same sound.

They were getting ready to enter the last cave, no more than a low, over-hanging shelf of rock and wind-piled dirt. They stopped in their tracks.

Looking over at each other, they said in a low chorus, "Water."

It was an unmistakable, rushing sound, filled with the surging power made only by a great body of water.

While they were in a valley, Cathleen knew they were vulnerable to the oncoming threat.

She grabbed Jason's hand and shouted to Parsons.

"We'll be back! Get to the In-Between until I call for you!"

Conjuring a Time Thread usually took a few minutes to plan where you wanted to travel, but Cathleen didn't have that luxury.

She snagged one, just managing to place her target as an hour ahead.

There was the compression of time and space upon their bodies and the feeling of falling at hundreds of miles an hour. Because of the pressure and speed, they both squeezed their eyes shut, opening them only when they stopped hurtling through the void between then and now.

Jason felt Cathleen's hand slip out of his after giving it a last squeeze.

He opened his eyes to find they stood in the middle of a wildly swaying rope bridge. He looked down, instinctively grabbing for the thick, rope hand-rail, running down both sides of the swaying structure, mirroring Cathleen's quick movement.

A deep gorge below was filling rapidly with swirling, dark green water. The sweeping tidal surge inundated and dislodged boulders and rocks, while pushing massive tangles of trees before its incredible force, like piles of paper Mache.

Cathleen stood a foot away from Jason, but he still shouted to be heard. He asked if the torrent of water might be the frozen wave they'd encountered earlier, but her answer was ripped away by a wind gust.

They searched the deluge for any sign of the Historian. He entered the green depths earlier, to locate the power source holding the waters against the will of nature.

A choking stench, laced with the pungent smell of decay, drifted over them from the other side of the bridge. The winds relentlessly hammered at their bodies while they clung to the wet rope railing, mesmerized by the green waters engulfing the world below.

Jason, intently watching the scene below, yelled over the howl of the gale, "I think we're standing at the doorstep to hell, love."

Cathleen nodded in agreement, yelling back, "This must be the bridge the Guardian saw on that parchment. I figured the water was close enough for us to hear and made this bridge our destination when I caught the Thread."

They both knew it was unlikely they'd spot the Historian in the chaos of the churning waters. Neither wanted to turn their back on the other end of the bridge. They slowly began to move backward, picking their footing carefully, to avoid slipping through the openings between links of thick, knotted rope.

They had another ten feet to go, constantly watching the other end of the dancing bridge, for any sign of creatures from the Dark Pit, just on the other side. Cathleen knew demons could only use this crossing, if a wizard, steeped in the Dark Arts, called them. Even then, the dark beings would need the wizard's close presence to defeat the powerful charms and wards barring their access. Parsons had explained this and another important facts as they walked earlier. According to him, when this bridge was stretched across this abyss over a thousand years ago by the original Council of Green Wizards, its sole purpose was to have access to the fourth realm by the Outlander Wizard Scouts.

They could cross over at will, stopping escape plots by prisoners of the Dark Pit, or interrupt demon crossings. These were pre-emptive strikes, designed to thwart these fiends summoned by Dark Wizards who operated covertly in the natural realm.

The bridge was something of a secret underground railroad, used by the Outlander Wizard Scouts. It placed many in great jeopardy and caused the death of numerous Scouts over the many eons of its operation.

This was the Council's preventative intervention policy at work, but when Cathleen heard the alarm in Jason's voice as he shouted out to her, she knew it didn't always succeed.

Chapter 11

Cathleen was placing her foot on the next rope rung of the bridge, when Jason called out. Becoming distracted, her boot didn't make a solid connection. The thickly twisted rope was damp from the higher altitude, adding to the slick surface of the bottom of her boot.

Jason reacted instantly, trying to catch her before her foot slipped through the opening. He swung his arm out to stabilize her where she struggled.

His movement caused the narrow bridge to swing more violently. He had to stop moving altogether, when he saw Cathleen was dropping further through the gap between rungs. To his great distress, one of her legs was dangling over the dark void.

Cathleen fought to hold onto the slick, rope railings. Her position on the bridge shifted when she lost her footing. She found herself slightly twisted and turned in the other direction on the swaying bridge.

With the wind howling around her, Cathleen felt her right hand slipping off the rough rope. The jarring movement of the slip finally caused her to lose her tenuous grip on the hand-rail. She reached out, but couldn't reconnect with the rope, and the wind-milling motion of her arm caused her to slip further through the gap in the rungs.

The squalls picked up noticeably. Cathleen had no doubt what forces were at play. Her eyes squinting into the sharp winds, she looked back over her shoulder to the other end of the bridge. There was another, who had no compunction about jeopardizing the life of the Protector and in fact, he purposely stomped onto the bridge, shaking both the wizard and her mate.

At first, Cathleen could only make out a wavy shimmer in the air near the other end of the suspension bridge. Slowly a form began to materialize. A tall, darkly robed figure appeared on the first rung of the rope bridge.

Cathleen was barely holding on to the slippery hand-rail with her left hand. Half of her body swung like an off-kilter pendulum in the frenzied air beneath her.

She shouted, "Don't move Jason!" Then slammed down a Dome of Protection over him, knowing she wouldn't be able to defend against the approaching being if she covered herself.

This was surely a wizard with prodigious Dark powers to break through the wards holding back his kind. Cathleen watched his slow approach, looking for any clue to defeating him, or at the very least, defending against him. She chose the only viable action, if she was going to survive against his magic.

Looking back at Jason, she saw the deep distress in his face. He stood very still inside the Dome, waiting for her next move. "Jason," she shouted, "I need to get off this bridge, but I'll join you soon. Keep backing up until you're on the ground and wait for me. The Dome will drop as soon as you're safe."

He knew better than to question her and nodding to her began his slow progress toward the edge of the bridge and safety. He suspected what Cathleen planned to do. When he heard the words of the Old Tongue lifted in the rushing air, he wasn't surprised to see she'd vanished.

Jason turned his full concentration on the last few feet of the swaying bridge. He understood the Dome protected him from the approaching being, but it wouldn't help him if he slipped. The movement of the rope under his feet became so pronounced, he wondered if it would flip him over and off, like a playground swing pushed too hard and high.

The dark figure stood in the middle of the bridge. Jason was sure he had everything to do with the unnatural things happening around him. Shooting a quick glance behind, Jason tried to gauge how far he needed to go before he reached the safety of the other side. When he turned back, he judged the wizard was nearly at the spot where Cathleen slipped through, before she disappeared.

There were two more rungs to go. Jason was about to place his foot onto the next rope rung, giving a quick glance at the approaching figure. Suddenly, a new sound cut through the roar of the wind and the torrent of waters below. It was a sharp, snipping noise, like rapid-fire from an automatic.

Jason didn't need to think, before he acted. He pushed back on his booted heels, bunching up his leg muscles and leapt across the opened space where the bridge had been. The feeling of nothingness beneath him stopped his breath, until he tumbled hard, onto solid ground.

It took a minute to start breathing again. He took some unsteady breaths and pushed himself to a sitting position. He realized the Dome was no longer around him.

Sprawled over the hard earth, he watched as the bridge continued its long plunge to the roiling waters below. He couldn't see it after a few seconds, when it was lost behind the heavy curtain of spray created by the booming flood.

He got to his feet, searching across the newly created gulf between him and the other side.   The dark figure who had come from that evil border land, vanished along with the bridge.

Jason had a hunch Cathleen had something to do with the destruction of the rope expanse. He was amazed at her faith in his ability to jump the distance needed for safety. "She must think I have super-human powers," he whispered to himself. Oddly, he found he was only slightly shaken by the possibility of falling to his death.

He wondered when Cathleen would show herself, and then became conscious of the silence settling over the roar of waters through the gorge. He approached the edge overlooking the deep ravine, astonished to see that the raging torrent transformed into a sheet of green glass. Standing on the crystal-like waters were two figures. Even at this great distance, Jason recognized the woman with the long, auburn hair blowing in the winds as his beautiful wife, the Celtic Wizard.

Intuitively, he also knew the man standing beside her. "And there's the Historian, Will Farley."

Almost by saying his name, the Historian appeared beside him, along with Cathleen. Jason moved to Cathleen's side, putting his arms around her in a tight embrace.

The Historian looked away, appearing uncomfortable around their open affection toward one another. He cleared his throat loudly, breaking into their moment before he spoke. "The frozen wave has been released as you can see, as have the six others I found ringing the Isle like a chain of frozen waterfalls. I discovered the Protector when she entered the waters here. She joined me in my mission to find the wizard responsible."

Jason said, "I think he was the one trying to cross the bridge to get to me, when Cathleen took the bridge down. Am I right, love?"

Cathleen looked perplexed. "I didn't destroy the bridge, Jason. I began circling the isle with the Historian, almost as soon as I left you. I assumed you'd gotten yourself off it right after that."

"Well then, who brought it down and whose side are they on?" Jason asked, frustration in his tone.

A disembodied voice floated into their discussion. "You have all been very busy but have gotten no closer to uncovering the murderer of Bretton Clawson and night is already falling," it scolded.

Out of nowhere, the Guardian popped into their circle. No longer in the guise of the House Buddy, Parsons, he stood on his ridged tentacles, scrutinizing each of them. His eyes moving on their long stems like small balloons on a string.

"I have just returned from the Council and Sir Alex has decided to speed up your inquiry by offering you a dedicated Time Thread into the fourth realm."

"What? He wants us to go into the Dark Pit?" Cathleen demanded, shocked.

"Not precisely," the Guardian went on.

"The Thread, which has been looped around Sir Alex's personal Oracle's Signet Ring, will allow instant transport into the stronghold of a Dark Lord unknown to all, but the Council of Greens."

Cathleen spoke up. "Well, who is this Wizard?"

"As a young sorcerer, he was known as Calvin Boatright. He rose quickly in the ranks of the Greens, proving himself a kind of child prodigy in the magical arts. He was an avid learner and became the youngest Wizard ever to be accepted as an Outlander Wizard Scout. Over time, his reputation as an enforcer of the laws of the Mother, brought him to the inner sanctum of the Council, as a sitting member."

Jason asked, "So, what became of him?"

"It was discovered he was a fraud and a consummate liar. A secret practitioner of the Dark Arts. He'd been bolstering his reputation as a great wizard by using unholy spells and charms. He even used a glamour charm to gull the Sitting Council into taking him as one of them.

He was given a new name in the Council Book of Reckoning that would follow him into infinity, as well as the Dark Pit. You will know him as Calumny, The Deceiver."

While they took in what was said about this great and dangerous fraud, the Guardian reached into a sort of stomach pouch, pulling out Sir Alex's large ring.

They all leaned in to study this magical talisman. A forest green stone, set into a thick gold band, lay gleaming on the flat end of the Guardian's sucker-covered palm. Cathleen recognized the Arch Wizards personal runes, deeply incised on its hard surface.

The Guardian continued. "By slipping on the ring, the wearer will walk into the Dark realm, to search for answerers in this investigation. There is only one condition." They waited for him to go on, Jason looking apprehensive at the coming stipulation. "The Arch Wizard commands the Witch of Appalachia, wear this ring. No one else among this group investigating The Claw's murder, will have the right to wield its powers."

Chapter 12

This was Jason's biggest fear. Cathleen would have to face the dangers of the fourth realm while he was forced to stand down and wait. There was no way he'd let her face that evil place alone. *There must be a way I can be with her*, he thought. He looked over at the Historian, standing with his arms folded across his broad chest. He asked no questions but appeared to be waiting for the next boot to drop.

Jason spoke to the Guardian, getting closer to the Kraken-like creature was difficult, even for a man who'd seen his share of ugly! "I'd like to know if Cathleen will have other defenses for her safety when she enters the realm of the Dark."

Cathleen looked away from the ring sitting on the Guardian's upturned tentacle, at the sound of her husband's voice. She heard something in his tone, a resolve she was sure the others wouldn't pick up on. *He's planning something*, a smile twitching at her lips.

Jason would never take himself off a case willingly and he'd never relinquish his role as her back-up in a dangerous situation.

One of the Guardian's long stems waved in Jason's direction, a bulbous eye fixing on the inquisitive human. "I have also been given this, to place in her hands." With that, he reached inside the odd pouch once more, this time bringing out a fat, black candle. Turning his eye away from Jason, back to Cathleen, he spoke to her directly. "There is no light in the Dark Pit, or anywhere in the fourth realm for that matter. Therefore, not a glimmer will help you in the pitch-black air around the sprawling compound of the Dark Lord you seek. When the Council of Greens created this prison of exile during the Dark Times, part of their punishment for fallen wizards and intruding demons, was to deny them even a twinkle of the Mother's natural light, be that sun, moon, or stars. This black candle will shed light in that fiendish world, while remaining unseen by any of the ah...residents."

He held out the ridged tentacle where he placed the candle beside the ring, gesturing to Cathleen to take them. Cathleen gingerly removed the items of magic, avoiding contact with the Guardian's appendage, without appearing squeamish. She said, "I'll use these carefully, but won't the candle burn down?"

"Of course! And you must immediately leave the Pit when that time comes, else you will be blind as if locked inside your own tomb. Think of the candle as your bird in the coal mine. If it shows signs of dying, so shall you, soon thereafter."

With this sobering comment the Guardian vanished. The three were left staring at the space he had occupied, questions still forming in their minds.

Cathleen was the first to speak. "Master Historian, I don't much like the rules the Arch Wizard has tried to impose on our investigation. I propose the three of us use these charmed talismans and enter the Dark realm together. I can tell, Jason has had the same thought," she added giving her husband a small grin.

"I would agree wholeheartedly, Protector! The strictures forced on us and you seem false, somehow. Almost as if we were meant to fail. I believe the Arch Wizard has been taking some very dangerous advice. How shall we proceed?"

Cathleen called the Time Thread off the ring and into her hands. It was cold, crackling like shifting ice. Using the language of the Ancient Ones, she formed it into a slender rope, shimmering like mercury as it moved and lengthened, until it was long enough to secure around their waists.

"Sort of like mountain climbing," Jason noted. He'd done his share of that back in Iron Mountain, mostly searching for lost hikers off the Appalachian Trail.

Satisfied they could all pass unseen into the Pit, Cathleen threaded the end of the thin rope around the gold ring and shoved it onto her thumb. The Time Thread was already programed to bring the user to the boundary of the fourth realm. The Dark Pit of the Sleepless Dead would be waiting for them at the end of their jump.

When they found themselves standing on solid ground once more, a beam of light shot straight up, from the depths of the green stone, piercing the gloom around them.   When the flash dulled, it was darker than the bottom of a mud bog.

The three instinctively turned their eyes upward, to the night sky. It was void of any celestial bodies, as if none would shine their pure light upon the foul place. The empty dome was as dull as gray smoke.

Cathleen felt the vastness of the bleak sky, pressing down on them like the underbelly of a great beast.

They were still tethered together, as a deadening sense of emptiness settled heavily upon them. There was no sense of life in this new environment. The howling winds swept around them from every angle, enveloping them in odors reminiscent of open graves and rotting corpses. A profound stillness came over the three, settling over them like a heavy shroud until they barely breathed with the weight.

Cathleen struggled to rouse herself from the odd numbness that stiffen her joints and brought an ache to her muscles. She felt like she'd aged sixty years. She lit the stubby black candle with a wisp of Green Fire, whispering a reminder to the others, only they could see the pale circle of light it shed over the ground.

The tiny band walked single file away from the cliff overlooking the ocean of glassy dark waters. They heard the clatter of the destroyed bridge as it bumped off both sides of the expanse. Cathleen led them to a cluster of large boulders and rocks, forming a kind of stone shelter. They huddled inside the deep crevice they formed, speaking in hushed voices.

"Where to from here, Cathleen?" Jason asked as soon as the Historian was well inside the gap between the rocks.

"Protector," the Historian interjected before she could answer. "We need to locate the place The Claw was taken before he was murdered. That will tell more about who committed the deed and perhaps reveal the trader from among the Council."

"Why do you think he was taken to the Dark Pit to kill?" Cathleen asked.

"Because, while his subordinate was killed outright, there were signs on The Claw's body that Dark Magic was used as a means of torture, before he succumbed to the last sleep.

This would have been drawn out to inflict the most pain. He was a much hated and feared enemy of the users of Dark Magic and demon-spawn alike. This would be the only place to carry out such a gruesome task uninhibited."

"Makes sense to me," Jason added.

He went on, "The killer knew we'd likely be looking for a mortal with a grudge against The Claw, or maybe even an opportunist, happy to eliminate competition among the Scouts. In either case, the creatures from the Pit would remain free of scrutiny and they could continue using whatever methods they employ to enter other realms."

Cathleen was quiet a minute, her face shadowed and unreadable to her companions. "That parchment Jason found at Neidin's cottage, might have been a clue planted by The Claw before he was killed. It makes sense that he discovered the bridge was being used to cross over into the natural realm and he died, trying to warn the Council."

The Historian said, "This all points to an insider from the Greens, working with the Dark Ones. Someone among them had to have warned the Dark Wizard that The Claw was snooping around and discovered their crossing point."

Jason and Cathleen could hear the snarl in his voice.

Cathleen thought If he is right, this could be an orchestrated trap they were walking into.

Cathleen whispered back, "Taking out two Wizards, the Protector and the Council Historian besides, would be a real coup."

Jason asked if she thought the ring and candle would work as they moved further into the Pit. "I trust Sir Alex with my life," she answered without hesitation. Then adding, "But there are other forces at play, that he's likely unaware of, or I don't think he'd have sent me here. We need to move out and locate that murder site. Hopefully that will unmask the agent working on behalf of the Dark Ones.

Chapter 13

They removed the thin band created from the Time Thread, from around their waists, before they left the shelter of the boulders. With a few words, Cathleen had it looped around the heavy gold ring. She was relieved no light shot from its depths when she slipped it back onto her thumb.

Don't need a spotlight to announce us, she thought.

As they started to move out from the pocket of safety formed by the rocks, the Historian glanced over at her. He seemed to sense her discomfort. "The denizens of the Dark Pit would surely have loosed packs of howling banshees upon us, if our arrival had been detected," he said softly.

She nodded and they left the make-shift shelter.

They stayed close together, the Historian following a few feet behind Jason and Cathleen, acting as rear guard.

The chunky candle proved impervious to the howling winds that buffeted the trio with its gritty lashing. The small flame cast its thin but sure light over the ground, marking their progress through the constant night.

Cathleen whispered back to Jason to be ready to take the candle if she and the Historian had to defend against any demons or their wizard masters.

Jason understood he'd be little help in that situation. He instinctively reached for the talisman he always wore, hanging around his neck from a long, leather cord. His mother-in-law, Brighid, presented him with the wooden disk long ago. It was carved on both sides in magical runes, that sometimes irritated him if they pressed against bare skin. Brighid had instructed him to hold it in front of himself "in times of peril," as she gently put being attacked by werewolves, necromancers, or some other nightmarish creature. She concluded her instructions at the time, saying, "Then shout, "Cosc," dear." While he had no idea what this ceremony would accomplish magically, he felt safer as he pulled the disk out from under his sweatshirt.

Cathleen had seen the action from the corner of her eye, nodding approval to herself.

They walked for several minutes, readjusting their direction when they all spotted a spectral structure, rising in the distance. Its bulk appeared as a lighter shade of the darkness that surrounded it, giving it a blurred shape. Cathleen kept them close to the scattered boulders and low piles of rock, as they crossed the blown landscape.

She knew enough about the Pit to realize they were only crossing its boundaries and nowhere near the heartland. To her mind, the Dark Lord they sought would occupy this blighted area, to be closer to the bridge crossing and its ready access to the natural realm. That was likely why the Claw was so easily discovered while he hunted here. The Deceiver would have guards prowling the bridge crossing and they possibly fell upon the outnumbered Master Outlander Wizard Scout and his Orderly, during his reconnaissance of the area.

As they rounded an unusually large rock pile, an earsplitting siren blared, shattering the dense silence. Its echo bounced off the hard surfaces around them like shards of obsidian.

The Historian hissed, "Freeze!"

They all fought the urge to cover their ears, fearing any movement would give away their position.

"Some kind of intruder warning system?" Jason whispered.

"No," the Historian answered, his voice barely audible to Jason without the enhanced hearing of the wizards. "This is likely a call to a ceremony of some kind. These demon-lovers feel secure in their hellish home. They don't believe they have a need of warning devices. We may discover something at this gathering, however, to inform our investigation."

"I agree, but I don't fancy just walking into the party unless we have ample camouflage," Cathleen said in a hushed voice.

"We'll travel under a Shadow Wrap. When we get to their meeting place, we'll keep a Dome over us as well, for added protection."

Cathleen added ominously, "But remember, if there is a traitor on the Council of Greens among them, they'd have the Inner Eye and could discover us immediately."

A minute later, the Shadow Wrap in place, they jogged toward the rising spectral form, filling the darkness ahead. As they closed on their target, the massive structure remained only a paler shade of black, but its bulk filled the horizon in both directions like a sprawling city.

Jason moved easily under the Wrap, having used this kind of camouflage numerous times with Cathleen. The closer they got to the looming structure, however, the flimsier it felt to him.

He held the amulet in his left hand, finding reassurance in the heat it radiated as they closed on the target. He believed the disk held a singular energy that would act as a shield if attacked by any of these unholy beings, but that theory was, as yet, untested.

As he followed the candle's pale glow, Jason was suddenly jolted by a sensation, warning him of a new presence. He whispered to his companions. "Something's closing in on our left flank."

Cathleen and the Historian threw off the Shadow Wrap, springing into action. Arms outstretched, standing a few feet apart and facing opposite directions, the sacred Celtic Fire poured from their hands, flowing like molten lava. The land within this semi-circle, lit up with the greenish light. The combined fires caught a large presence in its fiery eye.

A tortoise-like creature, its scaly, thick body, glistening through a transparent hump of protective shell, scuttled over the rocky plain. The demon spawn turned an anvil-shaped head, toward the pair of wizards. Three, slow-blinking red eyes, made it appear unphased by the fiery display.

The head bobbed at the end of a muscular, accordion-like neck that appeared capable of extending, or contracting as needed. There were no obvious defensive mechanisms on the being, as it moved toward them at an unhurried pace. When it was almost six feet away from the cascading fire, it tipped back on stubby hind legs. The red eyes on the reptilian head, continued to blink like a bashful child, holding the two wizards momentarily in a mesmerizing stare.

Jason left the Wrap, moving directly behind Cathleen. He watched the monster closely, intuitively knowing what it would do next. He yelled out a warning. "Dome!"

Shaken from her hypnotic state, Cathleen slammed down a Dome of Protection over the three of them. A breath later, the sluggish creature's mouth, gapped wide, spewing a stream of black sludge, smothering the sacred fire burning around it and lumbering toward the three humans.

Chapter 14

The Historian turned slightly to look over at Jason, more than a little amazed at his unique gift to smell out danger.

Jason never talked about that particularly strange ability, attributing it to the well-honed instincts of a woodsman and long-time lawman.

The creature discharged a steady stream of dense muck, while the three watched it move like a mud slide, toward the shimmering Dome. Jason felt sure this beast would act like the reptilian creatures he was so familiar with in the first realm. The crooked mouth closed tightly as the beast inched its way closer to the Dome's edge. "Now, Cathleen!" Jason shouted.

Cathleen dropped the Dome of Protection at his first word, exposing them all to instant peril. She shouted out her spell in the Old Tongue, calling for a whirlwind. "Cuai feach!" she screamed into the opening mouth of the beast as it reared back again and loomed over them.

A gale force wind tore into the demon, hitting it so hard, it was moved several feet away before it was tipped onto the transparent shell on its back. Four stubby legs pumped the air for purchase, causing the creature to spin until it was a blur in the gloomy air.

When it stopped twirling like a top, the Historian sent a fiery bolt into the demon's exposed underbelly. A high, whistling screech tore through the silence. Another bolt caused the creature's body to shudder violently, until all movement ceased. Its jaws unhinged like a snake's, allowing black globs to drip onto the ground in soft, sizzling patters.

Though only a few minutes had passed during the attack, the three felt drained. Moving through this bleak realm, was proving an exhausting challenge to them all physically and mentally. Cathleen acknowledged that earlier her reflexes seemed sluggish and she felt tired, as if she'd been treading water the whole time. The others admitted the same lethargy had been affecting them as well.

The Historian stood opposite Cathleen and Jason as they studied the demon's still body. They all agreed it must have been a roving guard, not unlike the Outlander Wizard Scouts, and they were unfortunate enough to make contact with it.

"We need to move out. This thing might have contacted its wizard master, alerting them to our presence," the Historian was saying as he adjusted the leather sheath for the short sword he wore.

Jason noticed it when he first met the Historian. Now, he studied the wicked looking blade as it caught the light from Cathleen's candle. He noticed odd cyphers on the hilt and running down the blade.   At one time, Jason used cryptograms in his work as part of an elite military unit working behind foreign borders. His curiosity was roused when the big man tried slide the sword home, without Cathleen's notice.

Rather than leave the carcass of the beast exposed to discovery, the two wizards lifted it using strong air currents, into a deep hole Cathleen conjured for the purpose. With several waves of their hands, the currents pushed the black dirt over the remains, and the three resumed their trek.

In hushed conversation, Cathleen and the Historian voiced the same opinion. They believed they were about to discover the headquarters for the fallen wizard, Calvin Boatwright. They suspected the Deceiver's involvement in the murder of the Master Outlander Wizard Scout from the beginning but needed to uncover the evidence that would deny him continued existence on this, or any other plane.

Cathleen held up a hand and the little band halted. "When we get to the stronghold, I don't want to reveal our numbers. We'll split up. Jason will stay with me and we'll approach from the right side. Historian, you make your way around the back of the structure and scout the rear area, for a back-way in. If we run into any guards, we have to silence them, before they can sound any alarms."

"While I agree to your plan Protector, I would add one element. Send Jason in ahead as the distraction we'll need to enter without detection."

Seeing a flash of anger in her eyes at his suggestion, the Historian was quick to add, "This Jason is not one you call "husband."

Jason and Cathleen heard the hiss of the sword as it was smoothly pulled from its leather cover. They both took a step back, not knowing what the Historian's exposed weapon meant to their next actions.

The Historian didn't seem to notice their guarded reactions. He waived the short sword in three directions, chanting softly. Cathleen caught a few ancient Druid words and knew the Historian was conjuring a presence.

When he was finished, he said, "Turn around."

Standing like a kid's action figure was a perfect replica of Jason Tate. It stood with its arms held casually behind its back, feet slightly apart.

Cathleen and Jason approached it.

"It's as stiff as a board," Jason said, clearly not happy with having an identical twin.

The Historian touched the chest of the clone with the point of his short sword. An arc of green light shot into the chest. It blinked and turned its green eye on a clearly impressed, Jason. The black patch over its left eye was a replica of Jason's, making him wonder for a moment if there was an eye under it.

"I trust you know the story of the Trojan Horse. Designed by the Greeks to hide solders, it was a perfect ruse. The enemy took it into Troy, as a trophy of the war, when the Greeks pretended to sail away in defeat." the Historian remarked, a touch of smugness in his deep voice.

"And this is our Trojan Horse," Cathleen finished his story.

Giving her a curt nod, he slid the sword home, approaching his silent creation.

"A fitting plan for the Master Historian, wouldn't you agree?" he asked looking back at Jason and Cathleen with a tight smile.

"What are your orders?" the clone asked in a lifeless, robotic voice.

"You will move forward until you reach the enemy's citadel. There will be demon-guards, but you will destroy anything that tries to stop you from entering. Once inside, you must go directly to the main chamber and seek out Calvin Boatwright, the Deceiver. He no doubt, will be waiting for you. When you are in his presence, you will fade back into the ether from which you are created."

"Why will you have him vanish like that?" Jason asked. "I thought he'd actually be of some help inside the stronghold."

Cathleen interjected the answer. "Because we'll use the clone's diversion to enter the chamber without detection. The Deceiver will probably be very curious about this gift, falling into his hands. He may even think the clone is a magic user and therefore, more valuable to his plans to infiltrate the other realms with impunity."

The Historian didn't add anything to the explanation.

Turning on his boot he said, "Let's move out."

He had placed the Clone at the front as they walked single file, using whatever natural cover they could. Cathleen, trailing the others, swept any footprints away to help disguise their passage over the barren wasteland.

Jason turned back to Cathleen to whisper. "It's weird to be following myself."

She smiled up at him, giving his arm a squeeze. "The Historian must be impressed with you, to think you'd make a fine captive in the Deceiver's mind."

"Yeah. Guess I should be flattered," he responded flatly.

After walking several minutes in silence, the clone picked up his pace and the others jogged to keep pace. He stopped abruptly and turned to the Historian. In a more animated voice he informed him, "I am within six-point-four yards, of the front gates to the Deceiver's stronghold."

The Historian was joined by Cathleen and Jason in time to hear the clone's report.

They all looked around, perplexed at the emptiness surrounding them.

"It's been shielded," Cathleen blurted out, clearly unhappy with herself for not sensing the use of magic so near at hand. "He must have been alerted to our presence," she added.

The Historian, who never seemed concerned with any situation, merely grunted.

Cathleen held the candle higher to cover more ground with its pale light. All around them was the same black, cracked earth, strewn with rocks and void of any living vegetation. There was no sign of any structure, let alone a wizard's fortress.

The candle created an umbrella of light over the small knot of searchers. At the edge of the glow, was a heavy darkness. Cathleen could almost feel it push back against the flimsy light in her hand.

She said in a hushed voice, "Historian, use the sword to test for demon-spawn and to illuminate this phantom fort."

"How did you…" He stammered, but she cut him short.

"I am a Protector and you are too arrogant, thinking less of me. Now, use the sword," she hissed back at him.

The next sound was of silky-smooth steel being pulled from the scabbard. The sword glinted a flat pewter color in the candlelight, as he pointed it straight out in front.

The Historian joined Cathleen in measured, soft chanting, when she stood beside him.

Jason reached over, taking the candle from her hand. In times like this, he understood Cathleen was the only wizard in the family.

"Diche altair, bring discernment. Diche altair, bring clarity."

The two voices melded, not female, or male, not human, but a stirring, like wind racing along a battlefield strewn with moans and sighs. When they stopped chanting, the clone who was waiting silently, pointed to an unveiled, high-walled structure.

Studying the massive size outlined against a darker sky, Cathleen was again dumbfounded that she hadn't sensed its bulky presence.

This place keeps messing with my magic, she thought with growing alarm.

The clone resumed his task and began walking toward the fortress, seemingly undaunted by its looming dimensions. The others followed, watching the walls rise from the cracked, tortured earth.

Jason moved silently, stepping close to his wife's side.

"Cathleen, there's something fishy going on. Even though we all saw its silhouette earlier, you didn't know this fort was even here until the clone pointed it out. Now, suddenly, there's a huge fortress in our path."

"What are you saying, Jason?" asked the Historian who moved back to hear their conversation

"I'm saying, something here is messing with your magic and the clone is leading us into a trap."

Chapter 15

"That's ridiculous!" the Historian said, outraged that the clone he summoned would pose any threat. "My magic would have been tampered with for such an aberration and there is no evidence of that!"

Cathleen placed a gentle hand on his shoulder to silence any further outburst of anger. "Master Historian, earlier I expressed concern that my own magic was being altered, or subverted, in this place. I suspect that only the candle will remain untouched by the powerful forces of evil residing on this plane. Jason, have you felt anything about the clone besides your suspicions that he's leading us into a trap?"

Jason was uncomfortable in his role of Seer, having always down-played his abilities to feel danger. There were also his odd Walking Dreams. That's what he called out-of-body premonitions, when he saw a possible future if left unchanged by intervention, magical or otherwise. He took a deep breath of the rank air, ignoring the taste it left in his mouth. "Here's what I am certain of and you may not like what I say. That creature you conjured, my clone, is working for the bad guys and not you, Historian. Haven't you sensed the building excitement in his movements? When he first appeared, he had a flat, robotic tone to his speech. That's gone and he sounds more human. Plus, I find it amazing that a mere conjured creature could detect the stronghold of the Deceiver and neither of you super wizards had a clue it was right in front of us!"

The candle in Cathleen's hand was raised above her head. It threw shadows on their faces, giving the Historian an even deeper scowl as he contemplated Jason's argument.

Cathleen broke into the silence. "Jason's right. It's no coincidence that the stronghold looked far off no matter how long we moved toward it. An optical illusion, fooling our senses."

"But why would the clone even tell us we were near the Dark Ones citadel if he worked with them? We could have blindly walked right into it." the Historian asked.

Jason spoke up looking past the Historian. "Because he wasn't telling us. He was telling them!"

The others turned to follow his gaze. The clone stood a few feet from a double gate, likely barred with powerful wards. A horde of spidery figures, each the size of a small horse, surrounded him. They scrambled over the area by the hundreds, exiting large holes scattered over the hard ground. There was a cacophony of high chirping noises as the spider creatures clacked beaked mouths incessantly.

"Sweet Mother!" Cathleen shouted.

The Historian dropped a Dome of Protection over the three of them. The short sword began glowing a deep green in his big hand. "You were right, Jason. My clone was tampered with by the dark forces and now he's led us into an ambush. My sincere apologies."

Cathleen studied the spider creatures for weaknesses, knowing they'd be attacking any minute. "Historian, can you still communicate with the clone?"

"Yes, but what good would that do? He's lost to us."

"Not quite. Tell it to open the gates to the fortress. That should divert some of the spiders as they try to stop him entering, maybe even confuse the pack."

By the time she finished speaking, several of the spiders had reached their Dome. Surrounding it, they used sharp pincers at the ends of their front legs, to attack the shimmering sphere. There was a frenzy of activity around the Dome with more spiders joining in the attack.

A stringy goo was being extruded out of all of the hairy underbellies of the creatures. Cathleen suspected it was used to wrap their prey, once caught. She knew they wouldn't have much luck with the Dome, watching the sticky substance slide uselessly to the ground.

Jason looked back at the front gates. "You're right, Cathleen! The clone opened the gates, but now he's being carried off by dozens of the creatures. It looks like they're taking him down one of their holes."

Cathleen saw a look of alarm pass over Jason's face. She guessed he must have felt some fear for the clone's fate, as they both watched it being pulled down a hole by several of the huge arthropods.

The Historian grabbed Cathleen's arm, drawing her attention back to their own predicament. The spider creatures were moving around the Dome, some biting at it. They suddenly stopped, forming a tightly packed ring around the Dome. The Historian noted the change in their behavior and told the others it appeared to be some kind of holding tactic.

"We need to exit the Dome and get into that stronghold," he was saying.

"The Deceiver is known to keep souvenirs from attacks on the first realm, trophies honoring his great power. I'm certain he'll remain true to form and have something belonging to The Claw."

"That would confirm his involvement in the murder," Jason added, in Lawman mode.

Cathleen said, "We'll use the Shadow Wrap and leave the Dome. I'll create a diversion to get these thugs to move off long enough to get us out of here."

The men heard the determination in Cathleen's voice and neither offered any unwelcome objections.

Cathleen handed the candle over to Jason and raised both arms. She decided to call upon a long-trusted friend to help them out of this untenable situation.

After several words in the mystic language and others the Historian had never heard spoken in incantations, the constant chirping and clacking of claws changed, becoming high pitched screams. Hairy black bodies were flying through the air, one hitting the Dome with such force, it bounced off and back into the seething cauldron of hairy creatures. They immediately attacked the downed creature, pulling it apart on the spot.

Cathleen asked the Historian to cover them in a Shadow Wrap while she undid the charm for the Dome. Abruptly, the three stood in the midst of chaos and destruction. The large hairy bodies were still being flung through the air by some invisible force.

She took the candle back as they made their way around the turmoil that had erupted away from the Dome.

They moved quickly, avoiding deep burrows and moving toward the open gates.

Jason heard a flat voice calling "Master" over and over, when he stepped past another gapping entrance to a spider's lair. He shivered inwardly at the thought of seeing his face on the clone that was likely being devoured.

The trio moved past several spider guards, rushing from the fort to join the melee outside. Cathleen smiled to herself when she thought of what awaited the demon-spawn.

"The Geilt is a fine warrior for the Mother and her Protector," she said quietly to her companions.

The men turned their heads in the direction she was looking. At first, all they saw was a tight knot of spider creatures, until they spotted the flailing arms and flying club of the Geilt. They both knew his story well.

He shunned all contact with others, living a solitary existence in the wilderness of the third realm. Most in the wizarding community believed he was mad and as wild as his untamed woodlands, but his reputation as a powerful magic user, assured his privacy.

Jason knew Cathleen overcame these obstacles long ago, by keeping her word to the Geilt. She released him from his pledge of service after he helped with a dangerous investigation. This forged a bond of trust between them and he came freely to her aid whenever she called upon him.

The Historian watched the Geilt's effective combat methods. His only comment, another of his expressive grunts.

They moved into an empty courtyard, the hulking stone fortress curling around it in a dark embrace. The structure towered over the invisible trio, almost as long as it was tall. They instinctively crouched lower under their Shadow cover, feeling its evil presence like a force, pressing down on them.

Cathleen signaled and they moved up wide, granite steps. At the top, two spider creatures were weaving a sticky looking web across the entryway into the Great Room, just beyond. The webbing was so thick seeing behind it was impossible as they crisscrossed strands, strengthening them into a mesh barrier.

The Historian had been holding his short sword at his side. He brought it up to see it glowing a deep green. "It calls for blood," he murmured, holding the blade close to his face.

Without further comment, the Historian tore back his part of the Shadow Wrap lunging at the closest beast. Cathleen and Jason were stunned by his sudden actions, watching while the Historian moved with the speed of a riptide.

His blade, wielded like a scythe, sliced through the hairy legs and sinew on both the arthropods jointed legs. The demons toppled over onto their backs, where the soft underbelly was pierced over and over with the blazing green sword.

The attack had taken less than a minute. The frantic chirping of the creatures stopped abruptly, replaced by the howls of the Geilt, finishing off those that couldn't escape down their holes.

Cathleen and Jason threw off the Wrap and approached the hard-breathing Historian. "Can you cut through the web, Historian?" Cathleen used the Calming Voice to help restore order to the other wizard's mind after the blood lust took it. Killing was never the first directive of any Wizard of the Green, unless it was unavoidable.

Giving her a grateful look, he swung once through the thickly spun web. It fell to either side like heavy draping.

Cathleen put a restraining hand on the Historian's arm as he was about to enter. She noticed a warrior's fixed gaze had returned to his eyes. "We wait for the Geilt. The Deceiver knows what's been happening to his spidery guards and has likely been setting wards and spells around the place."

Jason moved up beside her, watching the Wildman finish off the last of the creatures that hadn't scuttled along the hard earth for the safety of their burrows. "The Geilt's finished with that lot, Cathleen," he said quietly.

They all turned back to watch the approach of the fur-covered woodsman. In one huge hand, he carried a matter-smeared club, in the other, the severed head of a spider creature.

Cathleen greeted him warmly. "Thank you for your intervention, old friend. You have helped us greatly."

The Geilt looked into Cathleen's wide hazel eyes almost longingly, saying, "This Geilt feels honor to be of service to Cathleen O'Brien. You call and I shall always answer."

The Historian interjected a question, nettling him since he watched the burly madman approach. "Why do you carry the creature's head, Geilt? Is it a trophy?"

"No trophy, wizard. Hard beak makes webbing. A fine weapon for Geilt," he added with a low rumble that might have been a chuckle.

Jason had been standing back from this little clique, watching for any other threats from the surrounding areas. Satisfied they could move without fearing attack from the rear, he let Cathleen know and they moved into the cavernous, Great Room.

A bleak feeling permeated the air. This was exaggerated by the gloom created by stinking torches hanging from sconces scattered around the walls. They provided a feeble light that was swallowed in the vastness of the room.

Even flame can't exist in a pure state in this evil den, Cathleen thought.

The Historian walked silently behind them. They moved slowly, each peering into the gray shadows crawling up the high walls, into the murky recesses of the ceiling.

The Geilt had taken guard position, shifting his club to a thickly muscled shoulder. The fingers of his other hand were tightly woven through the spikey black hair on the head of the arthropod. He casually swung it while he walked.

The Historian shot quick glances at the Wildman as he trudged behind. He was fascinated with the mystery of how such a low form of human, could have been befriended by the lovely, Cathleen O'Brien.

She has more powers than just her Protector's magic, he thought.

The small band was only at mid-point in the vast room, when the sound of maniacal laughter circled them, bouncing off stone walls and heavy tapestries depicting loathsome acts of evil being done to various life-forms.

Jason took hold of his wooden talisman, slipping it off his neck. Cathleen noticed his action, watching while he wrapped the leather strip around his hand, keeping the disk hidden in his fist. He cut a glance in her direction and saw her look of approval. Jason didn't need to understand the magic, he just needed to trust in it. Cathleen knew by the set of his jaw, he did.

The four automatically formed a tight circle, standing back-to-back, protecting their rear. The Geilt appeared calm, but the high pitch of the laughter felt like needles passing through the others' sensitive eardrums.

Cathleen spoke quietly, "That would be the Deceiver I guess. Geilt, any chance of you locating his inner sanctum in this pile of rocks? We need to scour this place for clues, if you can keep the Deceiver busy for a while."

The Geilt gave her a slight nod.

Cathleen and the others closed the gap he made leaving. Though there was no sign of imminent attack, she felt the air currents constantly shifting around them and knew unseen creatures were moving through the dense shadows surrounding them.

They'd have to work fast, while the Geilt bought them some time. "We should hear the Geilt's war cry any minute," Cathleen spoke softly. "When we do, whatever is slinking around us in the shadows, will run to their Master's aid. As soon as they leave, we need to locate the Deceiver's

Ceremonial Chamber. He would have taken The Claw's life in some sort of black magic ritual."

"Yes," the Historian added. "And any evidence of that crime will be there."

Jason held his amulet tightly listening to the others, adding in a cautionary tone, "Then all we need to do, is destroy the Deceiver before his creatures can stop us."

They stood in their tight circle, listening for the war-cry of the Wildman.

Chapter 16

The howl was like nothing Jason had ever heard in a lifetime in the Appalachian Mountains. It sounded as if it came from the belly of the dead earth they stood upon, raising the hair on his neck and arms and chilling his blood, like he'd stepped into a frigid river.

They all tensed when it seared the darkness once more, keeping their tight circle for a possible charge on their position.

"Cathleen, was that the Geilt?" Jason asked, his voice tight in his throat.

"No. That was the Deceiver calling to his minions. Let's move out. We won't be attacked until he gives the order."

The wizards each brought a small green flame to one hand. Cathleen handed the stubby candle off to Jason. He kept it raised above them as they shifted toward the rear of the Great Room.

A tapestry, so enormous, it was segmented into four, separate wall hangings, covered most of the back wall. A quick study by Jason showed It was filled with grisly scenes of torture of every living creature conceivable, including humans.

The Historian ripped the two center-panels from the wall, with a flick of his hand, revealing another, heavily-spun barrier to a passageway. This one was torn and shredded, the tattered fabric, waving in the shifting air currents.

They all saw the sticky webbing was speckled with coarse, black hairs.

"Looks like the Geilt found this first," Cathleen reported to them softly.

Answering the unasked question written on Jason's face, she added. "He has powerful magic, Jason. This would prove no barrier to him."

They entered a narrow corridor, following it until it opened into a wide crossroads.

Jason stepped around Cathleen and Jason, studying the dirt covered stone floor in the low flame of her Green Fire.

"The Geilt went this way, but there are dozens of pad prints, from the spider creatures, I would guess. There's also another set, but I don't recognize these."

Cathleen took only a second to make her decision on which way to go.

"The chamber the Deceiver uses for his rituals will likely be deep inside the stronghold. Let's go in the opposite direction from the Geilt. We need to locate our evidence of The Claw's murder and quickly. The Geilt can take care of himself."

The three turned left, away from the path the Wildman had taken. There were torches hanging along the black granite walls along the passageway. They burned low, their light quivering, as if afraid to disturb the bleak darkness.

Cathleen picked-up a low murmur, wafting like a bad smell through the thick air of the halls. It stopped for a few breaths and resumed, clearer this time. Cathleen whispered, "Stop."

The others listened and waited for her next move.

The Historian finally said, "Those are the evil words of Dark Magic, Protector." He then whispered his own words, reducing his small flame to a green dot in his palm. Cathleen did the same.

Jason asked if perhaps the Geilt had been captured.

Cathleen answered emphatically, "No way. He could blink out of here and return to his woodlands if he was captured. I understood most of what was being said in the corrupted Old Tongue they used. Unfortunately, I think they have another captive and they're preparing for a blood sacrifice. I think he's being tortured somewhere and will be taken to the Ritual Chamber when they tire of that." Looking over at the Historian, Cathleen asked in a frantic whisper, "Are there any other Outlander Wizard Scouts working this murder investigation?"

"The Outlander Wizard Scouts have all been assigned to patrol safer sectors until this case is solved. None would enter this realm, without the Arch Wizard's order."

"Cathleen," Jason interjected. "Let me go ahead and search out the Ritual Chamber. I'll hunt for any clues left behind in The Claw's murder. You two need to help whoever's been caught up in this nasty web."

"Jason…"

"I'll be fine, love. I have Brighid's talisman and know how to use it."

She gave him a quick nod and watched as he was swallowed by the gloom. The candle he carried gave a thin light as he moved away, showing little besides a fading form.

She couldn't share her Green Fire with him, but he'd proven he had uncanny vision in the darkness. Even with one eye, Jason could see better than she could, unless she used the Inner Eye. Just another question that floated around in Cathleen's head about her husband's almost-supernatural abilities.

The Historian moved several feet ahead, while she watched Jason disappear from view. She hurried to catch up, joining him near a stone staircase leading below.

"Must go to subterranean rooms, likely the dungeons," he said close to Cathleen's ear.

"If the Claw was held here for any length of time, it would have been in such a place, until the Deceiver called for his ritual death."

Cathleen was about to say something, when a chill ran through her body. With a jolt she grabbed for the Historian's arm.

"It's Jason," she said in a rush. "He's in trouble. You go below to the dungeons. I need to find him before he bites off more than my mom's charm can handle."

Without another word, Cathleen began to run back to the junction where Jason left them.

The Historian stood at the top of a flight of roughly cut, stone stairs. They appeared to be chiseled out of the very bedrock the stronghold was built over.

Peering down into the waiting darkness, his senses were so highly tuned they felt like new appendages on his body, groping for signs of danger.

He raised the low flame on his hand, going down several steps until reaching a landing. From this point, the stairs turned at a sharp angel, as they descended deeper underground.

He extinguished his green flame when he saw a faint light painting a shadow on the wall just around the corner.

Moving downward, his shadow now preceded him. Several lighted torches sputtered in their high brackets. The Historian noticed the stone walls oozed a thick, blackish slime.   Suspecting it was a destructive element, he was careful not to come into contact with any of the goo. He moved downward as quietly as possible, but the occasional scuffing of his boot heel on the pitted rock, was unnerving.

When a rank odor rose up to meet him, the Historian stopped, sliding his short sword out of its sheath. The hiss of the well-honed metal along the leather announced itself like the viper he named it for. The Cobra's Kiss felt good in his hand.

He picked up the sound of a slow drip, coming from somewhere deeper in the bowels of the stronghold. He used his Inner Eye since entering the vast stronghold, but hadn't detected any other life forms outside of the spider creatures. He knew better than to believe they'd be the only demon-spawn he'd encounter.

Every muscle was as taut as a bow string, notched with an arrow and ready to fly. Moving to the last step, he placed his feet carefully onto the damp stone floor. As if triggered by the touch of his boots, a low rumble erupted from somewhere in the gloom.

It sounded close, the stones echoing the threatening growl.

The Historian picked up the muffled movement of something heavy coming directly toward him.

Padded feet? he wondered, gripping the Viper's Kiss in his fist.

It was not in the Historian's nature to turn tail on any threat. He raised the Green Fire once more. This time, it was a full bloom of Sacred flame and he calmly waited for death to come calling.

Chapter 17

Cathleen chided herself for allowing Jason to convince her he'd be fine on his own, in the hellish place. She trusted his instincts with her life, but not with his own. She knew he had a keen sixth sense, but that wasn't magic. That was a primordial human trait, just more finely honed in some.

She took the same fork as Jason when they split up, straining to see or hear anything that might point her to his location. Keeping her green flame very small, it struggled against the smothering darkness of the passageways. She took some comfort knowing Jason had the charmed candle with him. That thought jogged her memory and she looked at the other item the Arc Wizard had provided for this hunt.

The ring on her thumb flashed a rich green when she waved it over the area. It winked back at her like a blinking cat in the glow of her fire. *Cat prints!* That's what made those other marks Jason discovered, she thought with alarm. Cathleen was even more anxious to locate her husband in the face of this new threat. A feline monster would make the perfect guard in these dark passageways, with their naturally enhanced night vision.

Jason's only defense was the wooden talisman wrapped around his hand. That meant close contact with such a beast for the amulet to do any damage. For a minute Cathleen wondered why her mother would have given him such an ineffective magical artifact to protect himself, knowing its limitations.

She was passing a series of empty cells, when a second, deeper chill, passed through her body. *Jason, you're near and in trouble!*

Cathleen stopped, letting her discipline override her need to run to her love's aid. She focused her senses on the pitch-dark outside the flame's light for movement, gradually becoming aware of a pungent odor.

She raised her flame over the filth-covered stone flooring. Several large paw prints were pressed into the thick layer of dirt. Just ahead of these, she spotted Jason's boot tracks.

Moving forward, she dropped a Shadow Wrap over herself, not wanting to give away her presence to the creature until she could strike. With her Inner Eye, she caught sight of a yellow glow, painting the stone walls on both sides of the passageway, straight ahead. It began to bounce around like a firefly as it moved down the corridor.

Cathleen knew this was the candle Jason held and though no beast could see the light from it, a feline monster could easily detect the being carrying it.

He's running!

Cathleen dropped the Wrap charm, not wanting to struggle to keep it in place while she ran. The awful smell was sharper and she heard a long, guttural rumble. She wasn't sure what she'd be confronting when she caught up with Jason's attacker, but she was ready. Her dad trained her to always be prepared with two plans. One to fight and one to escape. *No sense in entering the battle like a sightseer, but it's alright to leave like one,* was his advice in engaging an enemy.

Right now, Cathleen would have loved a bit more by way of useable training. She was going up against a demon-spawn from this Dark Pit and her life and her husband's, depended on her magic.

There was another growl vibrating around the close hallways and much closer.

Cathleen turned the Green flame of Celtic Fire, into a broader blaze that lit the area ahead. A few feet away, the yellow glow from Jason's candle suddenly shot up into a pillar of flame, as if responding to Cathleen's presence and the dire situation they faced.

The two humans stared at the crouched beast, caught between them.

The oval-shaped eyes were huge, nearly filling the angular, cat-like head. They glowed like chunks of red-hot coal. The entire creature was hairless and as translucent as a jelly fish.

Cathleen and Jason could see dark threads of blood, moving under the thick skin and around internal organs.

The beast was perfectly still. Its legs were drawn up in the pouncing position, muscles bunched in its haunches, at the ready.

It had an enemy behind and in front and Cathleen wondered if it was choosing its victim when she saw the long claws glint in the light.

Jason yelled across to her.

"Cathleen, I'm up against a wall and can't move. I think this thing's been herding me until I couldn't go any further."

"Jason, stay still and I'll drop a…"

Before she could finish, the beast let out a throaty roar. Jason was attacking it with the amulet and fire, both inflicting pain and damage to the enraged creature.

Cathleen was about to use her Green Fire to finish it off, when the beast fastened its powerful jaws around Jason's arm. The amulet was still in his hand, but hanging useless, as the huge head shook him while he dangled from long incisors.

Jason didn't scream in pain but roared back at the beast like a caveman might have with a Saber Tooth Tiger.

Cathleen shouted out every spell and incantation she could think of with no, or little effect. She could see Jason struggling to inflict his own pain on the creature, while being shaken like a caught rabbit.

He used the candle's long flame to continue his attack, burning the leathery hide which enraged the demon more. It was the only thing he could do to keep the jaws from clamping down harder and crushing his arm in his powerful grip. As it was, the sharp incisors pierced him deeply. His blood dripped onto the ground, spattering the walls as he was violently tossed about.

Cathleen felt helpless to rescue Jason from a certain death. Her magic was weakened in this dark realm, but there had to be something she was overlooking. A weakness in the Deceiver's fortress.

Then she realized it was a weakness in the Deceiver himself! In a flash of revelation, she saw it. He was an egomaniac. It would take the Deceiver's intervention to stop his beast, so she had to goad him into doing just that.

Cathleen called out to the traitorous wizard, careful not to call him by the name branded on his chest by the Council, several hundred years ago. "You certainly don't live up to your reputation, Calvin Boatwright. I was told you were afraid of nothing when you were a member of the Greens. It seems you've softened considerably, hiding here in your stronghold, using kitties and spiders to fight your battles, while you cower in a dark room somewhere!"

A strong vibration rippled through the passageway. The beast reacted immediately, dropping Jason onto the ground. It turned its hairless head as if searching out the source of the ominous sound.

Jason lay perfectly still. He knew cats liked to play with their food.

Cathleen felt a blast of icy air stir her long hair, accompanied by the sound of raspy breathing echoing down the corridor.

Jason cradled his injured arm, barely allowing his own breath, shallow. The cat creature must have been satisfied he wouldn't be interrupted in his kill, turning back to watch him for any movement. Its whip-like tail swept the floor as it twitched in anticipation of pouncing on his prey once more.

Cathleen knew a Dome of Protection might only be partially effective because of her weakened powers. She called for a Shadow Wrap instead, pulling from the shades of darkness surrounding them.

Jason's body immediately vanished from the scrutiny of the burning, red eyes. The dumb beast took a step back in surprise, cocking its huge head slightly, obviously distrustful of the new situation.

Cathleen used the unguarded moment to throw a spear of Green Fire into the hairless creature, aiming as close to the visibly beating heart as possible. The flame spread upon contact with the close organs, seeming to melt them with its heat. The beast yowled in fury as it crumpled to the floor, burning from the inside out.

Jason, who witnessed the bolt of green when it hit home, rolled aside to avoid the creature's flaming carcass. Cathleen ran over to him as soon as she was certain the beast was done for. Jason staggered slightly as she helped him get to his feet, his injured arm tucked close to his chest.

"Jason, I never should have let you go off on your own." Cathleen wrapped her arm around his waist, supporting him as he swayed in place.

"Your mom's amulet is pretty powerful, love, and for some reason that stubby candle shot out a good flame. I'll be fine. Just need to clean this bite."

Cathleen bent down to retrieve the still burning candle, pleased it hadn't gone out in the struggle with the Deceiver's house pet.

Using Jason's ever-present penknife, Cathleen tore off a long strip from the bottom of the T-shirt she wore under her sweatshirt. Whispering a hasty charm to ward off infection, she wrapped it snuggly around Jason's arm to stop any further loss of blood.

An oily smoke rose behind them, from the remains of the charred demon-spawn. The fine particles of its carcass hung in the air of the close space. They back-tracked down the passage and toward the stairs leading to the dungeons below.

Cathleen was anxious to find the Historian.

As they slowly moved through the thick gloom of the passageways, Cathleen's thoughts returned to the Deceiver.

He likely witnessed the short battle and was aware of Jason's injury. *He probably wanted to test the Protector's powers, without exposing himself.* Cathleen thought, he's a coward as well as a liar.

She asked Jason how he was doing. It was too dark to judge by his color, but she sensed his energies flagging as they made their way along the narrow stone halls.

After a few minutes of slow going, Jason spoke softly. He told her he was beginning to feel light-headed. "I think I'm getting weaker, love. That bite must have put a poison into my blood stream."

"I need to get the Historian to re-join us, Jason. That's the only way I can treat your arm properly. My healing charm is too weak here." She stopped and sliding her arm from around his waist, leaned him against a wall.

He heard her begin a Calling Spell she'd used in the past, to summon the Historian. Within a few heartbeats, the tall, rugged form of the ex-warrior, filled the passage in front of them.

"Protector, you knew I was below. Why have you…?" He looked over as Jason began to slide down the wall, sitting spread-legged in a near faint.

Cathleen rushed to his side. "Jason, it's no good! My magic won't hold. I've lost a good bit of my power in this place of the damned. I'm going to give you the ring so you can return to the Council Chambers. They can treat you there or send you on to the Healing Garden. I want you to ask the Arch Wizard to send another Council member, to help me sort things out here."

He offered no argument, knowing he was more of a liability now that he was badly injured.

Cathleen slipped the ring off her thumb, unwinding the shimmering Time Thread that would lead back to Sir Alex. The Historian helped her secure the Thread around Jason's waist.

"Tell the Arch Wizard I want Mercy McNaughton, the Council Scribe, to act as a temporary External Censor Officer under my authority."

After a quick kiss, she slid the ring onto Jason's middle finger, repeating the words to call the Time Thread. Jason vanished in the shudder that rippled the space around his body.

"What did you do to end the attack on Jason, Protector?" the Historian asked. They had resumed their search for the Ceremonial Chamber together.

"I called the Deceiver a coward, but Jason was already confronting the creature when I found him."

"Ah. I see. And was it some sort of feline by any chance?"

She shot him a quick look, noticing his face looked tense in the cool glow of the candle.

"Have you seen this creature yourself, Historian?"

"It's likely part of a cadre of inner sanctum guards. Like those coming up behind us right now."

Chapter 18

Cathleen and the Historian wrapped an arm around each other's waists and began to spin like a weathervane in a tornado. The extreme speed of this whirling motion, blurred their bodies until they appeared as one being, confusing the burning red eyes of the three hairless cat-creatures facing them.

The churning of the dead air caused the beasts to stop, their claws digging into the dirt floor. They backed up slightly, to assess this new intruder.

The Historian was armed with his short sword, while Cathleen conjured a Net of Nettles, ready to cast at the nearest beast. They kept up their spinning, until they were ready to strike.

The translucent bodies of the three demons were repulsive. They exuded a terrible stench that was filling the narrow passage with the smell of a cesspit.

The Historian had chosen his intended victim and breaking the spinning spell, plunged the sword deeply into its pale chest.

Free of the whirling motion, Cathleen threw her Net, watching it land neatly around the vulnerable body of the rear guard.

It struggled frantically against the weight, causing the spikey needles to work their way into its exposed flesh. The caterwauling from both beasts reverberated against the stone of the narrow passage, affecting the courage of the last beast.

Cathleen watched as the unscathed demon slunk back into the darkness, just as the Historian pulled his sword from the dead body of its pack-mate.

Cathleen turned to the howling monster she netted.

Forming a jagged bolt of Green Fire, she sent it hurtling, into the struggling creature. The flames finished it off, reducing its screams to a few soft screeches before it succumbed.

"One got away. Do you think it'll come back with reinforcements?" she asked.

He merely shrugged his answer. She watched as the Historian carefully wiped his steel blade clean of the enemy's blood and entrails using a piece of cloth conjured by him for the task and then reversing the spell.

Looking up at Cathleen he remarked casually, "This is dirty work, Protector. By the way," he added in a casual tone, "I overheard you tell Jason to ask that the Council Scribe, Mercy McNaughton, be sent here, under your authority as Protector. Do you really think the Arch Wizard will allow such an odd request to be answered?"

Cathleen merely looked back at him, feeling the sting to her pride as a Protector of the Green. Like him, she merely shrugged her shoulders indifferently.

She'd been fashioning small globes of Green Fire and setting them afloat. She planned to use them like scouts they could trail down the hallways.

Putting his sword back into its sheath, and saying nothing more about her odd request, the two moved off at a fast pace. They followed the green globes, floating along the dark ceiling like paper lanterns.

Abruptly, the lead fire orb vanished from sight.

"It's found a room!" Cathleen whispered, her anticipation rising.

The two rushed forward, following the lead orb into the middle of an octagonal shaped room. The pair turned slowly in place, studying the chamber. They were surrounded by eight walls made of a highly glossed, black stone. The mirrored surfaces reflected back, clear images of Cathleen and the Historian, standing side-by-side, over and over.

Cathleen called the other green orbs, assembling them around the ceiling where they shed an eerie glow over the scene. Like the hallways, this room was low ceilinged. The two immediately noted the iron studs driven into the reflective walls. Thick chains were looped through iron hoops and ankle clamps.

Cathleen had an immediate visceral reaction to the terror and suffering that radiated from every corner. She glanced over at the Historian, seeing his face reflected her own feelings of disgust and outrage.

Cathleen walked over to a low plinth set next to a large hearth at the back of the room. On top of the pedestal sat an oval-shaped stone bowl. When she reached in a finger to see its contents, it came away with rust-colored flakes. Dry Blood was her intuitive reaction.

The Historian was stirring the dead ashes in the roughly built hearth using the tip of his sword when Cathleen came up beside him with the candle.

She suddenly stopped his arm, silently pointing to something glinting back at them in the light.

He leaned toward the fire grate and picked out a round object. Turning it over in his hand, wiping off ash, he showed a gold badge to Cathleen. With a deep frown, he tucked it into an inner pocket of his leather vest.

His voice was strained with anger when he spoke in a low voice.

"The badge of his office as Master Outlander Wizard Scout," he said, looking into Cathleen's wide eyes.

They had discovered all the proof they needed to convict the Deceiver of the murder of Bretton Clawson. He would now face the ultimate punishment meaded out by the Council of Greens. Total annihilation.

"We need to carry out the Council's orders, now that there is certainty of guilt," the Historian said with steel in his voice.

Cathleen agreed, but added, "We will locate the Deceiver, but we also need to destroy his network of demons before we leave this place. We should wait to carry out the final judgement on the Deceiver, until the Council Scribe joins us. She can witness and record that our deeds are within the letter of the law of the Greens."

They continued to search the black-mirrored room for any other evidence of the fate of Bretton Clawson.

Cathleen returned to the wall with the ankles irons where the prisoner was likely chained. She bent down when she noticed scrapings on the reflective wall where The Claw likely was chained.

At first glance, they appeared to be marks left by the heavy iron links. Cathleen crouched down to eye level, discovering a clear pattern to the scratches. She called to the Historian.

"It's the secret Outlander code, used by the Scouts to communicate with one another," he told her.

The Historian leaned over her shoulder, studying the message.

"What does it say?" Cathleen asked.

After a few seconds to consider the coded marks, the Historian looked over at her.

"This is a cryptic communication, indeed. He speaks of discovering the "two faces of the Deceiver." His marks are crudely done and unclear. It might read, "Deceiver wears two faces. Beware...beware one who knows...no...beware writer of secrets." There is more, but I can't make it out."

Cathleen repeated the last words of the translation.

"Beware the writer of secrets? What do you suppose that means?"

The Historian was silent. Even in the gloomy light casting shadows around the room, Cathleen could make out the deep furrows of concern on her companion's handsome face.

Chapter 19

They left the ritual chamber with all the evidence they needed to carry out the Deceiver's punishment. Complete obliteration of his life and dark works.

The message scratched on the wall by the tortured prisoner, Bretton Clawson, was vague and unsettling to Cathleen.

She and the Historian silently followed the floating globes again, alert for any guards as they moved through the labyrinth of passages, back to the Great Room.

The Historian pitched his voice so that only Cathleen could hear his warning, with her enhanced audible range.

"The Deceiver has surely vacated this fortress, now that it's proven vulnerable to his enemies. He's likely assembled a large force of demon-spawn, waiting to engage with us when we emerge from here, as his rear action," the Historian said in a tightly controlled voice.

His remarks conjured a frightening vision for Cathleen, of row upon row, of huge, hairy spider creatures, sharp beaks clacking, alongside transparent, catlike monsters, hungry for the taste of flesh. And those were just the beasts they'd encountered so far. Cathleen searched her memory for the best wards to protect them when they exited the stronghold.

They entered the enormous Great Room, moving toward the doors leading outside to the courtyard. Keeping pace with her tall companion as they crossed the deep silence of the cavernous room, Cathleen had just placed a foot down, when she was suddenly jolted by a violent ripple beneath her boot.

She was thrown off balance and would have fallen with the sudden pitch of the stone, if not for the Historian's speed and quick arm around her waist.

He screamed out a levitation spell, sweeping Cathleen into the air, pulling her up and away from the writhing stone below.

They floated two feet above the quickly liquefying stone flooring.

From where she clung to the Historian's brawny shoulder, Cathleen watched as the solid, stone floor, transformed into a lake of boiling sludge. She caught sight of her Green Fire globes, suspended over the seething dark mass and had a flash of inspiration.

"Historian, we need to blow out the walls on either side of the iron doors and let this bubbling cauldron do some of our work for us!" she shouted, not trying to conceal their presence any longer.

With one arm wrapped firmly around one another, they continued to hang just above the bubbling, molten rock.

The sound of their voices calling to the ancient Druid gods, rose above the spattering and hissing just below their booted feet.

Another sound began to make itself heard above the Old Tongue, penetrating their concentration. It clearly came from the courtyard, as if the battle had erupted without them.

They finished their spell and with the last word, floated back a safe distance from the walls. Holding their free arms out in front, they pointed at the far doors and walls shouting together, "Saighean!" and focused an instant flash of searing light on the iron doors.

They were torn away with the ripping sound of shredding wood and the screech of twisted iron. Immediately following, Cathleen directed her fire globes to smash into the thick walls on either side of where the doors stood. These were blown apart like scattered confetti. Stone particles as small as grains of sand, rained down on a scene of mayhem among an army of creatures from the Dark Pit.

Cathleen and the Historian floated through the gaping hole they created. They carefully stayed above the scalding lava flow, watching it effectively pour over the ranks of spiders and large cat-creatures, along with some skeletal, human-like creatures they hadn't encountered earlier.

"Can you see the Deceiver?" Cathleen screamed over the din below to make herself heard.

The Historian answered, a sneer twisting his face, "He will be at the very back of this mob. Ready?"

Cathleen knew he meant to fly over the creatures caught in the flow. Below, she watched as the pale arms of the wraith-thin humanoids, worked furiously in an effort to save themselves. They were pulling others under and trying to stand on them above the inundation. The fiery lava ate away at this temporary reprieve, slowly dissolving everything in its deadly path.

As the two wizards passed overhead, several long, pincer-tipped legs reached up to snag a foot, dangling perilously close. The Historian mumbled a few words and they rose higher, out of range.

Cathleen picked up the sound of a human voice, barely audible with the clacking and desperate roars of agony from below.

Evidently the Historian heard it too. Taking a firmer grip around her waist, he guided them toward the edge of the courtyard.

A dense, acrid stench rose up from the creeping flow. It pushed the bodies of the beasts captured in the unyielding sludge forward, filling all of the open ground and any spider holes in its wide path. The mass finally slowed, coming to rest at the edge of the forest surrounding the citadel.

"Protector!" the Historian shouted in her ear. "The Deceiver has taken to the Chameleon Woods."

"Put me down here and you get ahead of him. We'll catch him between us before he can call for any of his minions," Cathleen directed him. She knew it wasn't a great plan to split their forces, but that seemed the only option they had. They didn't want to lose the Deceiver in the wilderness of that enchanted forest. If he made his way to the cliffs, he could slip into the In-Between, staying there indefinitely.

More importantly, they couldn't stay in the raw evil of this part of the Dark realm much longer. Their powers were inconsistent and constantly under siege from the place and the wizard who ruled here. The Deceiver owned this part of the Dark Pit and made its rules of magic.

The Historian set Cathleen down in a small glade, just inside Chameleon Woods. The silence was so complete she began to wonder if her acute hearing was being affected with the rest of her powers. She had to remind herself that here, in the fourth realm, there wouldn't be any natural life anywhere, not even in the woods. She looked around seeing the sickly trees and pitted ground that made up this forest.

Funny, I never noticed that when we were here earlier.

It felt as if she was seeing things as they truly were, not filtered through the machinations of the Deceiver. She took a minute to orient herself, looking around to be sure the Deceiver hadn't slipped in behind her, making her the hunted. With her Inner Eye, she scoped out a large swath of woodland and picked up a slight ripple in front of a dead tree stump. Remembering their encounter with the Forest Watchman, she immediately called for Green Fire.

"No need to go to those extremes, Protector. It's only me, Mercy McNaughton, Scribe to the Council of Greens. I believe you called for me to join you here?" The pretty Scribe stepped away from the dead trunk and closer to Cathleen. She was slightly taller than Cathleen's five-foot-four, the bulk of her muscular body gave her a good ten pounds over her too. She wore her thick, red hair in a single braid, trailing below her shoulders to a slender waist. "You seem surprised at my appearance, Protector. As the Council's chosen External Censor Officer, I must admit some surprise at your youth, as well."

"My apologies, Mercy. I have no doubt the Arch Wizard has chosen wisely in putting you forward to the Council as Scribe. I thank you for answering my call. Can you tell me, first, how Jason Tate is doing? Was he sent to the Healing Gardens by Sir Alex?"

"Your husband is well into a full recovery, Protector. He has been resting at the Arch Wizards personal retreat. Which brings me to your request. Why am I here?"

Cathleen's sensitive ears picked up a slight annoyance in Mercy's tone, but ignored it, knowing the Time Thread she had to use to get there was no easy ordeal.

"I've been told you might have information about the Deceiver that isn't public knowledge to any on the Council, except you and Sir Alex. I need that information now."

"Can you be more specific, Protector? My position as Scribe affords me insight into much in the Wizarding world that pertains to the Greens."

"I need to keep moving through this woodland, Mercy, so I have to cut to the chase. What do you know about the Deceiver's many faces? Is he capable of shifting into another form, or person?"

"I best walk with you since Sir Alex only allotted me one hour before I lose my Thread to return home. He was rather miffed that you took me away from my work, but truthfully, with the Council meeting being canceled by him, there wasn't much to do."

Cathleen wondered for a moment why Sir Alex would not bring the Council together considering their need to act in these dangerous times. They were entering a deeply shadowed stand of blackened trees. The bark on all of them was covered in a spongy fungus, oozing thick droplets of a foul-smelling substance. The leaves were curling as an oily sheen spread across the surface of each leaf. She couldn't understand why she never noticed all this when she passed through here earlier.

"Scribe, does the fourth realm change perceptions for an outsider?"

The heavy stillness imposed itself on the two young women and they spoke in hushed tones. "Oh, indeed," she answered softly. "We know The Dark Pit of the Sleepless Dead is a blight on any living thing within its evil sphere. When you first encounter this realm, things may not look much different from the first realm. But given time to adjust to the dark atmosphere, you'll begin to see the true ugliness around you."

Cathleen was about to comment on her own experience, when the sound of brittle tree limbs being snapped carried through the dead woods. They froze, studying the area around them. There was more movement and sounds of something big and heavy coming toward them, mowing down everything in its path.

"Protector, something is coming in our direction. What should we do?"

Cathleen considered her response before answering, "Wait."

Chapter 20

Cathleen and the Scribe, Mercy McNaughton, were under a hastily dropped Dome of Protection. A slight trembling of the earth tickled the bottoms of Cathleen's boots. Whatever moved toward them must be heavy. She concentrated her energies on her response to the imminent threat, but something made her instincts continue to buzz with warnings. *This creature is not the Deceiver, but likely only a minion,* she was thinking as she prepared herself to meet a demon-spawn.

Cathleen tried to ignore the warning signals bouncing around in her head. She slowed down her thoughts while they waited for the beast to show itself. The Deceiver escaped into these blackened woods, and while she came from behind the fleeing wizard, the Historian should be herding him away from any access to the cliffs beyond, turning him back toward Cathleen with his use of magic.

They believed he was heading for the cliffs, possibly to exit the fourth realm and enter into the In-Between. There, he could lie low indefinitely, returning to his stronghold when the search for him was abandoned. That could be eons later, but time means nothing in the In-Between.

A slight movement brought Cathleen's attention back to Mercy McNaughton. When she dropped the Dome earlier, the Scribe had gone very still. Cathleen glanced over at her, to be sure she was dealing with the sudden confinement. Not everyone welcomed this kind of sealed-in protection.

She was surprised to see an eager look on Mercy's face. Something about the tight smile playing at the corners of her mouth deepened Cathleen's uneasy feeling. Cathleen suddenly understood why her instincts were aflame with warnings.

Whatever was thrashing through the dead forest was most assuredly one of the Deceiver's demon-spawn, because the Deceiver himself now stood beside her in the sealed Dome. Cathleen saw the chilling truth of the situation she found herself in. The Deceiver used his dark powers to shift into the form of the young Scribe.

At least I know Jason got through to the Council Chambers, she thought while trying not to give away her alarm at the current situation. The scenario played out in her mind, while she watched for something to burst through the brittle trees surrounding them.

The Deceiver must have left his compound before the Historian and I were able to escape, intercepting Mercy when the Time Thread dropped her at the cliffs. That couldn't have been more than forty-minutes ago.

Long enough, she realized, for the fallen Wizard to make it to the cliffs. He just missed getting boxed-in between her and the Historian. Cathleen's thoughts flashed through her head, reconstructing all that led up to her current circumstances.

Now she'd need to confirm her suspicions. She reached over and grabbed the Scribe's arm. She almost let go, feeling the betraying, non-living tingle of a false body, masking the true one beneath. Unlike a clone, shifting into another's body was never skin-deep.

Cathleen believed the Scribe had either been murdered or was hiding somewhere near the cliffs. If it was the latter, the young Mercy was in mortal danger from the evils that roamed the dead plane.

Cathleen felt the intensity of the imposter's eyes on her.

She jerked her hand away, trying to hide her revulsion at the feel of the superimposed flesh. "You're safe in the Dome, Scribe," she mumbled lamely.

Her words were like the trigger on a gun. The Dome of Protection was blown apart like a piñata. Cathleen was thrown into the air, coming down with a heavy thud on the blackened earth. The air left her lungs in a long whoosh, when she was slammed on her back, stunned, her eyes unfocused. She became vaguely aware of having something settle over her mouth and nose.

Sleeping Mask Spell, she thought, tossing her head from side to side, struggling against its affect.

Before she passed out completely, Cathleen heard the Deceiver speaking to someone. *He's shifted back, but where's the Scribe*, she thought, her mind slipping away before she could fight off his spell.

The Deceiver raised his voice in anger. It was high pitched, like a Forest Hag's, but even more strident to her faded hearing. "It took you enough time to get back here! That annoying Scribe nearly fouled our plans. I was forced to use her image to shift, or risk being taken."

"All is well, Boatwright. Calm yourself."

Cathleen heard these words, fighting against the inevitable blankness seeping into her mind. They touched something in her memory, something familiar.

In a last spurt of realization, she saw clearly that all was lost to the Mother's Green Wizards if she was captured. She opened her mouth to call out a name, but her words were swallowed inside the fog that finally claimed her.

Nearly a mile of corrupt woodlands stood between Cathleen's inert body and the man she tried to call to. Her only ally, the Historian. He'd been moving with great stealth, not wanting to give away his position to any of the guard units he'd seen patrolling the area. These were not the huge, deadly spiders, or furless cat creatures they'd encountered earlier, but robust looking thugs. He watched one small group as they passed in front of the pitted boulders he hid behind. They must have been confident in their numbers, because they were talking in low voices about the prey they hunted. His ears perked up with the next comment.

"The Historian was a soldier-Wizard, known for his powers," one slightly hunched-back guard, was telling a band of five. "We can't be too careful hunting him down. So, keep alert you lot!"

The Historian drew in a sharp breath of recognition. They all wore a short tunic, cinched at the waist, over bulky mesh armor. The same garb as an acolyte training with the Outlander Wizard Scouts. He clearly recognized the Outlander insignia blazoned on the front as one of the men turned, facing his direction. They were all heavily armed, indicating they had not mastered the dark spells yet and needed the old-fashioned protection of steel. A good sign for the one watching them now.

The Historian studied the group closely, searching for a familiar face among them. He was well-aware there had been defections over the eons that the Outlanders operated on the borderlands. There was always lots of speculation as to their fates.

Well, now I know where some of the traitors have gone. He tightened his grip on the hilt of his short sword, scowling as they passed close by, unaware of sharp eyes following them.

The guard who spoke was obviously the leader of this band. They might have been doing reconnaissance for a larger group, or maybe for the Deceiver himself. The Historian thought of Cathleen, approaching from the opposite direction and headed straight toward them. He figured the Deceiver had somehow slipped through their pincer trap and was likely conducting his own hunt for him and the Protector.

What a prize she would make, he thought with dismay. He faded away from the rocks, moving ahead and hoping to intercept Cathleen O'Brien before she walked into a trap.

The sounds of the traitorous Outlander Wizard Scouts laughing at a rough comment brought a hissed curse to his lips. "Your days are numbered. I shall snuff out your worthless lives, if it is my last act," he vowed softly.

Chapter 21

Mercy McNaughton was small enough to squeeze herself into the crevice of the large boulder. She remained still, afraid to come out until the Protector or the Historian showed up.

When she dropped from the Time Thread onto the cliffs bordering the Chameleon Forest, she had been greeted by two Outlander Wizard Scouts. They told her they were sent to guard her until the Protector arrived to take charge. After pacing the cliffs under their watchful eyes, Mercy grew annoyed with the arrangement. She was about to give the Scout with a slight hump a good piece of her mind. After all, she was the Scribe to the Council of Greens and had important work to do back home. She had wondered why she was being called here by the Protector, in any case.

The Protector's husband, Jason, was adamant that the Protector requested Mercy to join her immediately. He offered no further information, even though Sir Alex quizzed him closely, before sending him on to the Healing Gardens.

She did notice how irritated the Arch Wizard was with Jason's lack of information. He gave her a severe look saying, "Get him to the Gardens," and huffed out of the room.

She was marching over to the two Scouts when they had both fallen instantly to their knees, heads bent nearly to the ground. She looked back over her shoulder. "What on earth…?" Mercy was saying when a darkly robed figure came up behind her, spinning her around with a flick of a boney, white wrist.

Mercy remembered how he scrutinized her face and body like a careful painter. When she tried to move away from his probing eyes, she found herself unable to lift a foot. She knew magic when it was at play, figuring the dark stranger must have cast a binding spell.

Now, hiding inside the deep fissure of a boulder, she shivered from both fear and the deep chill in the dead atmosphere of the place.

She recalled the smirk on the wizard's face as he introduced himself as Calvin Boatwright. His smug look had changed into anger when Mercy blurted out, "The bloody Deceiver!" He called out a spell, creating funnel-like winds from the dead air around her. Mercy was scooped up like a leaf and she understood her fate. He planned to toss her body over the Precipice of Doom and into certain oblivion.

The Deceiver had watched a moment as she spun like a grain of sand in the gale winds. He laughed and turned his back on her plight. Knowing she'd be dropped into the vast abyss, he walked away from her surprised shriek and toward the cowering men.

Fighting to keep her head, Mercy waited for him to move off, then called out her own charm. This funnel would disappear the second it deposited her into the endless void so she had to work her magic quickly.

Bending the strong gust that held her in an iron vortex, Mercy forced it to move away from the cliff's edge and curved it, to spit her like a cherry pit into the crevice of a huge boulder.

Mercy had hunkered down in the shadow of the rock, to see if the Deceiver would reveal his devious plans. The notorious wizard had ordering the Scouts to their feet. He began screaming in a high, whiny voice, about how inept they'd been in their efforts to capture the Protector, Cathleen O'Brien.

After they hastily retreated back to the woodlands like chastised children, the Deceiver began a chant. It was familiar to Mercy's ears, but it had been altered by the infusion of dark magic into each word.

The natural winds continually picked up the fine dirt around her hiding place, blowing it into the narrow crevice where she hunkered low. This caused Mercy's eyes to water and blink several times.

Earlier, with a last blink to clear her vision, she had looked across the barren ground to where the Deceiver was standing, only to find him gone. Mercy's hand had flown to her mouth when she saw what he had done. The Scribe had been stunned at the Deceiver's transformation, never having seen a real Shifter before. She had numbly watched as her body-double walked briskly toward the thick, dead woods beyond, to join the traitorous Scouts.

After what felt like a lifetime huddled inside the boulder's cold split, she knew she had to move. *I can't hide here forever*, she thought resolutely. She carefully slipped into the bleak surroundings, keeping close to the deeper shadows of the rocks as much as possible.

She weighed her options. *Returning to the Council Chambers on a Time Thread would keep me safe. But it would expose the Protector and the Historian to grave danger, if they didn't realize the Deceiver had shifted to look like me.*

Continuing that train of thought, she moved in the direction the false Scribe had taken.

Following the Deceiver could lead her to Cathleen O'Brien and maybe even the Historian.

His handsome face flashed briefly in her memory and she felt an unfamiliar thrill run through her body. She couldn't let anything happen to the mysterious Will Farley.

She picked up her pace, alert for signs of the corrupted Scouts. It enraged her to know two of that elite group of wizards had become followers and lackies to the Deceiver. *He must have prodigious powers indeed, to lure any from among this special force*, she thought, adding to her apprehension of dealing with him.

She wondered to herself. *How many dark creatures have these turncoats allowed to cross over from the Dark Pit?* She shivered again in fear of the possibilities. She knew little about the geography of the Dark Pit of the Sleepless Dead, or the borderlands she'd be crossing. She did know the Chameleon Forest she was entering sat on the edge of eternal darkness, created as the ultimate punishment for desecrating the Green Mother's natural order.

The creatures that inhabited the Pit were conjured in evil and sustained by evil. Fallen wizards and other miscreant magic users were sent here to live out their life cycles, no matter how long, or brief.

As she followed the Deceiver's meandering trail, Mercy's mind kept going back to the strange behavior of Sir Alex. Her drifting thoughts almost exposed her to her quarry. The Deceiver had shifted to his real body and out of hers. He stood directly in front of her in a small opening in the forest. He was very tall and wraith thin in his dark robes, reminding her of a cobra getting ready to strike.

Mercy crouched down, scooting backward into the thicker stand of trees, watching and listening.

He was speaking with one of the corrupt Outlander Wizard Scouts, the one with the hump on his back. "I have sent the Protector on to the citadel, where she will be held in the Eye of Despair. Given the right amount of time there, even her spirit will collapse into a deep hopelessness."

"But what good does that do us, Master?"

The Deceiver rounded on the cringing Scout and snarled between long, yellowed teeth, "I will own her then, fool!"

Chapter 22

Cathleen slowly entered into a semi-conscious awareness. Working its way through the fog in her brain, was a strange, prickly sensation, zapping every fiber of her body with minute jolts of current.

Very…old…magic, she thought, desperately struggling to focus her mind on her current situation. She was groggy from the Sleeping Mask Spell the Deceiver used to subdue her, but this was a new sensation seeping into her awareness.

Cathleen mentally reached for her Protector's deeply ingrained discipline. She pushed her mind to concentrate and reconnect her with the circumstances she'd find when she opened her eyes.

She waited for the prickly feeling lighting up her nerve endings to pass. *This is just the after effect of being exposed to magic*, she told herself as the tiny pin-pricks continued, unabated. Gradually, she conditioned herself to ignore the odd jolts, feeling her senses fully restored. Cathleen partially opened her eyes.

Without moving her head, she took in as much of her surroundings as possible, still unwilling to show she was fully aware. Her long hair concealed much of her face so she was able to hide her awareness, if she was being observed.

Cathleen expected to be held in a dingy cell somewhere beneath the great fortress. She was unprepared to see the truth of her confinement. She was suspended above the floor of the same ceremonial room she and the Historian had discovered. The site of Bretton Clawson's murder.

She heard the snapping and settling of a fire in the hearth. From her narrow view, it was making more shadows than it illuminated.

She was held in place by a beam of black light, pouring down on her from somewhere above. Cathleen felt a strange heaviness as it bathed her in a shower of darkness.

Her first impulse when she realized her situation, was to escape the pressing weight. As hard as she willed it, she was unable to move a muscle. Only her eyes showed any of the strain.

From somewhere in the room, she heard a snicker. Stepping out of a dark corner, the fallen Scout with the hunched-back approached Cathleen. He could easily reach up and touch her leg and she saw by the look on his face that he was sorely tempted, but she suspected she was off limits and was glad for that small mercy because he controlled his impulse. "You are back with us, Protector. The Master will be delighted. He wants to watch while you suffer. So, do I, for that matter," he added sneering up at her.

"You're a bigger fool than you look, traitor! Your so-called, Master, is using your weaknesses like his tools to keep you subservient to him. You have your own magic, wizard. Use it and free me now. I'll testify on your behalf and you'll be spared the penalty for desertion."

"Save your breath, Protector, I am lost to the Mother and there's no changing that now."

"Tell me at least, for any love you had for the Mother, what is this black light holding me?"

The fallen Scout hesitated, but then said, "Won't do you any good knowing, but if you're so inclined to know…it's the Eye of Despair that's holding you, Protector. Ever hear of it?"

Cathleen had indeed heard of the evil torture devise, but it was only a rumor used to frighten young wizards. Her own father had explained it to be a spirit breaker, capable of bringing hopelessness and desolation to any held in its grasp. Cathleen closed her eyes, not wanting to show the traitor Scout any emotion bubbling up to the surface, especially fear or despair.

"I'll leave you then, Protector. The Master will join you soon as I tell him you are awake and ready for his entertainment."

She heard his laugh echo through the narrow hallway until it was smothered by the darkness. There was no doubt the black light was beginning to have its desired effect on Cathleen. She suddenly had an overpowering need to cry out over the sense of injustice. How could this be happening to her? She was all alone in her suffering.

She shook her head with a jerk, trying to dislodge such maudlin thoughts. It's beginning, she realized, her mind nearly seized-up with complete terror. Finding a spark of resolve, she clamped her mouth shut tightly, stifling the sobs she desperately wanted to spill into her cage of black light. She was suspended in a current of gloom and despair, insinuating its power into every fiber of her being.

Her will power was epic in her parent's minds and, Jason commented often on the steel he felt in her nature. But then, they'd never felt the Eye of Despair, cutting through their emotional defenses like a jagged knife, parring away at self-control and purpose, killing hope and faith, like little princelings in their sleep.

Cathleen's head hung on her chest as she slipped deeper into her maudlin misery.

There was a sound coming from somewhere nearby and it jarred her from her lethargy as the Deceiver's ugly face sprang unbidden to her mind. "OK, you lump of camel dung, I'm getting ready for you," she whispered between deep breaths, trying to stop the sobs threatening to erupt.

Cathleen heard another sound coming from the passageway just outside the room. This one sounded hesitant as it came closer to the Ceremonial chamber.

Another Scout?

She struggled to prepare herself, knowing while she hung in the Eye of Despair what little magic she still had was unavailable to her.

I might as well have been a normal human. Being the Protector means nothing!

She couldn't turn her head but slid her eyes in the direction of the door in time to see a fiery red head of hair, bent low and creeping into the shadowy room. Cathleen felt a twinge of recognition and hope.

"Welcome, Mercy McNaughton," Cathleen managed to say softly.

The Scribe looked into the black stream of light and saw Cathleen hanging there like a marionette. "Protector! You know me then? I need to work quickly to get you free and then get us out of here."

Cathleen watched as the Scribe, knowledgeable of many arcane spells and charms, began reciting those she believed would work. An interminable two-minutes of listening to her chanting and Cathleen felt lost. *Or it might be the effect of the Eye of Desolation*, she thought, annoyed with the tears that threatened to spill from her eyes any moment in frustration. Cathleen blanked out the scene of the struggling Scribe. She focused her last mental strength to reach deep inside herself, finding the calm center she needed to help in her own rescue. She broke into the Scribe's next chant, saying they only needed to find the right spell to end the flow of the black light. "That's what keeping me trapped and making me lose control of my emotions," she said, a sob choking her voice.

"Of course! Can't very well free you while it's power still holds you fast." The Scribe thought for a second and then began an unfamiliar chant. Cathleen immediately felt its reach, as the black light trembled around her. Mercy, her arms outstretched, finished her spell with words Cathleen remembered from childhood when her dad tried decorating for the Yuletide.

"Sruth bhua. End your flow of light and flow of energies!" The black beam vanished, dropping Cathleen unceremoniously onto the hard floor. She should have been ecstatic to be released, but the vague feeling of doom and sadness clung to her like her own shadow.

Mercy was helping her to stand. The effects of the Sleeping Mask, combined with no muscle activity for nearly an hour, left Cathleen stiff and awkward in her movements.

"We need to hurry, Mercy. I can still feel the negative energies the Deceiver was forcing into my mind. Whatever I say, or do, keep me moving!"

Cathleen let out a low moan as they made their way down the corridor, causing Mercy to slow down. She was trying so hard to focus her mind, it actually hurt her head. It felt like there was a blockage between her and her ability to reason. She worried it was also blocking her magic, making it inaccessible to her.

Cathleen stopped. "Need to test my magic." She whispered the spell to bring the shadows of the passageway to her and formed a Shadow Wrap. Covering the two of them, Cathleen immediately felt some of her determination and hope returning.

As they crept toward the Great Room and escape, Cathleen became more and more aware of the reassuring tingle of the Mother's magic moving through her. That triggered a clearer thought for their next move. She laid a hand on Mercy's arm, stopping her.

"The Historian! He has no idea the Deceiver is a Shifter. He'll be taken in by him pretending to be you. We have to find him before they do."

"Yes, and you should know, Protector, the Deceiver lured at least a few Outlander Scouts to his dark kingdom. The scum follow his every command."

"I know. Two of them brought me here. We're nearly to the Great Room. We're bound to run into the traitors guarding the exit, but my Wrap will hold. Just keep close to me and we'll be okay."

They were a few feet from the gaping hole Cathleen and the Historian caused earlier. The two heavy doors they blew off were laying a good distance from where they once stood, looking like rafts, sinking under a smattering of ruble.

Cathleen spotted the fallen Outlander Wizard Scouts, one stationed in the shadows on each side of the gap in the walls.

The women stopped as Cathleen said a few words to make certain their Shadow Wrap was secure. She leaned near her companion's ear and whispered.

"This Wrap will slow us down. As soon as we pass the guards, we'll head for the dead trees and shed the Wrap there. If we're spotted and have to fight our way out, you take the Scout on your side and I'll deal with the other. This is a kill or die order, Mercy. There are no options."

Mercy was relieved to see the determination flare in the Protector's eyes. *She's finally back!* she thought with relief.

The guards were obviously bored from standing watch over the litter-strewn courtyard. They shifted from foot to foot, occasionally using a low whistle to get the other's attention when they needed to relieve themselves in the shadow of the building.

Cathleen could feel Mercy's body tense as one of the Scouts passed within two feet of where they huddled near a pile of blasted stone. This was an opportunity and Cathleen wanted to take advantage of it. She motioned for Mercy to stay put, while she crept out from under her side of the Wrap.

The Scout was obviously finishing up and tucking his shirt back into place. Cathleen moved to his left. Picking up a loose stone, she tossed it to his right, needing him to move deeper into the interior of the vast room where the corners were steeped in gloom.

The Scout's head snapped up with the sound of the rock hitting somewhere behind him. The hissing sound of his sword being pulled from its scabbard made Cathleen shiver. She knew this man would be highly trained in its use and didn't want to face its sharp edge until she felt her magic was fully restored.

She never gave such a notion a second thought, but that was before the Eye of Despair enveloped her with negativity and fear.

The man was moving on cat's paws, walking in the direction his trained ear correctly identified. Cathleen couldn't help but admire his keen instincts. This was the Scout that had the slight hump and seemed in charge, perhaps a superior officer in the old regiment he disgraced.

Keeping low to the ground, Cathleen saw the man throw something out in front of himself. The next moment, a red light flared into life, illuminating the area directly in front of him. It hovered a moment, then moved slowly in wider and wider arcs, lighting each area as it circled.

Hover Lamp, Cathleen thought, half ashamed with herself for not thinking the well-armed Scout would surely have been issued such a device.

She knew it would register any life form in the vicinity of the red glow, making her even more vulnerable to detection.

The Scout held his sword slightly raised at his right side and as soon as the Hover Lamp moved on, so did he.

Suddenly, he spun around.

Both he and Cathleen heard the noise at the same instant and both reacted by checking their unguarded rear and flanks.

Cathleen, using her Inner Eye, had a distinct advantage over the Scout. He did manage to land his Hover Lamp and redirect it toward the front of the building.

It flew past Cathleen so quickly the Scout never registered her presence, though she had taken the precaution of flattening herself against the wall and calling some shadows to herself.

They both saw the front of the ragged wall area was no longer under guard. The Scout sent the Lamp closer to the area where the other Scout should have been posted. He gave a long whistle, receiving no response from his mate.

Cathleen saw something move behind the perplexed Scout. At first she thought it was a glitch in her Inner Eye's ability, but she clearly picked it up again.

Mercy?

Cathleen saw a rippling in the fetid air. With the doors and half the front walls gone, the pungent odors from the forest and surrounding dead zones, filtered unabated into the Great Room.

The Scribe must have followed her to lend assistance, but Cathleen was clear in her orders for her to lay low.

The Scout sensed something too, because he stopped moving. His legs were firmly set in a fighting stance and she wasn't surprised when he spun around, wielding his flat sword expertly in a wide, slashing arc.

<h1 style="text-align:center">Chapter 23</h1>

The Scout was thrown slightly off balance when his powerful, wide swing met no resistance. He backed up toward the courtyard, holding his sword straight out in front of his chest. He was ready to defend himself, but still hadn't identified his attacker.

Cathleen was just as anxious to know who this unseen ally was.

Keeping to the shadows, she edged along the wall until she came up directly behind the Scout. Dropping her camouflage with a sweep of her arm, she threw a binding spell over the man, rooting his feet to the ground and freezing him in his fighting stance.

The thick air swirled in front of the captured Scout. A leg, an arm and then, the whole body of the handsome Historian stepped out of the distorted whirlwind. Cathleen didn't dare shout her relief, but his keen ears clearly picked up her whispered comment, "Thank the Mother!"

"Well met, Protector. You seem quite adept at springing traps like the one set for you by the Deceiver."

Cathleen would normally have been annoyed with the Historian's comment, but her relief at being reunited with her ally, was greater than her pride. "Historian, we can discuss my experiences later. Right now, come with me." She led him to the large pile of stones, where Mercy was still hidden under the Shadow Wrap. The young Scribe blinked her eyes when Cathleen dropped the spell and the shadows melted back into the woods around them.

"Cathleen, I was about to...Oh!" Mercy saw the Historian come up beside Cathleen and felt her knees get spongy when he smiled down at her.

"Greetings to you, Scribe," he said in his deep, smooth voice.

Cathleen saw the magnetic draw these two had to one another, but their newly discovered attraction would have to wait to be explored. "We need to move out from here. The Deceiver's stronghold is done for him, but he still has at least one traitorous Scout doing his bidding." Turning to the Historian, Cathleen said, "Let's finish the job we started earlier."

They stood side-by-side, arms extended, each bringing jagged bolts of Green Fire to their hands. They shot these across the courtyard and directly into the huge Great Room. The effect was immediate. An explosion of green flame burst from every corner of the mammoth structure, consuming every inch of stone laid and standing.

As the two wizards worked their destructive spell, there came a howl from within the conflagration. They continued to pour their green death and destruction, turning only briefly to look into one another's eyes.

"He deserves his fate and the Mother deserves Her revenge," Cathleen said and turned away from the Historian's look of approval. They stood silently after her comment, working systematically to destroy the last of the citadel that was the Deceiver's seat of power. They both understood, this was but one such evil kingdom in the fourth realm of the Dark Pit of the Sleepless Dead.

Only the Mother knew the true numbers of Dark Ones. Only the Mother knew the monsters they called with their twisted magic. Cathleen's thoughts turned to the Scribe, waiting while they finished raining down Armageddon on the enormous fortress.

The cautionary words found scratched on a wall by the murdered Bretton Clawson, could very well apply to her. "Beware of Writer of Secrets." A warning from the dying Master of Outlander Wizard Scouts. They easily described someone who kept the minutes and records for the Council of Green Wizards and was privy to all of their plans and secrets.

Cathleen felt uneasy thinking such dreadful thoughts of the Scribe. She'd proven herself loyal in so many ways already. It just didn't fit.

The Historian's deep voice cut through her reflections, "It's done Protector. Now we need to finish off the traitor Scout."

Cathleen dropped her arms, extinguishing the sacred Fire from her hands.

The Historian noticed the distant look on her face, wondering if she still suffered from the effects of the Eye of Despair. He knew it could have a lasting hold on a human spirit.

"Protector! Will! You've done well to remove his only hiding place!" Mercy said excitedly. She jumped up from the shadows where she waited. Relief was clear on her face as she brushed a curl of fiery red hair behind an ear, her eyes never leaving the Historian's.

Cathleen wondered if he noticed Mercy used his given name, rather than his title just then. She's totally in love with him. Not the reaction of a traitor in this situation.

The three turned their backs on the smoldering ruins and headed into the dead forest. Despite the corruption that lay all around them, Cathleen sensed something else, something living, not far ahead.

Walking single file, she led the others, her mind burning with questions and suspicions surrounding the investigation. She realized that while they solved the case of the murdered Claw, there were other mysteries, mysteries clinging like a fungus to the discovery. Was Sir Alex's secret agent working on this case too?

Making their way through the thick clusters of blackened trees, Cathleen began to think about the earlier warning his agent gave to Sir Alex, of a blood bath the Council would suffer.

The Arch Wizard was the only Council member who knew the identity of the agent supplying this information. This disturbed Cathleen's sense of efficiency. If something happened to him, the agent could fade back into oblivion and his confidences along with him.

Cathleen's mental ramblings were cut short, when she picked up a trace of magic. The use of spells or charms, felt like a hum, prickling the air around her.

Outlander nearby, she thought.

While the Scouts were Wizards themselves, they were low-level magic users for the most part. Their training being focused on martial, rather than magical, arts. Never-the-less, they had powers and as such, could pose a challenge especially when cornered.

"They have split up, Protector," the Historian was leaning down, whispering his observation to Cathleen. He obviously picked up the vibes radiating from somewhere nearby. Cathleen heard Mercy begin a charm for discernment, but her attention was drawn away by movement in the dead air. It brushed her senses as lightly as a feather. Glancing at her two companions she saw it had a similar effect on them.

Mercy was reaching into a pocket of the long dress she wore.

Cathleen noticed when they first met that despite the modern age, Mercy wore the traditional garb of a Scribe. A finely made wool garment of forest green, embroidered with the symbols of her rank as Scribe to the Council. Its wide sleeves looked like wings hanging down at her side.

But Mercy was no angel, unless she was an avenging one. Cathleen saw a white bone appear in her small hand. *Woodland Hag*, she realized. A powerful relic if used by the slayer of that hideous creature. Cathleen re-evaluated Mercy's powers, knowing not many wizards could vanquish those formidable Witches, taking a finger relic to boot. She didn't need to look at the Historian to know how he was armed. The hiss of his sword sliding free was clue enough.

For herself, Cathleen decided she'd vanish to claim the element of surprise. Drawing in the inky shadows, she evaporated like a mist, without a word. Her companions looking perplexed for a moment, quickly understood her ploy. They stood back to back waiting for the imminent attack.

A large rock sailed by the Historian's head, so close the breeze stirred his long hair in passing. Mercy had her back close to his and they slowly began to rotate to protect their rear and flanks. There was movement to their left, followed by a loud twanging sound. A barbed harpoon came hurtling toward them out of the woods.

Mercy was in the direct line of fire and would have been skewered like a kabob if the Historian hadn't acted simultaneously. He conjured a thick war shield, throwing it down in front of her, just as the wicked triple-edged tip slammed home. The shaft of the harpoon splintered with the force of impact, when it imbedded itself deeply in the shield. This demonstrated there was much power behind the launched missile.

Cathleen witnessed the attack, impressed with the Historian's quick thinking. Now she knew the location of at least one of the traitorous Scouts and moved off in that direction. He was crouched low, behind one of the many boulders strewn throughout the bleak landscape, even here, among the thick stands of dead trees. Rocks the size of a small cottage were scattered about as if the earth belched them up from its black heart.

Coming up behind the Scout, she began a soft chant, lifting the shocked man off his feet and turning him in her direction. She remained hidden by the Wrap, allowing her disembodied voice to be that much more frightening. He hung in space while she addressed him. His face looked shocked, then terrified.

"Outlander Wizard Scout, you have betrayed your oath to the Green Mother and to the Council of Green Wizards. You have committed the heinous crime of murder of the Master, Bretton Clawson. For these crimes you are sentenced to oblivion."

She lifted her arm and sent the dangling man tearing through the woods, slamming into trees and jutting rocks, on his way to the cliffs. Here he was dropped like a stone down the endless well to nothingness.

There was another traitor hunkered down somewhere to her right. Cathleen waited under cover of the shadows until he gave away his position.

The Historian pulled Mercy into a crouch beside him, just as another spear-tipped missile flew overhead. This time he motioned her to stay down behind the shield, flicking his hand to dislodge the first harpoon. Grabbing it, he stood up, making himself a perfect target for their attacker. He threw his arm back, screaming out a spell before sending the harpoon smashing through the dead trees, toward its mark.

Mercy stood up carefully at the sound of a soft thud and howl of pain.

The Historian placed an arm around her shoulder saying, "It's over."

Cathleen was suddenly standing in front of them. She'd witnessed the second Scout being impaled with one of his own weapons, but knew he wasn't their last threat.

"Nice work, Historian, but we still have to capture the Deceiver. Any ideas of where he'd go to hide on this lifeless plain?"

Mercy spoke before he could answer. "There's only the In-Between, Protector. He can stay there for eons, waiting out the clock on the mortals searching for him."

The Historian added, "I suggest we search there before he melts into one of its many catacombs. It would be like searching for one bee in a hive if that happens."

Cathleen felt an ominous foreboding listening to the Historian's description. She knew the In-Between was exactly as he described. A hodge-podge if cylindrical spaces, harboring beings in a cryonic sleep. They awoke after each cycle of one-hundred years of time as measured in the first realm of humans. She and her fellow hunters would all be dust by then and the Deceiver would be free to come back with his dark magic, to rebuild his evil world.

Chapter 24

"We can't do this alone, Historian," Cathleen said firmly.

"Scribe, you must summon a Time Thread and return to the Council. Make your report, but don't mention our search will include the In-Between. I think there is someone involved in this case that's very close to the Council of Greens and I don't want them having that information. Just say, we're pursuing the Deceiver and destroying his followers." Cathleen stopped speaking for a second, adding, "And Mercy, I want you to return here secretly, with Jason. He's likely fully recovered and we can use his special skills in tracking. We'll meet up with you at the cliffs, then we'll enter the In-Between together. Meanwhile, the Historian and I will search out any other defectors from among the Scouts."

"But how will you know we're back, Protector?" the Scribe asked

"I can always feel Jason's presence. I'll know he's here. Remember, not even Sir Alex is to know you two are returning, or that we're searching the In-Between."

The Historian and Cathleen accompanied the Scribe to the cliffs, where she would call a Time Thread for her trip back to the Council's stronghold. A few muttered words of her spell and she vanished in a shimmer of air.

Cathleen looked over at the Historian, noting the look of concern on his face. "She'll be fine, Historian. And if all goes as planned, she and Jason will be back soon to help us finish this investigation."

Cathleen and the Historian began hunting down the remnants of Outlander Wizard Scouts that crossed over to the Dark. As they searched the wind-blown and blackened woods and plains, Cathleen wondered what the Deceiver had offered the turn-coats, that they would betray all that was once sacred to them.

Her speculation was shared by the Historian who had been entertaining the same questions. He confided, this was not the first time in the history of the Greens that Outlander Scouts had deserted their posts, but it certainly was the first, where they joined the Dark Magic Users.

The pair spoke in hushed voices, scanning the area around them. They'd gone back to the Deceiver's citadel and were searching an area in the vicinity of the destroyed fortress. Here, they uncovered a well-concealed barracks building, obviously used by the Scouts. Five bunks were made up and looked used.

"There will be at least one left undiscovered as of yet, Protector."

Cathleen nodded. He could be hiding anywhere in the vast, desolate landscape. A place he was well acquainted with. They moved on, entering to the blasted wastelands behind the smoldering remains of the Deceiver's castle.

After covering a mile of brittle, thorny brush, they came to a pool of dark water on the far-side of a small clearing. The polished onyx surface reflected the jittering movements of an enormous moth. Its rounded body was covered in black fuzz, delicate antennae jutted out from a narrowly shaped head, appearing too long for the body.

The creature sipped from the oily edges of the pond, skimming close to the surface. Occasionally, tiny wavelets rose up from a long, darting tongue, splashing miniscule drops onto its fury body.

The giant moth moved off, lighting on a nearby rotted log for a second, before repeating the same action, over and over. Cathleen and the Historian found themselves fascinated by the moth's odd ritual, watching closely. There was a kind of magical precision in its movements.

After taking a last drink, it settled down gently on the log, facing their direction. It appeared to be drying its wings with a slow, fanning motion.

In a flash of intuition, Cathleen understood what they'd been watching. She touched the Historian's arm very gently to avoid any startled response. He looked down into her wide, hazel eyes and saw the alarm she was desperately trying to transmit. He stepped closer to hear her muted warning, "Dragon Leach."

Cathleen felt certain the creature was aware of their presence. Like several species in other realms, it used body camouflage to conceal its real form from possible predators and prey alike. That would explain the vague jittering in the air around it, when they first spotted it at the pond. It would have been enough to fool their Inner Eye from discerning the true creature.

"This would be a good time to get out your sword."

Cathleen was already bringing Green Fire to her hand. Her spell began shaping the small flames into jagged spikes. They leapt around her palms, anxious to be freed.

The Dragon Leach kept its perch on the hallow log until the Green flames sprang to life in the human's hand. As if a visual cue had been given and received, the round, fuzzy body of the charming moth, began it lengthen and fill-out. It jumped off the log onto the ground, where the two wizards watched its alarming metamorphous.

The fuzzy black hairs on its body, began to shift into glittery, black scales. Cathleen and the Historian could hear them snap into place like fine armor.

The creature's spindly thighs and slightly knobby lower legs were bulked up with heavy muscles. Its delicate feet widened, with three, thick toes, armed with grasping talons. The slightly elongated head, lengthened more, into three feet of snout and deadly looking teeth.

Cathleen noticed one long incisor was broken at the point. *Likely in a battle with the Mother knows what*, she thought as she marveled at the transformation from benign insect, to massive monster.

The Historian's stance was almost casual as he took a position on Cathleen's right. His body exuded the assuredness of a seasoned warrior. His whole focus was on the monster taking shape a few yards away.

Cathleen knew very little about this kind of demon-spawn. Her father, Liam, had shared only one story about a Dragon Leach he'd encountered once, while hunting down a necromancer. He told Cathleen it was well-documented that the Dragon Leach was susceptible to extreme cold. Therefore, he cast a freezing charm, causing the beast to become deeply lethargic in the chilled temperature. It eventually slipped into a comatose state and was easily dispatched.

Her father always held that simple was better, less bells and whistles to break down.

Cathleen's attention was brought back to the present crisis when the creature reared up to its full height. It gave out a roar that lifted the hair on her neck and arms. With the great jaws opened wide, a gout of blood-red flames shot across the distance and directly at their vulnerable bodies.

The Historian, watching for just such a move, conjured a transparent shield at the last instant, covering them both completely.

The fire sizzled upon contact with the invisible buffer, diverting harmlessly to the ground on either side. The beast closed his great jaws, seeing its fire never touched the humans. Cathleen stepped out from behind the protection of the shield, long enough to hurl several of the jagged bolts in return fire. They tore into the unprotected underbelly of the Dragon Leach, burning large holes in its leathery skin. The injury wasn't enough to bring the creature down, though it was clearly wounded and infuriated by the pain.

"We must destroy this creature now, Protector! My shield is failing!"

Cathleen looked down long enough to see the edges of the magical barrier beginning to quiver and fade. Soon that corruption would work its way to the middle of the shield and it would disappear altogether.

The negative effects of the Dark Pit were taking a huge toll on their magic, making them vulnerable and before long, defenseless. The incensed beast intensified its fiery barrage. Their shield shuddered under the renewed assault and Cathleen moved very close to the Historian, to remain behind their shrinking cover.

The shield faded enough that the Historian was forced to stand behind Cathleen. Suddenly, the Dragon Leach stopped its attack, turning away from the pair.

The creature's injuries finally appeared to have an effect on it, driving it into the inky waters of the pond behind it. It was obviously trying to sooth its burnt underbelly, moving deeper into the water, until it covered its broad middle.

Cathleen shouted, "Freeze the water!"

The Historian was quick to understand her meaning. Together, they worked to turn the dark pool into a solid block of ice.

The Dragon Leach showed immediate signs of distress, roaring in reaction to the deep cold settling around its lower body and rising rapidly upward. It tried melting the black ice holding it in an unrelenting grip, but its fire was useless against the combined charm cast by the two wizards.

They watched as the beast twisted its upper torso, stretching its long neck in an effort to free itself. Gradually, its bellowing and fire-blowing ceased altogether. The freezing cold had done its job, penetrating every fiber of the creature's body. The heavy head fell forward, causing the frozen jaws to shatter as easily as dropped pottery.

Cathleen and the Historian heard the sharp teeth clatter like thrown pebbles as they skittered to the sides of the frozen pool.

"Let's get moving, Protector. I have no doubt the Deceiver has other such pets scattered around this place."

They left the glade, walking until they reached a higher elevation and could study the surrounding area. Off in the distance they spotted the cliffs. Unexpectedly, they also spotted a thin trace of smoke, rising like a gray smudge against the featureless, black sky.

"Looks like we've found the last Scout," Cathleen said softly, knowing sounds carried long miles in the dead air.

"We'll need to cover a lot of ground to reach him. I suggest we use a quicker means of transport," she added.

Taking hold of his hand, they raised their free arms, making a windmill motion, calling for the Wind Charm. A sudden gust came roaring out of the endless dusk, picking them up like paper dolls, to be carried down, into the valley below.

Chapter 25

The Wind Charm accurately deposited the two wizards behind the Scout's camp site and down wind. Among their many magically enhanced skills, Outlander Wizard Scouts had heightened senses. They could smell a body's scent as easily as a shark could smell blood in the water.

They were standing on a rocky ledge, below them a naturally formed shelter of boulders jutted out of a shadowy hillside. The Scout had piled several dead branches to conceal his hide-away. He must have rushed the job, or the smoke would never have leaked out and been spotted. It was possible he'd become complacent, thinking the other Scouts dealt with the intruders, or the Deceiver destroyed them himself. In either case, this scout appeared relaxed, sitting in front of a dying campfire, sharpening his weapon.

Through a series of hand signals, Cathleen conveyed she would approach the camp from the front and the Historian should come in from behind the Scout.

He nodded, fading soundlessly into the gloom.

Cathleen climbed down off the ledge. She circled around to the front of the small firepit, where embers still glowed from the dying campfire.

She had the element of surprise and used it to her best advantage. "Drop your sword, traitor," she said softly, the threat in her voice loud and clear. The Scout had likely encountered much to fear in the dark world of the Pit, but the woman that stood inches from his dying fire, radiated an awesome power. He instinctively knew who spoke.

Laying his sword beside his leg, he spoke without rising. "Why is the Protector of the Greens visiting this plane?

"Why am I finding one of the Mother's elite forces here, in the black heart of the fourth realm?"

He started to get to his feet.

"Stay where you are traitor!"

"I think not, Protector. I know your powers are weakened in this realm, while I have been given more powers than I had as an Outlander."

He was up in a blur of motion, the sharpened sword in his hand. He leapt over the fire pit and swung his sword arm in a wide arc, sweeping across Cathleen's exposed neck.

It took him a moment to register that his blade moved through the young wizard's neck without meeting the resistance of bone and flesh. Too late it dawned on him that he hadn't connected with living flesh, but a projection, a hologram. He blinked and the physical Cathleen covered him in a Net of Nettles she held behind her back. She watched as it fell over his brawny body, piercing exposed flesh with its sharp thorns. The plentiful red berries hanging off the ropey netting would poison him if any burst during his struggle to free himself.

Cathleen knew the Scout was familiar with this particular conjured weapon, seeing him immediately react by going still.

Thinking he was subdued, she stepped around the fire pit to stand in front of him. That's when she saw the death-wish in his eyes. He bent his body and rammed into her mid-section, driving her into the white embers of the pit. She felt the air driven from her lungs, as searing heat penetrated through her sweatshirt.

The Scout picked up a booted foot, preparing to stomp it into her vulnerable stomach.

Cathleen fought back the nausea of being used like a punching bag and was about to rain a real misery of hurt down on the Scouts head. She was denied that pay-back, closing her mouth on a spell when the Historian stepped into view. He came up behind the preoccupied Scout, gathering the ends of the Net of Nettles into his strong hands. Drawing it tightly around the Scout's bulky form caused every berry to burst, shooting poison into the punctured skin and his open mouth, nose and ears.

Cathleen leapt to her feet, ripping off the smoldering top to beat out a small nest of fire that had taken root there.

She stood next to the Historian, watching the last of the traitors turn an ugly shade of puce. His skin began to bubble up and burst like the red berries that were killing him.

The Historian told Cathleen to head back to the cliffs where he'd join her later. He would meantime dispose of the putrid body remains.

"He was once an Outlander Wizard Scout and I will honor the time he served faithfully."

She nodded, feeling a sense of sadness she hadn't expected upon defeat of an enemy. The Historian's words reminded her that once the foe was a friend.

Using another Wind Charm, Cathleen flew over the desolate scene of the Chameleon Woods, heading for the cliffs. Jason and Mercy should have returned, but I can't feel him, she thought. Seconds later, she dropped soundlessly from her own flight, onto solid ground. She immediately melted into the shadows of some large rocks, scanning the area carefully.

The sounds of the wind tearing along the face of the cliffs and pushing against the implacable stone mounds almost covered the crackling sounds of a Time Thread, somewhere nearby. Cathleen stood still until she could safely identify the traveler, responding to something in her intuition nagging at her to be cautious.

She watched tiny dots of current dance in the air, as a Thread hung steady in the high winds. Someone let it go and carefully landed near the cliff's edge. Standing with their narrow back turned to her, Cathleen was at a loss to make an immediate identification. From the distance, the figure looked small, almost child-like. That's when it struck her.

"Parsons!" she shouted over the strong gusts whipping around him.

The House Buddy spun around so quickly, Cathleen was afraid he'd lose his footing, though House Buddies were known for their sure-footedness. They claimed their webbed feet, stabilized them on any terrain, which is why they went bare footed everywhere.

"Mistress, Cathleen! Delightful to finally rejoin you," he said as she ran over to join him near the cliff's edge.

"You must have been surprised indeed, when the Guardian took my persona after I hid in the In-Between! I fear my bravery was much lacking then."

Cathleen felt sympathy for his obvious embarrassment, but she still had an unsettling feeling of impending threat.

"Parsons, I'm happy you're back with us. Where is the Guardian by the way? Has he any intention of returning here?"

"Oh, indeed. In fact, I expect the Guardian to drop in any moment."

As if on cue, the crackle of another Time Thread, snapped close by.

Cathleen took Parson's shoulder, gently moving him clear of the endless abyss. The many-legged, creature known as the Guardian, needed a wider landing site.

According to the Historian, this Guardian's natural home was the lochs and deep-water lakes of the Emerald Isle. His return here was somewhat surprising to her. His presence on this dead plane, must be more important than any hardship the strange creature might suffer, she thought waiting for him to materialize.

Cathleen was convinced the Guardian held a secret status, working independently of any Council directives. She also suspected he sat as a member of the Council, under a different guise, ever alert for defections, or betrayal, by any of the others. She was sure the Guardian's only loyalty was to the Green Mother and no wizard or magic user, could shake that resolve.

A Guardian held that post for many life cycles in the natural realm, training another Guardian covertly, to replace himself over time. This individual would be chosen from among worthy Wizards sitting alongside him on the Council of Greens.

After being chosen and trained and bound to secrecy under pain of death, the recruit would assume the Guardian's role upon his natural passing. He or she, would carry on as a Council member, repeating the process into a distant future.

Having seen the true form of this Guardian, but not knowing what persona he wore as a Council member, Cathleen wondered if she'd ever look at the Council members in quite the same way.

The air crackled in front of the waiting pair. It condensed and rippled until the Thread was released and its passenger touched ground. The Guardian could not wear his assumed persona as Council member, or he'd blow his cover. He stood on his four legs, looking more like a beached octopus to Cathleen than a powerful magic user.

After greeting him, Cathleen made an offer. "Guardian, if you will allow me, I will supply you a suitable form so that you can operate comfortably here." Without waiting for his reply, Cathleen called for a charm that covered the Guardian in thick, coarse hair, knowing how this creature must detest the feel of the dead air on his sensitive, naked flesh. He now looked like a replica of prehistoric man. This was the first impression Cathleen had when viewing her handiwork. The transformation included joining the four legs into two, sturdy, short limbs and placing the eyes deeply, under a sloping forehead, rather than bobbing about on long stems. "There! I think you'll be better suited to this dreary place," Cathleen said assuring him at his awkward attempt to walk on two legs again.

"Yes. As always Protector, you display great insight for one of such few life cycles. Parsons, I see you have arrived in one piece. Good. Shall we proceed, Protector?"

Cathleen said, "Guardian, I sent the Scribe back to report, and..."

"Yes. She's to return here with your mate. I know all this, Protector. The Scribe and the rather unsophisticated Corky Cochran, the Sargent at Arms, are both vying to become the Guardian upon my passing from this realm.

They are both eager to show off their clever skills to the Council, knowing I sit among them. I fear the Scribe may be delaying her entrance here, to gloat over saving your mate and returning him unharmed to your side. We should proceed without them!"

The Guardian's haughty attitude wasn't in any way affected by his new primitive exterior.

Cathleen stared at the hairy secretive being a second longer, then made a decision. "As Protector, it falls to me to lead this expedition to find the Deceiver. We three will wait until Jason and Mercy show up, Guardian."

"Make that four, Protector," the deep voice of the Historian broke into the conversation.

"Oh, my! Greetings, Historian," Parsons shouted out, waving at the big man.

"I imagine you didn't think to see me again!" his smile stretched from tufted ear to tufted ear.

The Historian approached the small group, taking his place beside Cathleen. "I see you have given the Guardian a new form, Protector. It suits you well, Guardian. None will know you in this guise."

"Then how did you guess, Will Farley?" the fur-clad creature asked with a snarl in his voice.

"Easy. You still act like pompous royalty, pushing your weight around. Seems as if you've met resistance from the Protector. This is her investigation you see."

The Guardian's eyes glared out from under thick brows.

"I am only here to observe the Deceiver's destruction and offer aid as needed."

Cathleen had enough of the verbal sparring. She still felt distracted by a nagging sense of threat hanging in the air. "Alright you two. I have some questions that need answered, now. Parson's why were you sent back here?"

The small figure seemed to tremble at the steely resolve behind her inquiry. He stammered a reply. "Why, Mistress Cathleen, Sir Alex wanted me to give you something, but it must be done in private," he said looking around at the others nervously.

Cathleen took the House Buddy's spindly arm and pulled him toward the cliff's edge, knowing the wind would mute their conversation.

"All right, Parsons, what has Sir Alex sent to me?"

She barely registered the dull flash of metal as Parsons' arm swung out from his side. The curved blade missed her heart by a hair's breadth, when she leaned back at the waist and away from the killing thrust. The momentum of his lunge caused Parsons to lose his balance. He was falling forward toward the vast expanse and the howling winds.

Cathleen threw herself at him, grabbing his thin arms and carrying him to the ground.

They rolled to an abrupt stop, Parsons under her, his eyes round with fear and shock. The knife still clutched in his fist, the webbed fingers curled tightly round the hilt. Cathleen's weight kept him pinned to the ground, unable to move.

The Historian and Guardian witnessed the attempted assassination from where they waited, several feet away. Running to her side, the Historian looked down with rage at Parsons, his own blade drawn and ready to use. The Guardian reached down and touched Parsons on the forehead with a stubby finger.

The House Buddy spasmed once under Cathleen and then went rigid. The curved knife slopped from his open hand lying beside his tuft of red hair.

Cathleen got to her feet, eyeing the caveman-like creature beside her.

"Why did you do that? I wanted to question him!" she shouted in his face.

She was furious at his interference, fighting an impulse to use her magic on the meddling fool.

The Historian placed a firm hand on her shoulder, helping to calm her desire to attack the Guardian where he stood.

For his part, the Guardian shuffled back from the ledge. His voice was defiant, without a trace of regret.

"You were too easily gulled, Protector, by this being's sweet ways and unassuming appearance. I used it once to my own ends, as you might recall. Now it would appear the Deceiver has found a way to do the same. Look!"

Cathleen and the Historian snapped their heads in the direction the Guardian pointed, in time to see a dark, spirit-fog lifting from Parsons' stiff body.

It took form as it jetted across the open ground, away from the three, and directly toward Chameleon Woods.

A reedy voice, carried on the ever-present winds, reached their ears.

"The next time, my blade will taste your blood! I promise you, Protector. You, and every pathetic mortal that seeks my destruction, shall meet their own!"

Chapter 26

The wizards watched as the Deceiver rose to his full height. He raised both arms above his head, diving into a quickly formed wormhole in the heavy air and vanished.

Cathleen turned blazing eyes on the secret agent. "Guardian," she barked. "How did you know this wasn't Parsons?"

"It was simple, really. The authentic House Buddy has been decommissioned by Sir Alex. Sent back to wherever Sir Alex conjured him. It would seem the Arch Wizard did not approve my commandeering Parsons for my personal use. He found him less than agreeable after that."

"That's most strange," the Historian noted, his brow, furrowed with doubt.

"Parsons served in Sir Alex's household for at least five centuries. The Arch Wizard was very attached to the House Buddy."

"Strange, indeed," The guardian agreed curtly.

"And now, we still have the hunt for the Deceiver to undertake, Protector. What use will the Scribe and your mate be to this venture?" the Guardian demanded.

Cathleen didn't bother to respond.

They all began searching the unrelenting darkness around them, for any sign of a Time Thread.

Cathleen was standing next to the Historian, nudging his elbow to get his attention.

"I've a crazy plan for terminating the Deceiver, but I doubt the Guardian will like it much."

"Proceed. Our orders are clear and must be carried out."

"We have to get him to the pool of the Dragon Leach. We may be able to lure him into the waters and freeze him until he can be destroyed.

"What are you two hatching up over there?" the Guardian asked, approaching.

Before she had to answer, the Historian called out, "It's here!"

The familiar snapping and crackle in the air, brought the three together, watching for the passengers to drop any minute.

"Mercy!" the Historian was racing toward the pretty Scribe and steadying her with an arm round her slim waist.

Jason jumped away from the Time Thread as it lashed back and forth wildly, until it was pulled back into the continuum.

Cathleen ran into his arms where she held on to him tightly. She leaned back, touching his face, then kissed him. "Jason, thank the Mother you're healed and with me again."

The Guardian coughed loudly, interrupting the tender scene.

Jason pulled Cathleen back when he caught sight of the brawny creature standing nearby. Cathleen followed his alarmed look and reassured him the prehistoric man was the Guardian wearing yet another persona.

"Sorry, I had no idea you were rejoining us, Guardian," Jason apologized.

"No need to concern yourself, human. My kind looked upon evolving homo sapiens as an unusual experiment by the Green Mother."

Cathleen turned to the Scribe. The Historian was still beside her after their own reunion. Something quite out of character for the Historian, who cleared his throat gruffly, stepping away from Mercy when he saw Cathleen staring over at them.

Mercy immediately turned to Cathleen.

"Protector, I have done all you've asked, bringing Jason back here and presenting a rather bland report of our activities. The Council was none too pleased. I quote, Sir Alex, who called your efforts, "The most stunning lack of progress, of any ECHO officer. He said he hoped he wouldn't regret making you temporary Master of the Outlander Wizard Scouts, as well. But the hardest part, was getting Jason released to come back with me. The Arch Wizard refused him permission. So..."

"I jumped on the Thread before I could be stopped," Jason finished her story.

Cathleen smiled at her husband thwarting the Arch Wizard's efforts to detain him. He would prove invaluable in the next few hours and she always felt more secure working cases with him at her side.

"Thank you, Mercy. You've done well. Sir Alex obviously underestimates Jason's abilities. Which is what we'll be relying on, when he goes with me now to track down the Deceiver."

The Guardian spoke up, "Where do you propose to look, you and your mate?"

"I believe he'll try to hide in the In Between until we're all gone. That's where we'll start."

"What will we be doing here, Protector," the Scribe asked.

"I'm sending you three back to the Council."

They shouted in unison, "What?"

"This is madness, Protector," the Guardian was saying.

"I only just arrived back here and need to help," Mercy chimed in.

The Historian went very still.

Cathleen looked over at him. She knew what she saw in his eyes was understanding and agreement to this new plan.

He suspects there's a rotten apple on the Council and we need to unmask them, she thought. Her face closed off any emotion.

"There is no better plan than the Protector's," the Historian stated firmly.

The Guardian nearly growled his own response.

"It's ludicrous to divide our forces. Our combined magic will be more than sufficient to bring this Dark Lord to his knees. Sending the Scribe back is all well and good, but I am indispensable to this mission!"

"My decision, my plan. You return with the Scribe immediately and take on Jason's persona so the Arch Wizard thinks he's returned with her."

Cathleen turned to Mercy who looked confused by this turn of events.

"Mercy, believe me when I say, it's very important to have you back with the Council of Greens. In fact, when you get back, advise the

Arch Wizard to call a special meeting so you can update your report with new information."

"What will that be, Protector?"

"Tell them I've discovered there is a traitor among them."

The Scribe went very still. The Guardian had been listening to the conversation and suddenly was standing in front of Cathleen. Jason automatically moved closer to her side.

"What is this you're saying? A traitor among the Sitting Council? Now I know you have taken leave of your senses! You must have spent too much time under the Eye of Despair. It's affected your judgment."

The Historian moved like a shadow behind the Guardian.

"And how would you know about the dark light, Guardian?" he said in a low, menacing voice.

"Why, the Scribe included it in her report, though being fairly rattled at the time, she's likely not certain what she said."

"That's not true, Protector! I only reported exactly what you directed. I never mentioned your being held hostage. And I certainly never told them about the black light and the Eye of Despair. There would have been many questions and they were silent after I spoke."

"My theory is proven," the Guardian said in a clipped tone of voice.

"The Scribe can't recall the particulars of her presentation, but I was there and remember all of it."

Cathleen saw this was deteriorating into a 'he said, she said' stand-off. "All right. The plans have changed in light of this. Mercy, you will return alone, to alert the Council to my suspicions about a traitor in their midst. The Arch Wizard will have to sort that out. Guardian, you may stay and accompany us, but your behavior will be closely watched. If I suspect the slightest chance of mischief, I'll dispatch you back to the Lochs myself and you won't enjoy the trip. Historian, you'll remain to lend your magic to mine and to monitor the Guardians behavior during our time in the In-Between."

A minute later, Mercy was gone and the small group followed Cathleen back into the gloom of Chameleon Woods.

"We need to find that log where the real Parsons passed into the In-Between. I believe that's a portal site," Cathleen said quietly over her shoulder as she moved deeper into the woods.

Jason walked slightly ahead and to her right, scouting the ground for signs of their earlier passing. "There it is," he said, pointing to a huge stump, lying on its side, covered in a bristly moss and spongy fungus. They approached the front of the decomposing tree base, the opening tall enough to walk through in a crouch. Huddled together, they were peering inside when they sighted movement, not far from the mouth of the dark interior.

A round head, covered in a mop of white hair, popped out of the hallow log. They all stared as the head swiveled around on its long neck, until it faced the four searchers. "Greetings wizards and less than wizard, but more than mortal. You are just in time for the crossing."

Chapter 27

"My name is Maximillian. Most call me Milly. I am Gatekeeper to the In-Between, assigned by the first sitting Council of Greens, during the Dark Times. My purpose is to open the portal for the Mother's own and deny entry to any from the dark realm."

It was a long-winded introduction, but Cathleen and the others were too fascinated by the speaker's appearance to interrupt. When his head finally stopped revolving, they watched fascinated as the bush of white hair jumped with static electricity, sparking and dancing, within the constant electric charge that came off his body.

When he was completely outside the log's wide opening, the wraith-thin being, began a whispered chant.

Cathleen suspected it was meant to close the portal.

Milly came to stand in front of the curious group.

He had the look of a young boy who grew too quickly for his clothes. The frayed cuffs of his pants came to just above his ankles, his sharp elbows stuck out of his rough-spun top.

In spite of the mop of white hair, Milly's face was youthful, almost cherubic in its sweetness.

Cathleen addressed him warmly, taking an instant liking to the odd little man.

"Milly, I am Protector of the Green Mother. I was appointed by the Council of Greens, to find the murderer of Bretton Clawson, the Master Outlander Wizard Scout. His killer is a fallen wizard, condemned to the Dark Pit. I believe he managed to escape through this portal to the In-Between."

"That is quite impossible, wizard! I have been here at my station for eons. Except for that brief cycle of time, when I passed a House Buddy named, Parsons, through and then had to help him find his way out of the Labyrinth of Mirrors. It seems he wandered into the maze, soon after I opened the portal for him. A rather peculiar experience for me, as Parson's kept changing. At one point, I spotted his form in some of the mirrors. He had more legs than he started with!   Peculiar, like I said. And he wasn't all that grateful after I rescued him!"

The others all shot looks at the Guardian, recalling how he used the timid House Buddy for his new persona before Cathleen discovered his ruse.

"And there were no other times you left your station?" Cathleen asked.

"Oh, perhaps to visit with Dunny for a bit. He's such a jolly fellow!"

Memories of the big Rock Goblin flashed through the listeners' minds. Jolly wasn't exactly how they remembered the lumbering Dunny. Cathleen looked intently at Milly, "We need you to allow us to cross, Milly. Time is very important to our mission."

"There is one among you without the Mother's magic. I'm not certain how he'll fare in the In-Between." Milly walked straight over to Jason, his rough-made sandals, slapping on the hard earth, while his baggy pants, flapped around bare legs. He took Jason's hand in his long, stringy fingers. The Historian automatically moved his own hand to the hilt of his sword.

Jason stood motionless, allowing the strange, white-headed creature to run his other hand over his open palm. All the while sparks danced around the snowy head.

"Ah! There is something new to me, lurking beneath your mortal surface, human. You appear to be Oracle and Searcher, both. Gifts from the Mother to certain mortals. He may pass." He made his pronouncement, swiveling his head to look back at Cathleen.

She let out the breath she'd been holding, not having a plan that didn't include Jason.

Milly's comment wasn't a surprise to Cathleen. She felt the unique stirrings of power in her husband many times during their years together.

The Historian relaxed his protective stance and nodded at Jason who returned the gesture. It wasn't lost on her that the Historian was ready to protect him if needed.

"Milly," Cathleen said firmly. "Now that you've found us all suitable for the crossing, we need to leave immediately."

"Of course, Protector."

The group moved to the mouth of the rotting trunk, standing close together.

The Historian looked over at Cathleen and Jason, whispering, "The tree lived well over one thousand life cycles, according to our history of the In-Between."

That comment made Cathleen realize that she knew very little about the strange land they were about to enter. She looked back at the Historian, finally understanding why he had been the one to answer her summons at the beginning of this investigation.

Milly's mumbled chanting became louder bringing about an immediate ruffling in the air around the wide opening.

Peering into the depths of the ancient tree trunk was impossible. It remained a solid wall of black. Watching closely, Cathleen saw the opening expand enough for her to enter. Jason followed, with the Historian after him and the Guardian entered last. The second his hairy, prehistoric foot touched the ground beyond, the portal began to spin at a dizzying speed, closing with a soft swoosh of air.

They all stood still, trying to adjust to the creamy light that surrounded them completely. Their own shadows were lost in the wash of brightness and all but the Guardian were blinking furiously, trying to adjust their vision.

Jason's voice seemed to float over to the others, as if he was waking from a dream.

"There's something moving toward us. It's wrapped itself in this light."

Cathleen didn't question him, but the look she gave the Historian made him slide his sword out of its sheath.

The Guardian was unarmed, but Cathleen suspected his ability to shift was all he needed to protect himself. She'd mentally written him off as an ally if the going got rough. Glancing over at the stooped shouldered creature, she said, "Guardian, you've traveled on this plane before. What do you think is approaching?"

"Nothing good, I can assure you, Protector! We must avoid being caught out here in the open. This awful bright-light transmits the presence of warm-blooded creatures to the pack of hunting Swallowers that inhabit this place, among other nasty beings."

Cathleen turned to the Historian and asked him if he had any knowledge of these hunters.

"They are not unlike the slender fish found in the deepest seas of the first realm. They have incredibly large jaws and their stomachs are able to expand, allowing them to swallow very large prey."

"Sounds delightful," Jason said looking nervously around himself.

"Guardian, do you know anything else about these Swallowers that might be useful to us if we encounter any?" Cathleen saw her question implied more trust in the Guardian than she actually felt, but it played on his big ego and made him more forthcoming with information.

He described their habitat as "No more civilized than a mud wasp's, mere holes in the fabric that passes for atmosphere in this ghastly place."

Turning back to the Historian, Cathleen's face reflected the frustration she felt with these less-than-helpful answers.

"Protector, I can tell you the Guardian is correct about the burrowing nature of the Swallowers. They bore into the elastic world we find ourselves in. There is no real ground, no actual sky above us. Only an infinite stretching of the In-Between as it floats, sandwiched between each reality as we understand them. Earth, celestial dome, they mean nothing here on this plane of existence."

Curious to test out the elasticity of the ground they stood on, Jason brought his leg up and slammed it hard on the surface. He was immediately launched into uncontrollable summersaults until the Guardian intervened, catching his arm to stop his cartwheels.

Cathleen and the Historian had watched the gymnastics with open mouths. When Jason finally stopped moving, he told them he still felt the vibrations throughout his body. "I feel like a tuning fork!" he said.

Cathleen got the group moving. The clock was ticking on this case. They only had a limited time they could search the In-Between. Milly instructed Cathleen that he could only open the portal once more, before the next moon cycle in the first realm. He explained, "Even here, on the fourth plane, we are interconnected with the Mother's power to the realms of life. I will open the portal in twenty of your hours, Protector, after that, well, there won't be an after, after that!"

Chapter 28

The Guardian was assigned point because of his prior experience in the In-Between. They were deeper into the interior of the oddly unfixed land, without the benefit of any true features to help give a sense of position.

They all experienced the springy nature of whatever passed for ground in this dimension. In light of his experience earlier, Jason was extra cautious about how hard he stepped down on his booted feet.

They'd been walking for nearly a quarter of an hour. The only sign of life in the glare of the ever-present light was a colorless, amoeba-like creature the size of a large, ocean stingray. It was swimming in the currents of air that continually shifted around them, from every direction. Taking no notice of the four hunters, it curled its wide body like a soft taco and plunged into an unseen hole in the colorless ground.

Jason had seen many strange creatures during his times with Cathleen on her investigations, but like many good hunters it was the environment of the different worlds that stirred his curiosity.

"Historian," Jason called quietly to the man walking behind him. "Can you tell us anything about the odd movement of air that seems to be constantly swirling around us."

"The realm of the In-Between is shaped like an oval eye. Think of yourself in the middle of that eye," the Historian answered promptly. "It is continually spinning, but at such great speed, as to produce its own gravity, not unlike the first realm, earth. What you are feeling is the endless movement in the atmosphere of the In-Between. It is never still, always churning, like a captured cyclone that can't be stopped."

"How wide is this area we're crossing now?" Jason asked.

"The In-Between is no more than a half-mile across. If we split up, we could see each other clearly in this light."

The Guardian seemed to be ignoring any tidbits of conversation he might have overheard, but he looked back over his heavily muscled, stooped shoulders and snorted. "You seem well-informed Historian, though you have never left the Mother's bosom of the first realm. Or have you?"

Cathleen didn't miss the inuendo in his question but decided to shut down any bickering between these two powerful wizards before it escalated. She called back to the two in a decisive voice, "We need to find the Deceiver's lair and we have only a limited time to complete our task before the portal closes." She added the last bit to remind them they were all in peril in this strange place. "Because the area to be covered is so narrow, we'll split up and stay in touch visually. When the Deceiver is found, we'll shoot off a flare of Green Fire.

Jason and the Historian will search the area to our left. The Guardian and I will search the grounds on this track. Let's not forget, we may feel alone on this plane, but the Swallowers and other creatures, are likely aware of our presence."

The two men peeled away from the others without speaking. Jason gave his wife a quick backward look and caught up with his partner.

"Do you think it was wise to split our forces, Protector? The Deceiver will likely use the Swallowers to his advantage and..."

"And we are all capable of handling ourselves, Guardian! We must finish this now. We know he is guilty of murdering The Claw and we are here to mete out his punishment." They walked on in silence. The Guardian, reluctant to stir Cathleen's temper, kept up with the fast pace she set.

They already passed several holes in the spongy ground, but no toothy head poked out at them. Cathleen looked across the distance to see Jason and the Historian. With her keen vision, she watched as the Historian poked his sword into holes like the ones she'd passed.

"Guardian, what can you tell me of the Deceiver's history before he fell from the Mother's graces?"

Cathleen suppressed a smile as the Guardian puffed out his hairy chest, amused at his arrogance, even in a caveman body. "I can tell you he was greatly admired by the Sitting Council for his many skills as a wizard. But, like all mortals seeking self-glorification, he began to believe he was above the Mother's laws and the laws of the first realm. That's when he murdered and manipulated his fellow wizards, trying to usurp the powers of the Council for his own ends."

Cathleen held up her hand before the Guardian could go on. She spoke softly, "The air streams have changed. There's something big taking shape straight ahead. It's coming in our direction!"

The Guardian moved so fast in response to her warning, Cathleen barely registered he was no longer beside her. The thick covering of hair on his body bristled with anticipation as he planted his heavy legs wide apart. The form coming toward them spread out like spilled milk and transformed into twenty, tooth-filled mouths, open and ready to eat. Cathleen began the spell to bring Sacred Fire to her hands, when she saw the Guardian, standing with his brawny arms outstretched looking like a primitive traffic cop.

What's he doing? she thought frantically.

The Swallowers honed in on the burly figure of the Guardian and when several made contact, the air was filled with a sizzling sound as thousands of volts of current tore through the long, eel-like bodies.

Cathleen was so relieved to see her companion was handling the charge, she lost sight of one that split from the pack and came in behind her. She felt herself jerked backward when the hood of her sweatshirt was sucked into the large mouth of the beast. She couldn't use her fire, so threw herself onto the ground and bounced several times on top of the creature clinging to her. Luckily, this dissuaded it from trying to swallow her head, only an inch from a gapping mouth.

When she sprang back to her feet, the Swallower was still on the pale ground, allowing her to direct Green Fire at the slender body. Unlike the creatures the Guardian was dispatching with his magically infused volts, her Fire only slowed it down. It wriggled around a few seconds but appeared unscathed by the flames.

Cathleen spoke a few words in the Old Tongue, freezing her attacker in mid-air, mere inches from her face. This close-up, the Swallower resembled a cross between a piranha and a bug-eyed cartoon character. She turned in time to see the last of the beasts being destroyed by the Guardian. Cathleen was sure he'd begin to brag about his feat, but he was oddly quiet.

"If you are unhurt, Protector, I suggest we keep moving. The rest of our party has also been under siege by these foul creatures but seem no worse for the trouble."

Cathleen immediately looked across the distance, picking out the figures of the Historian and Jason. The Historian must have given Jason the knife he had tied to his thigh, because she could make out his efforts to wipe it clean on a cloth he handed back to the Historian.

"Guardian, I had the oddest feeling that the Swallowers were not attacking you, so much as they were answering your call. You appeared to have some power over them. Care to explain?"

"You are experiencing the Deceiver's web of lies and misconceptions, Protector. He has likely seeded the path to his hide-away, with many such deceits." He turned on his flat, hairy feet and began to walk away from the questioning look in Cathleen's eyes.

Chapter 29

Jason and the Historian were on the lookout for the Swallowers but weren't too concerned with what Jason referred to as 'air fish'.

The Historian smiled patiently at Jason's description because he knew nothing in the In-Between could be categorized so benignly. They were bound to stumble across some creatures here that had passed through the portal without the knowledge of the simple gatekeep, Milly. He'd already allowed the Deceiver to pass without challenge and now he could be anywhere in the bland landscape.

He turned toward Jason who matched his long strides easily and said, "I think you should take my knife," and slid it from his thigh sheath.

"It's not as formidable as my sword, but it's just as wicked if applied properly."

"Thanks. I feel better with some kind of weapon."

Jason had the knife in hand a few minutes later when something flew out of the glaring light, taking the Historian to the ground. When they stopped bouncing, Jason saw a being the size of the wizard, sitting squarely on his chest. The Historian's arms were pinned to his sides, by two of the creature's rubbery appendages. There was no way he could reach his sword.

It moved backward, using its hind legs to drag its victim toward a newly visible hole in the spongy ground. Jason lunged at the creature's back. The knife gripped in his hand was every bit as sharp as promised and it bit deeply into the smooth, hairless back of the attacker.

It left deep markings all over the monster's round head, giving it the appearance of a crater-scared moon. The head spun around and Jason was staring into a face as featureless as the In-Between.

Without hesitating, Jason put the knife deep into the area you'd expect to find an eye. He pulled it out in rapid motion, stabbing again and again until the beast went limp, rolling off the Historian and onto the ground.

The Historian reached for Jason's offered hand and pulled himself up.

"Jason, your courage as the Protector's partner is well known to the wizarding community. I can now attest to this myself. I thank you for coming to my aid."

"You would have certainly done the same for me. I'm just glad you gave me that knife!"

They both looked across to the others, seeing they'd been under attack as well. Jason's first response as always, was to run to Cathleen's side. He knew that would not be appreciated by her in her current role of Protector.

He looked across the barren ground a minute longer, seeing Cathleen and the Guardian were moving again. Taking that as his cue, he did the same.

Across the blank stretch of land, Cathleen and the Guardian spoke softly, believing it was likely they were being watched by creatures under the Deceiver's control.

The Swallowers were dangerous if they should reappear, but Cathleen had a suspicion the Guardian had some kind of influence over them, although he wouldn't confirm that.

But he did kill them before they could attack us in force, she was thinking to herself. She decided to tuck her suspicions away for the time being and concentrate on the primary objective of locating the elusive Deceiver.

She tried to keep track of Jason and his partner, noting they had moved much further ahead and were no longer just across from her and the Guardian. She was not aware of the attack upon the Historian, because she had been preoccupied defending against the Swallowers.

She glanced over at her prehistoric companion, noticing he'd slowed down, falling a few feet behind her.

"Why are you moving so slowly, Guardian? Is there something wrong?"

She stepped in front of him, making him stop. That's when she noticed a deep bite on his upper arm. He must have been mauled during her fight with the Swallower. She hadn't seen it because he kept to her right side, although the pelt of matted hair covered the deep tear which looked to go into muscle and down to bone.

"You've been badly injured! Why didn't you tell me?"

"Our only concern is destroying the Deceiver before his evil machinations can cause more harm to the Greens. I have sustained worse than this, Protector. We cannot be deterred from our hunt."

"Can I at least clean the wound? There's healing spells we can use to prevent further damage to you."

"I would have to revert to my real form, which would be most welcome, but if I do that, we lose more than just time. I am more vulnerable to the beasts that roam this dreadful place in my natural body."

Cathleen took her sweatshirt off. She still had her T-shirt, but immediately felt the chill of the ever-shifting air. She spoke a soft charm over the scorched garment causing a circular piece to detach from the bottom. She wrapped this tightly around the muscular arm of the silent Guardian, whispering a simple healing charm she remembered hearing her mother use for her many childhood injuries. "It's better than nothing and will keep it closed until we can get you back to the Council's physicians," she said and slipped back into the shortened fleece top.

"Thank you, Protector, and just in time for what lies ahead for us."

Cathleen turned to her left in time to see a darkly robed figure, sitting astride the back of a Dragon-Eel beast. It grew in size as it drew nearer to them, as did the one riding on its scaly back. She watched the slow, measured beat of its wide wings and the huge lizard-shaped head, moving from side to side, likely searching for easy prey. As it passed closer, she saw its sharp talons were already wrapped around something caught up in heavy netting.

"The Deceiver," the Guardian hissed.

The Deceiver and his creature moved rapidly across the pale dome, toward a row of newly forming thunder heads. These came out of nowhere, strokes of lightning relentlessly stabbing through them to the land below.

Cathleen heard the intermittent sound of shouts fill the swirling air.

"Guardian, he's captured one of the others!"

She looked in the direction where the two men should have been. As she hurried, with the Guardian trying to keep pace, she saw only one man was left. He was huddled into a ball on the ground, perhaps gravely injured.

Cathleen stopped short, the Guardian narrowly avoiding plowing into her.

"I have to go after the Deceiver! Are you able to help whoever is over there, Guardian?" she asked while moving off in the direction the wizard had gone.

"What if it's your mate?"

"I have no choice! You aren't in condition to follow the wizard to his lair and whoever is on the ground needs help, now! Go!"

Cathleen watched over her shoulder as she moved, to be certain the Guardian followed her orders. He lumbered across the flat, springy ground, heading toward the man left behind.

She couldn't allow herself to speculate on who was lying on the ground, or who had been taken by the Deceiver's beast. Her only concern had to be the prisoner the Dark Lord had taken.

Knowing that without her help whoever swung from the netting below the beast's scaly belly would surely die a gruesome death.

"Mother, help us all!"

Chapter 30

Cathleen used the swirling eddies of air to give herself some advantage of speed. She brought a heavy gust around and grabbing hold, forced it in the direction taken by the Deceiver.

The monster he rode was far more powerful in flight than her conjured ride allowed for, but that was all to the good. Cathleen couldn't take the chance of letting the wizard know he was being pursued. She'd keep him in view and have the element of surprise. While she held fast to her wind charm, she had to fight down the fear that began gnawing at her since first seeing the Dragon-Eel beast flying off with its captive. It couldn't matter which man it was, but her heart trembled at the thought that it was her love.

Earlier, in describing the In-Between in more detail, the Guardian explained how the featureless, seemingly endless plane actually curved into an elliptical shape. It was floating freely, like a small island between realms.

This information calmed her. She knew her flight would eventually take her over the scene where one of the men was taken. *I won't lose track of where I left the Guardian and the injured man in this dreadful place*, she thought, reassuring herself somewhat.

The Deceiver had a good head-start. Cathleen let out a long-held breath when she finally caught sight of a moving shape beginning to materialize in the distance. The beast's wings pumped in strong, downward strokes against the air's resistance. The sinuous tail of the creature acted like a rudder, cutting through the thick air in steady flight. It became clear to her that the Deceiver was directing his Dragon-Eel directly into the line of newly formed thunder heads.

These were the only such formations Cathleen had seen in the bland sky since arriving in the In-Between. The lightning she watched earlier, still shattered the grayish mounds of vapor, tearing through them, like claws raking a bloated body.

That's it! The bolts can be used as weapons, she thought, frantically trying to put together a plan of attack and rescue. Since she was unsure to what extent her magic was affected, or weakened in this strange place, she would improvise and use what she could find to manipulate to her needs. Cathleen pulled back on the speed she was traveling. She didn't want to overcome the Deceiver and his beast.

She looked for a pattern in the timing of the lightning, watching closely as the bolts pierced the dark haze of clouds. They appeared to be normal, electrically charged and random in timing, but the strikes were all concentrated around a particularly dense cloud bank.

"That's not just a cloud formation. There's some sort of structure built into it." Cathleen's whispered comment was torn from her mouth and carried away on the eddies of wind. As she floated closer, she was able to make out a pale dome, jutting through the largest of the gray cloud piles. She had to drop back to watch for the right time to move, or risk being caught spying.

The wizard flew directly into the mist when there was a pause in the lightening. Cathleen was relieved to see his prisoner still dangled from the Dragon-Eel's claws. The beast immediately disappeared from view and the air was frizzled by several flashing bolts when the mist closed behind them.

I can't just charge in, she thought, upon discovering the lair. Slowing her speed, she hovered near the entrance. She hung on the edge of the dense cloud, trying to listen over the constant moan of the wind.

Just as she was about to move into the gauzy mist, a reedy voice floated out to her sensitive ears. "You're a fool, Historian. I could offer you more power than you've ever dreamed you could wield. Between us, we could take over the Council of Greens and dispose of the uncooperative ones in the process. Their powers would become ours! I don't believe for a minute you are content with the measly role you play. No more than a history teacher to a bunch of doddering old sorcerers!"

"You know nothing of me, Deceiver. Your treachery has been recorded for all time and you wear your hated name upon your chest as part of your punishment. All magic users know you for the liar you are."

Cathleen heard a low growl. Now she knew who had been snatched and felt a twinge a guilt at her relief that Jason was safe. "Oh, yes, Historian. I know you. You are no more than a keeper of secrets and archaic spells and enchantments. You were once a wizard knight, a soldier of extraordinary skill and prowess. You can have all of that and more, if you renounce the Greens and join me. We worked together in the past, do you remember our exploits, Will Farley?"

"That was before you betrayed your sacred oath to the Mother. Before your cowardly murder of the Master Outlander, Bretton Clawson."

Cathleen had heard enough and was getting ready to launch herself through the solid wall of gray mist, when a phrase she'd just heard made her suck in her breath.

The Deceiver referred to the Historian as a 'keeper of secrets.' The exact warning scratched on the hearth wall by The Claw before his murder.

Could he be...?

Her doubts were put on hold when Cathleen heard a thud, followed by a moan. Any thoughts of the Historian being a traitor evaporated from her mind, while the sounds of pain filled the air. It was time to act.

The jagged bolts were crashing in their timed pattern around the entry way. The place the Historian was being held, was directly behind that electric shield. She'd have to evade the bolts, before she could control their explosive force.

Softly, she intoned a spell, conjuring a long conducting rod, hoping to redirect the lightening away from the hidden entrance, to the magically-infused shaft. She used the thick cloud as her ground and shoved the rod deep into it, making it stand firm with her spell.

To her relief, the lethal current was immediately drawn toward the enchanted rod.

Cathleen stepped behind a tower of lightning bolts, while the deadly current was diverted to the pole. Holding out her hands, she drew the jagged bolts closer to each other. With another flick of her hand they were gathered together, into a deadly bouquet. "Now I'm ready," she breathed.

With a wave of her hand, the deadly garland moved in front of her body. Reaching out, after protecting herself from the danger with another charm, she grabbed the sparking bundle like a fist filled with sparklers. They sent a harmless tickling sensation up her arm and through her body.

The entry to the Deceiver's rounded hideaway evaporated, as the cluster of lightning bolts grazed its misty fabric. Cathleen watched as the dome began to disintegrate as jolts of current ran through the conjured structure like veins in a pale body. The glaring light of the In-Between broke through the gray barrier of thinning clouds, allowing Cathleen to locate the prisoner.

Laying on his side, the Historian looked like a huge fish caught up in the heavy netting. As Cathleen moved to free him, he shouted out a warning.

"Behind you!"

Cathleen instinctively jumped to the left, barely avoiding the wide maw of the Dragon-Eel beast. When the creature's jaws snapped together on empty air, it swung its long head behind, looking in the direction Cathleen had thrown herself.

The Historian was struggling to free himself from the heavy net. His magic was useless under the charmed netting.

Suddenly the beast let out a deafening roar. He looked up in time to see Cathleen sitting astride the scaly back of the surprised creature. As if not amazing enough, the Protector was clutching bolts of lightning in her hand.

The Historian watched an arc of current as it moved through her and into the Dragon-eel creature. The beast reared back, whipping its long tail, trying to toss Cathleen from her perch.

The struggles of the beast faltered and then abruptly ceased, a rush of dead air leaving its slack jaws. Cathleen still held the jagged bolts, their power coursing through her now. Her long hair floated straight out from her head and her eyes shot out green beams like lasers searching out a target. She turned to the Historian. He had stopped struggling under the net and was staring dumbly at her, as if the Mother Herself stood before him.

Cathleen mumbled a few words. Suddenly, the searing current that ran through her body slipped out of her open mouth in a slithering, snake-like movement. It kept moving until it was lost in the bright light of the In-Between.

The Historian had witnessed much in the way of magical feats, but this display of Cathleen's powers impressed him deeply. The Protector came over to him and waved a hand over the heavy ropes. The net flew off, landing several feet away. She looked around and then back at him where he sat, half hidden in the mist that still hung over what remained of the dome.

"I think the Deceiver has met his match, Protector," he said springing like a cat to his feet, a rare smile on his face.

Cathleen asked if he had any idea where the wizard would run.

"I would say he returned to the Dark Pit and the fourth realm. He probably has more ways to go to ground in his familiar territory."

Cathleen began to move when the Historian spoke again. "Protector, I have never seen the magic you controlled with the lightning. As you might imagine, I have a vast knowledge of spells and wards dating back to the beginnings of the magic of the Greens. But your magic, it was not from current enchantments, nor was it a part of the ancient. Am I correct in believing your spell was infused by the powers of others of the Green Mother's Magic Users?"

Cathleen didn't want to take the time to explain about her mother's highly unauthorized, This and That Magic. "Later," was her cryptic answer. She took the Historian's arm and grabbed hold of another wind gust. They flew in silence until she saw Jason and the Guardian below.

Jason was sitting, propped against a small mound of spongy ground likely formed by the Guardian. The Guardian looked very natural squatting nearby in his caveman form.

They were deep in conversation, until Jason felt Cathleen's nearness. He looked up in time to see the two wizards touch ground. Cathleen ran over to Jason. He quickly assured her he was only stunned when the Deceiver's creature took his legs out from under him with his heavy tail.

The Guardian stepped close to the Historian. "You are safe then, Historian! The Protector has not vanquished the Deceiver though, from the look on your face."

"We believe he has crossed back to the Pit and is no longer on this plane."

"Will that nincompoop, Milly, let him pass through from here unchallenged? He is a less-than stellar gatekeeper to my mind," the Guardian grumbled, his heavy brow furrowed until his eyebrows joined into one thick brush.

Cathleen and Jason joined them in time to hear the last of the conversation.

Looking at the Guardian, her face was set in determination.

"The important thing is that we have the Historian back with us, safe and sound.

The Deceiver will find a way to gain entry back to the Pit to gather up more demon-spawn to put between himself and us. But I assure you, this wizard will meet the Mother's revenge for his murder of Bretton Clawson and his other crimes.

We are the instruments of her justice and we're going to deliver it soon!"

Chapter 31

Cathleen and the others held hands in a close line. The Guardian conjured the Time Thread that would take them back to the fourth realm and the Deceiver's ruined stronghold.

Asking the irascible Guardian to get them back to the cursed ground had the expected effect of giving him an ego boost. Cathleen was regretting the persona she placed upon the multi-limbed form of the Guardian. Realizing he felt both uncomfortable and irritated, she needed to highlight his importance to their mission, even in his current primitive form.

While they traveled within the cocoon of silence, Cathleen thought back on her mother's abilities as a wizard. Her advice had proven important in life as well as in magic. She warned Cathleen never to underestimate the need to share the successes in life with others, especially those working on the margins of any enterprise. Cathleen had forgotten the Neanderthal creature with his thick, ungraceful body, his hairy hand gripping hers, had needed to be recognized for his value. *Thanks mom*, the Celtic Wizard thought as they eased down in front of the gateway into the fourth realm.

They would need to have Milly open the gate onto this plane, though it was clearly visible on the other side. The gate spun at a rate so fast it was invisible to the naked eye. Even with the Inner Eye able to discern the blur of motion, they dare not try to pass through its deadly rotation.

Jason nudged Cathleen's arm, pointing at the figure of the Gatekeeper.

He was curled around himself like a sleeping pup, lying on a small pallet across from the gate. He wore a sweet expression on his face, gentle snores slipping from his round mouth. Thick strands of snowy hair floated angelically around his head, adding to the peaceful image he created in sleep.

Cathleen shouted out his name, "Milly! You need to let us pass!"

A pencil-thin arm reached down and pulled the blanket over his head, until only the white mop of hair could be seen.

"Milly," this time Jason called and the long limbs jutted out from beneath the blanket and long fingers curled back the cover until his eyes could see.

"Is that you, mate of the Protector?"

Jason assured him it was and that his party needed to cross over from the In-Between immediately.

Milly threw off the blanket, nearly tripping himself in the process of running to open the gateway.

They all stood expectantly while he began mumbling the proper spell. He stopped, shaking his head when he obviously used wrong wording, and began over.

After another two tries, Milly got the spell right and the whirling vortex slowed to a standstill, allowing them all to pass through onto the dead ground of the fourth realm.

Milly was quicker about closing it off than he had been with allowing them entry.

"Can't be too careful who gets in or out, don't ya know?" he said smiling broadly at the annoyed faces looking back at him in exasperation.

Milly seemed immune to the critical looks he was getting and began asking them how their trip went. While Jason tried to answer politely for the group, Cathleen watched the strange little man. She noticed while he was trying various renditions of his spell to open the gateway, he kept rubbing the back of his head, giving it little shakes from time to time.

When there was a break in Jason's comments, she came close to the Gatekeeper and asked, "Has the Deceiver been through here, Milly?"

"Why, I...I...can't recall, Protector. I must have fallen asleep and..."

"Milly, turn around please, I want to check something."

He did as Cathleen asked. The others sensing something was amiss, quickly joined her, forming a small circle of onlookers.

Cathleen raised her hand and with small sweeping motions, moved the thick bush of snow-white hair about, until she saw what she was searching for. "It's called a 'Monitor Minion' and can be used to spy on other magic users without their knowledge of its presence."

No one spoke, but there was an odd change in Milly's breathing.

Cathleen spun him around to face her and saw he was clutching frantically at his throat as if someone was choking the life out of him. His milky skin was turning a shocking shade of puce.

She immediately shouted for the Historian to remove the spy Minion, even if meant ripping tufts of his snowy mane out by the roots.

Without hesitating the Historian reach into the thick mass of white, gripped the disk-shaped device in his broad hands and gave a huge tug.

The scream far out-sized anything they expected from the small figure. His head swiveled around on the long neck, until he faced Cathleen, who held him by his thin arms, staring into his round eyes. His cherubic face transformed into a mask of pure loathing.

The Historian dropped the disk onto the hard ground, stomping on it with the heel of his boot, until it was reduced to dust. He swept this up with a wave of his hand and blew it out into the perpetual gloom.

The effect was immediate as Milly went limp in Cathleen's hands. Jason reached for him before he could fall to the ground. Carrying him back to the cot, Jason looked back at the others.

"Cathleen, is he still under the influence of the Deceiver?" he asked.

"Not now. But there's no doubt the Deceiver has drained him of some of his magic, like a leech siphons the life blood from an unsuspecting victim. We'll let him rest. He won't be needed to open the gate to us and he'll be useless to the Deceiver if he tries passing through again, to the In-Between."

Cathleen asked Jason to take point, to pick up any kind of trail left by the dark wizard. She knew Jason's skills as a tracker were somehow enhanced by his ability to sense the touch of magic on any surface. He described it as a shock that ran through him. That skill was Jason's Inner Eye in her estimation, making him a valuable asset to the team.

The Guardian and Historian moved off in opposite directions, leaving a quarter-mile of uninterrupted blackened ground between them. This positioning extended their front as they moved forward. Cathleen stayed several yards behind her fast-moving husband, as he easily covered the hard, dead ground like a sprinting deer.

They moved silently in this line formation, wrapped in the eternal gloom of the fourth realm.

Cathleen thought back to the beginnings of this foreboding place. When the Dark Pit was placed here by the ancients, the Green Wizards were a mere fledgling group of followers of the Green Mother. They had remarkable powers conferred on them, using them to promote and protect the natural life forms in the first realm.   Even in those distant times, evil was alive and walking freely among the innocent.

Cathleen's mental rambling was interrupted when Jason gave out their warning whistle. She hurried up to where he crouched, his palm flat against the black earth.

"He's here. Beneath our feet." He added softly, looking into her wide eyes.

Cathleen sent a narrow bolt of light in both directions, alerting the other trackers to Jason's discovery. The Guardian and Historian both used a Wind Charm to rejoin her and Jason where they huddled together. When they landed simultaneously, it was the Guardian who spoke first, nearly pushing the Historian aside with his heavily muscled body.

"What have you found, Protector?"

"I didn't. Jason has a keen sense of magic radiating from any surface and he might have located the Deceiver."

"Is he in some kind of underground bunker, Jason?" the Historian shouldered his way to Jason's side, forcing the Guardian to take a step back.

Jason looked back at the hardpacked dirt, answering, "I don't know if he's created a bunker, but he's definitely beneath ground. I can sense the recent use of magic and there's some kind of vibration, like a low hum, coming up through the ground."

That brought both the Guardian and Historian down to a crouch, beside the others. They placed their own hands, palms down as Jason had done, nodding agreement. Cathleen stood up, followed by the others.

"We'll need to infiltrate his hideout before the Deceiver can act against us. I'll take the Historian down there with me, to study the layout of this fortification. There are bound to be some of his demon-spawn hanging around for just such an incursion, so if any escape our efforts to destroy them, you two will need to step up and finish them off."

Jason still had the Historian's sharp knife and slipped it out of the thigh sheath. He looked over at the Guardian who was whispering under his breath. He figured it was some kind of conjuring spell.

When the Guardian finished there was a spike of bright light in the clingy gray air and a solid looking creature stepped out of it to stand close to the hairy Guardian. More wolf than dog, its ears brushed past the shaggy middle of the Guardian.

"Early man. Early dog. Very good, Guardian," Jason said smiling in appreciation of the well-suited form of weapon.

The wolfish beast was heavily built, with powerful looking jaws in its large head. The golden eyes shone with an intelligent awareness of every nuance in its environment. It stood very close to the hairy legs of its master, awaiting his order to kill. This was a hunting dog and he would fight beside the Guardian until his last breath.

Chapter 32

Cathleen asked the others to step back. She began searching for the opening to the underground bunker. There would be a concentrated afterglow of magic that would indicate an often-used passageway beneath them.

Using her Inner Eye, she focused on the small area found by Jason and extended her search in widening circles. There was a remote chance Jason's sensitivity was off, just as her own magic was affected in the blighted realm. This might prove a futile search.

"Protector!" Her concentration was shattered by the Historian's warning shout.

Cathleen was quite a distance from the others when his voice rang out. Spinning around at the yell, she witnessed the Historian and Jason being sucked through the black ground, as if they were bits of bread crumb on a kitchen floor. A heartbeat later, the hairy figure of the Guardian followed them down without so much as a grunt of alarm. The three vanished completely within that beat.

Only the fierce looking wolf breed was left. He was backing away from where the others stood just a moment earlier. The large head hung down, his long canines bared in a snarl and his hackles bristling down his muscled back. Cathleen murmured as she approached the confused and intimidating animal.

"What took them?" she asked automatically searching the ground around her.

The enormous wolf turned a baleful eye on the Protector. To her great surprise, he answered.

"You have been naive, yet again, Protector. The Deceiver is clever beyond your limited, human imaginings. He has led you out here to a killing field of his own design. It is well that the Mother endowed me with powers equal to his machinations. That is why I am called the Guardian."

"You! But I just saw you taken below."

"You saw what I allowed. There is something you don't know about my position, Cathleen O'Brien, but circumstances force me to reveal myself more fully, else you continue to stumble around in the darkness of unawareness.

I am an extension of the Mother's own powers. She placed me within the Council of Greens at their own dawning, where I have functioned as Her agent of reason and caution, since before the antiquity of the Dark Times.

I do wear many guises to suit my purpose. Your comrades believe they have been taken, along with the Guardian in that odious caveman form. And that is exactly what the Deceiver will think as well!"

"Your role as you describe it is mostly secretive and deceptive. Tell me, if you're the true Guardian, what just got sucked down below with Jason and the Historian?"

As if trying to test her patience, the huge mongrel plopped down on his haunches, his heavy body thumping loudly in the silence.

Cathleen saw a sharp gleam in the golden eyes looking back at her. Oddly, she found it comforting to see its light in such a dead world.

"I opted to trade places with the caveman creature after I brought this mongrel into existence. Don't feel badly not to have recognized the switch. It was too instantaneous even for your remarkable skills with the Inner Eye.

I placed the ferocity of the hunting wolf into the creature below and he will prove an asset to the Historian and your mate when they engage with the Deceiver's beast."

"Beast? What kind of beast is down there with them?"

The huge, primitive wolfdog jumped up without answering. Its head drooped downward, moving with its long snout brushing along the ground, sniffing in a sweeping pattern. He stopped, turning his golden eyes back to Cathleen.

"There is much you should understand before we pursue the rescue of our friends, Protector. After he was sentenced to continue his life cycles in the Pit, the fallen Wizard, Calvin Boatwright, discovered a way to tap into the evil resources of the dead realm.   They should have destroyed Boatwright, the Deceiver, when reports from loyal Scouts began surfacing. They warned how Boatwright was freely making forays into other realms, including the first realm of humans and natural life. The Council members dithered and procrastinated. They told themselves and the others, he would never forsake his code entirely. The beast your mate and the Historian will face, is the one the Deceiver has become."

It was obvious to Cathleen, he was finished with his explanations, as the wolfdog lowered his head to resume sniffing the ground.

His voice rumbled in the heavy air as he raised his head and spoke again. "The Deceiver is near, but his form is unknown to me."

Cathleen heard enough. She moved nearer to the enormous creature, almost dwarfed by his size. She raised both arms, hands held flat over the dung smelling earth. Her charm was one her mother taught her. The words were as ancient as the magic they called into play.

"Iamarta Saighean. Bring magical light to this dead ground, oh Mother."

A burst of searing light shot out from her hands, piercing the dirt below and reducing it to an ashy smoke. A hole began to form as she repeated the spell once more. Moving the power of small suns over the ground, the black earth evaporated into tiny particles, swept away in the constant winds.

The Guardian came closer to Cathleen. His muscled, wolfish-body twitched with the promise of impending attack.

For her part, Cathleen used a wind charm, floating down to depths that made her chest tighten.

From the corner of her eye, she saw the Guardian, still in his form as a prehistoric canine, floating slightly to her left. She noted the creature's ears were flattened against his head and the golden eyes, were bright with anticipation. After several minutes of a controlled fall, Cathleen realized they had entered a corridor to another place. Where is this taking us? she thought, beginning to feel too vulnerable by not knowing her final destination.

After the Guardian described the many deceptions carried out by Calvin Boatwright on his way to becoming the Deceiver, Cathleen knew one thing for certain. The Historian and Jason didn't have a chance of surviving his magic without her intervention.

She looked over at the falling wolf-creature appearance worn by the Guardian and knew he had more secrets to share.

Chapter 33

Jason was still fighting his way back to consciousness when he felt someone shaking his arm. "What…" he said groggy and rubbing a small knot on his forehead.

"Jason, are you aware enough to understand me? We are no longer in the fourth realm."

The Historian's voice was pitched to the softness of silk moving across a smooth surface. He purposely concealed his words for Jason's ears alone.

"No longer? Where are we?"

Jason accepted the strong hand of the other man to regain his feet. Allowing him a moment to orient himself, the Historian continued to explain his theory.

"We have been taken through some kind of time-space channel, formed by the Deceiver's magic. It links the fourth, to the first realm. I suspect this was how the Deceiver carried out his nefarious acts upon the natural realm, without risking detection or apprehension, by the Outlander Wizard Scouts.

It's also likely that Master Bretton Clawson, discovered this tunneling and ended up being captured in the process. I believe we've discovered, quite by accident, the same space channel. The important difference for us is, we aren't prisoners. Yet."

Jason was about to ask about the others, but the Historian continued. "However, of some import to our situation currently, it appears the Guardian has vanished. He stood beside me seconds before, leading me to wonder if he's still with the Protector, above, or has been taken here, below."

Jason had questions about this new circumstance, including how Cathleen could possibly find them. The Guardian's whereabouts were troubling too, because now she'd be alone in the cursed fourth plane, with only the huge hound for an ally.

Jason was now fully aware of his surroundings. Looking around he guessed they were in a cabin as indicated in the roughly-hewn plank walls and flooring.

It was no more than a single room. An alcove was carved out of a small area near the back for a cot. He was struck by its simplicity, almost as if some hermit might live there. It had the feel of a hunters lay-over place, for extended hunting trips.

We're in a wooded area, he thought intuitively. There was only a single window, set in the wall near the front door. The glass seemed very old and practically opaque, making it difficult to see clearly to the outside. The door was made expertly from a heavy wood, fitting snugly into its frame.

Jason watched the Historian try it, only to find it locked. "We'll wait a moment longer in here, to see if we have any guards, Jason," he called over in a subdued voice, attempting to see outside.

Jason moved toward the alcove when a glint popped out of its dark interior. He frowned when he spotted something familiar. He'd seen it last on the finger of the Scribe, Mercy McNaughton. The ring Cathleen had slipped onto Mercy's finger when she ordered her to return to the Council of Green Wizards and report on their findings. When Mercy was told to return there a second time, Cathleen met with stiff resistance from the Scribe.

Jason stepped into the sleeping area, taking the heavy gold ring off a three-legged stool near the cot. He was certain it was the same ring sent by Sir Alex for Cathleen's use. How did this get here if it was on the Scribe's finger?

His thoughts were interrupted when he heard, "Jason, I believe there is a guard outside this cottage, but we must escape before the Deceiver returns. What have you there?" the Guardian asked, looking into Jason's open hand.

"It's the Arch Wizard's signet ring. And the last time we saw it, it was being put on the Scribe's finger for her return trip to the Council." Jason let that fact take root in the Historian's mind before he continued. "The fact that it's in this place, can only mean one of two things. That Mercy somehow was captured by the Deceiver, or, she's working for him as a double agent."

The Historian was silent. When he finally spoke, his voice was colorless and unemotional. "If it is proven the Scribe is a traitor, she will meet a similar end as the Deceiver. Do you recall the warning The Claw scraped on the hearth where he was murdered? Beware the Writer of Secrets, it read. Who better than the Scribe to be privy to the Council's closely held secrets? It falls to the Scribe to sit at every Council meeting, taking notes and recording all that is said."

For all his summary of evidence against the pretty Scribe, Jason sensed a deep conflict inside the Historian. It wasn't lost on him, or Cathleen, that the Historian was fond of the pert Mercy McNaughton.

"Historian, we won't make any judgements until we have all the facts. For now, we have to find our way out of here and somehow, get in touch with Cathleen."

While they were making a more thorough search of the small cabin for possible clues to its owner, the Historian stopped and looked at Jason. "There is one other who's present at the Council meetings. He would have the same access as Mercy to all ..."

He was cut short by a thunderous roar.

They went to the small window, but it presented only a blurred figure off to the side of the cabin. Whatever it was, appeared to be crouched low to the ground.

"Historian," Jason whispered close to the other's bent head as they peered out.

"If this is the natural realm, did that thing out there cross over with us somehow?"

"It would seem so and it is none too happy about finding itself here."

They watched through the blurry window, trying to determine how formidable this new enemy would prove. They would soon find out as the creature moved to the door. After a few shoves, it caved in as if made of straw. A cloud of dust rose up from the cabin floor, obscuring the creature for a second.

Jason had the knife the Historian had given him, holding it at his side, ready to fight. He slipped the heavy ring onto his finger to keep it safe.

The Historian was speaking in the Old Tongue. Jason was familiar with many of Cathleen's favorite incantations and he caught enough of the words to know he was conjuring something. Suddenly, the Historian stopped speaking.

Standing in the doorway, they saw the slouch shoulders and thick legs of the Guardian in his caveman guise. He shuffled into the room on his flat, hairy feet and padded over to the pair.

The Historian and Jason stood behind a wall of Green Fire by then and the brute stopped short, throwing his head back in a deep howl.

"That's not the Guardian! It's the wolf-dog he conjured," Jason said with alarm.

They couldn't be certain how this creature would react to them if the wall was dropped, but Jason didn't want to wait any longer inside the cabin.

"Historian, douse your fire. Let's find out what he'll do."

The Historian muttered a few words and the wall collapsed like an accordion until it vanished altogether. The primitive creature made a rumbling sound and walked over to them.

The two men came to the same conclusion, which the Historian voiced at once. "The Guardian is not with us, Jason. He's switched his persona with the mongrel. The wolfish dog persona now resides in this prehistoric human body. That means, the Guardian is with Cathleen, keeping the body of the giant hound."

The object of this discussion solemnly watched the two humans discussing him for a minute, then crouched down, resting on his haunches as if sitting in front of a camp fire.

"Will he be of any help to us?" Jason asked, not really expecting a reply.

"It is my belief we will soon have an answer to that question. We need to leave here and follow the Deceiver's trail. I think I know where he'll be headed."

Jason shot him a quick glance and shared his own thoughts on the matter. "I'm thinking he's headed for the Council Chambers of the Green Wizards. Am I right, Historian?"

"They were promised a blood bath, Jason. He will surely be delivering on that pledge in person!"

"Do you think he's brought some of the demon spawn along to back him up when he makes his attack on the Greens?" Jason asked.

"He may not need them. If one among the Council is already held in his sway, the Deceiver will have the advantage of that duplicity. The traitor can strike with impunity until it is too late. Then, he...or she...can simply change sides openly and help destroy the others."

The hulking caveman got to his feet, made a loud snuffling noise and bolted through the open doorway.

"He's heard something, or smells something," Jason said. He'd used hunting dogs most of his life and knew when they picked up a scent. The caveman creature had all the instincts of a hunting wolf. The question was, whose scent was he on and could this band of two, plus a wolf, stop the massacre of the entire Sitting Council of Greens?

Chapter 34

Cathleen and the huge wolfdog landed with a resounding thump on a hard surface. It knocked the wind out of her and she gulped for air. When she regained her equilibrium, she shot back to her feet, looking around at their new surroundings.

"Guardian, are you OK? We're in some sort of cottage."

The bulky canine creature being occupied at present by the Guardian, got to his feet. Unsteady at first, after an energetic shaking from head to tail, it seemed alert and unharmed.

"We are no longer on the fourth plane, Protector. The smells, however, are quite familiar to me."

"Me too. Where do you think we've landed?"

"We are back in the Mother's beloved first realm of all things natural. The door to this cabin has been battered in. If I could hazard a guess, I'd say your mate and the Historian found themselves here, along with the caveman lout."

Cathleen vaguely wondered when the Guardian would forgive her for her choice of prehistoric man as his new identity at the beginning of her investigation. Sighing inwardly, she began checking out the small cabin.

"You're right about them landing here. I definitely feel both their energies. It stands to reason, anyone or anything that gets drawn into the space funnel we just traveled will end here. This is a long-used port of entry for the Deceiver, no doubt."

The shaggy animal walked outside, his long snout running along the packed earth like a vacuum. Cathleen watched for another moment, then turned back to her inspection of the cabin.

Walking to the back of the single room into a sleeping alcove, she stared at a three-legged stool by the cot. She felt compelled to hold her hand over the seat, receiving the expected tingle of magic.

Something of magic was placed here, but where is it now?

Whatever had been resting on the battered stool was no longer in the cabin, of that Cathleen was certain. She gazed back into the room thinking, when a deep growl rumbled through the still air.

She ran outside in time to see the huge mongrel shaking a limp object back and forth in his strong jaws. The speed of the moving head was too fast for Cathleen to identify what he'd snatched up in his mouth. Cathleen knew she had to rescue whatever it was, before it was too witless to be interrogated.

"Guardian! Drop what you're holding in your mouth!"

The large jaws opened wide and whatever the wolfish dog had captured immediately rolled itself into a tight ball. Cathleen approached warily, bringing a wisp of Green Fire to one hand in case she needed an immediate defense.

Like a contortionist, the creature unwound long, gangly limbs from around its vulnerable body. A round head popped out from under an arm, a mane of white hair springing back to life like a previously crushed marshmallow.

"Milly! What in the Mother's name are you doing here?" Cathleen yelled, utterly surprised to see the eccentric Gatekeeper.

"Protector, no one is as surprised as I am to be here, wherever 'here' is! I was at my post between the In-Between and the fourth realm when there was a ruckus coming from the other side. I opened my gate to be sure it wasn't one of your party. That's when two of the Grimm Vampire Faeries from the In-Between, swooped through!

They had to be returned to where they belonged to restore order, so I pursued them in the hideous fourth plane. I searched all through lunch and snack time, finally spotting them when they landed on a patch of ground and disappeared. I had to see for myself what new portal they were using to enter the first realm from the fourth. And that's how I got here. I was sucked down under the black earth, falling like a stone, for a lifetime! I was trying to orient myself when I was snatched up like a turkey drum!"

Milly shot the waiting mongrel a withering look.

The Guardian spoke up from where he sat nearby. "I thought it was another of the Deceiver's disguises and I couldn't take a chance he would escape." Looking over at a very ruffled Milly, he added, "Sorry about any discomfort, Gatekeeper."

Milly gave the large beast a wide-eyed look. "I don't recall a wolfish creature passing through my gate. How do you know me?"

"No time for long explanations, Milly," Cathleen broke in before the longwinded Guardian could begin talking.

"This is the Guardian. You can either be sent back to your post or help us find the rest of our party."

"Why, of course I can help. I know very little of this first realm, but I know much about the Grimm Faeries and the fourth realm. The Vampire Faeries were surely called by the Deceiver and crossed at his bidding."

Cathleen thought about that a second. "You think you can follow the Grimm to wherever they went, Milly?"

"Indeed! The founding Green Wizards endowed me with a special sense that alerts me to any trespass between the In-Between and the fourth plane, or the fourth into the first realm. I can tell you right now, your people passed this way and were closely followed by the Grimm Faeries. I just hope we aren't too late."

"Protector, the Gatekeeper and I can attack the Grimm Faeries from the rear, while you join your mate and the Historian. It is likely the Deceiver is using the Vampire Faeries to push the two closer to where he'll be waiting and cutting off any retreat for them. They will be in serious danger."

Without waiting for her reply, the great hound lopped off, its head high, sniffing at the wind.

Milly tried to keep up, finally calling to the Guardian in his high, plaintive voice.

"In your current form, Guardian, there's no way I can keep up with you."

The Guardian crouched low, saying, "Climb onto my back. You won't slow my pace."

Cathleen watched as the huge dog took off running, Milly's lanky arms wrapped tightly around his thick neck, his hands filled with tufts of gray fur.

She waited until she was certain they were safely away before conjuring a wind charm.

The Guardian and Milly both agreed on the direction she should take. She would let the gust of warm air lift her off the ground, but not before bending down to touch the Mother's natural earth. As the Protector of the Green, Cathleen was gifted by the Mother, to access extra powers into herself, with this close connection to the earth. Standing in the dimming light of a waning sun, Cathleen was whisked into the air. With her long, auburn hair streaming out behind her, she had once been told she resembled the beautifully carved woman on the prow of a Viking ship. In her Protector's heart, she felt just as formidable.

Chapter 35

Jason and the Historian were canny where the hunt was concerned. Both knew what it felt like to be hunter and hunted. They agreed that they found themselves in the latter category at the current time.

The big caveman lopping along behind them no longer concealed the Guardian, but a prehistoric wolf-like creature, never communicating in more than grunts.

The Historian spoke quietly to Jason while they passed through an open field of wild grasses, tarnished yellowish-green in the waning daylight.

"Jason, since the creature behind us is no longer the useful Guardian, but a mere wolfish dog, I propose that I send it to my rooms, near the Council Chambers. The Guardian will have to undo it when he joins us again."

Having warned Jason of his intentions, the Historian spun around, holding up his hand to stop the lumbering being. He quietly intoned the spell, shifting the caveman instantly to the rooms he saw clearly in his mind.

"He'll be fine there and safe from discovery. I'm sure he'd be no help to us now."

The Historian spotted the two Grimm Vampire Faeries a short while before when a fiery sunset touched their iridescent wings, lighting them like floating candles.

Jason suggested they find a place to hunker down until they tried to attack.

"I don't think they are going to attack us Jason. I think they are herding us like cattle, by the way they keep dodging away whenever we are close enough to engage with them."

"So, you think the Deceiver is waiting somewhere up ahead to close the trap. Then we better dispatch the little buggers, before they can team up with him. Let's stop moving and let them catch up to this point. We'll split up now and take them from their flanks."

The Historian gave Jason a sidelong look as they moved silently through some underbrush in a small stand of trees. "A fine plan, Jason," he whispered over to him. "But while I have the means to fight the Grimm, you would be defenseless. These are Vampire Faeries remember and not to be confused with the gentler sort."

"I'm not really defenseless. I have your knife...and this," he said holding up his right hand. The gold signet ring, snug on his middle finger, gave off a dull green glow in the dying light.

The Historian wasn't certain Jason could access the powers stored in the Arch Wizard's ring, but he knew the Protector's mate had some uncanny sense of magic. He gave his head a quick nod and they veered off in opposite directions.

They both agreed the Vampire Faeries were able to smell them and would end up at this jumping off point. Jason kept well-hidden, using the screen of trees they'd been passing through. He couldn't see the Historian, but was confident he blended into the shadows several yards away. He moved out of the forested area, into a shallow valley, surrounded by hill country, with occasional waist-deep swales caused by heavy run-off from the higher hillocks.

Jason had learned to move as silently as a wraith in the woods. He was crouching close to the ground as he followed one of these natural depressions in the earth. Evening settled softy around him. Stars were beginning to pop out like shards of glass, scattered in their uncountable numbers, against the blackness of the endless vault of night.

Jason was always at ease in the night, in spite of the black patch covering his lost eye. He felt his other senses spring into life, made keener by this one deficit. There were no sounds, but the sighs of the wind moving around the hills and stirring the long hair around his neck. Stopping to sniff the air for any scents that didn't belong in nature, he moved his head from side-to-side, searching for any peripheral movement.

There was a chance the Historian would pass him, but he was sure the savvy wizard would be moving in a similar fashion and the distance wouldn't be much.

He was getting ready to move away from the shadows of a deeper gulley, when he picked up a faint noise. The chirping voices of the Grimm Vampire Faeries signaling to one another. They knew exactly where he was and probably believed the Historian was with him.

He wondered why the Grimm hadn't split up, each following the different trails. It dawned on him slowly but had no less of an impact. Perhaps they had already dealt a mortal blow to the Historian. This may get dicey, he thought, slipping the knife out of the leg sheath supplied by the Historian earlier.

He snugged it tightly against the ring, feeling a jolt of magic when the two touched. Whatever happened to his partner, he had to face these Grimm on his own and then try to find the Historian. He couldn't allow himself to dwell on the possible fate of the wizard at the hands of the blood-drinkers.

Rather than stay in a place where he felt too boxed-in, Jason exited the trench. He tried to angle himself back toward to tree line and better cover. Up until then, he hadn't taken much notice of the ground beneath his feet. It must have rained recently in the hills. His boot made soft, sucking sounds when he moved. That's probably how they found me, he thought, angry with himself for not realizing the sound would be magnified in the stillness.

Making it out of the muddy depression, running in a crouch, he finally scooted into a thick patch of tall grasses and fern-like plants, not daring to move further toward the woods. Hunkering down, he listened for the chirping signals of the Grimm hunting him. The night was shattered by their piercing screams as the Grimm flew at him, attacking him from both sides.

Jason jumped to his feet, brandishing the sharp knife in front of him.

As if the attack released its magical properties, a bolt of jagged, green light, shot out from the emerald stone of the ring and down the blade of the knife. It caught one of the Grimm squarely in the middle, shredding its body like confetti.

The second Grimm opened a mouth full of sharp teeth, shooting out a long tongue. This aimed right at Jason's face, where it curled around the patch over Jason's empty eye socket.

Jason was momentarily paralyzed as the slimy tongue tried to drive itself into his skull. He jerked his whole body back, ignoring the feeling of acid that dripped down his cheek.

He stumbled backward until a strong arm caught him around the shoulders.

The Historian struggled to hold his own against the enraged Grimm, when it suddenly stopped its attack letting out a high screech. Jason and the Historian watched as the Vampire Faerie fell to the ground, its body becoming an ash heap under the Green Fire pouring from Cathleen's hands.

Without saying anything, she rushed over to where her husband was being supported by the Historian.

The acid from the Grimm's tongue had eaten a deep channel into Jason's cheek, but it was prevented from penetrating his skull though the empty eye socket.

"Historian, use one of your healing charms and quickly!"

Cathleen knew he would have knowledge of stronger spells, unknown to all but the Historian of the Greens. These would be from the time when magic flew like static in the air after a storm. A time before the first Green Wizards captured the powers for themselves. This old magic would carry the potency needed to heal Jason's wounds, but only an initiate such as the Historian could control it to his will.

Without further comment, the Historian closed his eyes momentarily, seeming to mentally pull the archaic spells from somewhere, deep inside his being. He began speaking in a strange dialect. Cathleen thought she recognized some words in the Old Tongue, but she had no understanding of their meaning.

The Historian stood in front of Jason who leaned heavily on Cathleen's shoulder. His eyes snapped open as a green blaze of light shot out of them, directly onto Jason's ruined cheek.

Jason began to stand more firmly on his own as the healing magic took effect, mending his face and purifying the eye socket of any of the venom from the Grimm's probing tongue.

As quickly as the light poured from his eyes, it vanished. The Historian had a small smile of satisfaction on his face and Jason knew it worked.

"Thank you, Historian," Jason said while he readjusted his black eye patch snugly into place. "I'm not that pretty, but I'd prefer to get my lines in old age."

Cathleen told the men that Milly and the Guardian were the ones who located them and that she'd sent them on ahead, to track down the Deceiver.

A wash of moonlight poured over the field, making the waving grasses appear like a restless dark sea.

"Where's the hairy guy that was with you?" she asked looking around for his sloping shoulders to surface.

After a quick explanation, the three set off in the direction of a hidden valley and the Council of Greens' castle stronghold. Cathleen was lost in thoughts of their last trip here, three years past, when she and Jason were married in her mother's ancestral castle, Brinnion Keep.

A wedding to be remembered had become a legend in the folklore of the magic users. A marriage where death and monsters were as evident as love and magic. A joining of the Witch and the Woodsman also brought out the dead from eternal slumber.

Cathleen wondered what she'd find today if not death and deceit.

So much in life slips into the same paths we've walked before, she realized as she matched the long strides of the rest of her hunting party.

Chapter 36

The night sky subtlety shifted from early evening to full darkness. Stars shimmered in their separate halloes, while a full moon floated high in its ethereal kingdom.

Cathleen took lead, with Jason and the Historian following close behind. They crossed low hills, carpeted with fragrant grasses and rich woodlands. The trees moved like night watchmen in the gentle breezes. Their destination was the secret valley of the Wizards of the Green Mother.

Since they were formed eons, upon eons ago, The Greens occupied this secluded area on the Emerald Isle. Its location known only to their tight clique and allies such as the Colossus Fairies and Woodland Elves, who held fast to the Mother's ways.

Other magic users surely knew of the existence, but the location of the hidden valley remained concealed from all. The Green Wizards employed the use of powerful wards and spells of deception to maintain this scared ground.

The Council of Green Wizards was so diligent in guarding this secret, if one among them fell away from his or her pledge to the Green Mother, powerful magic was used to cleanse any memory or hint, of its location.

The tiny band approached the valley from the west, coming down from the rolling hill country. Cathleen figured there was little over a mile left to travel in the moonlit night, before reaching Verdant Keep. Their castle was so named by the original Greens who built the castle-fortress, but was still called by this name into the present day.

Cathleen wondered if the Deceiver had been expunged of his knowledge of the valley, before he was sent to the fourth realm.

There was a good chance the Wizard Boatwright, shielded himself from that part of the penalty allotted him, using his own charms to minimize the effect of the memory erase.

There was another possibility, even more sinister in character. The traitor among the Council had prevented the vile Deceiver from receiving the full measure of his punishment before banishment. That possibility was all too real under the circumstances.

Cathleen shot a quick look over her shoulder. Jason saw her turn toward him, and she saw him flash his perfect white smile at her for the effort.

"Are we getting near, love?" he asked in a hushed voice.

"Not long now. If our timing is right, the Council will be holding a meeting to listen to Mercy's updated report."

The Historian heard the name of the pretty Scribe and lifted his head from his study of the ground they passed over. "Protector," he said coming abreast of Cathleen. She and Jason stopped together to hear what he had to say.

"I am aware that the Scribe, Mercy McNaughton, is a person of interest to you in your investigation. The Claw's message was explicit about one among us with access to Council secrets. I too, should fall into that category if we are to be thorough. But there is one other, we need to consider. He is…"

The Historian's words were cut short when the night sky was shattered by dozens of bolts of Green Fire from the direction of Verdant Keep. Bits of shouted spells and screams rode the soft winds like unseen hitchhikers.

"The Council is under attack!" Cathleen stammered in shock.

"The Deceiver must have brought other demon spawn besides the Grimm along with him," the Historian said, his handsome face twisted in anger.

"The Mother knows what we'll be up against!" he said turning to Cathleen with real concern on his face for the first time.

Jason took Cathleen's arm saying, "You two need to travel faster than I can without slowing you down. Go on ahead and I'll do some rear action."

While she hated leaving him on his own, she knew he was right. They had to move fast and a Wind Charm would be faster for her alone. The Historian was already calling up his own gust, cutting an anxious look in her direction.

"See you inside Council Chambers, Protector."

He was swept out of sight almost instantly. After a quick peck on Jason's cheek and a shouted, "I love you," Cathleen did the same.

Jason took the Historian's knife out of its sheath once more, the familiar jolt of magic shooting up his arm as it came into contact with the gold band on his finger. Not wanting to stumble blindly into one of the creatures called from the Pit, he moved quickly off open ground. He insinuated himself into the dense shadows, clinging like skirts to the rounded hills.

His plan was simple. Attack any of the rear guard, hopefully dispatching them before he was discovered, finding himself on the wrong end of that strategy.

The top-secret valley was no longer veiled in the night. It was bathed in garish lighting from above and below, by thunderous explosions of green, answered by blood-red bolts of fire coming from many directions.

Jason moved toward the battle, listening intently, as he tried to identify where the heaviest fighting took place. He picked out shouting and bombardment from every point, indicating the Verdant Keep was probably surrounded. This wasn't just a frontal attack.

He guessed the Greens must have spread out their own numbers, to cover the wider front created by the Deceiver's demon-spawn. There was no doubt in his mind they were sorely outnumbered.

As stealthily as a darker shadow inside the undisturbed gloom, Jason moved toward the left fortifications of the Keep.

He recalled the Historian telling Cathleen he'd see her inside the Chambers. He wondered if the former Scout would first seek out the traitor from among the Sitting Council members.

Neither Jason or Cathleen, suspected the Historian. Jason prayed that was the case since Cathleen would be fighting beside him. Moving forward, Jason shook off any concerns on her behalf, knowing his wife was as deadly as she was beautiful. Like her mother, Brighid, Cathleen had access to powerful and obscure magic, giving her an edge over most wizards.

The hidden valley gave up its secrets as the outline of a massive stone building hove into view against the night sky.

As he studied it, well-lit under the constant assault, Jason thought it looked like a replica of a medieval castle. Then it dawned on him. This was no modern copy, but likely a much older form of architecture, dating back to before the recorded times of Magic.

The grayish-green stone castle appeared unusually long, until Jason realized it employed a buttressing system at either wing, like huge arms holding it in place. The whole structure was aflame with light, either from the Sacred Green Fire, or deep-red flames and laser thin black beams that he hadn't noticed earlier.

Closer to the Keep, Jason thought he was imagining things.

The red fire became like a living creature, unnaturally curling itself around corners, climbing walls, insinuating itself inside windows and into turrets. The back of the castle was aflame, the high towers casting long shadows on the scattered debris on the grounds below.

Deceiver's magic-infused fire, Jason concluded as he watched.

As Jason came up to the footing of the nearest flying buttress, the blare from a horn cut through the sounds of combat. Moving in a low crouch, he stopped, straining to locate the source of the signal.

He looked up at the top of the buttress, spotting a natural balcony, built into the shape of an eye. It jutted out from the façade of the giant, stone arm, casting deep shadows below where Jason hid.

Standing on the wide ledge of the balcony was a man Jason intuitively knew was the Deceiver.

The wind lashed his tall frame, whipping long dark robes around an emaciated body. The wizard's black, shoulder-length hair blew straight out behind him like a pirate's sail.

The skull of some creature was cupped in his hands. While Jason watched, the Deceiver blew into the top of the head. The lower jaw dropped open wide and the deep sounding horn resonated over the battlefield.

He's calling in his troops. This will be a massacre if they answer!

As quickly as he could move undetected, Jason found his way through several outer rooms, to a spacious waiting room at the front of the castle. Intricate wall-hangings covered much of the stone walls, with wall sconces bathing their beautiful artistry in soft lighting.

Jason padded soundlessly over thick carpeting, likely among the more modern amenities added over many countless eons. He came to a set of heavy double doors.

The noise of screamed orders and the blasts of fire bolts shook the high, stained-glass windows set into the cathedral ceilings, throughout the anterior room where he stood. A bright light shone from under the ornately carved wooden doors that he suspected led into the Council Chambers. Jason was sure he heard voices as he got closer but wasn't sure if he'd find friend or foe. "Only one way to find out," he whispered to himself, reached for one of the brass handles and pulled.

Chapter 37

When Jason rushed inside the Council Chambers, he struggled to keep from squinting. After being in the dark for so long, his eye reacted to the unnaturally bright light flooding the room.

Gripping the knife tightly, he was reassured by the tingle of magic rushing through his arm when the hilt came into contact with the signet ring.

He felt better prepared for what he would be facing, since beginning this investigation with Cathleen.

Jason 's eye finally adjusted enough for him to recognize two figures, sitting at a highly polished U-shaped table.

"Milly!" he said moving toward the figure with a hallo of floating white hair.

The little Gatekeeper appeared in a deep trance and looked unseeing, into Jason's face.

Moving down the length of the table, Jason stopped in front of the second figure, the Scribe, Mercy McNaughton. He called her name softly, hoping for a response.

He tried again, "Mercy, can you hear me?"

The only sound he heard was the muted noise of the battle, now raging outside the thick walls.

Jason found himself in a quandary. He knew he'd have to leave these two in their vulnerable state, if he couldn't rouse them out of this sleep-like stupor. If the enemy outside made it into the Chamber Room, they'd both be slaughtered.

He was about to make his next move, when the ring on his finger shot a bolt of green, piercing the searing glow enveloping the room. The sharp edges of the bolt, cut through the charmed light, causing it to shrink away from the touch of its power.

The laser-like beam moved around the table, burning away the unnatural brightness, until it touched the Scribe's head, exploding on impact.

Jason watched unmoving, letting the jagged bolts go where they chose. Another bolt hit Milly in his narrow chest.

Jason took a step back from the table, waiting for what would follow. It was clear now, the sharp light flooding the room was set there to hold the two in place. The ring responded to his need to free them.

Mercy's eyes blinked rapidly and she sprang to her feet. She reached out to balance herself on the table. Milly followed suite, giving his round head a few shakes and sending tiny sparks flying from his snowy head.

"Are you two alright?" Jason asked, looking from one to the other.

The Scribe caught sight of Milly, a look of confusion crossing her face. "What trickery is this?" she asked, looking at Jason.

"The members were all sitting in Council when this one popped into our midst on the back of a large wolf! The wolf spoke in the Old way, warning of impending doom. Perhaps it was a threat against the Greens!"

Turning like an agitated cat to face Milly with her suspicions, Mercy blurted out, "Are you from another realm, little man?"

Milly stretched his long neck in a vain effort to appear taller and more dignified. Both were futile efforts for the lanky, puff-headed being.

"You have no memory of my position, Scribe? Humph! I'll repeat myself then. I am Maximillian, known as Milly, appointed Gatekeeper separating the fourth realm from the In-Between. I have served the Council of Greens since before you were a single mote of stardust, wizard!" Milly's cloud of white hair bristled with indignation.

Jason quickly intervened before the exchange could escalate into more than words between the two magic users. "Now that you know you're both working for the Greens, use some of that energy to help the Council members, fighting out there! I need to leave you, so I can find the Protector and the Historian."

"The Historian is here?" Mercy asked. The thought of the handsome Council member seemed to refocus the Scribe as she pushed away from the heavy table. "I shall accompany you, Jason. My help may be needed," she said looking up at him.

"As will I," Milly interjected, heading on his spindly legs to the wall directly behind the Arch Wizard's empty chair. "I saw the Arch Wizard run through here as the battle commenced outside these walls." Milly pulled aside the heavy tapestry, revealing the secret passage. Opening this with a jumble of words, he reached up on tip-toe for a torch, sputtering its light from an iron sconce.

Jason spoke up, "All right you two. You can come with me if you follow orders. But first, Milly, where did the Guardian get off to?"

"The Guardian? Here also?" Mercy asked.

Milly was quick to share his important information with the Scribe. "He's taken the form of the giant wolfish-dog you seem to recall, Scribe, though you didn't remember me. I tried to explain our mission, but that Council member, Corky something, silenced me somehow with his long staff, leaving me as mute as a doll. That's how you came to be sitting mutely, Scribe! You objected to the accusations against me and the Guardian, being made by him. That villain silenced your voice too and bound us both to the chairs. Alas! The wolfish Guardian deserted me to my fate, bounding off into the night through that high window, yonder!" Milly was pointing to a shattered stained-glass window, fifteen feet off the floor.

Jason asked the Scribe how this wizard had the authority to restrain them both.

Mercy explained, "Corky Cochran is the Sargent at Arms for the Council. He was appointed after Sir Alex became Arch Wizard. He also acted as bodyguard for him. Sir Alex became increasingly fearful after the threat of a blood bath was made against the Greens."

Milly piped up, "It was as if Cochran wanted to stop us from warning the others of the impending attack. Soon after the Guardian leapt through the window, the first wave of demon-spawn attempted to storm the Chamber room.

Perhaps the Guardian's wolfish form, helped him make good his escape. He's probably still running, poor creature."

Jason gave them a curt nod, saying, "Time to hunt. Milly, you lead with the torch. Let's move."

Still unsure about the Scribe's allegiance to the Green, Jason wasn't about to turn his back on her. For her part, Jason noticed Mercy had produced a ring similar to the one he wore, slipping it on her thumb.

Why would she have a signet ring like the Arch Wizard's? He was more than a little curious but stashed that question away. For now, he had to locate the Historian and Cathleen.

The passage they followed, led deeper into the heart of the massive stone castle. Various storage rooms and padlocked doors were scattered along the passageway. Jason knew there was no time to search every room, which Milly tried to do, leading them through the silent hallways.

Frustrated with the slow pace, Jason said in a hushed voice, "Milly, walk behind me. There's enough light from the other wall sconces," he added, not wanting to hurt the little man's feelings.

Jason decided using magic would speed his search for the others. Holding his arm straight out from his side, the knife reflected a dull glow in the torchlight. When it came into contact with the ring, the unmistakable pulse of magic surged through his arm and down to his fingers.

A jagged, green bolt shot from the blade's tip. It crawled up to the ceiling like a living thing, then bent itself around a sharp corner in the corridor.

The others didn't comment on Jason's newly displayed powers but picked up their pace. They followed the beam until the shaft of light expanded, covering several feet of stone wall where the passage came to a dead end.

Without warning, the spreading fire blasted a hole in the stone, large enough for a man to pass through.

Jason was joined by the others as he peered into the exposed room.

Standing in the middle of an ancient looking cell, three people turned toward the newcomers, a mixture of surprise and dread written on their faces.

Swaying between the Historian and Cathleen was the Arch Wizard, Sir Alex. Raising his head, he searched the faces of the three who burst into the room. When his bleary eyes found the Scribe, he said, "Forgive me Mistress. I did all I could to keep the evil doer at bay."

All eyes turned toward the Scribe, until Sir Alex moaned.

The Arch Wizard looked haggard and had aged a lifetime. A sickly sheen of perspiration coated his face, highlighting an ashen complexion. Dark stains covered the front of his green, velvet robes. The rich, gold thread of intricate magical symbols decorating it, were turned black in places.

Jason rushed to replace Cathleen's arm with his own, strong arm to support the injured man.

The Historian looked over at him saying, "Let's move him onto that table."

With a sweep of his hand, the implements of torture clattered loudly, spreading across the blood-stained stone floor. When they relieved themselves of their burden, the Historian and Jason rejoined the others.

Cathleen immediately turned to the Scribe. "Mercy, you need to explain yourself and quickly!" the command in her voice was clear and her eyes became a deeper, hazel green. She was furious at the secrets they kept uncovering.

The Scribe visibly tried to gather herself. "The true Arch Wizard was murdered during the time of my first shift to the fourth realm. I discovered this when you ordered me to return here, to give my report to the Council, Protector. I was told he disappeared without a trace, so I began searching for him. I found his mangled body in this very room. I removed his gold signet ring, hiding it on my person. I then replaced it with a fake ring, with a hint of magic, so it appeared authentic to any magic user. I used a Time Thread to shift the murdered Arch Wizard to Neidin's cottage, knowing she could conceal it from the Deceiver. I knew he would never attempt to enter her place of rest and peace. Sadly, she must have been lured away from the protection of her wards and likely met her own end at the hands of the Deceiver, or one of his demon-spawn"

Jason interjected what they knew of Neidin, explaining how she was destroyed long before he found the fake ring. "Likely the imposter posing as Neidin, took the ring from the corpse and kept it, believing it was the true signet ring," Jason concluded.

Mercy looked shocked at this news. "Jason, when I learned you found the false ring, I had to assume you hadn't found Sir Alex's body. I believed his remains had been destroyed. That's when I immediately conjured the clone of Sir Alex, leaving him here to confuse the spy and ultimately, the Deceiver. Sadly, his clone suffered the same torture as the true Arch Wizard."

Cathleen asked, "If you are wearing Sir Alex's real signet ring, Scribe, what is the power behind the fake one, Jason is wearing on his finger?"

When the Scribe looked at a loss for an answer, the Historian spoke up. "Jason has been touched with a singular power, a magic that is not of our own experiences as Wizards and Sorcerers. It is not unheard of that among humans sharing the Mother's first realm, a few chosen ones share Her gifts.

His is a magic rooted in spirit and passed from one to another within his heritage. Jason is in fact, a modern-day oracle."

Chapter 38

Cathleen never doubted Jason was unique in many ways and she always suspected some familial transfer of 'second sight' as some called it. His great aunt had the same walking dreams and could see into the murky future that would unfold without intervention. She knew she would have many long conversations with her husband about this newly named talent, but for now, they had mysteries to solve and knots to unwind.

The Scribe wandered over to where the Arch Wizard's clone was stretched across a heavy wooden table. The torturer's workstation. "You have served me faithfully and well, clone and I now release you from your worldly bonds." With those words, and to everyone's relief, the clone vanished.

Cathleen spoke when the last shimmer of the clone's departure disappeared. "Historian, you and Mercy will go back to the main chamber and…"

"How may I be of assistance, Protector?" a small voice broke into Cathleen's comment.

With the discovery of Cathleen and the Historian, and the vivid story told by the Scribe, no one took notice of the Gatekeeper. He was sitting with his legs drawn up to his chin in a corner, listening quietly.

"Milly! Have you abandoned your post?" the Historian asked alarmed.

"Not abandoned, Historian. I am here to lend my aid, as soon as it's called upon."

The answer brought a small smile to the big man's face, but he seemed pleased to have the gangling little Gatekeeper with them again.

Cathleen looked over at Jason, asking if the Guardian was with them.

"No. He escaped some sort of light-binding charm used by the Council's Sargent at Arms. Milly and the Scribe were frozen inside it, when I found them in the Council Chambers.

"He used it to silence us!" Mercy added angrily.

The Historian turned to Jason with a look of relief on his face. "Jason, I can finally tell you what I've been trying to say for hours! Corky Cochran is the other wizard I kept trying to name. He's at every Council meeting and privy to every secret agenda. And, as acting bodyguard to Sir Alex, he likely knew of plans Sir Alex wasn't even sharing with the other Greens."

As Cathleen listened quietly, some of her own questions were being answered. Questions seemed all she had uncovered for most of this investigation. Until now.

Everyone turned to her when she declared, "It's time to confront the Deceiver. He and his accomplice will begiven no quarter when we find him!

Mercy, you and the Historian must locate and assist the Guardian. It's very likely he's jumped from the frying pan into the fire!"

Mercy gave the Historian a quizzical look but said nothing.

For his part, the handsome Historian began a quiet spell and taking the Scribe's hand, they both vanished.

Jason asked Cathleen what her plans were for him and the Gatekeeper.

"Milly, you need to return to your post. If the Deceiver prevails here, you'll be the last hope of saving this realm from an invasion of demon-spawn he'll call to his side. The Time Thread I call will take you back to your gate. Go with the Mother!"

Cathleen stirred the air with her hand, causing a swirl of wind to enclose the Gatekeeper. When the white frizz on his head began shooting out in all directions, he blinked out of sight.

"It's just us now, husband!" she said as she stirred the air once more.

Cathleen reached for Jason's hand and the pressure on his chest, told him they were on their own Thread.

They landed behind the stonework of a long buttress. Jason recognized the eye-shaped window when he looked up. He saw the figure of the Deceiver standing on the wide ledge, arms raised, as he summoned his followers.

Cathleen had taken them back to that moment he first saw the evil one.

The sound of battle was coming from small pockets of defenders, scattered over the grounds in front of the castle. The Green Wizards were paired off, doing their best to stop the slithering, crawling and flying beasts, brought up from the Dark Pit to destroy every Wizard of the Green.

One enormous creature trampled the other demon-spawn, in its frenzied efforts to reach two wizards fighting close to the stone wing of the building.

It had many characteristics of a giant, saber tooth tiger, except for the row of spikes that sprouted from its muscular back. Like the other cat-like creatures Cathleen and Jason encountered in the Deceiver's stronghold, this one was also translucent.

Cathleen's theory was that without any natural light, the cursed darkness of the Pit formed these insubstantial looking beasts. Whatever caused it, they were all the more hideous for the oddity.

Cathleen and Jason watched the creature's progress toward the pair of Green Wizards, fighting for their lives. Its long claws dug into smaller demons, crushed under its weight and walked over like a bloody carpet beneath his padded feet.

Cathleen shouted another spell, turning the small fire dancing in her hand, into a veritable blow torch. The green flame exploded instantly upon contact with the monster, becoming liquefied and covering its body. Its roars were silenced as the liquid fire filled the gaping jaws.

The two Greens spun around, searching out their champion. They studied the shadows, but were drawn-back into another battle, the ally quickly forgotten.

Cathleen and Jason moved under a Shadow Wrap concealing their movements through the scattered battle front.

Jason clutched the knife and wore the ring, though now, he wasn't sure of its influence. Wherever his power came from, mattered little at the moment. He felt the same tingle course through him and that was enough.

Cathleen touched his shoulder, speaking close to his ear when he leaned into her.

"Two Vampire Faeries buzzing that pile of rubble to our left. Let's go."

Approaching undetected, Cathleen and Jason were close enough to see a wizard of the Green lying on the ground, his head in a pool of blood. A second one, blood dripping down his face, had created a Dome of Protection over himself and his fallen comrade. Knowing he couldn't fight while inside the Dome, he likely just hunkered down to wait for relief.

"As he weakens, so will the Dome," Cathleen whispered. "I'll take the one attacking now and you take out his buddy hanging by the castle wall," she added.

Cathleen threw the Wrap off herself. She charged the Phantom Vampire Faerie, throwing a sheet of freezing water over it as she ran. She knew this would damage its fragile, wings, causing the Vampire Faerie to fall to the ground where she'd deal with it.

As the frigid water drenched the creature, it let out a shrill howl of frustration, desperately trying to move its brittle wings. Within a blink, it was falling onto a pile of rock, blasted out of the ancient castle. One wing snapped off at the shoulder followed by a squeal of rage.

Cathleen quickly followed its fall with the death blow, pinning the voracious blood-sucker, with a sharp bolt of fire. A horrible stench filled the air as the creature's body contorted and contracted, then dissolved in the heat of her fire.

The Green Wizard watched from his Dome with wide eyes. He looked back at the fallen man, then at Cathleen and slowly shook his head. He mumbled a few words over his comrade and the body disappeared, sent Cathleen knew, to the second plane where his spirit would be renewed.

When the Dome dropped, Cathleen told the wizard to help his fellow Greens. She would join them all at the battle's conclusion, leaving no doubt it would end in the Council's favor.

Rushing over to where Jason faced the other Vampire Faerie, Cathleen arrived in time to see him standing over a quivering body.

Jason explained that the knife and ring still acted like one weapon, sending bolts of green where he pointed. From the gaping hole in the mid-section of the Vampire Faerie, Cathleen knew Jason used his power efficiently.

They left the twitching body of the Vampire, searching out other Council wizards still fighting amid the rubble.

The smoke was gritty and dense, permeating the still air with its acrid smell. Fires were scattered like smudge pots in an orchard. Cathleen was certain they'd been set by the Deceiver, effectively hiding his creatures from the magic the Greens would use against them.

She and Jason picked up the shouts of other defenders. Most of the Green Wizards were wheezing and coughing, which helped to pinpoint positions.

Spotting three wizards hunkered down behind the other stone arm of a flying buttress, they moved toward them at a run, struggling to keep under the Wrap.

The night was shattered with a constant barrage of spheres of Green Fire, hurtling toward the oncoming army of demon-spawn. These came in their hundreds, pouring through a wall of gray smoke.

Cathleen was only able to identify a few among their vast numbers.

Woodland Witches and moth-like creatures she knew could transform into the Dragon Leach, along with more of the Vampire Faeries. The rest were monsters from a child's night terrors, slithering, crawling or flying, with bared fangs, scaly or slimy bodies and grizzled, horned snouts.

This nightmare was coming fast toward the three defenders. Their constant barrage of fiery spheres never slowed down their momentum. Any fallen were trampled under, the sheer weight of the massed demons, pushing their remains deep into the earth.

Jason stood close to Cathleen.

"Jason, those three haven't a chance against what's coming at them! I need your help."

He waited inside the Shadow Wrap until the horde was nearly abreast of where he stood. The stirred air carried the pungent odor of the approaching, tightly packed throng. The smell was as repulsive as any Jason had ever encountered, evoking thoughts of hundreds of rotting corpses, lying under a July sun.

Jason shook his head as if he could clear the memory of the stench.

Cathleen was no longer with him but moved under her own concealment several feet away. She finished her spell just as the first beasts spotted a deep green glow, off to the side.

Jason, still under concealment, thrust his hand outside the covering, the ring and knife glowing green, like a beacon in the thick, gray air.

The lead-beasts turned in their charge, the rest following as one body, lured by the presence of a Green Wizard.

In his other hand, Jason held tightly to the Time Thread Cathleen called, instantly blinking out of sight.

The creature's murderous rampage, carried them swiftly to the gaping hole where Jason stood a second before.

The monsters were fueled with a blood lust, their sole purpose to kill. This effectively blinded their instincts to imminent danger. They pushed aggressively from the rear, until all were hurled into the oblivion prepared for them.

Cathleen had a grim smile on her face, listening to the howls, roars and screeches as the army of demon-spawn, plummeted out of existence on the natural plane, carried by her spell to be deposited in the depths of their special netherworld.

Cathleen knelt. Placing her hands flat on the rich earth that closed over the abyss, she thanked the Green Mother for blessing her power.

Getting back to her feet, she ran to where Jason would be waiting.

The In-Between was the last place the Deceiver could possibly run, with his forces so diminished. He would go where he could lay low for as long as he needed, without fear of being discovered.

Cathleen was not about to let him avoid his just punishment for the murders of Bretton Clawson and the Arch Wizard, no matter how long it took. She resolved she would not lose him because of her own mortality.

Chapter 39

The Guardian was weary of his crude, wolfish identity, but admittedly found it served him well. He was fleeter than any gazelle, his powerful jaws were enough deterrent to turn aside, or destroy, any number of demons already.

He felt fairly confident as he bounded away on four muscular legs, the sounds of battle becoming whispers on the night wind. His leap to freedom through the high painted window, was almost exhilarating. Unfortunately, it dropped him in the middle of a small cluster of demon-spawn answering the Deceiver's summons.

With the appearance of giant river rats, they all turned their beady red eyes on the Guardian as he tried to regain his footing. He'd killed several of the pack when he landed on them. The fight they gave him was short-lived as he neatly tore into those attacking him and watched the others as they squealed and abandoned their mates.

He knew the Protector had joined the battle to save the Greens and was up to her Inner Eye in demon-spawn, but he had a bigger prize to pursue. He regretted that it might appear he quit the field of battle himself, but then, there was no time to dither about appearances.

The Deceiver was on the move and so need he be! Finally pausing in his head-long dash, he stopped by an icy stream for a much needed drink. Studying the velvet dome above, the Guardian calculated nearly an hour had passed, since he began his hunt.

After making good his escape from the spell that froze the Scribe and the Gatekeeper, the Guardian hid until he caught sight of the Deceiver making his escape from the Council's citadel.

It was likely the Dark Wizard would head toward the porthole between the fourth realm and the In-Between. Once there, the Deceiver could cross into the stark brightness of the In-Between, hiding among the oddities of that alternate space, for as long as he wanted. He could out-live any mortal searching for him because that space existed without the measure of time.

Crouched over the fast-moving water, the Guardian's canine ears pricked up at the sound of a low hum.

The air ruffled around his long snout, drawn back now in a vicious snarl as he anticipated an enemy.

"Guardian! Well met!" the Historian called out. His arm was still comfortably stretched across the Scribe's shoulders, as they approached.

The wolf's hackles were raised, and the glint in his golden eyes was fierce. The Historian and Scribe kept a respectful distance.

"What is this, then?" the Guardian asked gruffly.

"Why are you not assisting the Protector and her mate battle the Deceiver's hordes?"

"Cathleen O'Brien sent us to find and assist you," the Scribe answered for them, adding, "When you leapt through that window, leaving the Gatekeeper and me behind, the traitor was revealed as Cory Cochran, Sargent at Arms to the Council."

"This is no news to me, Scribe. I have had my sights on him since the Arch Wizard foolishly appointed him to his station. He had the gleam of avarice and ego in his eye. I'm just surprised that Sir Alex was taken in by him.

"Guardian," the Historian said, "The Arch Wizard has passed into the next realm. We believe the Deceiver had him dispatched by Cochran, just as he did Master Bretton Clawson. It would have been easy for Cochran to carry out the nefarious deeds, considering his good standing in both the Council and with the Scouts, as something of a legend himself. He would have easy access to both his victims."

The huge canine growled deeply in his broad chest. The news about the demise of Sir Alex was jarring enough, but tying two murders to the same wizard, was astonishing he told the pair. "Have those fools on the Council lost their collective powers?" he asked, his eyes flashing with his disgust and anger as he continued.

"They have been naïve in believing Cochran could change from a trained killer, to mild, Sargent at Arms. He was well-bloodied over many years of battling demon incursions. How would he pass from that role, to take up the yew branch as the meek Chamber peace maker?"

"Guardian, Milly has been sent back to his post as Gatekeeper, by the Protector. I believe that's where she and Jason will be traveling next. They mean to prevent the Deceiver from using the gateway to cross over to the In-Between," Milly warned.

The Guardian gave a snort, saying, "That's exactly my own belief. The dark one will try to lose himself in that vast nothingness until we are all dust."

The Historian spoke again. "We three must return to the citadel of the Greens, to help secure the castle from any demon stragglers and insure the immediate installation of the new Arch Wizard.

According to the Mother's Law of the Greens, this transition of power to a new leader must take place as soon after the predecessor's death as possible. Sunrise must find a New Arch Wizard in command of the Council."

The Guardian, surprisingly, didn't offer his opinion on this turn of events. He moved within touching distance of the Historian and Scribe saying, "Climb onto my back Scribe, while the Historian takes hold of my scruff fur."

A few breaths later, they found themselves transported into the shadowy woods to the left of the great stronghold of Verdant Keep. The battle appeared to be winding down, bodies of creatures lying scattered around the grounds, most in some stage of disintegration.

The Guardian stood still while Mercy slid off his back to stand by the Historian who surveyed the scene of carnage. "It would appear only a small knot of demon-spawn remain," he noted.

"Wait! There's a wizard with them, Will. It's Cochran!" Mercy said excitedly.

The name was barely spoken, when the Guardian launched himself out of the shadowing trees, hurtling directly toward the traitor. He moved in a blur of speed, carrying him headlong into the standing wizard. The Guardian's body mass was twice that of the lanky, Corky Cochran's, but the watching Historian became alarmed when he caught the betraying shimmer of a protective shield.

It was too late to stop the attack.

The enormous wolf barreled into the shield with such force he was thrown backward, landing with a hard thud on his side. He lay still, momentarily stunned by the force of the impact.

The Historian grabbed Mercy's arm as she was about to run to the Guardian's aid. "Wait," he hissed in her ear. "Let the traitor drop his shield, as he'll have to, in order to deal with the Guardian. We'll move around and come at him from both sides. Prepare yourself, Mercy."

The Historian moved off, the Scribe close on his heels. They split up, each looping around the remnant band of demon-spawn and their master.

Mercy whispered a spell to interfere with Cochran's control over the demons, snarling and growling around him. Using an obscure charm, she hoped he couldn't reverse its effect fast enough to regain control of the monsters. Though their numbers were greatly reduced by then, with Cochran's direction and help, they would easily overrun the scattered outliers defending the castle.

Standing among his beasts, the conspirator dropped his shield. He moved confidently toward the huge, wolfish body stretched out to his full five feet on the ground. Using the sharp end of his boot, Cochran rolled it onto its other side, likely wanting to determine its injuries.

A whimper of pain came from the panting, open jaws.

"Oh dear, did you break your back, Guardian? Coming to the Council with that imbecilic Gatekeeper, Maximillian, was only your first error in judgement it would seem. The second, was believing I had no options once I was unmasked to the Council members."

Cochran used his boot again, this time to kick the broken animal hard, in its rump. He smiled at the high whine of distress. "As Sargent at Arms, it was ridiculously easy for me to gather intelligence about the Green

Wizards. I heard every scheme against my master, Calvin Boatwright, better known as the Deceiver. A reputation he enjoys greatly, by the way. He was always very grateful for this information. In fact, since I encountered him, eons ago in my Outlander Scouting days, he's rewarded me with wealth and power beyond my dreams as a mere Wizard of the Green."

Cochran looked around at the restless beasts awaiting his word. "You can feast upon this mangy cur before we attack the last of the Greens." He was turning away from the Guardian, when he realized the horde hadn't moved toward the defenseless victim. He had given them an order and they ignored it. "What's wrong with you scum of the Pit? I command you! Devour this dog where he lies! I don't want to see a tuft of fur left!"

Slowly, the gathered creatures turned to face him like one hideous monster, eyes gleaming with unhinged ferocity, jaws foaming and dripping with thick saliva.

In a commanding voice of the Sargent at Arms he once was, he shouted. "You will devour the beast, NOW!" Within a blink, the demon-spawn fell upon Corky Cochran with hundreds of tearing teeth and ripping claws.

The Scribe could only look on for a moment, the sight was so horrible, his screams, so piercing in their agony.

Chapter 40

The Historian hoped the impulsive Scribe waited for him before attacking the traitor, Corky Cochran. It was said that Mercy McNaughton had an almost encyclopedic knowledge of the spells and wards used by the Wizards of the Green Mother, but he'd never witnessed any magic performed by the pretty Scribe.

He'd moved off a few yards after they split up when he narrowly missed stepping on a creature slithering along the forest floor. He was about to step over a large log, when his keen eyes caught the movement of leaves and grasses beneath him.

Not a reptile of this natural realm, its flat, fan-shaped head was being used like a wide shovel. Pushing into the soft earth, it cut a deep trench, where its body, as thick around as two of his own muscular thighs together, glided noiselessly through the low, dirt walls it created.

The Historian stood perfectly still, watching it slither past until he saw the tail end. Based on the time it took to pass him, he guessed it was at least twenty feet long. He noted that its scaly body appeared swollen in several places.

It has eaten, he thought grimly. After the beast passed, the Historian realized what he was seeing. That was the Fiach Dubh, the Dark Hunter that swallows death. The Historian had never encountered this mythical creature before, known to invade battle fields and sights of carnage and death. He heard tales that the power of the spirits rising in the aftermath of combat was enough to draw this carrion eater from its hole in the In-Between. "Missing in action," was clearly explained in this light.

This means the Gatekeeper is back at his post, he realized, somewhat relieved as he stood silently observing the slow passage of the creature.

The Green Wizards allowed this harvester of the dead entry into the natural realm. It cleansed the earth of the signs of battle and bloodshed. When it was finished, or had its fill, it simply vanished, returning to the glaring numbness of the In-Between until called again by those dying violently in war.

Watching the thick tail slide by, the Historian reflected that this creature would be needed until men and magic no longer existed.

The snake beast finally moved out of sight, the deep trench it left behind, easy to follow. The Historian knew it would lead him to the recently fallen, fearful the Scribe might be among them.

He hung back in the shadows until the soft shifting of dirt finally stopped. Crouched low, inside the cover of the trees, the Historian heard a woman scream, followed by the beginning of a shouted spell.

Before Mercy could finish, the Historian burst from the gloom of the woods.

"Mercy! Let it be! It does the work of the Greens." He quickly took in the scene of the tattered remains of the traitor, Corky Cochran, surrounded by a pile of demon-spawn, a foot deep. He surmised Mercy and the revived Guardian had dispatched the brutes, but wasn't certain how the turncoat met his end.

The Dark Hunter seemed confused by the life it encountered, promptly changing direction, back into the woods.

The Guardian padded over to the Historian. His thick fur was matted with blood, but he seemed unhurt so likely it wasn't his.

"Greetings Historian. You are late to this game, but the little Scribe has done for both of us it seems. I owe her my very existence."

Mercy joined the two saying, "I only did what you would have done, Guardian. I'm just relieved the spell I used was so effective with the demon-spawn."

She explained to them that she altered the creature's response to a kill order, so they'd look upon the traitor as their prey and not the fallen Guardian.

The Historian stepped close to the petite Scribe. "Well done, Mercy. You have saved the Guardian and destroyed an evil at the heart of the Council."

The Scribe bent her head, the heavy braid of red hair barely hiding the blush spreading across her cheeks. She knew he could hear her rapid heartbeat, from the smile on his handsome face.

"We need to find the Protector and her mate to share this news," the Guardian huffed, clearly uncomfortable watching the human's too human interaction.

The Historian knew any feelings he had toward the pretty Scribe would have to wait to be explored. He turned to the Guardian saying, "Yes! They will surely have tracked the Deceiver to his last hiding place. I'll call a Time Thread so we can travel to the In-Between."

"Ah, exactly my own conclusion," the blood-spattered creature responded.

"There exists one small problem, however. I cannot accompany you. I shall return to the Council Chamber and try to bring order to the remaining wizards. By now, the surviving Greens have defeated the remnants of the traitor's army, and they'll be wanting a cohesive mop-up strategy."

Mercy interjected, "A plan for moving beyond the current situation is definitely needed, especially in light of the defection of the Sargent at Arms and the death of the Arch Wizard. But I'll need to stay behind too, Will Farley," she added softly.

"My position as Scribe demands I record all that transpires regarding the Wizards of the Green. I will also help explain the betrayal of Corky Cochran, the death of Sir Alex by his hand and support the Guardian's directives to the remaining wizards."

The Guardian gave a low rumble in his massive chest, approving the Scribe's alliance with him. "I can only retain this current identity for another cycle of heavenly movement in this realm. I must return to my beloved Lochs and my role as Guardian, in the interest of the Green Mother," the Guardian added solemnly.

It was true, each had a separate role to play. The Historian knew his would take him back alone, to the strange environment of the In-Between. He would need to locate the Protector and Jason quickly, or be forced to begin his pursuit of the Deceiver on his own. He felt more than capable of bringing the dark wizard down, but he also knew his foe was devious in the extreme. That thought jogged his memory and he blurted out, "The Dark Hunter!"

"What? You've seen Fiach Dubh, Historian?" the Guardian asked, his golden eyes alive with interest.

"He's here. Or he was here, searching the battlefield for fallen victims. His trail will lead me to the portal he used to enter this realm. I can better calibrate my Time Thread to find the Protector and Jason."

The Scribe moved closer to the Historian.

"May the Mother protect you, Will Farley. Come back to me, to us, quickly."

Even in the shallow light of the moon, Mercy's flush warmed her face. The Historian reached out a broad hand to gently stroke her cheek.

His smile was the last thing she saw when he blinked out of sight.

Chapter 41

Returning to the In-Between via the Time Thread was the easy part for Jason and Cathleen. They landed almost directly across from the Gatekeeper's station, causing the gawky Milly to spring up from his seemingly endless nap time.

"Protector! Jason! I was lying here thinking of ways to capture the Deceiver if he attempts passage through my gate."

"Of course, you were, Milly. Jason and I need immediate entry to the In-Between. I believe the dark wizard has already crossed back from the first realm."

"Oh, there's little chance of that happening, I assure you! I am most vigilant in these perilous days. But why would that scoundrel want to venture there to begin with, when he has a fortress in the fourth realm?"

"I suspect he'll be hiding in that timeless space, biding his time until the search ends with my mortality. So, Milly, think carefully on this question and your next answer. Has the Deceiver been prowling about your post?"

Milly shuffled his narrow, flat feet, raising a small cloud of pinkish dust around his scrawny ankles. "Come to remember it, when my eyes were resting briefly, I may have heard words whispering with the wind. They sounded distinctly like the Old Tongue to me. I don't think that's very helpful, but I believe the words made me fall into a deeper sleep, something I never do when I rest my eyes."

Jason exchanged a look with Cathleen as he came closer to the Gatekeeper. "Milly, the Protector and I will need you to close the gate after we go through."

As if that had been the plan all along, Milly murmured a few words and the mystical gate vanished.

Turning to Jason, Cathleen confided she now knew the words the Gatekeeper used, just in case they needed to get out in a hurry. Jason understood she'd not willingly deprive Milly of his pride in his role as Gatekeeper.

Leaving the chatty Milly behind was something of a relief for the pair as they silently wended their way over the spongy ground. The glaring light created the odd sensation that it permeated the very air they breathed.

"Let's stay close together, Jason. This place is like a beehive remember, and has lots of worm holes for this creep to hide in."

Jason slid the Historian's knife from its sheath. Having used it extensively during his part in the investigation, it was second nature to him by now. When it came into contact with the replica of Sir Alex's signet ring, a laser-thin green bolt shot out, scorching a nearby mound of spongy, pale dirt.

Cathleen's only reaction was a tight smile and a nod of approval.

They walked in silence, covering nearly three miles over the uneven, shifting ground before Cathleen finally held up her hand. A few seconds passed before a loud popping sound alerted them a Time Thread was about to deposit a traveler.

The Historian materialized like a mirage out of the brash light enveloping them.

"Your trajectory here was remarkably correct, Historian," Cathleen said admiring his ability to control such an unpredictable outcome.

"I came as quickly as I could, Protector. I found the Gatekeeper in his cot and confirmed you'd already passed through. I used the Thread to catch up quickly with news and assistance.

The Scribe and Guardian are back at the Green's Council Chambers. They'll be trying to bring command, over the chaos of the battle and to determine the number of casualties. By the time we're finished here, I believe they'll have restored order among the other wizards."

"What happened to the traitor, Historian?" Cathleen asked.

"Corky Cochran is no more. Destroyed by his own demon-spawn when Mercy called down a powerful spell to confuse their loyalty."

"Good. One less to hunt. Let's get going. I think the Deceiver will be even more dangerous, now that we've reached the end game in this drama."

The small party moved at a jog, trying to cover as much of the narrow land of the In-Between as possible. The scenery was hypnotically monotonous in the glaring light, flat and unbroken by any natural vegetation or formation, save the occasional mound of spongy earth. A half-hour later they came to a sudden halt.

Standing side-by-side, they all felt the rolling movement of the whitish ground beneath their feet. Cathleen squatted down, holding her hands over the spot. "This is no earthquake," she muttered to herself, picking up the distinctive markers of magic in play. The ground trembled a second longer, before a deep, droning noise shattered the pensive silence.

They all scanned the area for its source until Jason called out, "There!" pointing to a large swath of shifting ground.

A sand-colored object gradually pushed through the springy ground, several yards away. It rotated slowly, using its triangular shape to move the ground aside like a drill-bit through soft wood.

The three watched intently as the thing rose eight feet, before coming to rest. Sitting there, it was a striking incongruity in the naked environment. The side that eventually came to rest facing them was covered in symbols, obvious mystical cyphers and characters.

In a hushed tone, the Historian told the others these were the personal runes and markings of a Dark Magic user.

While she studied the scene in front of them, Cathleen noticed a slight vibration radiating from the cone at the top, disturbing the air around it.

Slipping into her Inner Eye, she immediately saw a dark, shadowy aura surrounding what she believed was a space-time travel machine. Her next thought was about the identity of the wizard inside.

The Historian stepped closer, speaking softly.

"This is obviously not an object natural to this plane. It clearly is a construct of the Deceiver. I have no clue to its purpose, but I'm certain those are his signature cyphers."

Jason picked up the hushed comment and decided to test a theory he'd been chewing on while he waited for the two wizards to take action.

He held out his hand, sure the knife was in close contact with the gold ring and aimed.

A green shaft shot from the knife tip. When the beam penetrated the vibrating aura, it ate through to the wide base of the pyramid.

Cathleen and the Historian quickly joined Jason's assault. They added their own Green Fire to the attack, pealing away the outer walls like layers of old paint, until they reached the transparent inner shell of the wedge-shaped craft.

Bathed in the green glow from three fiery-shafts, the interior of the pyramid sprang into view. A tall, darkly robed figure was exposed to the attackers. His back was turned away from the three, as he bent over something vaguely familiar to the Historian.

Cathleen signaled they should keep up their bombardment of the magically fortified wall. She had no doubt the figure inside was employing Dark Magic to hold off their own magic. Finally able to peer inside the newly exposed cabin, Cathleen was anxious to interrupt whatever the dark wizard appeared to be conjuring at the moment, before they had to face it. Focusing her mind on powerful invocations, she was startled out of her intense concentration when the Historian drew in a sharp breath.

He finally got a clearer look at the pile of debris the wizard stood over. It was the unique uniform worn by the Outlander Wizard Scout lying at his feet.

"He's captured a Scout!" he hissed between clenched teeth.

"Are you certain?" Cathleen asked

She studied the slumped figure anxiously. There was no need for the Historian to answer.

"Time to negotiate, Cathleen," Jason said turning to her. "This is now a hostage situation. I may be able to get him talking, while you two work your magic."

Cathleen gave a quick nod, knowing this was the only option in light of this new situation. She trusted in Justin's savvy when it came to dealing with the criminal mind. He'd proven his talents far outweighed any lack of magical talents.

The Deceiver now held an Ace up his wide sleeve. A kidnapped Scout, whom he certainly would not hesitate to execute. Negotiating for his freedom would have a cost, but at the moment, Cathleen knew she'd have to pay, or the Scout would pay with his life.

Chapter 42

Jason slid the knife back into the sheath, immediately interrupting the bolt of green power. He turned the heavy gold ring, hiding the large emerald stone inside his palm. Both objects would draw unwanted attention from the Deceiver. He had to at least appear conciliatory in negotiating for the Scout's release.

Cathleen signaled the Historian to cease the assault on what she believed was a capsule used to shift in time, conjured by the Deceiver. A movable environment, where the murderous wizard could hunker down for eons, in the In-Between. He could hide from Justice by simply out-living it!

With the other streams of Green Fire extinguished, the glaring light surrounding them seemed more intense to Jason. Readjusting slowly to the brightness, he moved a few feet closer to the target. He kept his hand on his thigh, hoping he could pull the knife in time if he needed to defend himself with more than words.

The light inside the capsule's cabin was dim, but the occupants were clear enough. *He must sense movement*, Jason thought, watching closely as the dark figure turned slowly in his direction.

The Deceiver's voice was a thousand fingernails on a chalkboard in Jason's ears. Any human tonality had been corrupted by an all-consuming evil, until it became the screech of a Ghoul.

His red eyes looking directly at Jason, he warned any further attack, would mean certain death for the Scout. He sneered, adding he would ensure it would be a particularly gruesome death!

The threat resonated loud and clear from inside the capsule, freezing Jason where he stood. He fought the urge to cover his ears, not wanting to present any weakness to this callous murderer.

Watching and hearing the maniacal Deceiver, it was obvious to him the Deceiver relinquished his humanity for the sake of greater magic. Jason knew this being before him, was only wrapped in a human form, like a mummer in a grotesque play.

As uncomfortable as it was to watch, Cathleen was relieved the fallen wizard was focusing all his attention on Jason for the moment.

Without turning her head, she spoke quietly to the Historian, standing rigidly at her side. "If Jason can't draw him out of there, he'll simply relocate with the time capsule, somewhere else on this plane. Be ready to throw a Binding Spell over the machine."

She didn't want to expose Jason any longer than needed to the sociopath, Calvin Boatright.

They heard Jason's firm voice, feeling the vibration of his words in the bright air around them. "Greetings from Cathleen O'Brien and Will Farley, but you likely know them as the Protector and the Historian. You, Calvin Boatright, known as 'The Liar' and the Deceiver, you now stand in their crosshairs."

The wide forehead furrowed deeply, drawing the heavy brows into a single black line. The nostrils of the Deceiver's long nose flared, making Jason wonder if he would breath out fire with his next breath. Blood-red eyes filled with incredible hate toward him, but Jason suspected they would look the same toward any of the Mother's natural creatures.

"You now have a choice to make, Boatright," Jason said, careful not to call him by anything but his human name. He hoped it was insulting to his sense of being all powerful. This type of egomaniac always enjoyed having a reputation as fierce and powerful. "You can surrender the Outlander Wizard Scout immediately, or face the lethal consequences for his abduction."

Again, a shrieked response from the Deceiver assaulted his ears. Jason felt physically buffeted by the words while he stood quietly and listened.

"If these two have sent you to barter for the release of this insignificant Scout, tell me, who are you and what is your title?" the Deceiver scratched out the words in the stillness around them. He went on speaking to Jason, a sneer dripping from every word. "You are unknown to me and surely, don't sit on the Council of Greens, or I would have been informed."

"Oh yeah. About your spy. He's dead. Discovered and destroyed! Your army of demon-spawn…also obliterated. But you would have known this if you hadn't deserted your Pit scum and run from the battle. You now have two minutes to release the Outlander Wizard Scout."

Jason turned his back to the Deceiver, feeling his red eyes burning holes through his back in sheer loathing.

Cathleen and the Historian stayed in place as Jason nonchalantly stepped between them. Cathleen never took her eyes off the creature inside the capsule. Barely moving her lips, she said, "That went about like I expected. You've softened him up I think."

Jason's mouth twitched with a wry smile.

The Deceiver was still scowling ferociously when he raised an arm over the inert body of his hostage. The Scout began to rise from the floor, though his body was completely limp and drained of color. He hung like a tattered kite from a tree limb.

Jason studied the captured man, wondering if they were already too late to save him. The Scout was maybe thirty-eight or forty. His uniform was covered in blood and badly torn, but there was an obvious insignia on his sleeve.

He heard Cathleen murmur, "Seabhac."

When Jason glanced over with a questioning look, she said, "Hawk Scout. The hostage is a Hawk in the ranks of the Outlanders. Meaning, he's performed many demon-interventions in the Borderlands to earn that high distinction in rank."

The Historian listened to the hushed comments, adding, "His name is Liam Thresher. An old friend, from my own Scouting days."

The Scout was hung in a calculated fashion, so the trio could study the many wounds on his body. Blood oozed from a deep gash in the meaty part of his thigh, spreading in an ever-widening puddle around his dangling feet.

Cathleen counted no less than five other slashes in his uniform, though these were shallow and weren't meant to kill him. These were given during torture, not battle. Her resolve became a granite-hard loathing, directed at the evil sorcerer staring brazenly back at them.

The shrieking voice penetrated her head like a nail being driven in slowly. Cathleen suspected the Deceiver used this trick of sound to cause as much discomfort to his enemies as possible. "This Scout will soon pass into the next life," he was saying. "When I was banished to the fourth plane, my puny mortality dropped away and I gave myself to the undying, Dark Powers. Your magic and threats hold no fear for me."

The Deceiver abruptly dropped his arm, causing the unconscious man to end in a heap of twisted arms and legs. A long moan escaped the Scout's slack mouth in response to the jolt of pain that tore through his wounded body. The Deceiver must have used magic to amplify it for the effect on his audience.

"Enough!" Cathleen shouted, outraged by the mistreatment of the Scout. Before Jason or the Historian could stop her, Cathleen was in front of the transparent wall. She was deeply into the words of her spell, drawing them out in slow, deliberate enunciation. "Sciotan Saighean! Sciotan Saighean! Sciotan Saighean!"

This invocation was dangerous, to both her and the object of her wrath. A wrong inflection placed on a word and she'd be eviscerated on the spot. Learned from her father, Liam, Cathleen knew he only turned to this spell in the most extraordinary of circumstances. It called for the extreme transformation of the sacred Green Fire, altering its natural shape and elements and calling a completely new entity into existence.

The balance had to be weighed carefully in words, since the whole enchantment could just as easily turn upon the wizard using it. She planted herself in front of the transparent wall, so the Deceiver would get the full effect of her casting. Two short columns of Green Fire shot up from Cathleen's upturned palms. She shouted a string of twisted sounding incantations, totally unknown to the Historian, looking on in astonishment.

The flames started spinning, until barely visible as shapes. They began to lengthen, then compress, repeating the process over and over.

The three watchers saw the fire transforming, until it was dense and hardened, like coal into diamonds, over eons of time.

Cathleen kept up her eerie chant, her voice taking on a high, crazed pitch.

The natural, jagged form of the twin flames was altered completely, their shape lost to the relentless pressure her spell exerted upon them.

As Cathleen called out a string of words, interspersed with odd clicking sounds, the thick pillars morphed yet again, into boulder-sized green pods. These floated above her head and would crush her with their weight if she lost control over her casting.

The Deceiver recognized her imminent danger, calling out his own curses to take control of the boulders suspended above her.

Her concentration remained unbroken, even as the Deceiver's screechy voice rose. His fury was nearly incandescent, when he found her magic too powerful for him to disrupt. Cathleen was gratified to see uncertainty take root in the Dark Wizard's fiery eyes. She stared openly at him, a small smile playing across her lips. She was close enough to the sheer wall to see his boney fingers curl into tight fists.

Cathleen knew he'd be trying to decipher the strange combination of sounds and words, to mount a counter-defensive spell. When she was sure of his undivided attention, she moved her hands, letting the huge pods fall to the ground to either side of her.

A burst of light sprang from her empty hands, warming the inert shells with an intense heat. The pods immediately began to quiver, glowing a creamy yellow. Small cracks began to show, moving like worms under the thick, green skins.

The watchers waited, holding their breath as the pods rocked back and forth, like giant jumping beans, jittering with life.

Chapter 43

The Historian was riveted to Cathleen's every gesture, scrutinizing each word of her spell casting. With the exception of a few word-combinations, the incantation was completely unknown to him. He intuited this was a very personalized casting.

Jason was used to hearing words that sounded more like animal calls, or noises that could never pass through a human mouth. But this was foreign, even to him.

He felt the Historian shifting closer, from the slight springiness in the ground nearby.

Still watching Cathleen, the Historian murmured, "Jason, this is new magic she calls into existence. None I have experienced before. Prepare yourself for what might follow."

Without acknowledging he'd heard the warning in the Historian's words, Jason turned the gold ring outward and gently slid the knife from its sheath.

Inside the capsule, the Deceiver drew closer to the transparent wall, staring out at the quivering pods. The glow from Cathleen's hands grew more intense than the brightness of the In-Between. It washed over the shells, a glaring color in the lifeless landscape. The pods shuddered violently. Deeper fractures were beginning to show under Cathleen's potent energy.

From their posts, several feet away, the men heard loud cracking sounds, as one, then the other pod, began to break apart. The two held their breath, waiting to see what monsters Cathleen had conjured with her magic.

Her searing light abruptly stopped, and Cathleen lowered her hands. She knew what would follow and carefully stepped further back, to safely observe.

There was one, strong tremor from inside each shell, before they exploded, the contents pouring out. They came in a flood from each shattered pod. Mandibles clacking aggressively, black, six-foot bodies, sectioned into three parts, moving with the speed of six legs. Each creature displayed a pair of thick wings attached to its mid-section, shinning with the luster of old leather in the light of the In-Between. Their elbow-shaped antennae were in constant movement, as the strange insects appeared to communicate with each other.

Jason was fascinated by the crawling, flying, throng of dark beings. He shot an incredulous look at the Historian. "Soldier ants on steroids?" he asked, never having seen Cathleen conjure these strange beings.

"No, my friend. The Protector has called for the mythical army of Umaih, Lord of the Crypt. It is this massing of creatures that scour the four realms, searching out the buried to clean their bones and rid the worlds of the dead. These belong to the Lord Umaih, as does Fiach Dubh, the snake creature we encountered, as it swallowed the dead around the Council's citadel. I might have guessed the Protector would entreaty this Lord for his aid. He's already made his presence known with his Dark Hunter."

The Historian watched the massing army in amazement for a second before speaking again. "I admire the Protector's courage. She took a great risk seeking help from this entity. We can only wait for her signal to render any assistance at this point."

The men watched as several of the winged creatures began crawling up the three sides of the pyramid jutting out of the ground. The pods continued to disgorge a seemingly endless stream of wasp-waisted dark bodies. These milled about, stepping over one another, or pushed into the throng, covering the time-travel machine in a blanket of undulating, dark bodies. Still others began to encircle the capsule in neat rows, upon rows, of clacking, restless creatures.

Cathleen finally allowed herself a sigh of relief as she observed the movements of the giant, ant-like creatures. She was well aware only Liam O'Brien ever dared to implore the mercurial, Umaih for his assistance. Her father's reputation among the old gods and demi-gods, likely saved her from the tearing jaws of this ravening horde.

The numbers crawling and flying around the capsule swelled by the Nano second, as more and more joined the shifting scene of trisected bodies.

Cathleen was mentally preparing for the appearance of the mythical Umaih, focusing back on the history taught by her father about the elusive Lord of the Crypt.

His army of creatures evolved from the wasp, beside the Mother's natural ant family, one-hundred and forty-million years ago. But this army had no queen. Umaih alone ruled over every facet of its existence, dictating the fate of each of his creatures.

That black mass, now covered all of the triangular time capsule, leaving exposed a portion the size of an oversized porthole, facing Cathleen. She had a clear view of the capsule's two occupants, noting the Scout had managed to shift himself into a slumped, sitting position, obviously trying to distance himself as much as possible from his captor. His bloodied head was turned, resting against the wall of the cabin. He looked exhausted by the effort. His eyes were squeezed shut, likely against the pain he experienced, forcing himself to move.

The Deceiver's focus was entirely on the insect army, swarming over and around his escape vehicle. He took no notice of the injured man. The Scout didn't look like he could do anything to challenge the Deceiver's attempt to leave, but Cathleen was glad to see he showed signs of awareness. She might need him to help himself, when the time came.

A thought, so glaringly obvious, jarred her own consciousness. *Why hasn't the Deceiver just transported himself out of here?* That's when it dawned on her. The army of insects was doing more than covering the capsule. They were smothering it and interfering with the Deceiver's magic.

They're holding the machine back from doing its vanishing act.

She could still hear the drone coming from the machine and feel the strong vibrations under foot, as it sat on the springy ground of the In-Between.

The Deceiver's shrill voice rang out. He was shouting a string of curses on Cathleen and the horde she caused to appear. His face appeared permanently contorted into a mask of pure fury.

Cathleen took several quick steps backward when the pyramid began to buck like a rodeo long-horn after the wizard's last dark spell was called. She had no doubt the former Calvin Boatright, was a powerful wizard. He already used his dark magic to inflict chaos on the Council of Greens, attacking them in their stronghold and leaving death and destruction in his wake.

Cathleen was relieved to see that despite the jarring movements the pyramid was firmly rooted in place. The injured Scout, unfortunately, was being tossed about like a rag doll, leaving a thin trail of blood wherever he landed.

The ant-like creatures clung to the capsule and to each other, without a single one dropping to the teeming army below.

The bucking motion stopped as quickly as it began.

He's working hard to come up with magic to use against Lord Umaih's army, she thought, gratified with her choice of allies.

Cathleen watched the Deceiver's mouth closely. He was murmuring again, raising his arms slowly from his sides. The capsule shuddered violently, as if trying to tear itself loose of an unseen vise. His voice became more and more strident with frustration.

Cathleen heard him use a string of unfamiliar words, only two were familiar.

Cosmic winds! Is he trying to harness the solar winds?

This invocation, reaching into the cosmos to harness a natural power, was only performed by the highest-ranking Green, the Arch Wizard. Even then, he or she only called on such vast powers in cases of extreme demon incursion, to sweep immense evil from the natural realm of men. It would be closely confined to a specific area and closely monitored by other wizards of high-rank.

Cathleen was stunned at the audacity of the Deceiver to invoke such powers.

She turned back to the two men, knowing they'd be riveted to the scene and her actions. They were in mortal danger if the wizard succeeded in this spell.

Before they could react, Cathleen dropped a Dome of Protection over them, securing it with a binding charm. They looked perplexed, but when they saw she was doing the same for herself, that look turned to deep concern.

She felt the air begin to stir around her own Dome, her binding spell giving the slightest quiver. Looking back at the Historian and Jason, she saw they experienced the same change in the air currents.

The solar wind stream was charged with particles released into the upper atmosphere of the sun and filled with kinetic energy. Cathleen had no experience with its ferocity, but on this flat, open plane, it could travel unimpeded, sweeping all before its deadly surge.

The brightness of the landscape gradually dulled, until it appeared they were on the brink of a heavy storm. Another shudder, this one much stronger, brought the beginnings of chaos to the thousands of insects massed around the pyramid. Their ranks were broken as the wind picked up in force, the whooshing sound, turning to a continuous roar.

Within two heartbeats, Cathleen heard the unstoppable power of harnessed solar winds, tearing at the ground. The supple land began forming a swirling vortex, pulling the ant-like beasts into its irresistible gravity.

The winds were clearly being manipulated by the Deceiver's spell as they scoured the area closest to the capsule, moving back into the ranks and scooping up the long bodies by the hundreds.

The Deceiver still shouted his incantations, but now, his words were lost in the fierce clamor of the solar winds and the sound of the brittle black bodies being pulverized in the churning vortex.

Cathleen knew all was lost, if the Deceiver was able to strip the army off the escape module. She didn't dare step out of her Dome, even for a second, knowing she'd be swept away like a mote of dust in a cyclone.

Without turning, she could feel Jason and the Historian were still safe, but the winds were growing increasingly more powerful.

How long will the Domes hold? It's never been tested like this. Her fear grew as she watched the creatures covering the triangular machine, losing to the ever-greater force and being sucked into the churning funnel.

The Deceiver knows I can't act unless I drop my protection. I need the General of this army to show up and quick!

"Umaih, I call to you! Your own servants are being destroyed!" Cathleen's scream was swallowed in the sound of a world being shredded.

The two men watching from their shuddering Dome, crouched lower.

They both jumped to their feet when a powerful blast struck in front of the humming capsule, creating a crater, inches away from the facing wall.

They could see Cathleen hadn't left her Dome. The Deceiver was staring down into the great chasm formed at the foot of his capsule.

The explosion was followed by a gritty, threatening voice.

"You have brought disarray and harm to mine and the Mother's and now you shall pay!"

The winds stopped and all waited for the next scene in this drama to begin.

Chapter 44

Hearing tales of the terrifying, Lord of the Crypt, Cathleen was totally unprepared for the slightly stooped, elderly man, standing outside her Dome. He was no taller than she when not including a mass of wild, steel gray hair, shooting off in every direction.

Wearing an ill-fitted, tweed jacket, over baggy trousers of an undetermined color and a threadbare green turtle-neck sweater, he looked every bit an Emeritus Professor of Philosophy.

This impression was fixed when he leaned closer. He studied her with serious gray eyes, peering out from behind thick, round lenses set in a wire frame.

Not waiting for her to speak, Umaih blinked out of sight, only to reappear inside Cathleen's Dome. "I have chosen to come to you in your father's favorite guise when he called upon my services. I assume you are like-minded, daughter of Liam O'Brien."

Cathleen stammered, "Of...of course! You do me great honor my Lord and I thank you for your timely intervention."

"You misjudge my purpose, child. It is not for you alone I have entered this vast and dreary plane. I am here to make the scoundrel skulking inside the capsule, pay for bringing my army of Cleaners into disarray. I must reclaim those caught up in the fantastic vortex created by the Solar winds. This wizard has distorted the cosmos for his own, nefarious ends. That shall not go unpunished!"

"My companions and I are on a mission as well, my Lord. The Deceiver has brought destruction and death to the Mother's own Council of Green Wizards as you are aware. He now holds an Outlander Wizard Scout hostage, inside the time voyager devised by the Dark one. He will certainly add his murder to that of Bretton Clawson."

"The Claw? The Claw has been taken from the living? I was unaware of this loss. He was an old comrade, encountering me and my army of Cleaners after many a battle. His was a courageous spirit. So, daughter of Liam, what is it you propose?"

"Simply put, my Lord Umaih, I need you to open that capsule so we can extract the Scout and destroy the Deceiver, before he can vanish from this place."

The Lord of the Crypt gave a sharp nod, reaching for Cathleen's hand. Within her next breath, they blinked out of sight, reappearing inside the Deceiver's pyramid.

The Deceiver jumped back from the transparent wall. He'd been closely watching the new developments, momentarily disconcerted by the Protector's disappearance, along with her strange visitor. He let out a little yelp of surprise when the two reappeared three feet from his face.

Quickly recovering his haughty attitude, the Deceiver glared at his uninvited guests. His dead-white lips curled into a sneer, looking down his nose at the unimpressive, tweedy figure next to Cathleen.

The Deceiver leaned in slightly, studying the newcomers. He was so close Cathleen could smell the stench of the Pit on him.

"What is this dwarfish creature? Have you brought him as your champion, Protector?" he smirked.

Cathleen's face was closed. The Lord Umaih still held her hand in his small, dry grip. She took courage from that contact while the Dark Wizard leered down on her.

"No matter. The Solar winds have cleared much of my impediment and I am about to leave this bland realm. I'll deal with you Protector and your insignificant friend, after I deliver the killing blow to the Scout. He's outlived his entertainment value."

He began to turn toward that poor unfortunate, sprawled behind him, his blood dripping away his life force.

The Lord Umaih made no comment to the Deceiver's taunts, but before he could look away, locked onto the evil wizard's eyes, his round glasses glinting like twin suns off a still ocean. He squeezed Cathleen's hand, never taking his steely gaze off the Dark Wizard.

A shock of energy crawled up her arm like a living thing. Her body felt as if it was being flooded with power, moving back and forth between her and the Lord of the Crypt, as if she was plugged into a high voltage line. This was unlike other power sources she'd shared over the years. The lightning hot jolt left her tingling all over, ready to explode into action.

A quick glance at the Scout slumped in a corner of the cabin was enough to slow down Cathleen's thoughts and reactions to her super-charged magic. The air around the Scout's body began to stir. She watched as the shallow rise and fall of his chest created the odd rippling effect. The dying man looked to be immersed in a clear pool of water. His form began to dwindle until the Scout faded like an old photo, then disappeared completely.

The Deceiver, feeling no threat from that quarter and held fast by Lord Umaih's stare, ignored his prisoner, totally missing this vanishing act.

Cathleen, her hand still held in a firm grip by Lord Umaih, shot a glance outside of the capsule. Jason and the Historian crouched inside their Dome, but now they were tending the Scout slumped between them.

She turned her eyes back to her present situation hearing the Lord Umaih speak.

"I am here to collect my army and assist in your destruction, foul wizard."

The Deceiver snorted, "You are a mystery to me little man. Why the Protector has brought you to your death is inconsequential, however. You shall suffer with her, as all the Mother's faithful pets shall."

The capsule rang with another bark of his grating laugh.

The Deceiver looked over his shoulder, ready to make good on his promise to destroy the captured Scout. His head spun on his thin neck, searching the cabin. When he turned back to Cathleen and Lord Umaih, the Deceiver's face was contorted with rage. His eyes glowed a deeper blood-red, colored with the fierceness of a cornered animal.

The wizard instinctively shot a look at the two men in the shimmering Dome of Protection, spotting the Scout lying between them. "You shall suffer in his place! Both of you!" he shrieked. The Deceiver held his arms straight out, the sleeves on the black robe looking like unfolded bat wings.

Cathleen was able to recognize a spell from the antiquity of the Druid's Dark Times. She was searching her memory, trying to identify the key words so she could prepare to answer its power.

For his part, The Lord Umaih appeared totally unimpressed by the incantation, wearing a complacent smile on his face and seeming rather bored with the Deceiver's magical efforts.

This indifference moved the Deceiver to an even higher pitch of fury. He screamed out the incantation, its words bouncing off the surfaces of the capsule like a spray of bullets.

Without turning to him, Cathleen spoke in the Secret Tongue she knew Umaih alone would understand. Pitching her voice for his ears alone, though the Dark One would probably not hear over the sound of his own shouts, she shared her knowledge of the spell.

"He's calling for a demon-spawn to attack the Dome!"

Answering in the same language, Umaih told Cathleen he knew this, adding his own insight. "It will be a Red Dragon Serpent. You must take hold of the horns and twist!"

With that vague advice given, Cathleen suddenly found herself standing outside the Dome of Protection.

Jason jumped up when she materialized. The Historian continued to direct his attention to the Scout's injuries, shooting her a quick glance. His ministrations would be stop-gap measures. She was certain the Scout would need a Healer from the Healing Gardens, if he was to survive.

After giving Jason a quick nod, confirming she was alright, she looked back into the capsule's cabin.

The two occupants were squared off, the Deceiver, towered over the diminutive Lord of the Crypt, Umaih. Cathleen wondered if the Dark Wizard had any idea who stood before him.

Jason's shout broke into her thoughts.

"Cathleen!"

Her wandering attention almost cost her a severe injury, or worse. The Red Dragon Serpent Umaih said she would face slithered close enough to bite off a limb, if she hadn't been quick on her feet.

Cathleen used the springy turf to her advantage, with a powerful leap away from the Dome and toward a low mound created by the Solar Winds. Though this realm had no vegetation, or true environmental features, the spongy material comprising its ground tended to bunch up in places, with any shifts in the bright air.

Grateful to have something at her back, Cathleen studied the demon called to kill her and destroy the Dome and its occupants.

She recalled Lord Umaih's coaching her about grabbing the monster by the horns, "And twist!" she mumbled the key to those instructions.

The Dragon Serpent reared back on a muscular tail. Its front arms were short, but the talons that tipped the front feet, were long and sharp. Though Cathleen knew this was a dumb beast, it was still unsettling to see how closely it scrutinized her. *Its sizing me up,* she thought, doing the same to it.

The cat-like eyes were mustard-yellow, shot-through with red. They were deeply set, over the long snout of its massive head. Above them, two curved horns protruded from the skull. A thin line of grayish smoke leaked from the beast's flaring nostrils.

An alarming thought flashed through Cathleen's mind, *Where there's smoke...*

While the creature supported its bulk with the thick tail, Cathleen noted the underbelly of the beast was covered like the rest of the body, in heavy, iridescent-red scales. She saw no obvious, vulnerable spot anywhere on its armored body.

The horns are my only option, but how do I get that close? Unless...

Jason watched as his wife successfully avoided the creature's jaws and saw-like teeth, standing with her back to the small mound. He knew she was looking for a weakness, but from Jason's vantage, there was none.

He turned to the Historian, still working to staunch the wounds of the Outlander Wizard Scout. "I'll be back."

The Historian looked confused, knowing they were basically locked into the Dome by Cathleen's Binding Spell.

Jason answered his unasked question, using the knife and ring to create a narrow beam of power. He immediately cut enough of a hole at the bottom of the Dome, for his slim body to squirm through. It sealed itself up as soon as he was outside.

Standing behind the Dragon Serpent, he put two fingers into his mouth and gave a shrill whistle. The monster's head swung around, spotting Jason as he slowly stepped away from the Dome. The massive jaws opened in a roar, followed by a blast of fire and the sharp smell of Sulphur. There was an undertone of its last meal of flesh too, shreds hanging in places from its teeth.

Jason barely avoided the fire stream by a scant few feet. He jumped to the left after anticipating the direction of the strike by studying the focus of the unblinking, golden eyes. He felt the searing heat on his face, rapidly blinking away tears from the super-heated air

Cathleen took advantage of Jason's risky diversion. Snagging a gust of wind, she launched herself onto the scaly back.

The creature reared up, reacting to the impact of her landing. She began to slip down the long body, toward the heavy tail. The scales on its back were placed too tightly for her to find a hand-hold.

Diving forward as far as she could reach, one of the monster's horns snagged on her sweatshirt. She was just able to wrap her hand around the top of the stout bone.

Hanging on like a one-handed, rodeo champ, she was tossed and twirled on the back of the demon-beast. Fire and smoke spewed from its mouth, its roars deafening in the close air of combat.

Jason dodged for shelter behind the Dome, knowing he might become collateral damage otherwise.

The beast began to tire from its angry gyrations and slowed down its whirling movement.

Cathleen immediately made a grab for the second horn and with her heart still racing in her chest, murmured a spell for strength. "Roe Neart, my Mother!"

She felt a renewing strength in her arms with her prayer for strength and resolutely clamped her teeth together. Holding the horns tightly, she gave a strong twist, bringing the head of the Dragon Serpent around until it almost faced her. She reared back and with her powers amplified by her invocation, twisted harder still.

The snap was loud and final.

She jumped off the falling beast as it crumpled beneath her.

It was laying on its side when a few bolts of Cathleen's Celtic Fire, erased all traces of the monster from the pale ground.

Jason ran to her, taking her into his arms. "Well done, love!"

"Thanks to your help, sweetie. Let's get the Scout out of danger!"

After dropping her Binding Spell and removing the Dome, she asked the Historian to take the Scout to the Healing Gardens straight away.

"Then return to the Council, Historian. Mercy and the others will need your guidance and help, to begin the recovery process and return to order. There are several injured Council members to see to and the dead to bury."

"And what of both of you and our mission?"

"The Deceiver will never leave this plane alive. I promise you. But there's no time to lose for the Scout!"

Cathleen and Jason watched as the Historian wrapped the injured man in a travel cocoon, hearing the familiar pop when they vanished from the In-Between.

Chapter 45

Cathleen turned her attention back to the capsule, several yards away. She was alarmed to see this unique time machine pulsating, trying to tear itself from the ground. The once transparent wall portal was now almost opaque and she could no longer make-out the occupants.

The hum became so pronounced in the dead atmosphere of the In-Between, she felt it in her teeth. She looked over at Jason, his own jaw clenched in reaction.

"Jason, Lord Umaih must be working to affect the spell the Deceiver's attempting, to make his escape. I need to get back inside the capsule. I'm sending you back to the Council Chambers where…"

"No, you're not! We're doing this together!"

Without another word, Cathleen reached out, linking their arms.

She was almost done with her incantation, when the spongy ground beneath their feet began to quiver. One violent shake knocked them to their hands and knees.

They instinctively turned away from a blinding light erupting around the capsule. The deep drone they were hearing for so long, transformed into the sound of a million bee swarms massing around them.

Cathleen and Jason huddled closer. Their eyes squeezed tightly against the searing glare, while they covered their ears to block the penetrating sound.

As quickly as it began, the light and noise disappeared. They staggered to their feet, desperately trying to regain their battered senses. Turning back to where the pyramid shaped capsule stood, they saw only the emptiness of the In-Between.

"They're gone. The Deceiver and Lord Umaih!" Cathleen cried out.

Her voice was filled with disbelief at the possibility that the Lord of the Crypt had been defeated by such a nemesis.

"It doesn't make sense, Cathleen. How could the Deceiver get the best of Lord Umaih?"

As if in answer to his question, the bleak air of the In-Between began filling with a chittering sound, growing louder and louder until it smothered the two with its weight.

The ant-like Cleaners from Lord Umaih's army suddenly appeared, suspended in the pale sky. Their numbers cast deep shadows, darkening the area around the two humans until it appeared like the darkest hours of night.

Cathleen pulled Jason closer to shout into his ear.

"These are the same creatures sucked into the vacuum created by the Solar Winds. When the Deceiver lost control of the vortex, it likely freed them, returning them to this plane."

While Cathleen and Jason watched from within the shadowy gloom, the giant-insects began dropping to the ground like a torrent of black leaves. They were in a frenzy of movement, crawling over one another and clustering together.

Jason took hold of Cathleen's arm and without warning, dragged her to the ground. She knew they were far enough away from the Cleaners to be safe from them and was taken off guard.

Then Jason shouted, "In-coming at three o'clock!"

Cathleen cut a glance to her right, barely catching a blur of movement as three spheres of blood-red fire balls streaked across the sky, bursting among the tightly packed Cleaners.

The chaos was immediate and catastrophic. The surviving creatures scuttled off in every direction, trampling to dust, the body parts of destroyed insects.

Cathleen hastily threw a Dome over herself and Jason, not wanting to risk being crushed or attacked, in the ensuing confusion. She suspected the Deceiver was attacking, as retaliation for being forced to remain in the In-Between by the Lord of the Crypt. She didn't have any idea where Lord Umaih had gotten to.

Huddled inside their Dome, they watched the destruction as more fireballs raced across the pale sky, before landing erratically within the surging mass of creatures.

"They have no leader without Lord Umaih!" Cathleen shouted.

"They're at the mercy of the Deceiver's fire. He's trying to bury them here, in the In-Between. He could raise them for his own use later! I have to stop that from happening."

Cathleen knew he wouldn't argue, but his apprehension was written clearly on his face. She reached over and touched his cheek where an eye patch covered the empty socket, before slipping out of the Dome.

The beasts had begun to move toward the deep chasm created by Lord Umaih. Cathleen saw there was a pattern to the volley after all. The fireballs were being lobed in a pattern that was forcing the shattered army to shift closer and closer to the edge of the huge cleft in the spongy earth.

Is the Lord of the Crypt destroyed? Cathleen thought frantically.

Holding up her hands and drawing several of the mangled bodies to herself, she used them to camouflage her presence. Hidden, among the dead and dying of the giant insects, she was eventually caught up in the surge moving inexorably toward the crater.

Another sound began to filter through the clacking of mandibles and shrill chirping all around her. Cathleen heard the distinctive, croaky voice of Lord Umaih. "Your escape capsule is destroyed and you are unable to leave this endless realm, Deceiver!"

Her relief was short lived when the Deceiver shouted over the rest of Lord Umaih's threats. "As your army falls, so shall you, Lord of Insects!"

Careful to remain concealed, Cathleen worked her way toward the sound of the voices.

She distinctly picked-up words in the Old Tongue. Not knowing the magic used by the old Lord, she figured he was calling to his remaining Cleaners.

If he can't control them, they'll all end up buried here, she thought.

As if on cue, Cathleen heard the ominous scratching of brittle bodies, being shoved over the precipice by those scrambling behind them.

Holding tightly to the dead Cleaner's body, she managed to weave her way deeper into the middle of the frenzied creatures. Cathleen pushed herself up on the Cleaner's back. Standing among the great throng, the sounds of the fallen being crumpled in the bedlam, completely drowned out the voice of Lord Umaih.

While she watched the scene with growing concern, a shadow blotted out a patch of the ever-present glare. Cathleen looked up. A thick cloud of greenish vapor hung above the confusion of black bodies. It began to spread like a stain across the featureless sky, before dropping down upon the mass of seething bodies.

All movement abruptly ceased. The army of Cleaners froze in place, a ceased-up engine, dead, yet alive. An eerie silence replaced the uproar of a moment earlier, only to be shattered by the Deceiver's scream of outrage. His plan to bury the army of Cleaners had been neatly thwarted by the Lord of the Crypt, who managed to save most of his scavenger army from annihilation.

Cathleen was the only being stirring in a sea of rigid creatures. She inched ahead, climbing over rigid bodies. She used the shouted curses and bursts of fire hurled between the Dark Wizard and Lord Umaih, as cover for her movements.

She needed to see! She climbed onto the back of one of the Cleaners. Laying herself flat against its shiny back, she whispered a few words, raising her odd mount slightly, above the blanket of immobile bodies. Scanning the area, she eventually spotted the Deceiver.

He floated above the chasm, standing on an airstream. He must have been enjoying the sight of the panic-stricken Cleaners, as they fell into the abyss. His colorless face had turned crimson with fury, at the meek-looking Umaih's minor victory.

Cathleen needed a way to communicate her presence to Lord Umaih. Searching from her slightly elevated position, she finally spotted the diminutive Lord.

She watched as the green vapor cloud, continued to waft over the Cleaners, stupefying any still moving. Umaih strangely resembled a charming fountain nymph, with the green mist gushing from his round mouth.

The Deceiver, obviously unaffected by the green mist, kept hurling fiery bolts at the small Lord. Umaih was unhurt, standing behind a low shield, created by hardening a mound of spongy earth.

Cathleen was floating her ant-creature over the tops of the other Cleaners when one of its legs snagged in an open mandible. There was a loud snapping sound when it broke off.

The Lord of the Crypt clamped his mouth shut, jerking his head in the direction of the noise. Unfortunately, this tipped off the Deceiver to her skulking about. He quickly followed suit, facing out over the silent, black field. He finally found Cathleen, huddled among the silent army.

The Deceiver shouted, his voice grating like steel wool against her ultra-sensitive ears. "If you have come to aid this wretch, you have saved me the task of hunting you down, Protector!"

Cathleen crouched lower, clinging to her mount. She whispered a charm learned as a child, to make her father's fishing hole more fun.

A ripple was immediately set free, running through the inanimate Cleaner bodies, several feet from her hiding place. This was followed by a second, stronger wave, undulating the mass of bodies like boats on top of strong sea swells.

Cathleen spread the rippling movement until the Deceiver screamed out in frustration.

"You won't escape my wrath, Protector! You insult me with your child's play!"

The Lord Umaih interjected, "Child's play that has caused you to lose her none-the less," he chuckled loudly.

The Deceiver turned his rage on the tweedy little man.

He floated back to the ground, planting himself to stand on the back of one of the giant ant creatures. He began chanting in the strange language again, but this time Cathleen recognized a few of the words.

Good Mother! He's calling on something from the Tome of Diabolic Enchantments!

Cathleen knew from years as her father's Apprentice, this book of spells and incantations was condemned by the Council of Greens, after its discovery eons ago. No Wizard of the Green was permitted to invoke the evils resulting from these dread curses.

Cathleen wasn't sure if he was calling a demon-spawn or creating something even more deadly to hunt her down. She guessed she wouldn't have long to wait.

She shot a look at the alarmingly quiet, Lord of the Crypt. He appeared unperturbed by the prospect of her facing something conjured from the notorious book.

As the last word of the Deceiver's summons was screeched into the heavy air, a subtle stirring could be seen among Lord Umaih's army. The spongy ground beneath their great weight shuddered, followed by a terrible roar as the quaking terrain rose upward. The frozen creatures dropped to the sides of a slowly rising, ash-colored mountain, creating thick clusters of black bodies surrounding it.

Cathleen looked at Lord Umaih, trying to gauge his reaction. He appeared calm, intently watching the pale earth being ripped open.

She knew the Lord of the Crypt would not be idle during her battle with this new threat. He needed to regain full control of his army and would not stand by without aiding his ally in this effort.

Cathleen's attention was drawn back to the immediate danger. Her Inner Eye was translating the full scope of what she was actually seeing.

The mountain developed into a broad, hunched back, with patches of grayish skin showing through clumps of bristling, soot-colored hair. It plowed through the earth, revealing the massive arms of the monster that answered the call of the Diabolic Enchantments.

Cathleen saw its knobby gray head, hairless and hanging down, almost shyly, on a massive chest. The face was hidden in the shadowing from its jutting forehead. Cathleen had no doubt the Deceiver had summoned a formidable beast to do battle with her.

As if reading her mind, the Dark Wizard called out to her. "This is an old acquaintance of yours, I believe. But you will not find him so friendly now, Protector! I have called him from his home in the Chameleon Woods. My powers have a long reach as you shall experience firsthand."

Cathleen had to admit, there was something unsettlingly familiar about this giant. He finally stopped rising, though she knew already he'd be enormous. She didn't want to engage in a pitched fight until she satisfied her need for information. The Deceiver would no doubt be using his powers to enhance the warrior he'd chosen to destroy her.

The giant stepped onto the pale ground, his movement causing a tremor that rattled Cathleen's teeth. *Guess this is it* Cathleen thought grimly.

The monster finally lifted his face, looking around. When he squarely faced her direction, Cathleen was as stiff with the tension as the frozen creatures around her.

She took a long look at the giant's impassive face and blurted out, "Dunny!"

Chapter 46

The enormous creature she called to could have been carved from the granite of Mount Rushmore. His deep-set black eyes focused on Cathleen, but there was not a glimmer of recognition in the empty gaze.

At first, Cathleen felt relief, thinking the Deceiver had unwittingly called the friendly Rock Goblin, Dunny, from the Chameleon Woods. That feeling faded as he continued to give her the cold, blank stare of a killer.

Cathleen was faced with a difficult conundrum. She had to do battle with the simple, non-threatening creature and she had to win. Any feelings of compassion toward Dunny would have to die with him.

The Deceiver called out to her, "Ah! You do remember the helpful Rock Goblin! I have made a few alterations in his disposition, however. The spells I've used will be unfamiliar, even to you, Protector. While you found him so agreeable earlier, I believe his disposition is not quite so…sunny…shall we say?"

Cathleen guessed the Deceiver used a signal word to rouse the altered Dunny into attack mode.   He suddenly burst into action, his thickly muscled legs carrying him to within reach of her tense body. She felt the breeze from his huge hand as it passed over near her shoulder. She bent backward at the waist to avoid a sweeping arm as he tried to scoop her up from the ground.

Unphased by his near miss, the Rock Goblin made another grab, moving incredibly fast for his lumbering size. When she threw her body to the side, trying to roll away from him, Cathleen's attacker snatched a foot as it flew past his massive body.

The blood rushed to her head, while she hung by one foot. The giant deftly caught her other foot and held her like a newly plucked chicken.

"Dunny! Let me go. I don't want to hurt you!" she screamed.

His response was a violent shake that left her rattled and dizzy.

The giant turned on his wide feet and began stomping heavily toward his new master. He intended to deliver her as ordered.

The Deceiver stood behind his own shield, using several of the fallen Cleaners. Their hard bodies effectively took the brunt of any damage from the lightning hurled by Lord Umaih.

Swinging under the giant's arm, Cathleen could see the two magic users had come to a stand-off. In her current inverted position, she realized she'd be the pawn in the game between two kings.

She didn't believe the Lord of the Crypt would put her life in danger, but neither would he act to save her if it meant sacrificing his army.

She thought glumly in the glare of reality, *I'm just another wizard to the great Lord Umaih!*

She screamed again, telling the slow-moving giant that she was his friend, tossing in Jason's name in hopes he'd recollect his kindness toward him earlier.

Dunny came to an abrupt stop. Cathleen felt very woozy, her head spinning like a weather vane in high wind. The Rock Goblin raised his arm, bringing her close to his lumpy face.

She was sure the beady eyes held a spark of a rudimentary thought as he studied her. His bushy eyebrows knitted together, under the deep frown of his protruding forehead. She wasn't certain if he remembered her or was seeing a rabbit he'd snared for supper.

Cathleen took this opportunity to get through his rock-hard head that she was not the enemy. A successful appeal was her only hope of avoiding being taken captive by the Deceiver. The memory of the Eye of Despair flashed a vivid feeling of utter hopelessness through her entire being. She knew this was a residual effect of her experience.

"Never again," she murmured to herself to boost her resolve.

Using a spell to give her voice a calming effect, she returned the Rock Goblin's frank gaze as best she could, while hanging like a rag doll from his big hand while he studied her.

"Dunny, it's me, Cathleen, the Protector."

She thought she saw a glimmer of recognition in the flat eyes.

"Dunny, the Deceiver took you from your home in the Chameleon Woods. You shouldn't be here. I can send you back before it's too late, but you must put me down."

The gray arm began to slowly come down.

Cathleen began to call a Time Thread before she hit the spongy ground, wanting to transport the giant back to the forest that was his home.

An angry cry shattered her concentration. She heard the Deceiver shouting his own spell in the odd language. Regrouping her thoughts, she finished her charm and grabbing the vibrating Thread from the air, spun her hand to wrap it securely around the giant's body.

"This will carry you home, friend! Just close your eyes and when you open them again, you'll be in your woods."

Like a small child, the Rock Goblin obediently shut his eyes. Cathleen heard him speak three words before he blinked out of sight.

"Dunny goes home."

Cathleen knew the next threat she faced wouldn't be as easily swayed as the Rock Goblin. Luckily for her, the Deceiver underestimated her power to influence the stone giant. She suspected the condemned Tome of Diabolic Enchantments needed a wizard of more extraordinary talents the Deceiver possessed.

His vanity will be his downfall she thought with conviction.

She watched the Dark Wizard raise his arms above his head, jagged bolts of red fanned out, shooting from his fingertips. The pale dome of the In-Between was being scorched by the red spikes. Long, strafing lines, now marred the blank sky like the contrails of passing jets.

Materializing out of the glare, a Dragon Snake, the size of a city bus, hung directly over the Deceiver's head. Cathleen didn't have to understand the strange language he spoke to the beast to know, this was her new opponent.

She was calling a Dome of Protection, but found her magic faltering as it had before in this realm. She felt like the air itself, was drawing off her power, dissipating it until it weakened all together.

The Dome was only partially in place, when the Dragon Snake came for her.

It folded its wings tightly along the sides of its body, going into the deep stoop like a hunting raptor.

Cathleen looked for the horns on this beast, but found it was as armored as a tank instead. She'd need a different tactic to defeat the oncoming demon-spawn.

Seconds before it hit the unfinished Dome, it made a graceful half-turn in mid-air and using its thick tail, swept Cathleen out from under her partial shield.

Cathleen found herself snatched-up in the horny talons of the creature, stunned by its efficiency in catching her. The long tail whipped through the air like a boat's rudder, steering them toward the Deceiver's battle station a quarter-mile away.

The Dragon pumped its short wings hard, trying to gain altitude while carrying a new burden. As it struggled to gain airflow under itself, a thin beam of green light shot into its underbelly. The smell of its burnt flesh drifted down to Cathleen, where she hung beneath the beast's only vulnerable spot.

Seeing the green shaft, she knew Jason was out of his Dome of Protection and was using the gold ring and knife, to produce the bolts. The beast was struck again, but this time the thin shaft was aimed higher, scorching the Dragon's bony eye ridge. There was a horrific scream from the creature when the hot ray pierced the golden cat-eye and burned its way through, exiting from the back of its anvil-shaped head.

Before it could plummet back to earth, landing on top of her, Cathleen jumped clear as the talons contracted in death. Jason was at her side, helping her to her feet an instant before the large Dragon Snake smashed into the springing ground, bouncing several times, before coming to rest.

Cathleen and Jason were panting from the adrenaline rushing through them. He slipped his arm around her waist, letting her lean on him for a moment, while they watched the great beast fade back into the nothingness it came from.

Across the field of frozen Cleaner bodies, they heard the unmistakable screech of the Deceiver. They knew he would never stop his attacks on the Protector until she and her mate were annihilated.

Chapter 47

"No time to lose, Jason. We need to end this now with the Deceiver! I'm needed back at Verdant Keep." She grabbed hold of his hand and pulling him closer, began a chant.

Jason heard this one used just recently by the Historian. Cathleen was calling for the creation of a clone. He was expecting the Protector look-alike, but was totally unprepared for another and then another.

They all had the vacant look in their eyes of such creations. Cathleen was betting, however, that none of them would get close enough to the Deceiver for him to identify the counterfeit ones.

The three clones stood in an orderly row in front of them.

Cathleen looked back at her husband. "You'll always know which one is me, but whatever you see happening, don't try to intervene. It would only expose my identity to the Deceiver. He's watching closely, so I have to mix things up a bit."

He gave a curt nod and she joined her three clones. She smiled over at him and at an unheard signal, the four linked hands.

Cathleen and her replicas began moving in a slow circle, gradually speeding up until they became a streak of color in the air churning around them.

Abruptly stopping, they turned as one and began moving toward the Deceiver's barricade. While they climbed over mounds of hard-shelled bodies, Cathleen kept a keen watch on the pale sky, anticipating an attack at any moment. Her hunch proved accurate. A shape began to materialize above the Deceiver's position.

She and the clones kept moving, using the hard bodies as shields as much as possible, closing the distance between them and whatever lay ahead.

Cathleen programmed her clones to mimic her movements exactly, so she wouldn't be too obvious in her difference. She felt the Deceiver's keen eyes roaming over each of the copies. He lingered for a second longer when he studied her. Even at a distance, his power had a physical effect on her and she shuddered.

The shape, hanging like a tattered bedsheet above the Deceiver's head, was becoming more defined by the second. Cathleen signaled the others to stop. Mirroring her every gesture, they all waited to see what evil would answer this summons. Cathleen knew Milly, the Gatekeeper was determined not to allow anything from the Dark Pit, entry to the In-Between.

That's exactly why the Deceiver would call upon a truly ancient evil to destroy her. This would be a creature from a time before the Green Mother released Magic to Her followers. Its Dark powers would have formed and come into being, along with the four realms.

Guttural sounds floated over the silent grounds to where Cathleen stood waiting. They grew louder as the vague mass, now hovering in front of the Deceiver, grew more defined taking on a silvery sheen even at this distance from her.

Cathleen noted a clear distortion in the air around the growing form, as if this being was sucking the currents into itself. *Is the air itself being used to infuse this creature with life?* Cathleen felt a pull on the pale breeze that blew around her, answering her question. She tried to follow the Deceiver's bizarre, relentless chanting.

The demon he summoned came more and more into the present. A sudden wind blew up around him. His robes swirled around his legs, while his lank, black hair was pulled back, exposing the dead-white of his lean face and scrawny neck. When the wind settled, the creature was fully formed. Its silvery body stood in front of the Deceiver's blinking eyes.

Cathleen studied this new adversary intently, searching for characteristics she might recognize as weaknesses, for the inevitable battle to come.

The creature stood rigidly on two beefy legs. It was at least seven feet tall, judging from how it towered over the tall Deceiver. The brawny body was covered in fish-like scales. From her vantage point, Cathleen counted four claw-tipped appendages extending from its hands. An extremely long neck, thick with muscle, carried the weight of a huge head.

The odd shape of the skull caught Cathleen's attention. It had a pinched look, as if extruded through a narrow pipe, making the lengthy, toothy jaws similar to the maw of a Nile crocodile.

The creature continuously whipped a thin, spike-studded tail behind itself, reminding her of a cat ready to pounce. *That thing could cause some real damage,* she thought watching the tail tear up the earth with each aggressive sweep.

More than this creature's physical features, Cathleen was concerned with a vibe she was picking up from it. That tingle in her senses was far more disconcerting than the formidable weaponry it would use against her.

After a minute of observation with her Inner Eye, Cathleen determined this was no dumb beast. This beast once walked the earth as human. She watched closely as it began a careful scan of its surroundings, ignoring the Deceiver's presence completely.

A thin membrane covering black, reptilian-shaped eyes, slid back into the lower lids, while it calmly considered the frozen Cleaners covering the ground.

Cathleen believed there was a keen intelligence shining out of those tainted eyes. She watched its measured scrutiny of its surroundings and knew she was right.

Cathleen felt the breath of evil roil under the glossy hide. She knew it was ready to destroy and would relish the opportunity.

While it stood near the Deceiver, it wasn't lost on her that the creature he called, maintained an aloof distance from him.

Who's calling the shots here she thought with renewed concern. This monster is not going to follow any cease and desist orders, that's for sure!

"Arrakta, I welcome you, oh great and fierce Lord."

The beast spun toward the simpering wizard.

Cathleen noted the splayed feet were three-toed, with curved spikes protruding from the heels, just like the lethal-looking tail. *Dear Mother! Even its feet are weaponized!*

A deep baritone voice erupted from the beast, startling the Deceiver who unconsciously shuffled back a foot. Arrakta leaned in, roaring into the Deceiver's face. "This is a field of dead Cleaners before me. I have no interest in the dead bugs of the Lord Umaih!"

The monster's voice was more of a hiss, each word seemed to drip with venom.

"If it pleases you, mighty Lord, his army is not dead, but frozen. More importantly, your enemy, the Lord Umaih, has allied himself with the Protector of the Green Mother." The Deceiver was nearly breathless when he finished his rapid explanation, but Cathleen could tell Arrakta's interest was piqued. A wicked gleam flashed from its obsidian eyes.

The long head turned back to the rigid bodies. As if showing off his powers, a stream of clear liquid shot out from the open jaws. Upon contact, this burned through the carapace of the nearest frozen soldier, leaving a hole in the body and penetrating the three bodies under it. It took a scant few seconds before the four Cleaners dissolved into a black puddle.

He can liquify the whole army of Cleaners, Cathleen thought with growing alarm.

"Where is the insignificant Protector of the Green, wizard?"

The Deceiver unconsciously shifted back another foot, before stammering his reply. "I'm not certain my Lord, which of the four clinging to the bodies of the Cleaners is the true Protector and which, mere clones. A cheap trick of the wretched Protector, my Lord," he added, weakly excusing his ignorance. Trying to deflect any anger, he quickly added, "The Lord Umaih is close by, however, and surely aware that you answered my call."

"Silence, wizard!" Arrakta roared.

A few drops of venomous spittle flying from his elongated mouth, hit the ground near the Deceiver's foot. The acid ate small, deep holes into the spongy earth, causing the Deceiver to shuffle side-ways like a crab.

The Deceiver might be regretting his choice of demons about now. Got to make my move soon, before this creep can do more damage to Umaih's army.

Using her mental link to the clones, Cathleen decided to test Arrakta's response to a challenge.

She had three chances to formulate an attack plan that could destroy the monster before she had to expose herself to his wrath.

Her first impression, that this demon felt human-like, still nettled her.

This could be an ancient wizard from before the Dark Times, when evil strode freely and unchallenged, across the first plane. The lore of the Green Wizards recounted many tales of human Magic Users succumbing to the temptation of unlimited powers offered by the Old Gods and Demons that always were and always would be.

The Green Mother, awakened from her deep slumber in the heart of the Healing Gardens, responded to the terror being inflicted on the natural realm. She released the Magic of the Green Wizards and together, they beat-back the dark forces.

Cathleen believed this creature was summoned using the archaic language of the Dark Magic Users from that time. It would be far more powerful than the cringing Deceiver, watching it fearfully now, from a safer distance.

Cathleen sent a signal through her link to the clones, pleased with the quick reaction to her command.

The one nearest her left, advanced toward the imposing monster. She moved out slowly at first, gaining speed until she was a blur of motion.

The beast turned his body to face her fully.

Cathleen saw his mouth beginning to drool, droplets of venom hissing on the ground around him. The deep voice boomed out clearly over the field of hard-shelled bodies. "Ah, yes! The Protector's first clone approaches."

"Uh, oh," Cathleen murmured.

Chapter 48

She wasn't sure how the beast, busy twisting the head off one of her clones, had identified her so quickly. It was like he had the Inner Eye. *Dear Mother! If he has that gift, he was once one of ours. One of the original Greens and among the Mother's most gifted!*

Her thoughts tumbled around in turmoil. She struggled to concentrate, distracted by the crunching of her clones' body as the creature methodically destroyed her. The slow and deliberate movements of the monster displayed a frightening detachment on its part.

Watching, transfixed, Cathleen couldn't imagine one of the founding Green Wizards being so consumed with evil, that he was literally transformed into the being she now faced.

She struggled to quell a rising apprehension at facing such an opponent. If this being possessed the Inner Eye, it likely already scoped out her position. As if verifying her suspicions, she watched as the monster turned its long head slowly, until it stopped directly across from where she stood among the Cleaners.

He threw aside what was left of her clone, narrowly missing the cringing Deceiver. Catching sight of the Deceiver's worried look, the great beast stepped closer as if to taunt the frightened wizard.

"You disgust me, wizard. How did you come to call one such as I, being the cringing weakling I behold standing here?"

The Deceiver answered in a whiney voice. "My Lord, I found the summoning spells on parchments, secreted away inside the Green's citadel, when I was still one of them. I planted a spy among the Council members after I learned they planned my punishment. I ordered him to bring it from my hiding place after I was banished here by those fools."

Even to Cathleen's ears, this explanation sounded like a boast of his own powers to this maniacal Dark Lord.

Arrakta shot out a clawed hand, snagging the Deceiver by his robes. "Do not presume to preen your ego in my presence, wizard. You are nothing to me," his words hissed between rows of teeth.

The Deceiver gave an awkward bow, hanging a foot off the ground. He was mumbling some sort of wordy homage to the beast that the great Lord Arrakta, ignored.

He dropped the Deceiver like a sack of stones and dismissively turned away. He was looking back in Cathleen's direction

She felt his dark eyes on her. No doubt remained in her mind he had picked her out from her clones for his personal attention. While she frantically reviewed her magical options, she wasn't prepared for the creatures next move.

Its deep voice rolled like a thunderclap across the field of black bodies. "While you have little to fear at this point, Protector, the same cannot be said for the human you left unprotected behind you. A misjudgment that he shall pay for!"

In the heat of the moment Cathleen hadn't moved Jason far enough away to keep him safe, when all this began. Her glaring misjudgment might cost him his life. She had to distract the beast from attacking Jason, barely visible across the wide field of frozen Cleaners. "Arrakta, as an apprentice, I was taught the Old Ones were powerful but their newly acquired Magic was won at the cost of their humanity. Have you ever seen yourself as you truly evolved?"

Cathleen pointed to the creature. Suddenly, a wide, full-length mirror hung suspended before the vainglorious beast.

A low snarl, building to the roar of a mighty wave, flooded the silent grounds. The sound was like a physical presence, as it washed over Cathleen's senses. Her hair stood on end as if Arrakta had reached out and touched her body with his unholy clawed hands.

His rage was followed by the sound of breaking glass, when a long stream of the caustic venom shot from the narrow jaws of the monster.

The smell of corrupting bodies was so overpowering Cathleen shut down that keen sense, until the stink was dissipated by the restless winds of the In-Between.

Arrakta easily reached a row of twelve soldiers with his vile sputum. The bodies liquified into a single pool and every Cleaner close enough to fall in, was devoured by the same deadly fluids.

Cathleen was getting ready to try a Net of Nettles on the beast, when a high screeching sound, vibrated the liquified pond of Cleaner remains.

She'd all but forgotten the petite Lord Umaih, turning in time to see him waving his arms above his head. His curses in the Old Tongue fairly sizzled in the air.

The Deceiver was in the direct path of the oncoming Lord of the Crypt. He moved closer to Arrakta, drawing back from the approaching Umaih as he came steadily toward them. He was shouting out his spell with an energy that belied his small stature and prim looks. Fire was shooting from his fingertips, glinting off his round glasses while he moved like a small engine.

Cathleen thought he wouldn't stop until he was on top of the beast and the cowering Deceiver. As quickly as the air erupted with his loud spell casting, Umaih halted his charge, still several feet from the pair. Slowly, he turned to look out over his unmoving Cleaners, a tight smile on his mouth.

Cathleen studied the creatures, watching as bent antennae began to quiver. They were beginning to communicate with each other. They stirred as a single being, moving like a vast, dark ocean, rising up, higher and higher, flowing forward in a solid wall of living destruction.

Cathleen sent a mental alert to her two remaining clones. They all fought to get a hand-hold on the Cleaners they suddenly had to ride. She took a second to link with the two, ordering them to hang on tightly.

We'll be OK, just don't let go!

The Deceiver shook off his abject fear long enough to call up a Time Thread. The humming sound barely filtered through the scratching sound of hard bodies rubbing against one another.

Just as he went to grab the Thread and escape the threat, a long arm snatched him from behind. The Thread vanished immediately as the Deceiver found himself staring at the opening jaws of Arrakta. "You called me to your defense, yet have little faith in my abilities, Deceiver. Liars and turncoats all meet the same end and you are doubling deserving of yours!" The great maw opened wide and the Deceiver's head disappeared into the dark hole.

Cathleen heard screams as the teeth slowly ground back and forth, a sawing motion that prolonged a grisly death. Engrossed in his punishment of the Deceiver for trifling with his powers, Arrakta appeared to have forgotten the oncoming flood of Cleaners. Cathleen was wondering how such a vast threat could be overlooked when the beast tossed what was left of the Deceiver's gnawed body aside, turning his full attention to the incoming surge.

By then, Cathleen and her two clones were each securely riding a black mount, straddling their mid-sections like horses. The powerful movement of the bodies propelled her to the top of the wave, her two clones just slightly ahead of her.

Cathleen needed to get Lord Umaih's attention before they all came crashing down on the monster. The fact that Arrakta seemed unphased by the approaching deluge, was making her very nervous.

Using magic to pitch her voice to find Umaih's ears alone, Cathleen asked him to take his army into the great chasm he created earlier.

"This is no common demon, Lord Umaih. I know it was once human and I believe it was among the first Wizards of the Green. Your army of Cleaners is no match for his powers and will be destroyed unless you can hide them from the beast. I will fight at your side to defeat this monster, but you need to act now!"

Lord Umaih made no reply, but Cathleen felt the moving wave change direction toward the deep depression in the earth where the Deceiver had hoped to bury the Cleaners. Oddly, that would prove to be their salvation.

Cathleen hurriedly drew the clones back to herself. The three were carried on a gust of wind to join the Lord of the Crypt where he stood. His small, age-spotted hands were directing the vast army of Cleaners toward the rift like a Maestro at his podium. With the last row of Cleaners into the chasm, he sealed it with a ward against entry by any but himself. Shifting his eyes over to Cathleen and her two clones, he said, "That will hold them safe until I release them."

Cathleen was anxious to safeguard Jason as well against the beast. It had half-devoured the Deceiver, before tossing him away like a fish bone. Cathleen was certain there wasn't a scrap of humanity left in the hideous creature. She had to get back to her husband before Arrakta fixed its attention on his presence once more.

Jason still had the gold signet ring of the Arch Wizard and the Historian's knife, but she doubted their power against such a towering evil as he'd be facing. "Lord Umaih, I must secure the safety of my companion."

"Yes. I see him off in the distance. I will keep this one busy until you can lend assistance."

Cathleen used a Wind Charm and she and the two clones streaked across the creamy sky, landing near her anxious-looking husband. They fell into a tight, but brief embrace, both understanding the threat hanging over them.

"Jason, I need to get you somewhere safe. I want to send you back to the Green's Chambers on a Time Thread. You'll be safe with the Historian and the others."

"Not going to happen, love! I've been watching this guy you're up against and even from here, I can tell he's got you out gunned."

"I've got Umaih with me and he's…"

"He's one little man with magic, but if I'm with you, there'll be one more. This ring has more than proven I can wield some power using it. I'm going back with you and we're going to kick some monster butt!"

Cathleen knew when she'd lost an argument with her husband and the thought of him using his new-found powers, fighting beside her, was something of a rush.

"OK, Sheriff. But stay close and no rodeo tactics!"

Chapter 49

Leaving the two clones where they stood, Cathleen used the Wind Charm to land herself and Jason near the Lord of the Crypt. He was busy casting another spell and took no notice that Jason accompanied the Protector.

The two humans watched as tongues of Green Fire flickered in his small hands.

He mumbled another charm over their swaying dance and the flames rose up and locked together, creating a solid pillar of green. Lord Umaih spoke again, this time Cathleen clearly understanding what he called forth.

The fiery column shifted and spun. Umaih, his hands still raised and open, shouted a single ancient word. "Amhailt!"

A howling erupted from the spinning tower of flame. An arm shot out of the whirling mass, followed quickly by the phantom Umaih conjured from the fires. This presence was from a dark place, well known to the Lord of the Crypt.

Cathleen shivered involuntarily, noticing Jason had a similar reaction. He unconsciously rubbed his arms in response to the extreme cold the being radiated.

"A Phantom from the Underworld, Jason," Cathleen leaned over to whisper.

Jason nodded his head in agreement, stepping closer to her.

Speaking the same language used to call him, the Spirit addressed Lord Umaih. His weak voice was nearly smothered, beneath the sounds of a wind that had risen, buffeting the empty plains of the In-Between.

Cathleen translated his words to Jason as the phantom addressed the Lord of the Crypt.

"You have summoned me from my restless journey, mighty Lord, and I have answered. What service do you require of me, during my sojourn in this dreary realm?"

Cathleen and Jason studied the Specter, as yet unnamed by Umaih.

Its arms and upper body were naked, the lower trunk and legs were still inside a burial shroud. From what they could see, it was terribly emaciated and covered on most of the exposed body with terrible, black boils.

"Why has he called a plague victim, Cathleen?" Jason spoke close to her ear, but Umaih heard never-the-less, spinning around in their direction. "This Phantom carries more than the Black Death, human. It carries the memories of the beast standing across from us."

An incredible thought flashed inside Cathleen's head. She knew how to answer the riddle of the ghost hanging in front of them in his winding sheet. "Lord Umaih, I believe you have called the lost human spirit of the monster Arrakta. As a human wizard he succumbed to the evils that once freely roamed the Mother's worlds. He willingly forfeited his humanity, trading it for the powers that ultimately corrupted him, body and soul. His body succumbed to mortal illness, while he transformed his essence, into this evil creature before us. Is this correct, my Lord?"

"I expected you would puzzle this out for yourself, Protector. And now, we unleash what was the man, upon what is now the monster!"

Puffing out a blast of greenish mist, Umaih propelled the Phantom closer to the beast. Arrakta was trying to break the wards protecting the Cleaners, appearing to have given little notice to the arrival of Cathleen and Jason.

Jason removed the knife from the sheath and made certain the gold ring was in close contact. He felt his hand tingle and nodded to Cathleen that he was ready to move in when she gave the word.

The Phantom of the man Arrakta had once been floated above the scaly figure of the beast. The movement caused it to look up. The monster appeared to study the apparition for a moment, before opening its toothy-jaws in a blood curdling roar. The spirit was unmoved and unmoving.

Its presence though seemed to focus the creature's attention on the three others. Black eyes burning with hatred looked from one to the other. The long tail whipped the ground in such a fury clouds of pale dust rose higher than its burly thighs.

The deep voice boomed out across the field. "What game do you play at, Umaih? This specter is of no use to your survival, or that of the Protector and her mate. They will dance with death, though I may sup upon their tender flesh before."

His guttural laugh stirred the air around the Phantom.

The Lord Umaih called over to the beast. "Do you truly not recognize the shade of your own, once-human self, beast? The Evil Ones gave nothing away without a high cost! You were seduced by their empty promises of an immortality without the weaknesses of all humans. The Evil Ones watched gleefully while you twisted in your own sweat and filth. When you expired, they separated your blackened heart from the human remains, instilling the Dark powers you so desired. Your reward for losing your human nature was to become a beast of the night, as hideous to behold as you are to smell! I sent my Cleaners to remove your corrupted flesh from the Mother's earth, but even they recoiled at touching you. You have no human heart, leaving your Phantom to roam eternally, until you are destroyed in your beast form and your heart reclaimed by the Protector."

"Huh?" Cathleen murmured, wondering if she had heard correctly. How was she going to reunite this monster's black heart with his human shade and free the Phantom from his endless wandering? She guessed the Lord of the Crypt would provide that answer, or at least she fervently hoped he would! She glanced over at Jason, he'd obviously heard that comment, raising his eyebrows with his unasked questions and concerns.

The Phantom began to drift down, coming to rest in front of the beast. That creature backed away a few feet before opening its maw and spitting out a stream of foul-smelling venom at the opaque spirit.

The Lord of the Crypt chuckled at the effort, lost as it was on the ghost. "You spit upon your own lost spirit, Arrakta! In life, you were considered a fine man. A man who might easily have risen to Arch Wizard of the Council of Green Wizards, at their genesis, many centuries ago. Your death was as shrouded in mystery as this shade floating before you. As Lord of the Crypt, I am privy to the shadowy elements of every death, including yours. Do you wish to know your name when you lived in human form and grace?"

The phantom began to quiver, finally vanishing from sight. For some reason, this seemed to amuse Arrakta and inspired a throaty laugh from the beast. "I have no need for such trivial information, Umaih. Rather, why don't you choose whom should die first; the Protector, or her mate?"

Riveted to the conversation and long dialogue from Umaih, Cathleen and Jason didn't notice that the beast had drifted closer to them until he stood literally within spitting distance.

Arrakta's long tail flicked out, and he pivoted slightly. It connected with Cathleen, wrapping like a boa constrictor around her waist and dragging her back to the beast in one blur of movement.

The barbed tail easily pierced her thick sweatshirt, ripping the light T-shirt beneath. Her struggles caused long scratches and cuts along her rib cage and back.

Jason sprinted across the open ground, throwing his full weight into a tackle, lunging at the beast legs. The unexpected move brought it down hard. They all bounced on the springy earth, but the weight of the beast brought them to rest quickly.

Like the careful woodsman he was, Jason had been studying the beast's body, searching out points of vulnerability. Every animal had at least one weak spot.

Now, he was ramming his knife over and over, into the place he'd identified, just below the scaly arms. Each time, stiletto thin beams of Green Energy shot deeply into the monster, searing its innards with magically intensified energy.

In response, the beast uncoiled its tail from around Cathleen's body, dropping her onto the ground near Jason. She knew she was bleeding. She felt warm rivulets running down from her ribs and back, into the waist of her jeans.

Rather than lay in harm's way, possibly tripping Jason as he danced around the monster like a graceful matador, she rolled herself away from the active battle.

Arrakta was spitting his poison in a constant stream, but Jason was prepared for that response. He kept to the rear of the great beast, just behind its left shoulder. Every time it raised an arm to strike out, Jason flew into the gap with his knife. The bulk of the monster made it impossible for it to move with the same alacrity as the human. It became negligent with frustration, leaving itself wide open to Jason's deadly jabs as it swatted at Jason like a fly, never connecting.

They were going around in circles. Cathleen had to interject herself and fast, before Jason's strength gave out. The monster would have ten times his energy and Jason already showed signs of tiring, moving more slowly in his tight circle.

Looking back at Lord Umaih it appeared he was patiently waiting for her to finish the job.

He's not going to help, she thought amazed and alarmed.

Cathleen crouched down and placing her hands flat on the colorless ground, she prayed to the Mother for enhanced strength. Though this wasn't the natural realm of life, the Mother's influence was felt on every plane of existence.

Back on her feet, she mentally signaled for the two clones to join her in battle, sending a Wind Charm to scoop them up. They had no magic, but they did possess enhanced human strengths and responses. Cathleen decided to conjured weapons they could wield effectively in conflict. A battle mace for one and a broad sword for the other. She was ready to have them annoy the beast to death at least.

Jason held his own. She could see his attacks were finally having an effect on the beast's movements.

The tail was no longer lashing about, but was being dragged like inconvenient, extra weight. Arrakta was covered in oozing gashes in the soft spots under both arms. A steady flow of rancid smelling fluid seeped onto the ground and under Jason's feet.

Cathleen used their private whistle to call Jason away from the fray so she could jump in. Without hesitating, he fell back, out of the way of the grasping clawed hands.

He saw Cathleen move just beyond striking and spitting range, of the enraged beast. He noted her flushed face, watching as she lifted her arms for spell casting. That's when he saw the dark red splotch covering the front and sides of her sweatshirt.

Chapter 50

It felt like a belt of sharp spikes was cinched tightly around her waist and back. Cathleen struggled to keep her attention fully focused on the beast she was facing off with. From the corner of her eye, she caught Jason moving closer and knew he'd seen she was injured.

"Jason, no! I'll slow down the bleeding." He stopped, but she knew he'd jump back in if she lost ground to the monster. She was relieved to feel a calming surge beginning to flow throughout her body, stemming the steady loss of blood.

She used her link to call the waiting clones into action.

Arrakta spun in place as the first clone attacked, barely missing sweeping her feet from under her with the deadly tail.

She moved so fast Cathleen wondered if the Mother had also given them heightened abilities for the life and death battle.

A cloned Cathleen bent her knees, making a fantastic leap and landing on the beast's back. Bracing her legs tightly around the thick upper neck of the monster, she began to hack away with the broad sword. Most of her efforts were deflected by the rows of thick scales covering the neck and chest, so her best thrusts only left nicks in the beast's armor.

Arrakta, once an ancient human wizard, knew how to kill men.

It reached back with a clawed hand, seizing the clone's arm where it was wrapped around its neck. It plucked her off its back, dangling her from his strong arm.

Still gripping the sword in the other hand, she doubled her efforts with the weapon, landing some deeper gashes on Arrakta's chest with well-placed upward thrusts under the scales.

 Her efforts were short-lived. The beast reached in with its other clawed hand and broke the clone's back with a single wrenching blow.

Jason watched the combat closely, unable to suppress a groan at witnessing this brutal killing. Even though he knew she was just his wife's clone, witnessing her destruction was unnerving.

Cathleen signaled to the second clone to engage with the enemy.

Responding immediately, she used the spongy ground to launch herself like a champion pole-vaulter, sailing over the head of the beast to land directly behind. She carefully side-stepped the thrashing tail.

The beast made a quick turn, facing off with the last clone.

She clutched a heavy wooden handle, a thick chain attached to a heavy spiked ball, swinging below it. Holding her arm to the side, never taking her eyes off of Arrakta, she began a slow, rhythmic swing, until the ball was hissing through the air around her.

Without letting go of the handle, the clone directed the ball to lash out at Arrakta's powerful, lower legs.

The sound of breaking bone and ripping tendons was quickly covered by another ferocious roar, this one laced with scorching pain delivered to the beast.

The clone leapt clear of the retaliating tail, pounding out furiously and gouging out chunks of earth. The beast's heavy jaws opened wide only to bite down hard on empty air, as the clone moved fluidly around it.

Cathleen watched the monster grow more frustrated with each cascading blow from the battle-mace.

This was all the diversion she needed to finish this being for good.

She signaled to Jason it was time to move in for the kill. She watched as a surge of power shot from his right hand.

Cathleen took a second to study the combatants, before she jumped into the fray.

The beast was fending off blows from the spiked ball, using its lethal tail to keep its attacker too far away to cause serious damage. For her part, the clone showed signs of venom strikes penetrating her clothes in several places, slowing her barrage considerably as it ate through her flesh.

While only a replica of her creator, the clone could feel the pain of her injuries. Though unlike her mistress, she was fashioned for battle and stopping her assault was not an option.

Cathleen motioned Jason to cover the beast from its left flank, while she moved off to the right.

Arrakta stopped pounding the ground with the deadly tail when it sensed a new challenge. The beast's narrow head turned from side-to-side, its beady black eyes watching the pair move to out flank its position.

A glint of anger flared in the close-set, ebony eyes.

"Ah! I am presented with two Protectors but identifying the true Green Wizard will pose no challenge. Your mate is an inconvenience to me, as I want to give the Protector of the Green, my undivided attention."

The beast turned away from the clone, disregarding her blows entirely and squarely facing Cathleen. Maniacal laughter exploded from the broad chest, making the creature's scales shimmer. "The smell of a frail human is strong on you, Protector. It is but slightly tinged, with your feeble magic," the beast hissed, mocking her powers.

A thin cord of drool seeped through a double row of teeth protruding from its bottom jawbone. "Who shall be the first to die?" it mused, turning away from Cathleen, to Jason.

 Suddenly, it was airborne, lurching itself at the second clone. Before either Cathleen or Jason could react, it connected with the last of Cathleen's replicas, its clawed hands wrapped around the slender waist.

The ripping sound was like hearing a steak being pulled from the haunch of a living steer. Cathleen felt her own innards clench, watching the clone's body torn in half.

The sight proved too much for Jason. Even knowing this was only Cathleen's conjured-body double being destroyed, he was overcome with utter outrage at the act.

He slammed a shoulder into the thick torso of the beast while it was still in the act of destroying the clone.

The momentum of his run, combined with his well-muscled body weight, shifted the monster off balance. It was forced to widen its leg stance and use its tail as a counterbalance to the hit.

Jason took advantage of his surprise assault, pushing this knife upward, between the armored scales covering the creature's chest. He watched the gratifying surge of destruction, shooting from the ring.

Arrakta was howling with the newly inflicted pain. The full-on attack lasted less than thirty seconds, before the beast was able to use its splayed feet to regain its footing.

It lunged at Jason, taking him into a one-armed embrace meant to break his back.

Cathleen, stunned momentarily with Jason's attack, threw a dense smoke screen at the combatants. The confused beast, snarling at the gray cloud covering it, loosened its grip as expected. The smoke diminished its ability to see almost totally.

Cathleen used her enhanced strengths to free Jason with a hard pull on his legs, as he dangled from the monster's arm. He slid out like a banana from a peel. Cathleen quickly continued her spell to draw him over to her side.

"Jason, thank the Mother you're not hurt!" she said in a rush. Her voice was filled with as much irritation as concern. Jason began to speak, but she held up her hand, stopping him. "Time for words later. Right now, I need to do this." Before he could object, a Dome of Protection was dropped over him. From outside the protective shield Cathleen looked deeply into his forest green eye. "I'll finish this job, knowing you'll be safe. I love you, Jason. Stay put, so I'm not distracted!"

Jason knew better than to go against a battle directive from his wizard-wife, especially in highly dangerous circumstances. He also knew he'd softened the beast up a bit for her and gave her a thumbs up to send her back into battle.

Chapter 51

As she approached the cloud of thick, gray smoke her spell created to envelop Arrakta, Cathleen was already casting another she'd learned from her father many years ago. In a vulnerable predicament, her dad used the incantation to save them both from the superhuman speed of a charging Woodland Witch and her pet Bone Crusher. Recalling her terror, watching as the pair of killers raced toward them, she remembered how his spell slowed the advancing attack, turning it into slow-motion video. The Woodland Witch looked as if she was slogging through a mud bog, while the frothing slobber from her Bone Crusher, became a frozen trail behind its shaggy head. Her dad amusingly had a named this magic as his "Swamp Soup" spell.

She was sure she had chosen the right spell to stop the attack Arrakta would make any second. Using her Inner Eye, Cathleen watched the frustrated beast slapping at the dense smoke, trying to clear its field of vision. The long tail pounded furiously on the ground, muffled sounds of frustrated snarls, filtered through the persistent gray fog.

Arrakta gave a loud roar as the smoke began to thin and it spotted Cathleen standing just outside the dissipating mist.

Revenge glared hot in its wild eyes.

Cathleen was speaking the last words of her casting. The air around Arrakta immediately began to thicken into a heavy muck.

The beast fought against this new impediment, trying to move a leg and meeting with invisible resistance. It was powerfully built and strained to push its body closer to Cathleen. The sight of the despised Protector of the Green inspired greater efforts by the creature.

"You once were a free and honored wizard, Arrakta," Cathleen called out to the beast.

It struggled to reach out a long arm toward Cathleen, while she was taking backward baby steps to heighten it's frustration.

"You sacrificed your humanity for your power and look at you now. Struggling like a fly in a honey pot!"

The beast suddenly halted its revenge-fueled charge on her.

Cathleen heard it spout a string of words, only recognizing the words 'Dark Fire' and 'dome.' She spun around in time to see ragged, black flames, cascading in sheets over Jason's Dome of Protection. She could barely make-out the figure of her husband, instinctively crouching inside. The igloo-shaped safe place was beginning to show signs of stress cracks as it shuddered under Arrakta's black fire.

The beast was trying to break through Cathleen's spell and destroy the Dome. Jason would be totally exposed to his wrath and incinerated on the spot.

Bringing Green Fire to her hands, she abandoned her duel with the beast. Running flat-out toward the Dome, shooting bolts into the dark flames.

Incredibly, the black flames recoiled from her assault, reforming into a funnel above the shaky roof of the Dome.

Cathleen was nearly in front of the Dome when Arrakta's voice range out. She had no trouble interpreting these words. The great beast had called upon his own human spirit to come to his aid.

What's he doing, calling his shade? she thought, a knot of concern beginning to root in her stomach. How could he use the miserable, wandering spirit?

The Dark Fire was a heavy presence hanging above the quivering Dome of Protection. Jason was close to the curved membrane of the conjured fort.

His hand was tightly wrapped around the hilt of his knife. He peered out to meet Cathleen's eyes, immediately understanding she was about to act.

He dropped to the ground in a tight crouch as Cathleen's hand jerked upward, ripping away the top of the Dome.

The Dark Fire was snuffed out like a candle's flame when the force that tore off the roof of the Dome, blasted the black fire out of existence.

Cathleen was gratified to hear the outrage from the screaming beast, though her relief was short-lived. She was watching to make certain the fire was destroyed completely, when she heard Jason call out to her.

He was standing inside the partial Dome looking back at her and repeated her name.

His voice sounded hollow, without any feeling. It was the voice of a dead man.

The beast, Arrakta was still working his evil upon them and Jason was still his target.

Cathleen studied her husband's face a moment longer and breathed out the truth that stared back from his vacant eye.

"The shade of the beast!"

Chapter 52

Without the protection of the Dome, Jason was exposed to Arrakta's immediate retaliation. Cathleen had seen body possession by a restive spirit before, but never dreamed she'd see this horrible form of control befall her husband. Not while she was standing a foot away!

There was a heartbeat of indecision, as she watched Jason's body being lifted and slowly floated out the topless Dome.

Cathleen dropped her spell, dissolving its shimmering protection completely. Calling out to him, she saw a flicker of recognition in Jason's eye. The rigid look of his face softened, but quickly reset into the expressionless look of an undead.

"Jason, come to me!" she shouted, her voice sounding more like a plea than a command.

Arrakta still struggled behind her, making little progress through the thick sludge of restraining air. But while the beast was in control of Jason, she was in a weakened position.

Cathleen had to secure Jason before Arrakta's influence grew too great over the phantom. As long as Arrakta's human heart beat inside the monster, it would rule the spirit it condemned to wander.

Cathleen's thoughts raced.

The phantom's search for peace is futile until the heart is torn from the beast and permitted to die with the spirit. This was what the Lord of the Crypt was trying to make me understand.

Cathleen watched as Jason floated just out of reach. Arrakta was demonstrating his ultimate power over her, even as he struggled against hers.

She turned to the Lord Umaih, watching the drama unfold from behind his improvised mound shield.

Pitching her voice for his ears alone, Cathleen shouted across to him.

"My Lord Umaih, I need your help to drive the shade of Arrakta from Jason, while I obtain his human heart from the beast."

Cathleen blinked and Umaih stood in front of her.

"Your mate will be consumed by this shade, Protector. With every beat of Jason's heart, Arrakta's ghost is a parasite, absorbing his life force. When your mate is completely drained of this vigor, the spirit will depart, leaving Jason a withered husk, taking his place to wander without peace."

"But I thought the spirit wanted release, to find a peaceful rest in its death!"

Cathleen couldn't hide the desperation in her voice. How could she have misread the situation so completely!

"This is no innocent mortal's spirit. This is the spirit of a human wizard who sought immortality and supremacy through magic. Arrakta's human nature was corrupted by greed and arrogance as his magic grew more powerful.

The beast will reclaim the spirit that once made him human and leash it like a dog to be led at his side. I fear your mate will be lost to you forever."

Cathleen was stunned by the revelation, now so glaring it couldn't be denied.

She stepped away from the Lord of the Crypt, turning her back to him.

He took no offense at this gesture, understanding the Protector was preparing herself for the ultimate battle. A battle, not only to rid the Mother's realm of the beast, Arrakta, but to save her mate from becoming an enslaved spirit to the beast.

Cathleen closed her eyes, searching deeply in her memory. She began to chant softly, the language of the mystical Druids, slithering on the thin air into the ears of the Lord of the Crypt.

"Tribhas, Tribhas, Tribhas!" she finally shouted the third time to end her spell.

A tight smile came to Umaih's ancient face. He knew she had called down the spell for The Triple Death. The three natural elements of the Mother's making would now be at her command to help destroy the aberration that was the monster, Arrakta.

When she turned back to Umaih, he saw her eyes were entirely filled with the color of the Mother's Celtic Fire. The Protector's face was set in a fierce determination and showed no fear.

 Walking directly toward Arrakta, Cathleen saw the powerful being was nearly free from her spell. It was moving its heavily muscled legs easily and readying itself for combat.

Umaih heard Cathleen's clear, commanding voice.

"Arrakta, the Three Deaths have been called down upon you. I present you with the first!"

The beast's opened its long jaws, roaring his loathing of the Protector, seeing only that she stood alone and unprotected. Its whip-like tail thudded into the pale earth and it launched itself directly at Cathleen, where she stood unmoving, six feet away.

Dual streams of enhanced Green Fire shot out of her hands and were directed into the monster's mid-section. Cathleen held the beams steady as they began to eat away like lasers, at the hard scales protecting the heavy torso.

Her eyes began to glow an even deeper green. The watching Lord of the Crypt saw surges of energy snapping in the air around her head.

Suddenly, added to the constant fiery blasts, the wind that was humming softly around Umaih's ears began to howl like a thousand unleased Banshees.

The hurricane-force gusts tore into Arrakta. All the while, the beast thrashed futilely, trying to put out the Sacred Fire eating through its armor, down to the exposed flesh beneath. The winds increased in volume, the sound warping into a long, continuous howl.

Umaih, staying a safe distance, knew the howl was a mixture of wind and Arrakta's pain and frustration, as it began to turn in frenzied circles, with the madness of a rabid creature.

Cathleen let the two elements rage freely as she called for the third of the Three Deaths.

Opening her mouth wide, her glowing eyes rolled back into her head. She appeared to have lost consciousness.

She stood spellbound, fire coming from both hands, gale-force winds, tearing at the air around her and the beast. Abruptly, sea green water gushed from her open mouth, with the force of a mighty nor 'easter. The thick jet squarely hitting the beast in its broad chest.

Arrakta was pushed back by the enormous surge of power.

Umaih, watching while the magic fairly sizzled in the air around Cathleen, saw the physical strain the beast exerted, struggling to keep its footing.

Cathleen never faltered. Maintaining the spell of Three Deaths could only be achieved by a wizard of vast magical resources.

Umaih realized the woman known as the Protector, was this and much more. More than even the Council of Greens recognized.

Umaih turned his attention back to Jason. It was time for him to intervene on behalf of the young man. No longer floating toward the beast, under siege as it was from the Three Deaths, Jason was standing near the sealed-off chasm.

The Lord of the Crypt was unhappy in this new role thrust upon him. Dealing with the dead was his only purpose in the Mother's service. For a moment, he speculated that he might let the human die, then this would feel more natural to him. He sighed deeply, knowing this was not to be.

He flew on a downdraft from the Protector's battering wind, reaching her mate quickly.

His presence took the possessing shade by surprise. It was engaged in its own struggle, trying to keep control over the human host who had a strong, independent spirit of his own.

The Lord Umaih was a being of little patience. He took a moment to assess the condition of the Protector's mate. Mumbling to himself, he declared him still alive, though still battling the influence of the beast's human spirit.

"Shade of the wizard, now known as Arrakta, eons ago you welcomed the Darkness into your magic. I command you to leave this human. He is not for you, nor is he for me, Lord of the Crypt."

A shudder ran through Jason's stiff body when Umaih identified himself to the ghost.

"Leave this puny host and let the Protector secure your heart from the beast that holds you in its sway even now. When you were dying, you used the Black Arts to keep your heart alive and created the beast, Arrakta. That evil act caused you to wander as a shade in the shadow world for millennia. You are guilty of bringing this abomination forth, where it taints the Mother's world with its evil. Simply put, you need your heart returned to your ethereal body, where it will join you in death. Only then will you find peace"

Jason's body shivered and his eye popped open. Lord Umaih saw the light of human thought brighten the forest green pupil and knew he had succeeded.

"Welcome back, human. I'll answer your questions when all is completed here."

Jason looked across the pale ground, spotting Cathleen several yards off. He gasped when he saw what was happening to her and around her.

"No need to concern yourself about the Protector, human. She has already proven herself more than a match for the beast, using the dreaded Three Deaths to conquer it."

Jason watched as Arrakta struggled under the deluge of water, while Green Fire ate away at its protective scales, exposing grayish flesh to the ravages of the flames. The beast curled into itself as the heavy legs became blackened and twisted under the heat of the fire.

Finding he couldn't stomach watching any longer, Jason turned back to Umaih who'd been observing his reaction. He began to speak, when a shrill cry rang out. The heavy wind carried it over to where the two stood.

When the cry ceased, Umaih and Jason were staring at the scene of destruction Cathleen had wrought.

"It is time to free my Cleaners so they may begin their work once more. Be assured, human, they shall not be interested in you."

He gave a wry laugh and turned away from Jason to unseal the chasm and release the giant, ant-like creatures.

Jason turned back in time to see Cathleen drop her arms, the flames immediately extinguished. He saw her mouth was firmly closed and the jet of water stopped as well. The wind had dropped back in volume to a soft, persistent hum.

Cathleen must have felt him watching her. She turned fully toward him, standing for a moment to compose herself after using the powerful incantation of the Three Deaths. Jason saw she held something in her right hand, carrying it close to her chest as she walked over to him. He noticed a subtle movement under her hand as she came up to him.

"Come on, Jason. Let's give this back to its rightful owner.

The spirit of the man Arrakta once was floated over to stand in front of Cathleen and Jason. Cathleen held out her right hand, cupping it from beneath with the other. "In death as in life, your heart will be with you always."

A pitiful sob came from the phantom when it saw the heart beating a rhythm of life that he no longer possessed.

Cathleen began a soft invocation and pushed the heart through the ectoplasm that once was flesh and blood.

She felt a jolt of numbing cold as the heart was drawn into the shade's body. "I need to tell my tale of death and corruption before I can find my rest," the shade said.

They stood quietly, knowing this story would be his last words.

<h1 style="text-align:center">Chapter 53</h1>

Jason listened closely while the phantom explained to him and Cathleen, how he was drawn into the murky waters of Dark Magic. His voice was weak, but easily penetrated the thin air of the In-Between. "I was once a wizard of great repute in the wizarding community. My growing ego led me to seek more and more power, doing anything to enhance my magic until I could be more powerful than any living wizard. By the time my physical self was sickened in a deadly pestilence, I had enough knowledge of the Dark Arts to create a new being. It would hold my magic and save me from the eternal sleep of other mortals. I called the beast, Arrakta, after a demon spawn wrote that name in the blood of my closest wizard competitor."

Cathleen asked how it created the beast.

"At the moment of my last human breath, I caused my heart to be ripped from my chest and placed in the creature you have slain. I passed through the veil, becoming this shade you see.

The beast howled when it saw me cross over the barrier, but soon, a new life-force surged through it with the beating of my heart.

I have been punished fully for my actions. I have been shunned by all other shades because I lacked my human heart. I have had to witness the horrors the beast, Arrakta has committed. At last, I shall join the spirits and rest in the peace of magic."

At the conclusion of the long story, the ghost of the ancient wizard faded into the white space. Jason could hear a faint thumping and then, only silence.

Cathleen and Jason both took a simultaneous deep breath, smiling at one another at the similar reaction of relief.

The investigation into the murder of Bretton Clawson was over, the Protector's role was finished. What lay ahead was for others on the Council of Greens to address. Foremost among them, electing a new Arch Wizard.

They turned to watch the Lord of the Crypt, calling his army of Cleaners from their enforced confinement.

Thousands upon thousands of midnight-black creatures, climbed over the ridge of the deep gorge. Their antennae waved restlessly like wheat stalks in a strong breeze, as this remarkable army was busy assembling and communing with one another. The clacking of their mandibles filled the air, generating a riotous symphony.

Cathleen imagined they were celebrating their liberation by their Master, the Lord Umaih.

As the black horde climbed over one another in the mass effort toward freedom, a question popped into Jason's mind.

"I wonder if they're hungry, after being locked up like that,' he said. A hint of trepidation was not lost on Cathleen, who immediately grinned up at him.

"There's nothing to fear from this lot, sweetie. We have to get back to the Council and make sure the Greens are working to regroup. I think Lord Umaih has already said his goodbyes."

Jason shot a look in the direction of the old Lord, spotting him astride one of his legions of Cleaners. He'd more or less accepted the fact that they were scavengers of the dead. He watched as Umaih held up an arm, holding a branch of the sacred Yew tree. It glowed a vibrant green, reminding Jason that The Lord of the Crypt was doing the Mother's bidding.

Jason felt Cathleen slip her arm through his and he held it close to his side, drawing her nearer.

"He's off on his own business, sweetie and we have to be too."

Cathleen called up a Time Thread, manipulating it for their return trip to the present day, inside the Citadel of the Greens.

The humming of the Thread was nearly drowned out by the incessant clacking of the Cleaners, but Jason felt himself sucked into the center of its vortex. As usual, the pressure on his body was nearly suffocating, and gratefully, over as quickly as it began. He heard the gratifying 'pop' of their re-entry into the first realm, the natural world of the Mother.

Cathleen looked over at him, checking that Jason was alright after the jump. Time Threads were hard on the mostly unprotected human body.

When he smiled down at her, she was relieved and started to check out their surroundings.

"This is the hallway, just outside Council Chambers. It's pretty quiet in there," she said pressing her ear close to a wall panel.

She decided to move, entering the Chamber Room through the door reserved by custom for the Arch Wizard, followed by the Sargent at Arms.

Cathleen told Jason the special door was charmed by the Arch Wizard, binding it to the wall. She added that all the magic placed around the castle was now in question.

Cathleen flicked her hand, opening the iron-banded door and moving back the wall-hanging as they entered. After the gloom of the hallway, it took a moment for their eyes to adjust to the Council Chamber. The spacious room was bright, with dozens of torches placed in gold sconces around the circular walls.

Sitting in the Arch Wizard's chair of power was Mercy McNaughton, Scribe to the Council of Green Wizards.

"Have you been elected then?" Cathleen asked without preamble.

"It would appear so, Protector," she answered with a touch of smugness in her tone, putting Cathleen on guard.

"Where is the Historian, Mercy?" she asked.

Looking around the table, she added, "And for that matter, where is the Guardian?" noting a flash of annoyance pass over the Scribe's pretty face.

Cathleen caught Jason's eye and signaled him with a small gesture to remain where he stood. She needed to sort out this newest twist in the Council's saga.

The Scribe seemed to struggle with her answer and Cathleen caught a look of anxiety tighten her bow mouth. "They are being held in the dungeons. Soon, they'll receive the punishment unanimously agreed to by the Council."

Both Cathleen and Jason were stunned. These were respected and valued members of the Council of Greens. Will Farley's unimpeachable record as an Outlander Wizard Scout alone had earned him accolades and admiration from the elite magic users of the first realm. His current service as Historian was a testament to the esteem felt toward him by the deceased Arch Wizard. The Guardian was set upon this plane to act as a liaison to the Mother's magic users and to oversee the Council's works against the Dark Arts. What had transpired to negate all of that in the eyes of the Council of Greens?

Cathleen focused long and hard on the young woman sitting so uncomfortably in the head chair.

"Mercy," she said, while looking around the room at the many empty seats.

"You don't have near a quorum to vote on any matter that would come before this body. Half of the Council of Greens were either killed or are being treated for their wounds in the Healing Gardens."

The Scribe sounded prickly when she answered. "This is Council business, Protector, clearly outside your purview. But I can share this much intelligence, uncovered by me and reported back to the members."

"All six of them, you mean?" Cathleen interjected mockingly.

The sarcasm seemed to hit home and the Scribe flushed a deep red.

"Our numbers are not relevant to the issue of deceit! The Historian and Guardian have been found guilty of spying for the late Deceiver. We believed Corky Cochran, the late Sargent at Arms, was alone in his plot as a double agent. We were wrong! While the Historian was supplying the Deceiver with sensitive information concerning Council business, the Guardian schemed to betray the late Sir Alex into the hands of Cochran to be murdered."

Cathleen glanced over at Jason. His lie-o-meter must be spinning! she thought.

"But the Arch Wizard wasn't killed. He lives!" Cathleen said firmly.

She pointed dramatically toward the heavy tapestry on the wall and the hidden door.

Mercy automatically spun in that direction, giving the Protector time to whisper a conjuring spell.

She summoned the same clone Mercy created of Sir Alex, in an effort to hide the Arch Wizard's murder and confuse the Council spy. He would show no signs of torture, however, to maintain the ruse.

Cathleen was convinced Sir Alex's' murder was carried out by the Magic User now posing as the Council Scribe, Mercy McNaughton.

The heavy tapestry rustled and a hand poked through, sweeping it aside.

The Arch Wizard, Sir Alex, stepped into the room and headed straight for his chair. The chair Mercy McNaughton's imposter currently occupied.

In her agitation, the fraud shouted out, "But…how? He's dead! You're dead, old fool! You're dead!"

The pretender Scribe was nearly incoherent with panic. She leapt up from the throne-like chair, knocking it over in her haste.

Cathleen was suddenly standing directly in front of her wild eyes. "I will ask this only once, imposter! Where is the true Scribe, Mercy McNaughton? Lie and you die. Jason can smell a lie a mile off."

Cathleen moved closer to the cringing girl's face. Her eyes flashed with pent-up anger at the unfolding charade of twisted events and misleading stories.

There was Dark Magic at the heart of the Council and it fell to her to root it out before it poisoned the whole body of Greens.

The six Council members hadn't uttered a sound during the tense scene playing out before them. Only one person took note.

Cathleen felt Jason lean close, whispering in her ear.

"The members haven't so much as blinked, Cathleen. They're all staring off into space like zombies."

Cathleen hadn't noticed the others since she so focused on the so-called Scribe.

Glancing around the horseshoe shape table, confirmed Jason's observations.

From the corner of her eye, she saw the Scribe edging closer to the hidden door.

Rather than keeping her from bolting from the Chamber, Cathleen turned her full attention to the six remaining Council members.

Without turning to face him, Cathleen called back to Jason.

"Jason, please release the Historian and the Guardian from the dungeons and return them to this chamber. Stay alert for the fake Scribe.

I need to break the enchantment placed on these remaining members, then I'll find the imposter.   We need to know her true identity and find the real Mercy McNaughton."

Chapter 54

Cathleen turned her attention to the six wizards scattered around the Council table.

They had all changed from their battle gear and were dressed in their long, formal robes. Each garment was richly embroidered with runes detailing their personal history in the Mother's service, dating back hundreds of years in most cases. Though not immortals, as that would be unnatural in their human state, the Mother granted sorcerers elected to the Council of Green Wizards a lifetime that often encompassed many centuries, thus keeping vital continuity within the membership.

Looking at the rigid bodies and impassive faces, Cathleen knew this would not be an easy curse to lift. After studying the six and using several invocations to break their hypnotic state, she stepped closer to each one, looking for signs of human control trying to assert itself.

Of the four men and two women frozen in place, only one had even the vaguest glimmer of life in his eyes. Faigon Crampton, the oldest sitting member on the Council, seemed to be fighting off the effects of the spell.

Crampton 's age had long been forgotten, his robes reflecting uncountable feats of magic as a Green Wizard. Even his obvious infirmities weren't enough to remove him from active duty on the Council.

Cathleen addressed him respectfully. "You are a powerful wizard, Faigon Crampton, often praised by my father, Liam O'Brien. He called you the Mother's Sword Arm. I sense your battle with this curse laid upon you and the others. I can help free you all. I ask that you give me a single word, to direct me and I will lift the binding."

Cathleen watched the old wizard's face, hoping for anything that would indicate the spell's weaknesses.

The wizard's great age could be perceived in his eyes, red-rimmed and nearly colorless. Staring into them, she saw an oddity as the milky-brown pupils began to contract and dilate, as if responding to sudden light.

She blurted out, "It's the code. You're using your eyes to give me the word."

Cathleen knew from her mother's experience as an Outlander Wizard Scout, the Scouts were taught to use this silent code if they were unable to communicate verbally together. Situations like being incapacitated by another wizard's curse. In fact, it was The Claw who devised the spell. He called it 'Vision Speak.'

Her mother taught her this code when she was very young, wanting to keep her from blurting out comments about evil presences when among non-magic users."

Cathleen, looking deeply into Faigon Crampton's ancient eyes, recognized the coded contraction and widening of the pupil for the word for 'yes'. A few minute later, she had the key words to undo the enchantment.

The six responded immediately when the spell was lifted. Jumping to their feet, their excited voices bounced around the nearly empty chamber.

Cathleen held up her hands to signal silence.

"I understand what happened here, but our priority is finding the true Scribe and…"

Cathleen spun around when she saw the startled looks on the faces of the wizards. All eyes were drawn to the hidden door.

Jason, leading the freed Historian and Guardian, still in the guise of a giant, wolfish dog, stepped from behind the tapestry. The true Scribe was not with them.

The Guardian's golden eyes briefly scanned the room, as if searching out prey. They stopped when they lighted on Cathleen's face.

His voice rumbled up from his broad chest. "The Scribe is no more, Protector," he announced in a clear voice, tinged with obvious distress.

"Her spirit was driven from her mortal remains by the being now possessing her physical body, stealing her identity. Her lifeforce has long passed from the realm of the living."

A deep stillness filled the air. Cathleen believed the fake Scribe was merely shifted into Mercy's identity. She never believed her to be dead.

The Guardian's enormous head hung down, while he waited for his news to sink in before continuing. "We were both taken almost immediately, upon our return from the In-Between. The Scribe was reporting to the six remaining Council members, when an enchantment caused all present to freeze in place. I suspect the hex was prepared like a bear trap, to be triggered when we stepped foot in the Council Chambers. The Scribe and I were taken to the dungeons where we were separated."

The Historian interjected, "I was subdued upon my own return and held in the cell where we found the Arch Wizard's clone. I was unaware of your capture, Guardian and never suspected the Scribe had been taken as well."

Cathleen waited for more information from the Historian, but when he stopped speaking his mouth was tightly drawn into a thin line of anger. She turned her eyes back to the Guardian, who resumed his report.

"My cell was across from Mercy McNaughton's. We discovered our magic was blocked by the strong wards placed around us. When someone entered her cell, I was unable to intervene and save her from her fate. Her screams filled the darkness. When they ceased, a deep silence came upon me and I understood she had passed from this life."

Cathleen's jaw was clenched, fighting back her own scream of rage at what had befallen Mercy.

"I could not see the killer as they stood in deep shadows to work their torture, but in the end, I saw the body of the Scribe rise from the cell floor. A dark smoke swirled around her head, using her open mouth, it entered the corpse. The door to the cell flew open and the imposter walked out in their new guise."

Cathleen asked the Guardian why he believed this Dark One was using Mercy's body to pass among the others.

"There is to be an election of a new Arch Wizard. Can you imagine the power and control this evil one would have in such a position? All manner of demon-spawn would be welcomed into the Mother's natural realm."

Jason was standing close to the Historian during this account of the death of the pretty Mercy McNaughton. The big man's hands ball-up into tight fists. His fury was palpable.

Cathleen was very still, stunned by the news of the young Scribe's torture and death. She gave herself a mental shake and turned back to the waiting Council members.

"You have all heard!" she said firmly. "There is a Dark Magic user here, in the citadel. You need to pair-up and scour the rooms for the creature posing as Mercy McNaughton. Be watchful for any demon-spawn they might have called to serve in this plot to destroy our Council of Greens. This wizard will use the Scribe's residual memories of the grounds and layout of the castle, so don't enter anywhere without using a personal ward for protection."

One of the women asked Cathleen what action they should take if they found the impersonator.

"Kill them so dead even their shadow will be destroyed before they fall!"

The wizards paired up, with Wizard Crampton insisting to a very junior eighty-year-old, he was as fit as any to tackle the search.

Cathleen suspected he'd likely said the same, over many life-times of dedication to the Greens. She watched as they split off in different directions, covering the castle proper. She intended to search the grounds surrounding the hulking edifice.

"Historian, I'd like you to go with Jason, while I keep the Guardian with me. We will use the front gates as our starting point. I believe the imposter will want to shed the Scribe's body as soon as possible."

"Why would they do that, Protector?" the Guardian asked.

Cathleen looked over at the shaggy creature sitting beside her. His head came up to her shoulder.

"Because, her body will slowly corrupt, even with magic to control it. They'll need another body and soon."

Looking over at the Historian, Cathleen saw the flinty spark of hatred, swirling in the depths of his dark eyes. He hadn't said a word since listening to the report of Mercy's gruesome murder from the Guardian, but his stony silence spoke volumes.

Cathleen now had second thoughts about teaming him up with her husband. She worried he might become reckless in his actions and put them both in danger. Before she could reverse her orders, the Historian and Jason were heading toward the front doors.

The Historian was a professional hunter and she would have to trust in his innate sense to do the right thing when it came to confronting a powerful enemy.

She watched a second longer as the two men disappeared into the waiting shadows of the night.

Chapter 55

Cathleen understood hunting for a wizard came with its own very specific challenges.

Unless you knew them well, you could be blind-sided by an unusual spell with unfamiliar elements of magic, or a creature manifestation you'd never before encountered.

This particular wizard had the advantage of intimate knowledge of the Greens and the echo of memories that wouldn't fade for quite a while from the body they possessed.

There was also the possible moment of hesitation Cathleen feared would endanger her husband and Will Farley. If the Historian saw the body of Mercy McNaughton in front of him, his growing emotional attachment to her could make him reluctant to attack.

She knew there was nothing she could do to control such variables.

The Guardian padded silently beside her; his nose close to the ground, snuffling as they moved along the bank of a fast-flowing stream. The tracks of various animals coming to drink its cool waters marked the soft, black earth.

"There!" the Guardian's deep voice penetrated Cathleen's thoughts.

She leaned in to see a line of prints left by a small shoe. Her keen Inner Eye noted the ground around the prints was slightly swept clean, likely by the hem of long robes.

"You've found her trail, Guardian," Cathleen said in a hushed voice.

She scanned the area as they moved ahead, following the prints as they diverged from the stream bank, into the heavily wooded area surrounding the castle.

These woods acted as natural walls for the Council's fortress, concealing the aged, stone stronghold, within a thick circle of verdant trees and foliage. Over countless centuries, the Greens encouraged the growth of creeping vines and other plants that would attach themselves to the stone work of the castle. Even from a bird's view, it was a sea of green below.

The Guardian grunted his agreement adding, "I have sensed something familiar in this being we hunt. The Scribe's body is beginning to fade as you've predicted and now, there is an undertone. It is definitely female."

Cathleen stopped moving. "Are you certain of this, Guardian?"

"I am and furthermore this is an ancient we hunt. One of the first Magic Users to roam this realm."

Cathleen took in this new information, mulling over the ramifications of confronting old magic. Moving deeper into the woods, they were immediately surrounded by its clean, earthy smells. The occasional hoot of an owl watching from his perch and the scurrying of tiny feet through the underbrush were the sounds of normalcy in this otherwise unnatural hunt.

Cathleen was careful to use a muffling charm, quieting their own movements in the hushed environment of the night.

The Guardian continued to follow the now familiar scent of the Dark One. With her own senses in hyper-drive, Cathleen stopped when she picked up a faint sound. The Guardian stopped simultaneously; a huge paw held in the air like a pointer.

They were at the edge of a small glade. Flowering plants and young tree sprouts dotted the rare opening in the forest. The larger tree limbs hanging over-head, easily dwarfed its presence.

Cathleen touched her shaggy companion on a fury shoulder. He looked back, shuffling around to sit on his haunches, to face her.

"I think whatever we're following has doubled back and is now following us," she whispered to the wolfish creature sitting in front of her.

The Guardian's eyes darted to a stand of trees, to the left of the clearing. His long tail pounded once on the ground, the grasses dulling the thump.

"I fear I have misjudged this being's abilities. It shall not happen again, Protector. What action do you suggest?"

Cathleen proposed they split up after they crossed the glen and reentered the dark trees. "She will continue to follow you, when I double back and get behind her."

"This could prove a dangerous plan for you, Protector. Keep alert to any sign that she has sensed your presence."

They passed through the clearing quickly and were immediately lost in the shadows of the mature trees.

Cathleen moved right, while the Guardian kept a steady pace forward.

She took a deep breath and vanished. The Shadow Wrap she called to herself, made her feel less exposed while she looped back a short distance, toward the stalking predator. She waited a moment, allowing the skulking wizard time to cross the open ground to resume following her prey.

The distinct snap of a twig breaking under foot tickled Cathleen's ear. They had misjudged again! The Dark Wizard must have guessed at their ploy and instead of following the giant dog, she waited for the trap to be set in place. Cathleen knew her Wrap concealed her, but she still felt like the bait in that trap!

Unable to move, for fear of giving herself away, Cathleen stood frozen, listening for the sounds of the approaching wizard. Another noise, a muffled shuffling of debris beneath the trees, alerted her. The enemy was getting closer.

She needed to wait until the imposter Scribe was close enough to see before she could use her magic. She couldn't risk revealing herself until she was able to identify her clearly.

Because of the heavy tree canopy, there was little light from a waning moon. Cathleen didn't dare raise a small flame, instead she'd need to rely on her keen Inner Eye to pick-out the form of the false Scribe.

A flash of movement several feet from where she waited followed by a second blurring of the air could mean the Dark One was conjuring something to aid in her hunt. Not knowing what creature was being called, Cathleen had to interrupt the conjuring and fast.

Moving within the masking of the Wrap, she got behind a thick tree trunk and began her own magic. At her whispered invocation, a clone of the dead Arch Wizard, sprang out of the ground shadows, wearing his Council robes of authority.

His appearance had the desired effect on the enemy.

Cathleen suspected the Dark Wizard despised Sir Alex for his position on the Council. She guessed the sight of him would trigger the same rage displayed earlier.

Cathleen felt a ripple in the moist air beneath the trees, as the false Mercy McNaughton finally revealed herself. She was squatting close to the ground and sprang like a tiger at the figure of the Arch Wizard. Her weight and momentum drove him to the ground. Cathleen hadn't seen the curved blade until it flashed up and down, ripping into the clone's chest.

The Scribe's body had faded substantially and Cathleen recognize the wizard who had assumed Mercy's identity. She could barely credit her eyes, knowing this being served the Mother from the very inception of the Green Wizards in this realm.

"Neidin! Sweet Mother, she's alive!" she gasped, astonished at the revelation.

Not wanting to reveal herself to this savage killer, Cathleen watched with dread, remembering her first encounter with this ancient wizard in the Chameleon Woods.

After they stumbled upon her cottage, Neidin tried to subdue her, along with Jason and the Guardian, then in the guise of Parsons, giving them a spelled tea.

Cathleen recalled how the dark spirit that filled the beautiful woman, fled from the cottage upon her ruse being discovered.

After that incident, Cathleen believed Neidin had been destroyed by the Deceiver, who revived her body to use against unsuspecting enemies.

Neidin was pledged to offer 'a little nest of peace and safety' according to the ancient Druid traditions, to those serving the Green Mother.

The Outlander Wizard Scouts would have known of that custom and trusted her with their lives.

Cathleen and the others slipped that noose, and at the time, believed Neidin had passed from the Mother's realms forever. Watching this brutal attack on the clone of Sir Alex, any doubts that the Sorcerer Neidin had succumbed to the lure of Dark Magic, vanished with every slash of her lethal blade. This was no animated corpse. This was a willing participant in the annihilation of any in service to the Green Mother.

Neidin had been working with the Deceiver all along. But clearly, even the powerful Deceiver was beguiled by his ally's beauty and fooled by her willingness to help him. Neidin would surely have planned his destruction as her own powers grew.

Witnessing the savage attack, Cathleen's thoughts were as grim as the act she witnessed was gruesome. Neidin served no man, after she stopped serving the Mother.

The destruction of the Arch Wizard's clone was complete, its body hacked to pieces. The 'Wizard of Peace and Tranquility' as she was called, turned her cold eyes in Cathleen's direction, clearly sensing her nearness.

Ragged, orange fire shot from the tips of her fingers when she pointed them and the wicked blade at Cathleen's hiding place. She was taking a few, careful steps toward the large tree trunk, when a deep growl erupted from behind her.

Neidin spun around to face this new adversary, licking her lovely lips in anticipation.

She shrugged off the remaining traces of the Scribe's identity and gave a short gurgle of laughter.

Clearly, she was enjoying the prospect of another challenge to her powers.

The great head of the wolfish beast poked through a thick stand of saplings directly in front of her. Piercing, golden eyes appraised the slender woman, while thick drool dripped from the gapping muzzle.

Neidin stared at the animal, her fingertips lit like candles, topped with narrow shoots of orange flame.

Without breaking eye contact, the heavily muscled body smashed through the smaller trees as if they were mere twigs. The creature, unimpressed by her fire, launched his massive body directly at her.

Chapter 56

The Guardian watched Neidin's savage attack upon what was clearly a clone conjured by the Protector. He guessed Neidin was too far gone in her madness to notice this fact herself.

He recalled how he was in the guise of Parsons, the House Buddy, when he, the Protector and her mate, stumbled across Neidin's small cottage.   Though he knew her well, from the earliest days of the formation of the Green Wizards, she never guessed the elfish Parsons was truly the Guardian of the Green.

When he foolishly drank the tea given them on that visit, his unassuming appearance likely saved him from the slaughter he'd just witnessed. Clearly, she intended to destroy any Green Wizards or Scouts that fell into her hands.

He would have been incapable of defending himself back at her cottage. Luckily, the Protector and her mate were not taken in by her hospitality. He let his guard down believing she was serving the Mother as Purveyor of Peace and Comfort. He would not give her the benefit of any doubt, ever again.

The Guardian felt more secure in his present wolfish form, studying the murderous Wizard Neidin before his attack. The orange streaks of flames, shooting from her finger tips, painted her face in dancing shadows, giving her a crazed, wild-eyed look.

A short distance away, Cathleen watched as the two adversaries stood mutely, sizing each other up. She wondered if Neidin had guessed at the real identity of the shaggy creature she faced.

She noticed how Neidin cocked her head to the side, as if she questioned something familiar about her opponent. Likely, she sensed his magic and knew she'd felt its power before somewhere in the past.

Murmuring her charm, Cathleen finally brought the sacred Green Fire to her hands. She couldn't attack unless the Guardian was at a safe distance.

Seeing the great beast crouch low, heavy muscles bunching in his hind quarters, she knew he was ready to launch himself at the traitor.

Cathleen threw off the Shadow Wrap, waiting for her opening.

She guessed the Guardian would use his vast body, to drive the traitorous woman to the ground. Instead of trying to avoid his lunge, Neidin held up her hands, holding them flat, palms facing the charge of the shaggy creature. She screamed out a string of words.

Red flames fanned out like an accordion to either side of her hands, creating a wall of fire. The flames were alive with a charge of static electricity, causing them to jump and crackle, licking at the lower branches of nearby trees, while scorching the saplings to the ground.

Neidin stood securely behind her fiery creation, the garish glow revealing the sheer madness twisting her once, beautiful face.

The Guardian couldn't check the momentum behind his head-long charge. He hit the burning shield with such force he became airborne, crashing backward through the trees. His heavy fur set alight with flame, transformed him into a streaking comet before he landed several yards away.

Cathleen had her opening, though it must have cost the Guardian dearly.

She caused the Mother's Celtic Fire to form into javelin-shaped bolts. These, she proceeded to heave one after another into Neidin's body, as the wizard spun around to face her new opponent.

To Cathleen's mind, Neidin was a traitor to all she pledged to hold sacred. She deserved no mercy and she'd receive no quarter.

Cathleen steeled her heart against the screams and curses of the other wizard as watched her churn like butter, as she was battered by the powerful green spears.

Neidin's own blood-red fire was snuffed out as she spun her with dizzying speed.

When the ancient wizard was no more than a heap of settling, gray ash, Cathleen hurried to where the Guardian lay, stretched out on his side.

She kept a small flame in one hand to study the injured creature. She could see his body had been badly burned. In places, the thick pelt was eaten away by the fire, exposing scorched, pink flesh beneath.

While she was crouched down beside him, she felt a slight chill run through her. His presence was confirmed when a low whistle trilled from nearby.

Jason, she thought hurriedly getting to her feet, answering his signal.

She was joined a minute later by Jason and the Historian. They stood in a semi-circle, looking solemn while studying the injured Guardian.

"Unless he shifts back to his natural form, Protector, he won't survive the Time Thread to the Healing Garden," the Historian predicted gravely.

They watched the great beast's heaving side, as he obviously struggled to take air into his seared lungs. The stench of his burned fur and flesh was nearly overwhelming in the closeness of the woods.

Cathleen knew this could mean the end of the Guardian of the Green. She mentally began to run through some of the spells and charms she could use to cause him to revert back to his own body.

She moved closer to the massive head, the jaws slack and panting, taking in shallow breaths. His thick tongue lay like a slab of beef on the ground. She needed to work this magic or lose their comrade.

The spell was a simple one. One of her mother's favorite, from her This and That Magic collection of personal invocations. "Soeis bagair. Transform, shapeshifter. As the Mother brought you into this realm."

Nothing happened. The three hung over the shaggy form, mutely watching the dying creature.

Suddenly, the scorched limbs jerked and the massive body shuddered.

Cathleen repeated her spell and when she spoke the last word, the large, wolfish beast began to fade. Lying in its place was the creature of the

Lochs, his globular eyes white and unseeing on their long stems. The many legs were spread around him, stiff and unmoving.

Cathleen called for a Time Thread to transport the unconscious Guardian into the hands of the Healers. With the help of the Historian's magic, they secured the awkward body for the trip to the Healing Garden.

After the Thread popped out of existence, Jason stepped closer to Cathleen.

"Will he survive, Cathleen?" he asked softly, concern obvious in his voice.

He'd come to respect the somewhat haughty Guardian, for his loyalty to the Mother but also to Cathleen and the others involved in the hunt for the Deceiver.

"Only the Healers will have that answer, sweetie."

The three didn't speak on their trek back to the Citadel, but the silence couldn't still the questions that plagued Cathleen about the future of the Council.

Her mind was filled with the challenges looming ahead for the Council Green Wizards. The deaths and murders, the intrigues and traitors, all worked to undermine the mission of protecting the natural life forms in the realm of the Green Mother.

A new Arch Wizard would have to be elected and an interim Guardian, until the first Guardian to serve in that position was healed. If he was healed.

A well-vetted Wizard was needed to replace the fallen Scribe, Mercy McNaughton. Cathleen wondered how deeply Mercy's death would affect the Historian and if he would remain in his position on the Council. He could just as easily return to the Outlander Wizard Scouts and assume the leadership position for that decimated group of elite wizard soldiers.

Even a newly appointed Sargent at Arms would be on the list of wizards required to form a viable Sitting Council.

The over-arching question of how so many could have been deceived by the traitors among them could taint the very foundation of the Council.

Cathleen knew as Protector of the Green she would have to take a leadership role in reforming the Green Wizards. If they were to carry on in their centuries-old role as living barriers against demon incursions and rogue magic users, the Green Wizards would need a complete rededication of their powers to the Mother.

The safety of the first realm depended upon their vigilance and that would be impossible without cohesiveness within their exclusive group.

The three paused when they came to the edge of the woods. They stood together on the lush grass, leading down a gentle slope to the castle proper.

In the tender glow of a young dawn, the massive stronghold of the Green Wizards rose up before them. It stood proudly, like the rising Phoenix emerging from the shadows. A glow radiated from every corner, from the torches that appeared to float throughout the castle.

The time for rebirth was upon them and no one felt the weight of change more keenly than the Protector of the Green, the Witch of Appalachia.

Standing with the forest at their backs, Jason breathed deeply of the earthy fragrance. His connection to any woodlands always had a kind of magical effect on him, giving him a sense of peace like no other environment.

Cathleen glanced over at him, smiling to herself at the contented look she'd seen so often back in their home, deep in the Appalachian Mountains. She knew it wasn't an easy transition for him, going from Sheriff, to Demon Hunter. Yet, time and again, he amazed her with his easy acceptance of the unexplainable and mystical, in their life together.

Jason Tate was a man of some mystery to her, even after nearly five years together. This latest investigation revealed he had his own source of powers to tape into.

A vivid scene of Jason armed with the Historian's knife and Sir Alex's signet ring flashed in her mind's eye. Jason wielded his newfound power as if he was born to it, as she had been.

Cathleen would have to undertake another investigation as soon as she had seen the Green Council strong again. This would be a personal inquiry into the strange powers she'd witnessed. Powers wielded by her untrained husband, Jason.

One day soon they would discover together the source of his seemingly raw magic and work to refine and train it. Cathleen glanced up at Jason's handsome profile, dreaming of the day she might add Wizard to his name.

She knew his spirit was already blessed by the Mother. Perhaps one day he would hold Her most precious gift in his hands.

Yes, one day he'll rule the Celtic Fire beside me.

About the Author

    Francesca is part of a large Italian family where she discovered early on that a love of reading was as much a part of her DNA as her mother's skill at baking. Growing up in a house filled with laughter, screaming, banging pots, fighting and loving family bonds, shaped her life and heart.

    Having moved from the east coast where she was raised between New York and New Jersey, Francesca left for the mid-west where she spent several years outside the Chicago area raising a family of three children, completing her college degrees and writing introspective poetry as a young mother.

    Francesca has worked in local television, a small city zoo, founded a non-profit tutoring agency for an inner-city neighborhood which eventually served local school districts, worked for an International Evangelical Television and Radio Station and for a non-profit organization serving challenged adults.

Francesca Quarto resides in a small town outside of Indianapolis, Indiana with her husband Patrick. She still has a great love of the written word and while she enjoys her E-Reader immensely, she still treasures the excitement of turning the next page.

Tell-Tale Publishing would like to thank you for your purchase. If you enjoyed this book, please show the author your appreciation by posting an online review. If you would like to read more by this or other fine TT authors, please visit our website:

www.tell-talepublishing.com

***